Then Again, Maybe

by
Susan L. Tuttle

Bling!
Romance
Lighthouse Publishing of the Carolinas

THEN AGAIN, MAYBE BY SUSAN L. TUTTLE
Bling! is an imprint of LPCBooks,
a division of Iron Stream Media
100 Missionary Ridge, Birmingham, AL 35242

ISBN: Paperback 978-1-64526-289-3; eBook 978-1-64526-290-9
Copyright © 2020 by Susan L. Tuttle
Cover design by Elaina Lee
Interior design by Karthick Srinivasan

Available in print from your local bookstore, online, or from the publisher at:
ShopLPC.com

For more information on this book and the author, visit: www.susanltuttle.com

Brought to you by the creative team at LPCBooks:
Bradley Isbell, Shonda Savage, Linda Yezak, Jessica Nelson

Library of Congress Cataloging-in-Publication Data
Tuttle, Susan L.
Then Again, Maybe / Susan L. Tuttle 1st ed.

Printed in the United States of America

ACKNOWLEDGMENTS

Most people think of writing as a solitary journey, but it's far from that. I will always start my acknowledgments by giving thanks to my Jesus. He is my everything. Anything good you see in me has always been and will always be Him.

To my writing friends, you are invaluable in this process. Jessica R. Patch, thank you for your courage to look at my roughest drafts and offer "truth in love." Writing doesn't happen without you. I will always be grateful that God put you on the other side of that elevator door. To Joanna Politano and Dawn Crandall, thank you both for all the support, prayers, and brainstorming voxes. Your friendship means so very much. And Beth Vogt, thank you, thank you, friend, for your encouragement and help offered without a moment's hesitation. I so appreciate you!

To my amazing cousin and her hubby, Janette and Ken Stewart. Thank you so much for helping me with all the medical questions I had for this book. You took time from your busy days to supply me with answers to countless questions. If any details end up incorrect, it's all me!

To Linda S. Glaz, my agent. Thanks for your tireless work and belief not only in me, but also in the writing community. So many are blessed by you and your huge heart. You are a warrior for authors, and I'm so grateful you brought me into your world.

To my editors, Jessica Nelson and Linda Yezak. One word instead of fifty-two: thanks. ;)

And to My Love and my kiddos (Corydon, Ella, and Raleigh.) There, your name is in print! Thanks for how you all love and care for me in your own ways. I am blessed by each one of you and always remember, I love you MORE!

DEDICATION

To My Love. Our own journey had its fair share of ups and downs on the way to our "I do," but I wouldn't rewrite our story for anything. Thank you for giving me my own Happily Ever After every day. I love you MOST.

Chapter One

B elle Thornton's first mistake had been opening the door. Nothing good came from a doorbell ringing before a girl finished her first cup of coffee. But the good manners long instilled through all of her beauty pageant years trumped the common sense shouting for her to crawl back in bed, pull the covers over her head, and start again tomorrow.

She seriously needed to reconsider her priorities. The day had raced downhill faster than her baby girl chased the ice cream truck. Only two and a half and already Anna perked up to its siren song and the treats it held inside. That child loved ice cream more than a beauty queen loved sparkles.

After the incredibly kind yet no-nonsense surprise visit from the inspectors—one from the fire department, one from building code—left her with an expensive task list, she reheated her coffee. Perhaps this day could still be salvaged.

But she lived with a toddler who woke up on the wrong side of her twin bed. Definitely didn't help that even with all the windows open, it was about one hundred degrees in their tiny brick box of an apartment. Because of the broken air conditioner, she'd purchased a few portable fans, but all they seemed to do was move around the stale July air.

"No want toast." Barely tall enough to see over the counter, Anna's head of loose blonde curls bounced as she stomped her bare foot.

"Eggs?" Belle attempted.

This time the curls shook. "Nooo."

"Oatmeal and a banana?" Any one of those suggestions would work on a normal day, but this morning was like trying to guess which wire to cut on a ticking time bomb. Too many wrong guesses, and things would explode.

So she went straight for the sure thing. Reaching for a colorful box with a unicorn, rainbow, and leprechaun, she pushed away the internal voice chastising her for serving up sugar in the morning. Desperate times called for desperate measures. "How about unicorn cereal?"

And her tiny blonde went from near menace to cherub. "With mik." Now smiling, she perched herself on a chair at the table and plopped her well-loved pink stuffed unicorn in the seat beside her.

"Yes, with milk."

Crisis averted, Belle served her breakfast, settled onto another chair, and opened her laptop. Spreadsheets filled with numbers stared at her, and no matter how she manipulated them, they refused to add up the way she needed. The requests from the inspectors who'd visited lined up at the corner of her mind, adding pieces to a puzzle she could only find one way to solve. Which would require another visit to her landlord, Rick, unless a second solution popped up.

"Ah done." Anna plunked her spoon into the leftover milk.

The numbers would need to wait until Anna was downstairs in daycare. One of the perks of living above her fledgling business meant a short commute. "Time for us to get dressed then."

Grabbing her hand, she walked Anna to her bedroom and waited while she picked out just the right outfits for herself and Uni, her unicorn. Then they engaged in the morning's second battle over brushing teeth before turning YouTube to "Baby Shark" so Belle could get herself ready. A typical challenge to her sanity, this morning the song saved it.

Forgoing a shower—something she never would have done before Anna— she grabbed body spray instead and tossed her hair into a messy bun, a mom's survival hairstyle, though hers erred more on the side of messy than styled this morning. Oh, what her former friends would say now if they could see her. She cringed. She knew exactly what they'd say because she had been leader of their pack—one that deserted her right around the time she'd been left standing pregnant at the altar.

The past three years had taught her several lessons she'd never purposefully signed up for but would never exchange. Things like, outward appearance doesn't mean as much as outward actions. A person's situation doesn't determine their value. She was stronger than she looked. And parenting was equal parts exhaustion and reward. It was those—and other—lessons that led to leasing this building and opening AnnaBelle's.

The secondhand store-slash-educational space-slash-daycare was born from her struggles, its name a mash-up of hers and her daughter's. The rough-around-the-edges structure held a wealth of opportunities for other single moms, many made possible thanks to the volunteers from the retirement home next door. It had become a place filled with life, laughter, and second chances. Unfortunately, it needed its own physical second chance, something she assumed a landlord would handle.

Should have remembered what people said about assuming.

By the time late afternoon rolled around, she'd fielded three phone calls from roofers with booked-up schedules, two calls with inflated estimates on air conditioning repair, and one on a back-ordered window that was supposed to have been fixed last week. All this between unclogging the sink in the daycare bathroom and tightening the handle on a leaky faucet in the kitchenette/breakroom. And she still needed to line up workers to tackle the list left this morning. If she missed any of those checkmarks, fines would start racking up.

"Your face is too young for those wrinkles." Astrid Holmes strolled in, manicured nails a match for her red lipstick, gray hair in a hair-sprayed poof, and dark brown eyes assessing her from behind black-framed eyeglasses. "What's got you so puckered up?"

Wasn't any use to lie to Astrid. The old woman was a walking lie detector. "Everything." Belle straightened from behind her tiny desk in her closet-turned-office at the back of the building and started with the linchpin to today's troubles. "I had a surprise visit this morning from our local building inspector complete with the fire chief."

"Mercy. A man in uniform. Was he handsome?"

"I didn't notice."

"That's your problem. You don't keep an eye out for potentials."

"Because I'm not looking for one." Been there, done that, got the T-shirt and tossed it away.

Astrid merely gave her the look. "Tell me then, what did they want?"

"Seems someone called them about an exit sign that wasn't working and those crumbling steps out back. They came to check it, and one thing led to another. Now I have a list."

"Such as?"

Belle handed it off.

"Oh my." Astrid's mouth opened farther the more she read. "Are you going to speak with Rick?"

"I don't have much choice." Hopefully, he'd be as patient as he'd already proven himself to be. "If I'm forced to fix all of that, I'll miss my projected target for bringing the rent current."

"He's the landlord. He should be fixing this."

"Except I signed a lease that says otherwise." Because she'd wanted to open AnnaBelle's on her own. Well, she had, and now she was paying for that choice—literally. Still, her mistake was easier to accept than the pain from others letting her down.

She hadn't planned on this building being a mistake, though. Two years ago, it had seemed like the answer to all the question marks hovering over her plans. An expansive first floor big enough for how she'd envisioned AnnaBelle's layout, a small apartment for her and Anna in one corner above it, and a price tag she could afford. Everything appeared like it was finally coming together, so she'd penned her name on that thin black line.

Things were great. Until they weren't. As the snow began to melt, it became obvious she needed a new roof. One call to her landlord made it clear that signing the Absolute Triple Net lease he'd tweaked in his favor meant he wasn't responsible for the upkeep of this place—she was.

Astrid settled onto the edge of the desk and patted Belle's shoulder. "Things'll work out. They always do."

"I wish I had your optimism."

"I have a lot of years to stand on, all filled with hindsight. You're just getting started."

Really? Because it felt like an ending if she couldn't get things worked out.

Belle fiddled with a binder on her desk. "My hope is that Rick will continue to give us grace with our rent." He'd allowed it to slide while she paid for the upkeep around here. She'd racked up quite the debt, but so far he'd been generous with his patience. "The lotion sales are really picking up. I'm going to bring him new projections and pray he'll be understanding."

As a baby, Anna developed eczema. No over-the-counter or prescribed lotions seemed to help, and Belle struggled using such strong ingredients on her little girl. So she created her own thick lotion that cleared up Anna's issues. That small tube had morphed into a hobby that turned into a profitable—and growing—small business. Now she had several scents and even a few soaps and lip balms the women around here helped make. Those skin care sales padded her bottom line and extended her ability to teach the practices of small business to some of the ladies. Yet another way AnnaBelle's assisted single moms.

Astrid handed her the papers. "He'd better. You're paying for the upkeep of his building. Grace should be his middle name where you're concerned."

"I'd be happier if it was Charitable because I'm going to ask if he'll kick in some of the money. Adding all this stuff"—she shook the list in the air, wishing some of the biggest ticket items, like the new sprinkler system, would magically slide off—"has to be more than he expected when I signed that lease, and honestly, I don't know if I can swing it all."

She'd been saving for a new roof and air conditioning, the two big maintenance issues she'd previously hoped to accomplish this summer. If she had to handle these new items too, she'd be patching the roof and forgoing the AC fix. It still puttered away down here. She and Anna would have to keep running fans upstairs.

"You know the girls and I will help any way we can. The guys too." Astrid stood stoically by her side, the self-promoted captain from the rag-tag team of elderly volunteers next door.

"I know. I couldn't run this place without you." Then it hit how silent things were. "Did you get them all to sleep?" Quite the feat considering the *them* consisted of seven little ones under the age of five dropped off for today's daycare.

"We did. Fran, Margie, and Ruth are keeping a watchful eye."

Those cotton-tops could probably use a nap too. "If they don't nod off themselves."

They shared a quiet laugh, then Astrid squeezed Belle's hand. "You truly are doing a wonderful thing here."

No doubt she meant the words to soothe, but they added to her stress. People whom others had cast off found their place here. If she screwed this up and the doors closed in their faces … No, she refused to think that way.

Sighing, she stood and filed her paperwork in the dinged-up metal cabinet in the corner. "Did Anna give you any trouble today?" She'd hit the terrible twos early and was still clinging to them even at the halfway mark.

"She was sweet as pie, as always."

"For you."

"I'm not her mama."

"No. I'm the lucky one in that role." Even with the tantrums. Parenting was hard. Single parenting a level all of its own. Sure, sometimes a rogue thought or two popped up about having someone in the trenches with her, but total self-reliance proved far less dangerous to her heart and mind than a thousand of Anna's tantrums ever would.

Her cell phone dinged, and she picked it up. "You have got to be kidding me. I swear this day is out to get me."

"What?" Astrid leaned over her desk.

"Eric is staying in Haiti."

"Doesn't he fly in today?"

"Apparently not." She stood. "I have five women signed up for the free Lamaze class that starts Thursday and no one to teach it now." Because Eric Wassink's one-month mission trip had now become an open-ended stay. She couldn't be mad at him, though. He had warned her of the possibility when he left. "He's staying because the need there is too great. This is what happens when I take volunteers with big hearts."

She quickly texted him, then grabbed her purse and peered up at Astrid. "Do you mind handling things here? I'm storming the hospital, and I'm not leaving until someone agrees to help." This was a battle she could win, and she desperately needed one victory before bedtime.

"Of course I'll stay, but you've already asked practically everyone on that floor."

"And I'm asking again. It's a lot harder to say no to someone in person." Determination was a trait that had grown stronger in the past three years. She might have been forced to deal with being left behind or in a lurch, but that wasn't going to happen to these girls. And she most definitely wouldn't be the one to do it. "You sure you'll be okay?"

"I'll call in the reinforcements when the kids wake up if need be. Estee and Betty's bridge game can be interrupted. We've got you covered."

"Thanks, Astrid." Knowing her, she'd put on one of her mini magic shows to keep them entertained. Astrid had been a dancer who worked with a magician, fell in love, and married him. Through their years together, she'd become nearly as good as he was at the craft, and she loved showing it off to the littles here. No doubt she felt closer to Titus every time she did.

With a wave, Belle hustled out of the room, checked in quickly with who was on the register up front, and then booked it to her car. Traffic through the heart of Abundance was minimal this afternoon, especially since she headed away from the tiny downtown area. Revitalization had ramped up ever since local Harlow Tucker married Hollywood royalty Blake Carlton and they brought their annual charity event to town. Now colorful storefronts lined the shopping district there, which would be filled with locals and tourists mingling on this hot afternoon. If they weren't meandering along Rainier and Seventh, then they were driving south a few miles to Holland and its lakeshore to splash in the waves. Summer was what made winter in Michigan worth surviving.

She turned along a curve leaving town, cranked up her radio, and lowered her window. Surviving had been year-round for her ever since Micah Shaw pulled his disappearing act. If it weren't for her sister, Penny, and brother-in-law, Jonah, she might have become the hermit she desperately wanted to be in the aftermath of it all. Crazy to think that her and Micah's almost-wedding led to his cousin marrying her sister, but Penny and Jonah were proof that happily-ever-afters did happen for some people. In the past couple of years, they had lent their emotional support to all her endeavors. Jonah even offered financial support when it came to leasing this building, but she needed to stand on her own two feet. She sunk every penny of her pageant wins into this place, and like the black hole it was, the dilapidated building had sucked them all up.

Still, AnnaBelle's was the best thing she'd done outside of becoming a mommy. Both had been birthed during the same season in her life. Pregnant and basically alone, her pageantry past at least afforded more opportunities than many others in her situation. Even then, things became incredibly hard. The idea that one place could address so many issues had pricked her heart. She possessed a way to offer that place and the know-how to run it. She'd been good with numbers in school and could see connections and patterns without even trying. Marketing and business had captured her interest, so she'd majored in one and minored in the other. Most people only saw her as the former beauty queen she was, but that Miss Teen USA title had provided her with a free education, and now she was using it for more than her pageant resume.

Helping people like herself.

Each year she added to AnnaBelle's, and this year had been the prenatal program. Still, three years into her five-year plan, she wasn't completely on target with all her goals. Her burgeoning lotion line could bridge that gap if the sales continued to pick up. They were at that tipping point where she needed to spend money to make money, and those green bills were being rather elusive.

Much like the help she sought for the prenatal class.

Which was what brought her to Spectrum Hospital at one-thirty on a Friday afternoon. As she exited her car, a wall of heat wrapped around her. Even in the shade of the parking garage, the day was unbearably hot. Before she made it to the door, sweat slicked her skin like she'd run here rather than drove. She swiped it from her brow.

Inside she made her way to the nurses' station on floor three. Head nurse Lettie Rydel saw her as she stepped off the elevator. "Belle! What brings you around today?"

"Eric is staying in Haiti, so I'm back to square one over at AnnaBelle's."

"Oh." Lettie made a face. "I did hear that."

Belle hugged the wall as a laundry cart squeaked past them. "There's got to be someone else here who'll help."

Lettie tapped her lips.

"Please, Lettie? Even if you think it's a long shot. Give me a name, and I'll crack them. I promise." There weren't any other options.

Lettie's blank stare slowly morphed into a smile. "I'll do even better. I'll point you to some fresh meat."

"Huh?"

"Our new interns started at the beginning of the month, but one of them is actually a fourth-year transfer resident. Nice guy. Keeps himself in check around the nurses. Takes extra time with his patients. I bet if you asked, he'd be willing to help." She back-walked down the hall. "Let me track him down. Wait here."

The directive wasn't needed. Other single moms depended on her. So if Lettie knew someone who could help, Belle wasn't moving from this spot until she'd convinced him to do just that.

"Shaw, you coming with us tonight?" The slam of a cupboard accompanied the question.

"Ten bucks he says no."

Micah Shaw turned toward the deep voice who'd answered for him. It belonged to Garrett Ryder, who smirked from his perch on the counter of their resident's lounge. Sticking to the other end, Micah grabbed a pod for the Keurig. "Good thing no one's taking you up on your bet, because you'd win."

"After the day we're having, you sure you don't need a drink?" Another colleague walked past.

Need? No. Want? He swallowed the *yes* that would likely dog him all his days. Getting the two confused played a large part in how his life derailed, and it cost him more than he'd ever wanted to spend. He'd returned home with the burning hope to pay off that debt.

"I'm good." Micah lowered himself onto a chair.

"Suit yourself." Crushing his paper cup, Garrett tossed it into the trash as he exited. "We'll be at O'Doul's later if you want to catch up with us."

Three years ago, he'd have been the first one there and last to leave. Now he dug his fingers into the table to hold himself to it. Pictured his little girl who he'd never met. Thought of Belle, the woman who still held his heart even if she didn't want it. A possible future with them was worth infinitely more than one drink—and he knew now that he'd never stop with one. Dragging his hands through his hair, he groaned. Prayed. The temptation might never fully leave, but it did lessen every time he denied it.

The room emptied, and the quiet allowed his thoughts to wander. He closed his eyes against his last memory of Belle as she kissed him the night before their wedding. He could still feel her in his arms, something he'd never experienced with their daughter. Sure, his mom texted him pictures of Anna over her two and a half years of life, but he'd never held her. Never heard her laugh or made her smile like he used to with Belle. He'd walked away from them and now prayed Belle would allow him to walk back into their lives.

That familiar fear he battled too often bubbled like someone shaking a two-liter, then twisting the top off. He needed to keep things settled so he didn't lose control. He reached for his phone and tapped the first number on his favorites list. Two rings and a well-known voice answered.

"Hey there, Micah."

"Jonathan."

Jonathan Samuel. They'd been residents together in California. A year ahead in the program, Jonathan had taken Micah under his wing, and they'd become close friends. Married and with a six-month-old at home, Jonathan and his wife Stacey often invited Micah over to their tiny apartment. Seeing their marriage, watching Stacey's pregnancy progress, being close by for the delivery, all of it had provided Micah with an up-close look at what he was missing here at home. And while it had taken Jonathan nearly the entire three years of Micah's internship in California to pry his story from him, the details eventually spilled forth. Jonathan met each one with understanding and some pretty solid advice—along with a healthy dose of accountability. Which was what had Micah picking up the phone tonight.

Skipping pleasantries, Jonathan nailed the matter at hand. "Wanting a drink?"

"Been a long day and it's slightly half over."

"Tell me about it."

Propping his elbows on his knees, Micah squeezed the bridge of his nose. "Delivery of triplets, a mom with preeclampsia, and an emergency C-section that didn't end well." He still couldn't get one of the mother's cries out of his head. "It's hard to feel so out of control when you're taught to maintain it. Have it."

"Which is why you need to remember who ultimately holds that control." Jonathan's voice didn't waver, but it did soften with understanding. "I'm sorry it was a tough day. Ones like that are hard to let go of."

"Or forget."

"We'll never forget them, Micah, and we shouldn't. They're what make us better doctors."

Wasn't sure he entirely agreed, but Jonathan hadn't steered him wrong yet. He shifted on the bench. "Thanks for picking up."

"I told you I always would, as long as you keep up your end of the deal."

"I know." He'd always answer as long as Micah kept up with professional listening ears. "I've put a call in to a few counselors here. Hoping one is the right fit."

"Good." He waited a beat and then, "Anything other than work making you thirsty?"

Typical Jonathan. He knew there was, but he wanted Micah to voice it.

"I haven't spoken to her yet."

"You've been home two weeks."

"And working round the clock to learn the policies, procedures, and people at a new hospital. It hasn't been easy." Most thought he was crazy for transferring at the start of his fourth year of residency. Jonathan was one of the few who understood it was the opposite; he'd finally gotten his head on straight.

Jonathan chuckled low. "Something I believe you were warned about when you left California, but Belle and Anna are two of the three reasons behind your move. You're going to have to take that next leap eventually, and the longer you wait, the scarier it'll seem."

Not sure that was possible. There was way too much to lose once he landed that leap. Over here on this side, he could still maintain hope and hold on to the picture of his future he'd drawn that included Belle, Anna, and a little house overlooking the lake. He'd never been one with white-picket-fence dreams, but the first photo Mom had texted him of Belle holding their little girl changed all of that. It wasn't something he ever thought he'd be able to have, but three years, lots of long talks with Jonathan, and sound counseling convinced him to try. Persuaded him to believe that staying out of their lives wasn't the best thing for them.

Muffled voices slipped through the lounge door. Micah focused on the mottled gray floor. "The last thing I want to do is show up at her door with no sleep and no real time to talk to her. My schedule swaps to nights in a few days, which gives me nearly forty-eight hours off. I plan to see her then." Gave him time to get his head on straight if she did slam the door in his face—an entirely possible scenario and one he deserved.

"I'm holding you to it. You've lived in limbo long enough."

"I know." He'd called for accountability. Jonathan wasn't letting him down.

He did, however, switch topics. "How's your mom?"

The other reason he'd come home. When he left three years ago, she'd been more forgetful than usual. Fast-forward to this spring when Dad said he couldn't handle things anymore and was leaving. Mom's dementia had quickly deteriorated to what doctors considered the moderate stage, meaning she needed full-time care. Dad would handle her move into assisted living, but then he was moving on himself. While he hadn't filed for divorce, he considered their marriage over.

It all happened so fast. Coming home two weeks ago had been an unsettling wake-up call to Mom's diagnosis. "Settling into her new place. She still recognizes me but doesn't always remember that I'm grown. I often have to remind her of the same things repeatedly."

"I'm sorry, man. I know that's tough."

He swallowed past a lump. "Tell me all the new things Olivia can do since we last talked."

"Happily." Distracted by his favorite topic, Jonathan spent the next ten minutes on Olivia's newfound love of solid foods and her recent ability to roll everywhere, which had them installing plug covers, locks, and soft corners on every surface imaginable. Before disconnecting the call, they caught up on a few happenings at the hospital and the friends Micah had left behind. He stood to stretch.

Nash Holsten pushed into the small room, fresh scrubs and face. He'd taken half of someone's shift, so his day was just beginning. One look in Micah's direction provided ample info on the hours he'd missed. "Crazy day so far?"

Micah brushed a hand over his rumpled attire and filled him in on how chaotic it had been. "One of those days where you realize how precious life is and how quickly things can head south." His adrenaline was still coming down.

"Sorry I missed the excitement." Nash grabbed a water bottle from the fridge. "You transfer into the program and somehow have all the luck."

"Don't know if I'd call it lucky."

"All in how you look at things, mate." Laying the Australian accent on thick, Nash brushed by with a slap on Micah's shoulder. "For instance, you may want to try a mirror before heading out there."

The door swished shut behind him, and Micah quick-turned toward his reflection. Yep. A trip to the locker room was necessary. After exchanging his dirty scrubs for clean ones, Micah returned to the floor to tackle paperwork. If things remained quiet for a bit, he'd head outside for a walk. Stretch his legs and clear his head. Work on the best plan for how and when to approach Belle come Monday. About twenty feet from the nurses' station, someone called his name. Lettie waved from the opposite end of the hall.

"There you are." She switched her focus to the blonde leaning against the counter, whose back faced Micah. "Here's the man I was telling you about."

Lettie was talking him up to someone? Was she touring an expectant mom? Maybe someone scheduled for a C-section during one of his shifts. Pulling on a warm smile, he held out his hand as he reached the woman, and she turned. The shock on her face jolted to his heart, sending it into an erratic beat. "Belle?"

Chapter Two

Belle had heard of life moving in slow motion, but she'd never actually experienced it until this very second. Time downshifted as she turned, and a figure caught in her periphery. Every second dragged out. As much as she hoped she was seeing things, she wasn't. Micah Shaw stood in front of her.

That reality rooted her feet to the floor and her tongue to the roof of her mouth. Pretty sure her heart stopped too before pounding out a staccato beat that screamed, *Run!*

"Belle, this is Micah Shaw." Lettie's words dropped off at Belle's stiff stance. She must have noticed Micah stood in a similar statuesque state because her gaze bounced between the two of them. After an agonizing moment, she broke the thick silence. "Do you two know each other?"

Belle let her bolting figure answer.

"Belle?" Lettie's concern chased her down.

Dodging it, she kept moving. Not the elevator! She needed out of here. Now. Sweat pooled along her spine as she darted to the stairwell.

"Belle?" Micah's deep voice made a grab for her as well.

But she'd learned the art of leaving from him.

Tugging the door open, she raced through.

"Belle, wait!"

She couldn't. Wouldn't. Except his long legs had always moved faster than hers. She hadn't even made it to the next floor before his gentle hand ground her to a stop.

The familiar scent of cedar, Irish Spring soap, and the tiniest hint of antiseptic washed over her with a wave of bittersweet emotions. Slowly, she tracked her gaze up his lean body until it landed on those deep-blue eyes that taunted her memories and stared at her from their young daughter's face every single day.

Micah looked every bit as surprised as she felt. He released his hold as if touching her had been as unplanned as seeing her. Breath ripped from her lungs, and she couldn't seem to suck it back in. Especially when his gaze moved from surprised to something else. Regret? And ... cautious hope?

Hope?

That she wouldn't lay him flat right here in the stairwell?

"Belle." Her name scratched from his deep voice. The same one that used to send a thrill through her. And dang it all if the familiar sound didn't tug at her traitorous heart still. "It's …" His hand raked through his thick blond hair. Still wore it long and spiked away from his forehead in waves. His ever-present tan covered his strong face, strength that mimicked his steel will. Something she once found attractive, until he used it to cut her—and their daughter—completely from his life. Now that strength seemed to soften in his eyes, giving a vulnerability he'd seldom allowed to show before. He swallowed, his Adam's apple bobbing. "It's good to see you."

Seriously? *Good to see you?* That was all he could muster? Heat worked through her, stealing all remaining coherent words. She turned to keep moving down the stairs before she did something she'd regret. Or not regret. Because she itched to deck him, but the last thing she needed was to be arrested for assault.

That possibility didn't seem to faze Micah. His fingers encircled her wrist, and this time he held on. His touch remained loose enough that she could easily break away, but as her shoulders brushed his chest, the heat of his body stoked latent memories that momentarily paralyzed her. Her body, heart, and mind all seemed to be operating on different bandwidths, none of them connecting with the reality of the moment. She'd dreamed of this for years. What she'd say if she ever saw him again. How she'd look. Feel. Not one of those scenarios came close to the past three minutes.

Twisting her neck slightly, she hid behind loose strands of hair to study him further. Stubble covered his firm jaw and neck—a look she'd always loved on him. Yet she itched for a razor to shave it off because he had no right to look so good while she resembled something the cat dragged in. That thought set off an internal snort. She didn't believe in karma, but there was truth to the saying that you reap what you sow, and she was harvesting every claw-baring comment she'd ever made to or about another woman. Right now, she resembled exactly the kind of mess she used to point out to Micah to ensure he knew how lucky he was to have her coiffed skinny body on his arm.

My, how the mighty had fallen.

Still, she was thankful for the tumble because it made her who she was now.

Micah, on the other hand, didn't look like he'd changed a bit.

Overhead, the fluorescent lights in the stairwell buzzed. The awkward quietness sparked her frozen muscles, and she yanked away from him. "What are you doing here?"

"I took a transfer." His words were slow and measured, his tone calm, much like she used with Anna to ward off an oncoming tantrum.

Too bad for him that Anna's temperament mirrored hers.

"That's obvious. But what are you doing on the OB floor?"

"I switched to obstetrics."

He'd uttered all of eight words to her, and they provoked a million questions. But one thought rammed its way to the front. Lettie had mentioned the residents arrived two weeks ago. He'd been here. In West Michigan. And hadn't tried to contact her once—not even to see his daughter. Not that she'd have let him, but it still twisted the knife she thought she'd removed.

"I'd say we could grab a cup of coffee and compare notes on what labor and delivery is like, but you know what? I'm not really up for it."

He flinched, but she refused to feel sorry for him. What kind of man delivered everyone else's babies while walking away from his own?

Hurt eclipsed her other emotions, and she steeled her spine. This time she'd do the walking.

"I need to go."

"Belle, please wait."

At least he didn't reach for her again. Her heart was twisting in ways she could barely breathe through and, honest-to-God, she couldn't be responsible for her actions if he kept this up. She continued down the stairs.

He followed. "Please. We need to talk."

"No. We *needed* to talk three years ago, but you didn't seem to think so."

"I ... I'd like to see Anna."

She whirled on him. "Don't you *dare* say her name."

They slammed to a stop on a landing, and Micah tried again. "Our daughter—"

"No." She pounded her fist into her chest. "*My* daughter. You've done *nothing* to call her yours."

"I know." His hands raised, palms out as if she were a wild animal and he could capture her by using gentle tactics. But she'd fallen for his softness before. Had thought it was genuine. And he completely wrecked her.

Fire she barely restrained swept through her. She needed to get away from him. Now. But Micah took a step in her direction even as she backed away. "Leave me alone."

"Belle, please, I only want—"

"I don't care what you want." She flung the words at him. "Just leave."

But he stood strong.

Tears welled in her eyes. Why couldn't an ounce of this steel will to stay beside her have shown up three years ago, when she waited at the altar for him? Emotions choked her, but she would not break down in front of him.

"Belle?" Lettie stood above them. "Are you okay?"

No. Not even close.

"We're fine." Micah's focus remained on her.

"I asked her. Not you." Lettie's firm voice brooked no argument.

Micah's eyes flickered over Belle's, questioning who she'd side with. Asking for it to be him. To just give him a moment.

The fact that she could still understand him without words, that three years of extracting him from her heart hadn't worked, produced the only answer she could give. She peeked up at Lettie. "I'm fine. It was a minor misunderstanding, but we've cleared things up, and Dr. Shaw is leaving."

"Belle," Micah pleaded.

"I think that was clear, Dr. Shaw." Lettie started down the stairs.

Still holding her in his stare, Micah took one large step back, defeat and concern written in equal measures across his face. "Do you have a key card?"

She shook her head.

He faced Lettie. "Can you see Belle out of the stairwell so she won't be stuck? You can exit here, and I'll go up a floor."

Brushing past him, Lettie blessedly remained silent as she swiped her access card to exit the stairs. Behind her, Micah still stood. Belle didn't possess the energy to give him one last look. Stepping from the stairwell, they crossed to the elevators. No doubt Lettie had questions, but she refrained from asking them. Today, at least. Belle's reflection mocked her from the elevator's gold, glossy doors. The day she'd run into Micah again, she looked more like one of the crazy stepsisters than the princess of their broken fairy tale. Shouldn't matter. She wasn't in love with him anymore and wanted nothing from him, but boy, did it sting that this was the last picture he'd have of her in his mind. Probably figured he'd dodged a bullet.

With a sigh, she shook her head. Thinking this was the last time he'd see her was optimistic. He'd made it clear in their few shared words that he had an agenda with their daughter's name on it. As much as she wanted to tear his plans to shreds, that could one day drive a wedge between her and Anna. That was a risk she couldn't take, but she also couldn't throw open the door and let him waltz back into their lives. Could she?

"You sure you're okay?"

No. But this wasn't the time or place or even the person to have this conversation with. Lettie's concern was sweet, but they were more acquaintances than friends.

The doors opened. "I am."

Then she slipped past Lettie onto the elevator. If only her reawakened insecurities would slip away as easily.

Okay. He deserved every ounce of what she'd dished out. That didn't make it any easier to hear. Micah never thought returning to Belle and Anna's life would be easy, but he had thought it would be possible. Seeing her today planted the first seed of doubt.

If he hadn't wanted a drink before, he did now. Good thing he had plans to see Mom instead of going home to an empty house.

He stopped by the nurses' station to check in on his patients. Room 3502 was progressing as expected. Slow and steady for a first birth.

"Dr. Shaw?" The nurse in 3502 popped her head out of the doorway.

"Yes?"

"Her water broke. Do you want to check her?"

Maybe things were ramping up. "Coming."

Inside the room, soft music played. The mom's eyes were closed as she breathed through a contraction, but the dad's eyes were wide and wild. Earlier in the day, he'd seemed calm. Micah scanned the table beside the bed. Nice. Three Red Bulls and two Starbucks cups. Yes, they'd been here closing in on twenty-four hours, but at the rate the man was going, he'd be too shaky to hold his child when it finally arrived.

Within a few minutes, Micah had checked the mom. She'd gone straight from one contraction into another. Made sense. She was eight centimeters. "Won't be long now. You're in transition, which means it's the home stretch." He looked at the nurse. "I'll check her again in a half hour. My guess is she'll be ready to push."

"We'll get things set in here," the nurse responded.

Micah snapped off his gloves and dropped them into the container by the door.

"Um, excuse me?" The dad followed him over. He held out his hand. "Darrin. And that's my wife, Carrie."

Her name was in the chart, but Micah nodded as if it were new info. "She's doing great."

"Isn't she?" Darrin wrung his hands together. "Is everything okay? She's in a lot of pain."

Well, she was about to have a baby, so that was to be expected. Micah closed his mouth around those words, swallowed, then tried for an answer he could give. "It's too late to give her an epidural, but if you help her with her breathing, she's going to do fine. Labor and delivery is hard work, but the body is made for it."

Darrin turned gray as his wife let out a moan. "I wish I could do something more. Is there any way to speed this up?"

Looked like it was killing him to see his wife in pain. Micah gripped the guy's shoulder. "Just by being here, you're doing everything she needs." And so much more than he'd done for Belle. Every time he stood in an L&D room, he wished he could rewind time to be right by her side as she brought Anna into this world.

"Thanks." A little color returned to Darrin's cheeks. As another moan ripped the air, he rushed to his wife's side.

Micah exited the room and rubbed the nape of his neck. So much he'd missed out on, and judging by today's interaction, Belle would be fine if things remained status quo. He needn't worry that she'd slam the door in his face come Monday. She wouldn't even open it.

Movement down the hall captured his attention. Lettie, eyes on the chart she held, walked his way, and an idea struck. "Lettie!" he called. She looked up, spun, and hustled in the opposite direction. "Wait!"

He raced to catch her, running alongside until she stopped and slayed him with her eyes and tone. "What do you want?"

"For you to hear me out." He'd come home for a clean slate, not a muddied one, and today had pretty much tossed gobs of sludge all over those intentions. Convincing Lettie he wanted to help Belle might be the first swipe at wiping it off.

She rolled her eyes but then pushed open the door to an empty room. "You get two minutes."

No doubt it was more curiosity than kindness that had her listening, but he'd take what he could get.

The door swished shut behind them. "Belle and I share a past."

"I gathered. And I'm guessing it has something to do with her sweetheart of a little girl."

So, she knew Belle was a mom. That meant he could lay all his cards on the table. "You'd be right."

"Didn't look like I stumbled upon a happy reunion."

"Because I was an idiot, and that's why I came home. I want to make things right with Belle and Anna."

She tested him with the weight of her stare before nodding. "Noble. But she doesn't seem to want you around."

"No, she doesn't, but I need to be around her if she's going to see I've changed."

He hoped she'd agree. "You mentioned earlier that she needed something?"

"I don't think you're the doctor for the job."

"I am." Didn't matter what it was.

"I think she'd disagree."

"Probably, but our past shouldn't get in the way of any help she may need."

Lettie tilted her head. Outside, the overhead intercom squawked. An itch prickled between his shoulder blades. Finally, she cleared her throat. "Tell you what. You were the first resident I spoke to. If the others turn me down, I'll take that as a sign you're the one who's supposed to fill the slot."

Not the yes he was hoping for, but not the no he feared. "Mind if I ask what the slot is?"

She pulled open the door—"Lamaze class"—and let it close behind her.

Her answer stunned him into stillness before he shook it away to chase her down. Didn't need to go far. She stood in the hall with a wry grin on her face. "Relax, she's not pregnant."

The words registered, but it still took a moment to calm his pulse. "Then why a Lamaze class?"

"It's part of the business she runs. A little storefront where she provides opportunities for pregnant women and single moms. The Lamaze class is a new addition, and you'd be leading it with her. I'll let you know if I can't find someone else to do it." Chart in hand, Lettie disappeared into another room.

Leaning against the wall, Micah scrubbed his face with his hands, then tugged them through his hair. "You've got a crazy sense of humor, God."

His phone buzzed in his pocket. Mom's face flashed across his screen. He brushed away his heavy thoughts, inhaled, and answered. "Hey, Mom."

"They aren't letting me leave this place, and I need to go home and make dinner for you and your father."

This was a regular conversation lately. He'd remind her about Dad when they were face-to-face. It never went well over the phone. "Remember, Dad won't be home for dinner tonight, but I'm coming to see you when I leave the hospital."

Silence. Then, "Are you sick?"

"No, Mom. I'm a doctor, so I help people who are sick."

"You're too little to be a doctor."

Now wasn't the time to press her. She'd become agitated. Instead, he redirected. "I'm going to bring Chloe with me." Her white and gray puffball of a Havanese always brightened her nights.

"I've missed her. I have treats here for her."

"I know." He'd supplied them. "She'll be excited to see you and have a few."

A breath of silence slipped by. "So you'll come tonight then?"

19

"Yes. But not until after seven."

"And you'll take me home?"

Her voice held a childlike quality that deepened his desire to protect her—and hate the fact he couldn't. Not from the disease stealing her mind. Because this sickness warped what he *was* doing to keep her safe into something sinister. "Not tonight, Mom. But I promise you're safe there."

"I just want to go home."

"I know you do." A nurse popped her head out of room 3502 and waved at him. He headed that way. "I have to go, but I promise I'll be there soon."

"With Chloe?"

"With Chloe."

Because he was determined to be a man of his word.

Chapter Three

"**A**gain! Again!" Anna's excited voice drifted down the hall.

Belle stopped at the doorway to the small room she'd made into a daycare area for the moms connected with AnnaBelle's. A small rectangular table surrounded with tiny blue chairs stood on top of a colorful rug with all the letters of the alphabet woven into it. Short, wooden bookshelves lined two walls, meeting in a ninety-degree angle. Books and toys filled the shelves, and bean bags sat in front of them. On the other side of the room, a large whiteboard hung with another bright rug under it. She'd done her best with limited funds to make this a fun space, and it was—as long as no one looked up. The leaky roof had made a mess of the drop ceiling. Now most of the tiles needed replacing.

Still, she grinned at the sight in front of her. Astrid held court with the seven toddlers there today, and she had them spellbound by the simple coin trick she was performing. No matter how many times she pulled coins from their ears, hair, or—the all-time favorite, their armpits—they were as mesmerized as the first time they'd seen the magical feat.

Anna giggled as Astrid handed her the golden coin. "Go show it to your mama."

Turning, Anna's eyes lit as she caught sight of her, and she raced over. "Mama, yook!"

"Oooh, that's a shiny coin, Monkey." She took the treasure and marveled before returning it to Anna's chubby hands. "Go on and give it back to Miss Astrid."

"No. That's for her piggy bank."

Belle shared a look with Astrid, whose determined smile promised that arguing wouldn't do any good. "Then tell her thank you," Belle instructed.

"Thank you," Anna parroted, then took Belle's hand. "You pway with me now?"

"Sorry. Mama can't play yet, Monkey. I have a little more work to do." She shouldn't have stopped and let Anna see her, but it was hard to last an entire day without visiting. Especially when they lived, worked, and played at the same building. And after her run-in with Micah, a deep need to check on her little girl sprouted inside. With his return, a whole host of questions plagued her, but none of them compared to how his presence might affect her life with Anna.

Astrid quietly sidled up beside her. "You look worse than when you left here. Bad luck?"

"You could say that."

Astrid nodded to Fran and Betty, who were pulling out craft supplies.

"Anna, do you want to make slime with us?" Fran called.

Didn't have to ask her twice. Anna practically leapt to the table, and Astrid pulled Belle into the hall. "What happened?"

"Micah's back."

Astrid's thin black brows rose. "Anna's daddy?"

"That's the one." She started for her office. "But I don't have time to worry about him right now. On my way back here, Rick called and said he could meet with me. I need to print off my numbers and new projections."

"Think you should reschedule?"

"I can't." Besides, Micah wasn't about to disrupt her life all over again. She had too much to figure out. Why he'd returned home was a question she didn't possess the luxury of entertaining, but she wasn't naïve enough to think she wouldn't be forced to. For now, though, finding that answer would have to wait. "If we don't fix the things the fire chief and code inspector informed us about today, we'll be subject to fines." Even worse if she didn't get them handled. At least they'd given her three months. She'd need every single day provided. "I'm hoping Rick will handle a few items. If not, I'm on the hook for them all. Once I know his decision, I can start planning accordingly."

"Then go on, and don't worry about Anna. I'll watch her until you're back, and we'll even make dinner for you. After the day you had, you don't need to be worrying about that too."

If it weren't for the fact she knew Astrid would be dining alone tonight if Belle refused her offer, she'd turn her down. But the rest of Astrid's friends had plans to see the local high school play tonight, and she'd given her ticket to a new resident who recently moved in after her husband passed away.

"That sounds great. Thank you."

Grabbing the papers from the printer, Belle hustled to her car. Had to admit, it'd be nice to have a warm meal she wasn't responsible for tonight. While her nerves prevented her from eating lunch, her stomach seemed to overthrow them and growled for dinner.

She arrived at Rick's office and pushed through the front door. Krista, his receptionist, looked up from her desk. "Good afternoon, Belle. You're his last appointment for the day. He stayed late for you." Rising, she met her at the door that granted access to a hallway leading to his office. Opening it, she ushered her through. "Go on back."

"Thanks." Navy carpet with gray lines ran the length of the hall. Photos from various buildings around West Michigan graced the taupe walls that led to a conference room with two offices across from it. Rick's was the last door on the right. It stood open as if he anticipated her arrival.

She knocked on the dark wood casing, and he looked up from his desk. "Belle. Good to see you. Come on in."

He always said the right words, but something about him put her on edge every time she was in his presence. If she'd paid attention to the feeling early on, maybe she wouldn't have signed with him, but she'd been so intent on making AnnaBelle's happen that she'd been willing to ignore her gut. Instead, she played the apprehension off as an overall negative feeling stemming from how he reminded her of a dark-haired Micah. Both men carried their lean, tall frames with a similar confident assurance. They liked the latest fashion and their hair styled. Both even possessed a movie-star smile. Except Micah's had once stoked a warmth in her, where Rick's rolled in a cold front.

She refused to blame the man, however, for resembling the one who landed the final blow to her heart. Before Micah, it had been cracked. After him, it was in pieces. Made her current approach to life much more self-sufficient. Though she found no problem in asking Rick to help take care of the building he owned.

"Thanks for fitting me in." She sat in the tweed-upholstered chair across from his desk. "Hopefully this won't take long."

"No rush. I don't have anywhere I need to be tonight." He leaned back in his leather chair and crossed his arms over his chest, the navy sleeves of his button-up pulling against toned arms. She'd never seen one strand of his thick chestnut hair out of place, and this afternoon was no exception. His sharply defined cheeks and tight jaw were clean-shaven even this late in the day, which made her wonder if he actually grew facial hair or simply shaved again on his lunch break. And a faint dark musky scent permeated the room as if he'd sprayed the cologne he wore in the air.

"What can I do for you?" His voice always seemed an octave lower than one would expect from him.

"I had a visit from the fire chief and a code inspector this morning."

He didn't even blink. "Yes. I received a copy of their reports."

"Then you know all the items we need to take care of in the next ninety days."

"From what I could see, they were all items you're responsible for."

His response stomped out the little optimism she'd mustered up. "Right."

Didn't mean she couldn't still pose her question. There was a hundred percent chance that if she didn't ask, things wouldn't change, but that same chance dropped to fifty percent if she at least put the query out there. "I wondered if you'd be willing to pitch in for some of the repairs. They're a lot more extensive than most tenants have to deal with."

"Most tenants pay a higher rent for the square footage you have." He leaned forward. "And they pay it on time."

Okay, so that tactic shot her in the foot. "I know—"

He held up a hand with a smile he no doubt meant as comforting but landed more in the realm of insincere. "It's all right, Belle. I've told you before I believe in what you're doing, which is why I set the rent so low." Comparatively speaking, it was low. She'd be able to handle it too if the building itself wasn't such a money pit. "But I can't afford to keep it that low and cover the costs of upkeep to the building."

"Upkeeps that are far beyond anything I thought they'd be." Honestly, she'd have been better off to pay a slightly higher rent.

"I have to agree with you. I wasn't expecting quite as much to go wrong." Again, right words, but she didn't quite believe them. "Which is why I've let you run late on your rent, and my guess is that you're here today because the schedule you gave me in spring that outlined your plan to catch up has taken a hit after today's unexpected visits."

Give the man a gold star.

She bit her lip and swallowed those words. Her snarkiness still reared its head at times, but she'd at least learned to hold it in.

"It has." She pulled out her newest projections on the lotions, thankful that they looked even stronger than they had in spring. Sliding the papers to him, she outlined their estimations. "As you can see, the lotions are doing even better than I'd hoped. Making the building fixes that I'd already informed you about—along with these new ones—is definitely going to affect my bottom line, but I still should be able to catch up on my rent by the end of next year. November is what I'm now projecting, if not earlier."

His thumb rubbed against his bottom lip as he studied her spreadsheets. After thoroughly looking over each one, he tapped them into a neat pile and placed them in the tray on his desk. "Okay."

That was it?

She straightened in her chair. "You're good with all of this?"

"Like I said, I believe in what you're doing." He idly drummed his fingers. "And that's even without your lotion business, but those numbers alone are incredibly sound. Your growth so far is proven. You have solid leads for new sales.

Your repeat customers are over seventy percent, and they're already spending twenty percent more when they do return. Very impressive for as young as your company is." The drumming stopped. "So yes, I'm fine waiting for next November, because I like what I'm seeing. For me, business is about the long game, and this one promises favorable outcomes."

"Thank you." It wasn't exactly what she'd come looking for, but it did release some of the pressure. Things were still tight, and she'd still be making a few sacrifices, but the overall outlook wasn't completely hopeless. "I truly appreciate your willingness to work with me."

He stood and saw her to his office door. "Of course. It's my pleasure to help."

Was it the words, tone, or slick smile that hoisted her red flags? Whatever it was, she needed to set the feeling aside and focus on maintaining the goals she'd left on his desk, because if she missed their mark, then his comment would ring true. She'd be dealing with him for a long time to come.

Micah loved summer. Long days, warm nights, and lakes that weren't frozen. In winter, the day shift mimicked the night shift for all intents and purposes. He'd drive in with the dark and arrive home under it. He was a man who needed sunshine, and even though the clock neared eight p.m. there was still plenty of daylight in the sky. Enough to hop on the paddleboard Mom and Dad stored by the lake and work off today's tension coiling in his body. But not until after he saw Mom like he'd promised.

Typical for his drive home, his brain revisited each decision and action he'd enacted during the past twelve hours. Today, however, it was the final five that played through his mind. After Belle left, the parents in room 3502 welcomed a baby boy, and Micah went on to deliver three more babies after theirs. Like a drill on a bolt, each delivery tightened his muscles another notch. Not because they'd been difficult—they'd all been textbook. But because each time he placed that baby in its mama's arms, the pain he'd seen in Belle's eyes while she railed at him in the stairwell stared back at him. Before today he'd known he'd hurt her. Seeing that emotion on her face and hearing it in her voice not only gutted him but forced him to face his regrets in a new way.

Flexing his fingers on the steering wheel, he pulled up to Dad and Mom's house, shut off the engine, and stared straight ahead. With two stories of muted red brick covered with climbing vines, the house looked more like it belonged in Italy than East Grand Rapids. Detailed white stone outlined the long rectangular windows and created an arch over the front porch. Strange to be living here again. Even weirder without his parents inside.

Barking greeted him as he came through the walnut front door. Chloe. Scooping her up, he walked into the great room and dumped her on the couch. Several massive windows provided a perfect view of Reeds Lake just beyond their backyard, its water dotted with several white sailboats from the yacht club along the opposite shore.

This place would sell quickly once Dad put it on the market. First, he asked Micah to go through it, take what he wanted, and sell the rest. He'd already moved to Florida, so Micah was going room by room as he had time. Dad didn't seem to care how long it took, just said to call when the house was ready to be sold. For now, Micah could stay here.

Chloe yapped at him, and he pointed his finger at her. "You hang there while I change." As if she'd actually listen. She was used to someone with her all the time, so from the moment he walked through the door at the end of a shift, she stuck closer to him than medical tape on bare skin. He wasn't quite sure what to do with her. Dad didn't want her, and Micah didn't have the heart to bring her to a doggy shelter. Didn't love that she was home alone for hours on end, but it was the best he could do right now.

He headed for the stairs, stopping as he passed the closed door to Dad's office. It was a room he avoided, but tonight he reached for the knob. Turning it, he opened to the mahogany wood and navy tones. Dad's huge desk on one end, his built-in bar at the other. The smoky scent of hickory and tobacco from all the cigars Dad had smoked in here still hung in the air. Micah was shoved back in time three years to the night before his wedding. The conversation, hovering in the corner of his mind since seeing Belle today, now pressed in on him.

"You're really going through with it?" Dad reclined in his leather chair.

"I am. I love her." He swallowed, heart hammering, but he had to tell someone. Needed advice. Needed a father. "And she's pregnant."

No joy spread across Dad's face. Instead, he straightened. "Let me guess. You two decided to keep it?"

It? This was his grandchild.

"We have." And that scared the living daylights out of him.

After a long moment, Dad let out a deep huff. "You're a fool."

Micah tensed. "What?"

"If you think marrying her is going to make either one of you happy, then you're a fool." He stood, strolled to the corner, and poured himself a drink. Then he poured another and handed it to Micah.

Except he'd been trying to stop. He shook his head.

But Dad thrust it toward him. "Don't stop now. You're going to need this." He *shook it. "Go on, take it."*

Micah took the glass but only held it. "Kids weren't in our plans, but I love her. We can make this work."

Leaning against the bar, Dad pointed his tumbler at Micah. "Fool." He drew the word out. "You don't know the first thing about being a dad, and I certainly haven't taught you."

Because he'd been too busy keeping him at arm's length.

Dad tossed back his drink. "I'm going to do something I always promised I wouldn't. Give you advice." Then he looked him squarely in the eye. "If she wants to keep that kid, leave. You'll never be what they need."

Pain ripped through his chest. The beginnings of a panic attack. Was that really what his own dad thought of him?

A cool smile split Dad's face as he poured another drink. "You know I'm telling the truth because you know your life would have been better without me. Don't think you can rewrite history by giving it your own shot."

He wasn't wrong. The one thing he'd taught Micah about being a dad was how to resent his child. Made him always feel lacking but never sure exactly what it was he missed. Was that what he wanted to pass on?

His hand trembled around the drink, the amber liquid tempting him. Putting the glass to his lips, he made his choice.

One he deeply regretted. At the time, he'd thought it was right. Now he understood that while he had plenty of shortcomings, not one applied to how much he loved Belle and Anna. It wasn't up to him to decide if his imperfect love was enough for them. That decision belonged to Belle, and this time around, he'd let her make it.

But not without an extensive amount of convincing on his part. Right now, though, he had a promise to keep to Mom.

He changed quickly, grabbed his messenger bag, then drove over to Brookhaven. Dad had chosen a nursing home close to the house with a stellar reputation, and he was covering whatever Medicare didn't—no doubt to ease some of his conscience for leaving her. At least Micah hoped a part of him felt bad about packing up and moving south. Dad and Mom had never been close, but the fact that he walked so easily was unsettling.

As Micah reached for the glass door, his reflection mocked him. Guess the apple didn't fall far from the tree ... but hopefully, it could roll away and plant a new one.

Slipping inside, he passed by the front desk, the attendant there wiggling her fingers at Chloe. "Your mom is going to be so happy to see her," she said as she buzzed them into the area for memory-care patients.

"I have a feeling she won't be the only one." Whenever he let Chloe tag along for a visit, practically every resident paraded from their room to greet her. It lengthened his stay, but the way their elderly faces moved from lifeless to laughing was more than worth his time. By the time he made it to Mom, she was sitting in her doorway watching him.

She held out her hands. "Let me see my girl."

With a chuckle, Micah handed the squirming dog over. They both remembered each other without hesitation. "This dog has more bows than you do shoes."

Mom played with the edges of the pink and white polka-dotted bow between Chloe's ears. Never thought he'd be dressing a dog, but Mom kept Chloe styled, and he'd do no less. "She likes to look pretty."

"I think it's more that you always wanted a daughter."

Her clouded eyes cleared as she smiled at him. "But I was blessed with a son."

Something she'd always strived to ensure he knew. Dad, on the other hand ... Dad would have been fine if they'd remained childless. He'd definitely never been warm and cuddly. There was no tossing a baseball in the backyard. The only recurring feeling Micah received from his father was resentment. And while Mom struggled to remember Micah, Dad couldn't seem to forget him fast enough. Unless there was a specific reason, Dad didn't even speak to him.

Between Belle's mom and Micah's dad, neither of them had felt equipped to be parents. They decided even before the engagement ring was on her finger that married life would be the two of them alone. Then Belle discovered she was pregnant. Even more surprising than the two lines on her pregnancy test was her announcement that she wanted to keep their child.

But craziest of all was that a part of him—a part he hadn't even known existed—wanted the baby too. It freaked him out, and he'd done some stupid things. Like more drinking.

And spilling his worries to Dad the night before his wedding.

"Micah?" Mom must have said his name a few times. Now confusion deepened lines on her face.

He forced a tired smile. "How about we go in your room? I have something to show you."

Once they were settled in the tiny room that held her bed and dresser on one side, with a sofa and small table along the other, he opened the leather bag he'd slung across his body. "I haven't found your letters yet, but I did find this."

Every time he saw her, she asked if he found the letters her dad had written her because she wanted to pass them on to him. He'd yet to solve the mystery of where she'd left them and was starting to wonder if they even existed. So when he'd run across her journal tucked into the bottom of her bedside table, he hoped it would distract her from still wanting them.

Mom reached around Chloe, who sat panting in her lap. She grabbed hold of the dark green book and cracked it open, a smile on her face. She read the first page, her wrinkled hand tracing the words. After a long moment, she closed the journal and held the treasured item out to him. "Thank you for bringing this, but what I really want are my letters."

"You don't want to keep it, though? To read?" He had no clue what to do with what amounted to his mom's diary.

"No." She stretched closer to him. "You read it."

Something in the way she spoke the words stoked his curiosity. He took the leather book from her. "All right. Maybe I will."

That seemed to make her happy, because she smiled.

They visited for about an hour, Mom petting Chloe the entire time, then her eyelids began to droop. Micah helped her get ready for bed, tucked her in, and kissed her goodnight, remembering all the occasions she'd done the same for him. Didn't seem like life should move that fast.

But time never slowed. If anything, its speed increased with age. And that realization made him more aware of the moments like this he'd missed—and was missing—with Anna. He honestly didn't know if he had what it took to be the father she needed, but he intended to try. As he pulled out of the nursing home parking lot, Lettie called. He hit the button on his steering wheel.

"Hello?"

"Micah?"

"Hey, Lettie. What's up?" Though he hoped he already knew.

"The Lamaze class is yours if you were serious about taking it."

He straightened. God had heard his heart. "Absolutely."

"All right. It starts Thursday night at seven. She holds them right at AnnaBelle's."

Was that her store? He couldn't wait to see the place. Based on the name, a mash-up of hers and their daughter's, he loved it already. But, hold up. "Thursday at seven?"

"Yeah. Is that a problem?"

She knew his schedule. He started a night rotation later this week, but she remained silent as if she was testing him. He wasn't about to fail. "I'll make it work." He'd find someone to cover the start of his shift. "You'll text me the address?"

"As soon as we're off the phone."

"Thanks, Lettie."

"Don't thank me. This is for that little girl, so maybe she can get to know her daddy." She hesitated. "Don't make me regret this."

"I won't. I promise."

Because he was through with regrets. He'd come home to fix them, not add to them. Hopefully, Belle would let him.

Chapter Four

It was a triple espresso kind of morning. One shot for each restless night Belle had spent since running into Micah. Which only jumbled up her nerves more. Her anxiety level was at an all-time high. Wondering at what point he'd walk through her door or call with a demand to see Anna. Was he hiring a lawyer? Had he already done that? Maybe she should have stayed. Talked to him.

But what had he expected? That she'd welcome him with open arms? He had to know that wouldn't happen. The look on his face replayed for the millionth time across her memory. Micah had been nervous. More than that, he looked … ashamed. Worried. Like maybe, just maybe, guilt had eaten a hole through him.

As much as she'd dreamed early on about him returning for her and Anna, never once had she wanted the stimulus to be guilt. She'd wanted him to return because he realized he loved her. That depleted seedling of hope had sprouted into bitterness, which bloomed into anger over the months without him. Ever since Belle was born, people left her. Fine. She'd accepted that reality in her life. But her heart tore in two whenever she thought of Anna growing up without her father. How on earth could he leave their sweet little girl?

And how in the world would she let him back into her life?

Anna didn't know any different now. But if Micah came in and charmed her like he had Belle, then left again, Anna would feel that heartache. There was no chance Belle would allow it.

By the same token, how could she be responsible for standing in the way of Anna knowing her father? That could one day drive a wedge between them. Besides, if he did take them to court, he would look so much better on paper than she did. He made more money, held a steady, respectable job, and could easily afford a home with a huge yard. And working air conditioning. Agreeing to his possible demands could prove smarter than provoking him into a drawn-out legal battle that might not end in her favor.

Which meant talking to him was a must.

Maybe it was a quadruple espresso morning.

"Mama?" Anna wobbled into the room, her loose curls in knotted waves. Belle set aside her coffee and scooped up her daughter, planting a kiss against her warm little cheek. The imprint of her pillow still there, she smelled like Johnson & Johnson's lavender soap mixed with Downy April freshness.

"Good morning, Monkey." She walked her to the table and settled her on her booster seat. "Do you want some Cheerios?"

Anna nodded, snuggling Uni and her well-worn baby quilt.

Belle poured a small amount of cereal into a plastic bowl, added milk to a sippy cup, and put them in front of Anna. Then she grabbed a slice of toast along with her coffee and joined her. Sunshine streamed in through the top half of their windows, and fans propped open the bottom section. Even with them, the upstairs became unbearably hot. Unfortunately, the AC fix moved even farther out of reach this week. Probably a good day to spend outside. She'd help the grandmas set up the baby pools before sorting through donations this afternoon.

"Here." Anna held out a wet Cheerio.

Oh, the things that would have turned her stomach before having a child. With a grin, Belle snatched it from Anna's fingers with her lips. "Mmm. Thank you."

"Nother." Anna held out more.

"No, thank you. Mama has her toast. You eat your cereal."

Anna took a few more bites before offering her sippy cup to Belle. Okay. That was where she drew the line. Sharing food was one thing, but sharing drinks with a toddler? Not happening. "No, thank you."

Bringing it to her own lips, Anna chugged away.

The clock behind them chimed eight. Gave them enough time to cuddle through one episode of *PAW Patrol* before cleaning Anna up and heading downstairs to start their day. They settled on the couch.

Anna squished Belle's cheeks between her chubby hands. "Yuv you, Mama."

Belle was tempted to never teach her how to say her "Ls," the sound simply too cute. "I love you too."

"Yuv you three."

"Love you four."

"Yuv you more!"

"Love you more!" Their final words eclipsed each other, and Belle snuggled her close, turning on the TV. Twenty minutes passed quickly, which was about the time length Anna would sit still. Then they brushed her teeth, combed her hair, and darted to her closet to pick out clothes.

"I wear dis." Anna pulled on a pink ballerina skirt.

"You think so?"

Anna nodded, then reached for a blue-and-purple polka dot shirt. "And dis."

Belle put aside her chuckle for a smile, deepening it as Anna next jammed her green flip flops on the wrong feet. She'd inherited her Aunt Penny's love for color, while completely missing her classic style. Growing up, Belle had been so jealous of Penny's ability to choose her own clothes. Their mother had focused all her fashion choices on Belle, and the pressure of looking perfect all the time had completely undone her. When she finally broke away from it, that move cost her Mom's relationship—but gained back Penny's. It also supplied deep insight into what was truly important in life, so if Anna wanted to wear a flower shower cap, princess ball gown, and rubber boots, Belle would let her. They could hone her style as she grew older.

"You look beautiful."

"Thank you." Her sweet little voice rounded the words. While her vocabulary had exponentially increased over the past few months, her speech was still soft in so many spots. Belle recorded it weekly, never wanting to forget for one moment the little girl talk that would too soon stretch into a youthful sound. She held out her hand for Anna to take, and they skipped down the hall, picking up Anna's little satchel from near the door. "The Grands are going to take you swimming today."

"I go in a pool?" Anna bounced.

"A little one, but yes. Does that sound like fun?"

Anna nodded, her blue eyes wide. Together they clomped down the stairs to the breakroom. Astrid, Fran, and Betty sat in the tiny area, sipping their coffee. Close friends, the three women looked nothing alike. Slightly shorter than Astrid and round in every way, Fran was loud-spoken but soft-hearted. Then there was Betty, with her still-chestnut hair, always-smiling face, and too-thin body. So many of the retirees came and went throughout the week, but these three were a daily staple.

Anna toddled in and spotted Astrid. Grinning, she raced over and hopped onto her lap.

"Mornin', Little Bit." Astrid pushed away her coffee cake before Anna could snatch it.

"Good morning, ladies." Belle leaned against the doorframe. "I thought we could set up the inflatable pools for today."

"The men are already on it." Fran tipped her head of snow-white hair toward the door. Not a strand of the hair-sprayed poof moved. "Said they needed a project."

"I have plenty if they really mean it."

Betty stood and cleared their dishes with her right hand. She had struggled with a slight hunch to her back and numbness in her left hand since her twenties, due to months of radiation in a victorious battle against breast cancer. None of that slowed her down, though. "We'll send them your way, then. Though I have a feeling they'll put on their trunks and start a water war with the kids later. They think we can't hear anymore, but you can't miss their loud voices."

"Ha! Well, I won't stand in their way. In fact, I wish I could join the fun." No doubt with the smiles on their wrinkled faces, these ladies were looking forward to doing just that. Even better, they'd help make it. That group—affectionately referred to as the Grands since they'd become like adopted grandparents—rivaled the toddlers in creating unsupervised havoc. They also supplied plenty of laughter and love.

Every single day, Belle thanked the Lord for placing her here. Two forgotten groups finding a home with one another. The life they breathed into each other brought happiness to them all.

Belle walked to the front area and into the store, where she flipped the OPEN sign and unlocked the door. She hauled in donations left over the weekend before sorting and tagging the items. Mornings remained quiet while most of the moms dropped off their children, then attended classes at the community college twenty minutes away. By the afternoon, Nia would arrive for her shift at the store, learning the ins-and-outs of retail and helping cover their busier after-school hours.

Sure enough, around four, a group of teenage girls arrived. They strolled the aisles, choosing a few dresses to try on. As they exited the dressing rooms, they picked themselves apart. Belle wasn't trying to eavesdrop, but it was hard to ignore their conversation. Or the fact that the dresses they each tried would actually look stunning on the other.

Years ago, she would have added her own negative voice to theirs. Sometimes loudly enough for them to overhear. Sometimes quiet and snarky enough to yank vicious laughter from the girls she'd come with—not that she would have been caught dead in a secondhand shop like this. Still. She cringed at her old self. Life had definitely humbled her, and she was oh-so-thankful it had. Being snobby might be what Mom had taught her, but it would not be what she passed on to Anna.

Now she understood how razor-sharp her words could be, wounding without even a direct hit. But she also knew how one well-placed word of kindness could burrow into a person and unfurl courage, confidence, and beauty they didn't even realize existed inside of them. She could destroy or build others up.

Easy choice.

She slowly approached. "Girls."

They turned but said nothing.

"Those are beautiful dresses."

"Not on us."

She tipped her head. Years in the pageant world had given her an eye for fashion and body types. "Mind if I make a suggestion?"

They shrugged.

She'd take that as a yes. "I think if you swapped those dresses, you'd be amazed at the difference." She stepped closer to the petite, raven-haired girl. At least she assumed by the roots poking through her candy-apple red hair that it was originally black. "You've got this beautiful collarbone and toned arms, so the V-neck tank suits your body type really well." She turned her attention to the other girl, who had to be close to six feet tall. "And while you have broader shoulders, you also have killer legs, so the shorter skirt and capped sleeves on her dress will show those legs off while offering the proportion you're looking for."

"All right." Another shrug—but Belle also caught a hint of a blush on each of their faces—then they returned to their curtained dressing rooms. Tossing the dresses over the wall between them, they swapped the clothes, then snuck out to the mirror. Their smiles confirmed Belle's advice had been spot on.

"Now, how about some shoes?" She motioned them toward the shoe racks. "What size are you?"

They told her, and she chose two pairs of heels.

Both girls laughed. "You were right about the dresses, but ain't no way we can wear heels."

"Why not?"

"'Cause we don't want to trip," the redhead spoke.

"You won't."

More laughter.

"Hey, I was right about the dresses, so maybe I'm right about this too." She ran her hand over the shoes until she reached her size. "How about I give you a quick lesson?"

"In walking in heels?"

"Sure." She swapped her tennis shoes for the only pair in her size. Three-inch platform stilettos. "If I can walk in these, you can walk in those."

"We'll watch you first."

She stood and effortlessly strolled down the long wooden floor, turned, then made her way to the girls. "The trick is to walk lightly but confidently. Heel to toe. Give it a try."

Skepticism crossed their faces, but they took a few hesitant steps, resembling wobbly newborn foals more than confident young women.

"We are gonna break our necks." The shorter girl grabbed the wall as she tipped.

The redhead looked over her shoulder. "Maybe you can give us another demo?"

"Sure." Belle strolled toward the front of the store, then turned to face them. "It's easier than it looks. Just takes some practice."

The bell over the front door dinged. "Hello?"

Belle jerked around as the deep voice registered. Even recognizing it, she still wasn't prepared for the tall, broad form backlit by the afternoon sun. Her left foot tangled with her right. She windmilled her arms, hoping to regain balance, hopped to the left, and ran smack dab into the short stool sitting there. Her ankle twisted as she landed in a heap at Micah's feet.

This wasn't how Micah envisioned their second meeting, and it definitely wasn't like any of the situations he'd imagined for wrapping Belle in his arms again. "Let me help you sit up."

She brushed him away. "I've got it."

"Oh my gosh. Are you okay?" The two girls knelt beside her.

"I'm good. Just wanted to prove even if you fell, you wouldn't break your neck." She grimaced up at them, no doubt trying to hide any aches and pains. "I take my job very seriously."

Relieved laughter filtered through them.

Pressing her palms on the floor, Belle started to stand, but her face twisted and she paused.

"You're hurt." Her ankle, if he had to guess.

"I'm fine." Her gritted teeth didn't stop the flow of hurt and anger in her voice.

"Stubborn as always." He leaned close. "Let me help you."

"I'm good, thanks."

"And I'm a doctor."

"Of obstetrics." She enunciated slowly as if he'd lost his mind.

"Still went to med school."

She shimmied away from him. "Well, Doctor, your specific type of help would have been much more appreciated, say, two and a half years ago."

The teens watched their exchange with wide eyes.

Another girl hustled over. "Do you need me to get Astrid?"

"Could you?"

She nodded and quickly complied. Thirty seconds later, an older woman with sleek, gray hair, black-rimmed bifocals, and the brightest red lipstick he had ever seen jostled through the door and hurried to Belle's side. "What did you do?" The concern in her voice bordered on motherly. The way she knelt and took Belle's hand between hers nailed the feeling.

"I tripped."

"When *he* came through the door," one of the girls nicely supplied.

He glowered at her.

Astrid stood. "Let me guess. Micah?"

Holding out his hand, he switched to a smile. How could he not? Astrid didn't even reach his chest, but those hands on her hips said she was a force to be reckoned with. He rested his hands at his own waist as it became clear Astrid's weren't moving from hers. "Yes. Micah Shaw."

Belle pushed from the floor far enough to reach the stool that had tripped her and planted herself on it. "And he was about to demonstrate his amazing ability to leave, weren't you, Micah?"

He deserved her barbed-wire words. Had even tried to prepare himself for them. Didn't mean they were any easier to swallow now than they had been three days ago. Also didn't mean it would stop him from helping her. "I'm sure I can still be of assistance."

"Except I've long since passed needing your assistance." Slowly standing, she put all her weight onto her right leg. "I'm fine on my own." When she turned to Astrid, a wave of pain rippled over her face. "Can you help Nia watch the shop for a few?"

Astrid nodded.

"Belle—"

She silenced him with a scathing look. That fire provided enough energy for her to hop all the way across the room to an interior door. She wrenched it open.

And he let her. The teens had followed, ready to catch her if she fell. But he drew the line at the tall stairway beyond the door. She wasn't seriously going to try to climb that, was she? As she braced an arm on either wall and took her first hop, his own stubbornness kicked in. She'd been hurt enough on his watch. He wasn't letting it happen again.

A few strides carried him to her side, and he scooped her up before she had a chance to protest. Gasps escaped the girls' mouths, but they didn't stop him. Belle's arms wrapped around his neck. Out of reflex, no doubt.

"Put me down." Her tone dug into him as deeply as her nails at his nape.

"No." Her curves were softer than he remembered. But her blue eyes still held the same spark, and the scent of roses still floated from her. "So you can stop pinching me."

"It's nicer than what I want to be doing."

"I see you've maintained that pleasant bite to your words."

"And I see you still put your wants over all others'."

He peered down at her, his face so close to hers their noses nearly touched. Something that had once been so familiar now put a swarm of hornets in his middle. Reconciliation wouldn't come easily, but he refused to give up. "When I know it's what's best for the people I care for, Belle, I do."

"Leaving me pregnant at the altar was best for me?"

Sadness and guilt pressed in, taunting him to break their stare, but she deserved more from him, so he held tight. "I didn't say I always get it right."

Her eyes widened before she blinked and looked away. "Your coming back proves that."

So much he wanted to say. Instead, he focused on her swelling ankle. "You need to go to the ER."

She stiffened. "No."

"It could be broken."

"It's not."

"Which one of us holds a medical degree?"

She pierced him again with her eyes. "The one who can afford medical help."

He let her words sink in. Hated the picture they drew. "You don't have insurance."

"Brilliant deduction, Sherlock." She wiggled. "Now can you put me down?"

Not on her life. "What's upstairs?" He nodded to the landing.

Her lips flatlined.

"Her home," Astrid said from behind them.

"Astrid!"

"He's right about you needing the ER. You're right about not being able to afford it. So at least let him carry you upstairs and take a look."

He craned his neck to see her. "Thank you."

Those fists sat on her hips again, but the look in her eyes said she'd just as soon use them on him. "Don't thank me. This is for her."

Nodding, he started up the stairs. At the top, the room opened to dark hardwood floors and off-white walls that spread through a small kitchen and living area. He walked her to a gray couch in front of a bank of windows that overlooked the parking lot and a building across from it. Touches of pink scattered the area and toys littered the floor. He gently set Belle down, and his eyes caught on an unfamiliar eight-by-ten photo of his tiny blonde pixie.

Unable to stop himself, he picked up the frame and ran a finger over her precious smile. "She's beautiful." Was she here someplace? Belle worked downstairs, so it was entirely possible. His hands started to sweat.

Belle looked from the picture to him. "She is." And as if she had read his mind, she answered his unvoiced question. "Luckily, she's at daycare right now."

Luckily. Right.

Silence slipped in, easier than the millions of words still needing to be said between them. Then her sharp intake of breath as she moved to elevate her foot provided new focus. He sprang into action. Setting down the picture, he dropped to his knees and gingerly took her ankle. She gasped and pressed into the couch, her hands gripping the cushions. "Sorry." Causing patients pain was his least favorite portion of his job, though sometimes necessary. But his patient had never owned his heart before. This was near torturous.

She swallowed. "It's just sprained or bruised. I can handle it."

"How about you let me decide?" Though it wasn't really a question. As quickly and painlessly as he could, he manipulated her joint, asking questions and gauging her true response beyond her words. The pain was evident, but it didn't appear to be broken. Still … He stood. "I'll grab you some ice. If the bruising and swelling worsen, you will need to go in. I don't think it's broken, but there could be a fracture that will only show on film. For now, you'll need to stay off of it."

"Right." She laughed through gritted teeth. "I have all the time in the world to lay around."

"I'm serious, Belle."

"So am I." She stood. "I can get my own ice."

"Let me."

She turned on him. "You don't get to do this, Micah. Decide to leave. Decide to return. Decide you want to see Anna or that you want to help me." Two hops had her beside him, and she shoved both her palms against his chest. "I'm right here. I have a say too."

He gingerly circled her slender wrists with his fingers and tugged them down to her sides. "You do, Belle," he responded gently. "Whatever you want. Just tell me."

Yanking her hands away, she wobbled. He steadied her. She'd always been so tiny compared to his height and breadth, yet she'd somehow fit him better than anyone he'd ever met. He'd been an idiot to leave her. And he wasn't lying— whatever she needed, he'd do it.

"What I want?" Her body nearly vibrated with whatever mix of emotions she was holding inside. "I'm more concerned with what you want. Why are you back, Micah?"

Okay. Not at all the question he expected. *Why did you leave?* or even *why didn't you call?* topped that list whenever he'd thought about this moment.

As she cast a nervous glance toward Anna's picture, though, it hit him. She was scared.

He maintained his soft voice, wanting to assure her she had nothing to fear from him. "I'm not here to take her from you."

"But you want to see her."

"Yes. And you too."

That did away with her fear. But everything about her hardened. "Please tell me you don't mean *see me* as in date again because that won't happen. Ever."

In the context of this conversation, romance wasn't what he'd meant to convey. That hope filled his heart, though, and she must have seen that truth written all over him because she completely shut him down. He fully intended to circle around to that subject again, but right now, he focused on the door still cracked open while evasively maneuvering past the shut one. "Like it or not, Anna ties us together." A bond he'd frayed, but hopefully not severed. "I want to be a part of her life, which means I'll also be a part of yours."

Seemed like she was chewing on his response and wasn't quite in love with the taste. She nodded slowly, but the look on her face said her brain and her body weren't in sync. "I won't stop you from seeing her, but as far as you and I ..." She sighed long and hard as if she didn't have any more words for this conversation. Brushing her hair from her face, she turned toward the kitchen. "I need some aspirin and that ice."

"Please sit down. You can barely walk."

"I've got this."

"I know you do, but right now you don't have to."

Hesitation crossed her features for a brief second, but finally, *finally*, she gave in. That alone told him how badly she was hurting.

She hobbled to the couch. "Aspirin is in the top cupboard to the left of the fridge. Good luck with the child safety lock."

Two failed attempts said she wasn't joking. "This thing actually opens?" He yanked on it again.

"Take it easy. They were hard to install, and I don't want to have to do it a second time because you broke it."

Studying the stupid thing, he tried again. "It might be faster if I ran to Walgreens and bought you a bottle."

"Don't you have a PhD?"

"It's an MD, and it's not in baby locks."

She paused as if seriously contemplating not helping him. Then, "Press down on the triangle and pull the strap. It'll release."

40

"Says you." Wait. This time he squeezed the corners of the triangle as he pressed and pulled, and he met with success. "You didn't mention about the corners."

"Didn't I?"

That tone said she was enjoying this way too much, and he didn't mind one bit. He grabbed the meds and filled the glass by the sink with water, then brought them both to her. He studied her as she swallowed the two pills. "You're not hiding your freckles anymore." A small smattering covered her nose and cheeks, but most people hadn't a clue.

"Anna likes them."

She was his girl. He couldn't help the smile. "I always did too."

"I remember." The skin beneath them grew rosy, and she glanced away, no doubt running from the memory of how he'd place soft kisses against them.

If only he still held that right.

Clearing his throat, he took the pink throw pillows from the end of the couch and elevated her leg. "I see you still like pink," he said as he returned to the kitchen for a Ziploc and ice.

"Yep."

Makeshift ice pack in hand, he rejoined her and placed it on her ankle. "This should help."

"Thanks." She reached for a book on the side table, something to do with parenting, and cracked it open. "Anyway, I appreciate everything, but I can take it from here. I won't get off this couch. If I need anything, Astrid is here to help."

There was so much wrong with her plan, but he'd work it out with Astrid rather than argue it out with Belle. The best thing he could do right now was give her some space. Let her emotions settle, not to mention the physical pain in her ankle. They needed to talk, but a short reprieve might be a good thing for them both. It would definitely offer him time to regroup. He'd hoped to find common ground today. Instead, the gap between them felt wider than ever.

He moved toward the stairs. "I'm sure Astrid's great, but she doesn't know what that ankle needs. I'm going to run and grab something to wrap it and get you a pair of crutches. I'll be back in an hour."

"You don't need to do that."

"Do you have your phone on you?"

"Micah." When their eyes met, she must have seen his resolve. "I do."

He rattled off his new number for her to enter. "Call me if you need anything while I'm out."

She nodded.

He hustled down the steps, slowing as he passed Astrid. "I don't think it's broken, but she does need it wrapped. I'll be back."

Hopefully with the ability to convince Belle that he meant permanently.

Chapter Five

The hot morning had morphed into a scorching afternoon. It wasn't lost on him how stifling Belle's tiny apartment over the shop had been, so he grabbed a pint of salted caramel gelato, the one treat she used to allow herself. Even then, she considered a single spoonful indulgent. Now, he hoped it would soften her to his presence, much like the heat had softened the contents inside, because there was still so much about Belle and Anna's lives he wanted to know.

His cousin Jonah had filled in a few of those blanks when he'd called him over the weekend. That feat first required convincing Jonah he was home to stay, something he'd only marginally accomplished. Enough so that Jonah supplied basic details void of all emotions along with a stiff warning not to hurt Belle again.

A long road stretched in front of him full of people he needed to make amends with, but his first steps aimed straight for Belle and Anna. He'd hoped to see his daughter today or at least arrange a time to do so. But, as he'd come to accept, things didn't always work out the way he planned.

Astrid nodded as he strolled past. "That's still one of her favorites."

He smiled at the cold treat. "I'd hoped." Hand on the doorknob to the stairs, he paused. "Can you cover everything down here for the afternoon? Her ankle is worse than she's willing to admit."

"The girls and I will handle things for as long as necessary. We'll even get the men to pitch in—they'd do anything for Belle." She narrowed her eyes. "We all would."

"Sounds like we share that in common then." He stood tall and held her stare, unblinking.

After a long perusal, Astrid's demeanor softened and warmed, her ruby-red lips gentling into a smile, though a hint of wariness remained in her eyes.

Understood. It would take time for his new progress to erase his past mistakes.

"What are you waiting for then? We've got downstairs covered. Get on up there and handle the upstairs."

He opened the door and hustled up the steps. As he rounded the banister, he caught sight of Belle staring out the window over the parking lot. She hadn't moved. A sigh of relief escaped his lips.

"How are you feeling?" He dropped his bags on the counter, then crossed to her freezer.

"Like I should be downstairs, helping."

"The fact you're not tells me you're in a lot of pain."

"Or that I'm worried you'll go all caveman again and carry me back up here."

"That wasn't caveman. That was gentleman." Her freezer was bare. He tossed in the gelato and shut it. "But you're right. I would have. You need to take care of yourself."

"I need to work."

"Looks like you have a great crew willing to step in for you."

A tender smile slipped over her lips. Would the thought of him ever provoke that look? "They are great. This place has been as good for them as it has been for the single moms."

He grabbed his medical supplies, then joined her at the couch. "I'd love to hear more about AnnaBelle's. How about you fill me in while I wrap this up?"

"Trying to divert my focus from the pain?"

"First thing they teach us in medical school."

"I highly doubt that."

He chuckled, then ever so gently slipped her ankle onto his lap. He didn't miss her wince. "Tell me about this place."

With a swallow, she turned to the window. "It's a place to help single mothers."

"I can see that." Unwrapping the tape, he watched her. "Tell me what I can't see."

A slight hesitation preempted her response. "You know I never did anything with my degree."

"I do." It always bothered him. She was brilliant, but her mom had been more focused on her upward trajectory toward beauty queen. Made Belle feel as if the triple threat she possessed was beauty, dance, and song rather than beauty, heart, and brains. "You could have. Any company would have hired you in a heartbeat, and I'm talking Fortune 500s."

She cracked a shaky smile. "You were the only person to believe that."

"Oh, I don't know. I think somewhere inside, you believed it too." He wound the gauze around her ankle. "At least you should have."

"I did. When you said it."

Their shared stare held. Then she cleared her throat and broke the connection. "Anyway, I did look for work while I was pregnant, but it's difficult to land a job when you're already asking for maternity leave—not that any company would admit that's why I didn't get a second interview, but it wasn't hard to figure out their reason." While her words didn't come across as a swipe at him, he felt the punch nonetheless. "So I worked some as a cashier at our grocery store. Between that, my savings from pageant wins, and Penny and Jonah constantly dropping things off, I did okay."

She deserved better than okay, though. So did his little girl.

He desperately wanted to ask about those she hadn't mentioned—her parents. Yet something restrained him. Maybe the knowledge that they were already on tentative ground, and her mother always made her life shaky. So he stayed with safer questions for now.

"How did Penny and Jonah help?"

"In very sneaky ways." She played with the fringe on a pillow. "They'd wash baby clothes, then drop them off or put together new things—like a stroller— and show up with it. They knew I didn't like accepting their help, so they ensured I couldn't stubbornly return things."

His cousin had stepped in where Micah should have. He'd need to thank him. "Jonah's always been a determined guy."

"He sure has," Belle agreed. "Not everyone has that kind of help, though, or the opportunities I once did. They lack education or the ability to grow new skills. Even if they want to pursue something, they can't afford the cost of school, daycare, and just basic life."

"So AnnaBelle's was born."

"Kind of." She pointed out the window at the retirement home across the street. "When I wasn't cashiering, I worked at Brookhaven as their activities director."

This lifted his brow.

"What?" She shrugged. "I was good at it."

"I have no doubt. Just not an area I ever saw you interested in."

"At the time I took it, my only interest was in providing for myself and Anna."

This stalled his hands. He looked directly at her. There were so many promises he wanted to make, but they'd be empty ones to her. There was something else he could give her. Something he suspected she desperately needed. "Your selfless love is a beautiful thing. Our daughter is an incredibly lucky little girl."

Her big blue eyes widened for a split second, then she glanced away. "Thank you."

He finished wrapping her ankle and secured the tape. "So how did working at Brookhaven lead to this place?"

"Easy. It provided a light-bulb moment. Those retirees had too much downtime. Single moms don't have enough. It was like puzzle pieces created to fit. All I did was connect them."

"I think you did more than that."

Another shrug. She had no clue as to the impact of her actions. How special they were. "It morphed into more over time. At first AnnaBelle's was simply going to be a daycare and secondhand store. Then I started overhearing conversations between the retirees and my moms. There was so much wisdom and knowledge, so much life that they'd lived. They had more than babysitting to offer, and the young moms ate it up." She smiled. "It was good for both sides."

"Feeling like you have something to contribute gives you a purpose."

"Feeling like someone's willing to invest in you gives a sense of worth."

"And putting together those puzzle pieces created one amazing picture."

"Oh, we're not finished yet. I see a whole lot more of the picture that hasn't been put into place yet."

Micah slid her foot onto the pillows but remained by the couch with her. "Like the Lamaze class?"

"You know about that?"

"Lettie filled me in."

"Oh."

"And I'd love to help."

Children's voices drifted up from outdoors, slipping through the open window on a breeze. It kicked up the scent of roses too. From the flowers outdoors or her perfume, he wasn't sure. It was the only sweetness still lingering in the moment. Belle's walls had returned. "I don't think that's a good idea."

"Why? I'm more than qualified, and you need someone."

"Not you."

He suspected her answer applied to more than the class. But he wasn't accepting it. "Belle, I'm sticking around. I want to see Anna. Be a part of her life." And yours, he wanted to add but wasn't pressing hard right now. Especially with her reaction to that thought earlier. For now, he'd focus solely on building a relationship with Anna. If something with Belle grew out of that too, well, he wouldn't complain. "Helping with the class lets me help both of you. Plus, I plan on being around here to get to know her, so it makes sense that I pitch in as well. Besides, what good is knowing a doctor but not utilizing his skills when you so obviously—"

She held up her hand. "You can stop the babble."

"I don't babble."

"You didn't used to." The corner of her mouth lifted, but wariness still lined her eyes. "You're intent on being a part of Anna's life."

"I am. And I'm also willing for this to move at your pace. I won't press on when I can finally meet her. That timing is all yours. I only ask that you eventually allow it to happen and for her to one day know who I am."

Her focus slipped from him to something over his shoulder. He turned. A picture of Belle and Anna together on the beach hung on the wall. Belle's hair fell in curls against sun-kissed shoulders; her tender expression radiated love down on their little girl. The picture evoked memories of the warmth of her love, how it wrapped around him with one touch, one look. Now, as she blinked and recaptured his stare, nothing but its cool shadow remained. "Would you take me to court if I said no?"

Honest questions deserved honest answers. "Yes."

Strange. His response seemed to soften her resolve rather than hardening it. She nodded. "Okay. You can help me with the Lamaze class." Then she nestled into the corner of the couch. "We start Thursday at seven."

"I'll be here."

"Great." Her eyelids seemed heavy. Right. Pain meds always put her to sleep.

Making sure she had water, her cell phone, and the TV remote beside her, he moved for the door. "I'll head out and let you rest. You can call me if you need anything."

Her skeptical look answered before her words. "I'll call Astrid."

"Fine." He swallowed his frustration that she wouldn't rely on him. If he wanted to be mad at someone, he should point that finger directly at himself, because he created this situation.

He drove home and found Chloe had decided to create her very own version of Christmas in July with the white stuffing of Mom's favorite throw pillows. He groaned and scooped up the yapping dog. "Is this your way of telling me you're tired of spending your days alone?" Opening the slider, he let her into the backyard to do her business while he cleaned up her winter wonderland of a mess. At least Mom wouldn't remember the pillows.

Shaking his head, he opted for tired laughter. After the day he'd had, keeping his head in the right place and his hands off anything stronger than a cold can of pop required the last of his willpower.

After feeding them both, he took Chloe for a quick walk, then to see Mom. By the time he made it home again, he was spent. Collapsing on the couch, he patted his legs and Chloe hopped into his lap as he flicked on the TV. He surfed the channels. "There is nothing on this thing."

Chloe tilted her head as if she actually understood him.

He stretched his feet to the ottoman, knocking a book to the ground. Mom's journal. He grabbed it and started reading. Each entry intrigued him more.

Much like his own relationship with Dad, his parents' relationship was marked by an unspoken strain he never understood. Mom's words were like snatching a tiny piece of personal history that began to give bones to their hidden narrative.

My father always said that actions speak louder than words. And, as with most children, it's only now that I realize he was right—about oh, so many things. If only I'd listened, but I'm listening now, starting with that piece of advice.

For so many years, I allowed myself to choose actions that hurt my marriage and my husband—even before we were married. I could say all the right things on the surface, but it was my actions Todd saw. Oh, he made choices that hurt too, but I'm not responsible for his choices ... only mine. And now I want to live in a way that my actions show him I love him. To admit I was wrong. To ask forgiveness. And then to show him that I am here, no matter what—I choose him. Todd may never believe it or receive it, but still, I need to try. My love cannot be conditional on his actions. It must be unconditional. That's something I saw through my father. He loved me unconditionally. I wish I'd done more of that, and I wish Micah had seen it. Maybe it would have changed some of his decisions. But living in regret won't change the past, it'll only stifle the future. And that's what I hope for Micah—that he moves past regret. I know Todd and I weren't the best examples, but it's never too late. Never too late to love with actions that speak louder than words. To say you're sorry. To love unconditionally. And I pray that's what he learns from me now.

Micah closed the leather book. Mom's words worked something inside him. He latched on to them like a lost man stumbling upon a possible key to his encrypted map. Until this moment, he didn't realize how much he missed her—which sounded funny since she was still here. Except she wasn't. But he could hear her so clearly in the words he'd read. They elicited questions while also offering some answers, specifically on how to approach Belle.

Time to let his actions speak louder than words.

"Why didn't you call me?"

Even now, three years into repairing their relationship, Belle still marveled when she heard concern aimed at her from her big sister's voice.

"Because you have Jonah's dad there. You don't need all my drama visiting too."

"It's a welcome reprieve from talk about what's new in the world of garbage."

Belle chuckled. "You married the owner of a garbage company—the most successful one there in Chicago. You had to know the subject would come up. Especially around family, since it's a family business." One Micah had thought about leaving medicine for, until Walter Hamlin sided with Micah's cousin—and now Penny's husband—Jonah, over leadership in said company. "And trust me, that garbage talk has nothing on the stank happening here."

"You have definitely had a string of stinky days, for sure." Already aware of Micah's reappearance, Penny still had bounced between sheer surprise and utter outrage as Belle recounted yesterday's story. "I'd be happy to come over early and help you out for a few days. We could stay at my place. You could put your foot up, and I can chase Anna around." Two years ago, Jonah and Penny purchased a cottage in Holland on the shores of Lake Michigan. Each summer weekend they—along with Jonah's sister, Rachael, and her son, Gavin—traveled from Chicago to spend time in the sun, sand, and water. Belle and Anna often joined them for an afternoon. They'd try to get her to stay longer, but she didn't have the luxury of taking a full weekend off from AnnaBelle's. Especially now with the building's fix-it list looming overhead.

So as wonderful as that idea sounded, Belle couldn't accept, especially not with Penny seven and a half months pregnant. "You can't chase her around. Besides, don't you have a doctor's appointment Friday before you head over?"

"I can change it."

"Right. Like Jonah would be on board with that decision." He was incredibly overprotective in the sweetest of ways. Penny had definitely snagged the good cousin—even if neither of them pegged him as such at first glance.

"If it meant helping his favorite sister-in-law and niece—"

"His only sister-in-law and niece."

"He would."

Okay. She made an irrefutable point. Jonah would do anything to help the people he loved, and she was lucky enough to fall into that category. Still. "I really do appreciate it, but you need to take care of yourself and my niece or nephew. I still can't believe you didn't figure out what you're having."

"Or did we?" Penny teased in a slow voice.

"Penelope Thornton! Did you find out? Tell me right now."

"It's Penelope Black. Has been for nearly three years." She laughed. "And no, we did not. I promise. I want something else to focus on during labor than the pain you so generously told me about in great detail."

"Thought I'd help you be prepared." As much as any woman could be that first time. No one had been around to coach her or offer advice. She'd been the first of her friends to have a baby—not that any of them stuck around to congratulate her. And Mom was still in a huff over the fact that Penny and Belle had called her out on her awful behavior. Rather than making amends or a huge change in her life so she could be a part of theirs, Mom had basically walked out on them. Dad had tried to hold the family together, but in the interest of preserving his marriage, he wasn't around often.

"Um, Belle?" Penny's voice broke through. "You still there?"

She chased away the bitter memories with a headshake. "Sorry. I didn't sleep well last night, and I think it's catching up to me."

"You sure I can't come help?"

"Positive." She had things under control. Mostly. And she wasn't about to allow Penny or Jonah to think otherwise. Especially when they were successful at all the things she wanted to be succeeding at. Their own businesses, their relationship, even impending parenthood thus far.

"Okay." Penny gave in. "But I expect to see you for at least a few hours this weekend. Don't make me come hunt you down."

"As if you could. You're pretty easy to evade with that adorable belly of yours."

If smiles could be heard, Penny's would have shouted at her right now. "It is kinda cute, isn't it?"

The fact that either of them could say her big belly was cute testified to how far they'd both come. "It's beautiful, Sis."

They said their goodbyes and hung up. Belle didn't move from her chair immediately. Anna would awake any second—she was surprised she hadn't already—and would want her breakfast, but the thought of moving made Belle's ankle ache. She'd barely slept last night. She needed a few more pain relievers, but they didn't sit well on an empty stomach. Filling it required standing because no one was going to bring her breakfast. That buck stopped with her.

Sighing, she palmed the table and pushed to her feet, then grabbed her crutches from beside her chair. She swallowed against a wave of pain. Luckily on Tuesdays, Nia opened the store, so she wouldn't need to be downstairs any time soon. She could tackle her research and paperwork up here, though it promised to be a hot one. At least her tiny office downstairs offered sputtering AC. She planned on Anna hanging out at daycare, so she'd need to hobble down there eventually. The past several days left her physically and emotionally exhausted. She had no idea where she'd muster enough energy to survive today, but she somehow would.

Anna toddled from her room. "I hungry."

"Morning to you, too, Monkey."

She came over and held up her hands. "Up?"

"Sorry, sweetie, but Mama can't pick you up." Her heart twinged at Anna's pouty lips. "How about you go sit on the couch, and I'll come snuggle with you?"

Those rosebud lips pulled into a smile. "Okay, Mama." Her little Pull-Ups tail wiggled as she raced to their sofa. "Mik pweese?"

"One milk coming up." Thank goodness for sippy cups. She could manage that along with her crutches. Maybe she'd stick her coffee in one too. Navigating to the fridge, she paused and changed direction as someone knocked at the door. "Coming."

Wasn't quite eight a.m. Only person she could think of knocking on her door this early was Astrid.

She tugged it open and, sure enough, Astrid smiled at her from the other side. She held up a big brown sack from Panera Bread. "I have something for you."

Belle's stomach growled as the heavenly aroma of warm bread, eggs, and bacon drifted from the sack. "I can see that." As well as the coffee in her other hand. She leaned on the door so Astrid could pass. "How'd you manage this?" Astrid no longer drove.

"Magic." Astrid smirked.

"Funny." Belle closed her door. "But really, how?"

"I didn't." She set the items on the table and began unpacking them as if her answer made complete sense.

Anna shuffled over and inspected the collection of muffins and donuts.

Belle joined them. "Did you send Marv?" Out of the oldies crew next door, he was the one most likely to get behind the wheel. He loved any excuse to drive his black Cadillac.

"Nope." Astrid waltzed into the kitchen to grab a couple of plates. She returned to the table and scooped out some of the healthier offerings for Anna. "You eat this, and then you can have a donut." As if she caught herself, she peeked up at Belle. "As long as Mama says it's okay."

"That's fine." She agreed, mostly so she could keep questioning her suddenly evasive friend. Astrid's squirrelly responses sent up all the red flags, because she was nothing if not direct. "Then who?"

Astrid filled another plate for Belle and set it on the opposite end of the table, then took the chair beside it. "Come sit and eat."

If she weren't so hungry or so thankful for the wonderful-smelling food in front of her that she hadn't needed to cook, she'd be more able to withstand the temptation. But her empty stomach was messing with her mind. As if sensing her weakness, Astrid wiggled the coffee cup, and that sealed her fate. Belle hobbled over to the chair, grabbed the paper cup, and took a long drag. After she chased it with a bite of ham and cheese soufflé, she pressed for answers. "Are you waiting for me to finish, or are you going to tell me?" Though considering how funny Astrid was acting, Belle's suspicions led her to the one answer she didn't want to hear.

"Micah."

Yep. That was the one.

She set her fork down. "Is he here?" Because wouldn't that be about right? Here she sat, stinky and sweaty in worn-out pajamas and ultimate bedhead. Why not cement in his mind that she wasn't a hot mom but rather a hot mess?

Not that it mattered what he thought.

Okay. It did a little. But that was her pride talking and not her heart.

Astrid cut a strawberry in half. "He's not here." She ate the piece, dabbed her lips, and then continued. "He had this delivered. Did you know there's people whose job is to go pick up your takeout and bring it to you?"

"I did know that." She'd contemplated picking up a few shifts herself—either takeout or grocery delivery—if things didn't turn around here pretty quickly. "And you're saying Micah used them to send me Panera?"

"You and Anna." She nodded to the toddler, who was finishing her last bite of eggs.

"Awe done." Anna smiled, her blue eyes sparkling like her daddy's when he was after something too. "I have a pink donut now?"

That was the deal they'd struck. "Here you go," she said as she handed her the pastry on a napkin. "If you put your blanket on the floor, I'll turn on *PAW Patrol*."

"I can do it." Astrid situated Anna then rejoined Belle at the table. "To answer all your questions, Micah and I exchanged phone numbers yesterday. He called me last night and asked when you and Anna typically wake up. He knew you wouldn't sleep well and that your ankle would hurt even worse today. He wanted to ensure you could stay off it as much as possible, so he has lunch and dinner being delivered too."

So tempting, but she'd learned the hard lesson that giving into temptation could land her in places she never wanted to be. And she definitely wasn't inviting the man who'd provided that tutorial to her doorstep. "That sounds really kind of him, but I have it covered."

Her phone dinged a text from him as if he could read her mind from across town.

I figured your number hasn't changed. Hope your ankle is healing. Doctor's orders are to stay off of it, so to help, I've got your meals handled. Lunch is coming around noon, dinner at five. As long as that's all okay, tomorrow and Thursday will be the same. Unless I hear otherwise, I'll see you Thursday night.

Sweet, caring, and nonthreatening. With his few words, he'd let her know he was watching out for her but from a distance that respected her boundaries.

He was putting her needs first in every way. That was something new, and she wasn't quite sure what to do with it except embrace the space, because even with it stretching between them, Micah still managed to touch her heart. Inviting him any closer meant inviting inevitable hurt too. She set her phone down and looked at Astrid. "He's sending me meals for the next few days."

"Sounds like a boy who's got his priorities straight."

"Or a man who feels guilty because we never were his priority to begin with." Belle crossed her arms. "All of this is great, but it doesn't guarantee he's changed. For all I know, he could still be drinking." He'd flirted with a drinking problem before. She didn't think he still did, but that worry floated around with all the others. "Or decide tomorrow that Italy sounds like a good place to live."

"Italy?"

"He loves lasagna."

Astrid arched a brow over her black rims. "You know, for a girl who touts how people deserve second chances—and seems to have found one herself—you're awfully tough on someone seeking one."

Heat filled her cheeks. She lifted her coffee cup and drank the last sip rather than attempt to have the last word. Astrid was right, but Belle's heart wasn't ready to go there yet.

Chapter Six

Not only did doctors make the worst patients, they made awful patient advocates. Diagnosing and making decisions for his own care proved far easier than sitting by while another person made those calls about someone he loved. No doubt Mom's doctor had been happy to have that appointment over.

But between her waning appetite and increasing nausea, she'd lost too much weight. He'd done the research. There were several cholinesterase inhibitors to choose from, and the side effects she'd been experiencing could be eliminated by changing her current medication. They could also become worse, but until her doctor tried, they wouldn't know.

Dr. Cho made the change, after gently reminding Micah that he was Mom's son, not her doctor. All well in theory, but neither role contained a switch he could simply shut off.

Micah pulled in to his parents' drive. Beside him, the bag from Salvatore's made his stomach growl. Mom's appointment had run late, so his afternoon plans to tackle another room inside probably weren't happening. As he opened the front door to another Chloe-size disaster and her frenetic yips, he set that task in the definitely not-happening column. He'd have enough time to clean up this mess, walk her, and eat before heading to Lamaze class. First, he needed to call in dinner for Belle and Anna.

He set his takeout on the kitchen counter, then distracted Chloe with a treat before placing the order. He'd wanted to check in and see how her ankle fared, but something said to give her a little breathing room. Knowing that at least he'd provided her a break from making meals felt like he was tangibly helping, even if it might grate on her nerves to accept assistance from him. He was leaning heavily on the "let your actions speak louder than words" advice from the journal.

With sandwiches, soup, and salad on the way to Belle and Anna, Micah fed Chloe, then dug into his own cheesy layers of goodness. Lasagna might be his favorite meal, but Belle loved tacos. He'd stayed basic with his food orders for her in case Anna was a picky eater, but part of him was tempted to order her favorite meal. If she loved them, Anna must too, right? He couldn't wait to find out things like that. Like Christmas gifts under the tree, he desperately wanted to unwrap every little detail about his baby girl. But he had to have patience. Move at Belle's pace. His decisions were what led him to this place, and now it would be Belle's decisions that allowed him out of it.

After eating, he snapped Chloe onto a leash, then took her for a walk. Staying in shape helped him manage these longer days. Nights especially were tough. They threw his body completely off, and even though he should sleep during the day, he had too many things to accomplish. Sleep fell to the bottom of that list. He clocked enough to keep him coherent at work—or at least tried to. This past week proved tough, and he didn't see it changing anytime soon. Not like he hadn't dealt with sleep deprivation before. Med school taught him how to put his head down and push forward. His current goal was to make it to his scheduled vacation a month from now. He'd catch up on sleep then, and after that break, he'd be on an eight-week daytime rotation.

He grabbed the mail as they finished their walk, sorting through it as he entered the house. He'd used this address as his forwarding one, and mail was slowly making its way here. One envelope stood out, the handwriting on the outside familiar and expected. For the past three years, old family friend Walter Hamlin wrote him monthly, and for those past three years, Micah ignored the letters. Walter remained on the board of AllWaste, the business Micah's grandparents grew from the ground up and that Jonah now solely owned. It still pinched deep that Walter's deciding vote had prevented Micah from becoming co-owner. Granted, Micah could now see how Walter's choice had ultimately been the right one. Working for AllWaste was Jonah's path, not his. Had he tried to force himself into it, the end result would have destroyed more than their family relationships. In fact, it nearly had. Walter had done what Micah didn't possess the courage to do at the time.

Didn't mean it hadn't hurt or that he didn't feel betrayed by Walter. Which was probably why he still hadn't opened those letters. And he wasn't about to start now. Hypocritical? Yeah, probably, but at this moment all of his energy needed to be in repairing his relationship with Belle. Walter could wait.

His phone rang. He tossed the mail on the counter and pulled the phone from his pocket. Dad's name flashed across the screen. He debated answering, but while he had the luxury of avoiding Walter, he couldn't claim that with Dad. Too much still bound them, namely Mom.

He tapped the screen. "Hey, Dad."

"Micah." Dad's rough voice held evidence of all the years he'd been a smoker. "I have a Realtor coming to take pictures of the house on Monday. They'll let themselves in."

Not even a question about how Mom was doing.

"I thought you said you weren't in a hurry."

"I'm not. Just want to be ready to list it as soon as you're finished there."

"It may take a while." Best to prepare him. Dad never liked surprises. "My schedule is pretty full right now, so clearing things out may take longer than I originally thought."

Silence greeted him, and Micah steeled himself.

"Full because you're trying to work things out with Belle?"

"I am."

"Seems my advice fell on deaf ears."

"No. I obviously listened." Biggest mistake of his life. "Now I'm trying to fix the damage I caused by following it."

The clink of ice sounded as Dad no doubt swirled his Scotch. "You're trying to do the impossible. Nothing's changed. You're never going to be what they need. But you're intent on learning that lesson the hard way. I guess you're more like me than either of us care to believe."

Micah should have let the call roll to voicemail. Dad would have left the details on the house and skipped the undermining lecture.

"Trust me; I've learned a lot of things the hard way because of you." He withheld bitterness from his voice, managing to keep things matter-of-fact. "But I think the lessons were different than you intended."

Dad snorted. "Go ahead. Try and make it work with her. You'll soon see which of us is right."

There was no use arguing with him. Micah's energy was better spent in other places. "We both will." Chloe dropped a ball at his feet, and he kicked it across the wood floor. "I'll make sure things are clean before the agent comes on Monday."

"Good. Then let me know once you're finished there, and I'll have her set things in motion. Should sell fast."

No doubt that's what he hoped for. One less way he'd be tied to them.

They covered a few more points before Dad said his goodbye. Micah stopped him. "Before you go, do you happen to know where Mom may have put some letters Gramps wrote her?"

He gave a gruff laugh. "No idea. And I couldn't begin to guess."

"But you at least heard her talk about them, right? Or have seen them? I'm trying to figure out if they're even real."

"There's no telling if anything's real with your mother. I didn't understand her when she was in her right mind. I'm not even going to try now that she isn't." With no apology or awkwardness over his comments, Dad hung up.

Micah stared at his phone in disbelief and the beginnings of a new perspective.

His gut burned over how Dad treated Mom, but he couldn't miss the similarities in their actions toward the women they were supposed to love. Without trying and without explanation, they simply cut them loose. Didn't matter if their reasons were different, they'd produced the same outcome. Of *course* Belle was angry, but he understood that anger in a different way now.

Which meant that uphill climb he'd prepared himself for suddenly seemed more like the jagged face of a mountain he'd need to freehand. Hopefully, putting actions with his words would create a few secure handholds along the way.

A stir-crazy mind, sore body, and jumbled nerves did nothing for Belle's sunny disposition. "Anna, slow down." She hobbled after her toddler. Hard enough to keep up with her when all her limbs worked, but the past few days had about done her in. Anna seemed to understand Belle's weakness and knew how to exploit it. How on earth could someone so charming be so devious?

The bell chimed, and Micah walked through the door. Well, that answered her question. Her little gremlin hadn't fallen as far from the tree as Belle thought.

Micah's smile slimmed as one blue eye narrowed. "You okay?"

"I'm great."

"Pageant voice." He strolled up beside her and stopped, looking as put together as he always did. Gray skinny jeans, an untucked navy dress shirt with rolled sleeves, and retro Nikes. He'd given in to his curls today but shoved them off his forehead. Their softness played well with his day's worth of rough whiskers. "You're lying."

She opened her mouth to refute him, but he challenged her with an arched eyebrow.

Astrid interrupted their stalemate as she called from the hallway Anna raced down. "I've got her!"

That snagged Micah's attention. He peered around Belle's shoulder, a wistful look on his face. "Anna?"

"Astrid is babysitting while we conduct class."

She waited for him to ask to see Anna. His expression clearly showed his desire to, but he blinked it away. As he did, her lungs relaxed. She hadn't even realized she'd been holding her breath.

"That's kind of her." He casually stood with his hands in his pockets. There was nothing casual about his focus as it swung back to her, however. "How's your ankle? Have you stayed off it?"

"It's fine. And mostly."

"Mostly?"

"I live with a toddler. It's not like she has an off button."

His gaze tracked down to where he'd wrapped her ankle. She'd undone it to shower and did her best to replace it. Maybe he wouldn't notice.

"Before I leave tonight, I'd like to rewrap that. I didn't think I needed to tell you not to remove it."

"You didn't."

"Obviously I did."

Straightening, she started for the back hall. "I had to shower."

"Ever heard of a garbage bag?"

"Of course I have."

"Next time, use one."

She tossed him a mock glare over her shoulder. "You could use some work on your bedside manner."

"That would require your being in bed. Something else you've ignored."

"Not everyone can arbitrarily take time off."

"Being injured isn't arbitrary."

He had an answer for everything, a trait that had always sparked some fiery conversations between them. Ones that had made her think while simultaneously making her feel listened to. Micah had never viewed her as the blonde beauty queen so many others had. He challenged her.

Right now, though, she wished he'd stop.

She pushed open the classroom door, then leaned against it, looking at him. "Working is nonnegotiable for me. I'm on twenty-four-seven, Micah. I'm a single mom. It comes with the territory."

"A territory I want to help you with."

Each meal he'd had delivered these past few days backed up his words. She hated that she'd loved them all, but she blamed her exhausted, sore state. As if her body decided to lend credibility to her sad excuse, she wobbled.

"You're really not okay." Micah gently gripped her arm. "Come, sit." She allowed him to settle her in the office chair at the small desk in the room. He went to the bank of windows lining the wall. "Let's get some fresh air in here."

"No. The AC is on."

"Really?"

"Just enough to take the humidity out of the air. My money is better spent helping the moms than chilling them."

He strolled over. "Is that why your apartment upstairs was so warm?"

"Anna and I don't mind it."

He leaned against the wall beside her. "Pageant answer again."

Frustrating man. He'd always called her out on spinning her answers so she could evade questions she didn't like.

Thankfully, voices drifted down the hall, followed by the arrival of Sydney and Kim. Two of the young pregnant moms here for tonight, they stepped into the room, and their eyes widened as they caught sight of Belle's ankle. "Miss Thornton! What happened to you?"

"Stunt work gone wrong." Their mouths fell open, and she chuckled. "I'm joking, girls. I wish it was that exciting of a story. The truth is—"

"I startled her and she tripped."

Micah had just swallowed her embarrassment. What should have left a sour taste in her mouth produced a sweet one instead.

"Will you be okay?" Sydney asked.

"It's only a sprain."

"A pretty bad one. So how about we make sure she stays off it tonight?" Micah's grin had the same effect it always did on women. They warmed under it. Except his ulterior motive tonight was Belle's well-being. And that pressed heat against areas in her heart so iced over she'd lost hope they'd ever thaw.

"We can do that," Sydney agreed.

Kim added her nod as she held out her hand and introduced herself to Micah. Her personality far outweighed her short stature. Not quite five feet tall, Kim's wiry black hair fell in tight curls to her shoulders. Even in the struggle of being seventeen, alone, and pregnant, she maintained a genuine smile and encouraged every person who crossed her path. Belle loved working with her.

Sydney was her opposite in nearly every way. Tall, five years older, and redheaded, she battled depression and feeling overwhelmed. Belle had paired her with Kim, hoping the younger girl would rub off on her some. So far, there hadn't been any visible change, but that didn't mean it wasn't happening.

"And I'm Sydney."

Micah shook her hand next. "Nice to meet you both."

They made small talk until everyone showed up. Micah introduced himself to all the girls and, by the looks of it, wasn't struggling to remember their names or due dates.

Belle opened the class, then handed the reins to Micah before slipping to a chair to prop up her throbbing ankle. Nighttime proved to be the worst. She'd taken a pain pill shortly before Micah arrived, and now her eyelids felt as if she'd attached weights. The minutes slowly ticked past on the clock over the door, and his baritone voice lulled her into a near-sleep state.

The screech of chairs against hard floor startled Belle awake. She jumped to her feet before remembering her ankle. With a gasp, she gripped the edge of her desk.

Micah twisted around, eyed her, then finished saying good night to the girls who'd stood to leave. Based on the little she'd seen before she fell asleep, plus the encouraging words the girls offered as they exited, he'd done an amazing job. Of course, it might be the pain meds talking.

Once they were alone, he turned to her. "You look like you could use some help upstairs."

The memory of his arms around her Monday jolted through her, intensifying her internal battle over how to respond. She was exhausted, so his momentary help could be nice, but Anna would be upstairs by now. Yet, she should be tucked away, asleep. And Astrid would be there too, so they wouldn't be alone.

"I'd appreciate that." Accepting his help might be difficult, but those words came out easier than she'd expected.

Micah pressed ahead of her to open the door at the base of her stairs. Without even having to ask, he took her crutches as she reached him. Midway up, she swayed and he gripped her waist. She inhaled sharply, and he released. "Sorry."

"It's okay."

They reached the top of the steps, and Micah rounded in front of her, holding out the crutches. Belle took them, hobbled to the couch, and collapsed. Her armpits killed her and her ankle pulsed with each heartbeat. "This day and age, and someone can't invent something more comfortable than those torture sticks?"

"I could get you a cart to kneel that leg on."

Anna would think it was her new toy. "I'll stick with the crutches." She wouldn't be off her foot much longer anyway. Even if it ached like the dickens.

Astrid appeared at the end of the hallway. "Anna's asleep."

"Thanks, Astrid."

"It was my pleasure. That child brings me much joy."

Micah watched them, his face hopeful. No doubt he wished to someday say the same thing.

Astrid smiled as she started down the steps. "I see you're taken care of for the night, so I'll head home." She disappeared faster than Belle had ever seen her move.

Micah chuckled. "I like her."

"Most days, so do I."

"Not tonight, though?"

"No. Even tonight." She nodded to the kitchen. "She may have hightailed it out of here, but she also washed my dishes. I can't stay mad at someone who cleans my house."

His mouth swished to the side, and a mischievous gleam she hadn't seen for years reignited in his eyes. Pushing up his sleeves, he started in on the stack of toys littering her floor.

"What are you doing?" Belle straightened.

"Cleaning. What's it look like?"

"Micah. Stop. It's going to take far more than you cleaning my house to repair what's broken between us."

"Maybe." He tossed some blocks into the toy box. "But it's a start. Besides, these are trip hazards, and you don't have a spare leg." A laugh escaped her. It grew when he held up a tiny dress. "What on earth does this fit?"

"A Polly Pocket."

"A what?"

She pointed to a container beside the toy box. "Little dolls she plays with."

He opened it and pulled one out. "How on earth does she change their clothes? They're impossibly small."

"She's a determined child."

"She's double-whammied on that trait." He tossed a grin over his shoulder. "Has my messiness too. Sorry about that."

"Normally, I can keep up with things around here. But I've spent the past two days on the couch after work."

"As you should." He tossed the last toys into the bin, then started for her kitchen table. White tubs lined it. A few more were stacked in boxes along the wall. "I saw these last time. What are they?" He picked one up to inspect it. "AnnaBelle's Lotions?"

"They're an extension of what we do here." His quizzical look prodded her further explanation. "I started making them when Anna was born. She had eczema, but all the creams they suggested were too strong. I wanted to try a natural approach, so I did."

"You always were good helping me study chemistry."

"Oh, this wasn't like that. I studied a few essential oils and vitamins, then blended them together."

"I think it was a little harder than you're letting on." He unscrewed the top and inhaled. "This smells wonderful."

"Which one do you have?"

"There's more than one?"

"Several." She'd developed three scents before bringing on the moms at AnnaBelle's to assist. Things had grown since then. Lip balms, soaps, and four more scents. The branding. More was hopefully to come.

"But you just whipped them up?"

She shrugged. "It wasn't as hard as people think."

"For you. Most people don't have this ability, Belle." He put the one he held down and reached for another. "That was mango coconut." He inhaled the new one. "Wild basil and lime. I like this one even more." He capped it and reached for a third. "Do you only sell these at the store downstairs? Because you could easily branch out. Maybe even create a website."

It warmed her, his belief in her abilities. In her. Not that what he thought about her should matter a smidge anymore. But it did. "We're working on one. Right now we're primarily on Etsy and at local craft sales that pop up." His approving nod kept her talking like the children in daycare as they showed off their newest skills. "It's been a great way to teach the moms about small businesses from all aspects. Some love creating. Others love marketing. A few love the accounting. Everything we make is invested back into AnnaBelle's."

He smelled a few more, then returned to the wild basil and lime. "I'd like to buy this one."

"You don't have to do that. Please, take it."

"No. You worked hard, and you deserve the money for this."

"You already paid me by preventing medical expenses for my ankle."

"Which I caused you to sprain."

"Please. I tripped all on my own."

"I've never seen you wobble in heels. If I hadn't surprised you—"

"I'm not taking your money, Micah." Though right now, she could use every sale. But taking anything from him seemed … too vulnerable. Relying on herself was as comfortable as the yoga pants she swore she'd never wear. Now, she owned five pairs.

But with Micah it went beyond remaining comfy. If he saw vulnerability in her, he might think she couldn't adequately care for Anna.

He eyeballed her. She crossed her arms. He sighed. "Fine. I appreciate your generosity."

"You caught me at a good moment, I guess."

They shared a small chuckle, then he grew serious. He cast a glance down the hallway before his stare flickered back to her. Complete uncertainty met with wistful hope on his face.

All the years they'd spent apart couldn't erase the ones they'd had together. How intimately they'd known one another. They'd gone beyond the need for words. As much as she wished they weren't still connected, that bond was still there. "You want to see her."

"I do." His voice was low and gravelly as if the words lodged in his throat.

As if voicing them exposed his own vulnerabilities, and he feared she'd take advantage of his unguarded state.

But she understood what it was like for your heart to walk around outside your body. And as much as hers still hurt from his betrayal, she couldn't crush his. Not this way.

Protecting Anna had to come first. But if she was asleep, there couldn't be any harm.

Belle pressed to a stand and placed her crutches under her arms. "Her bedroom is this way."

His eyes widened. "You're serious?"

"Yes."

He followed. "I don't want to wake her up."

Belle cast a look over her shoulder. "You won't. She sleeps like a log." She stopped at Anna's door. "Something else she got from you." With a twist of the knob, she cracked the door.

Anna was curled in a ball under her pink unicorn sheet. Soft curls cascaded over her cheeks, puffs of air lifting them as she quietly breathed that slow, rhythmic breath of a contented sleep.

"It smells like cotton candy."

Belle peeked up at Micah, who was peering over her shoulder. His breath warmed her cheek. She shifted, allowing him space to move into the doorway. "It's one of the lotions. Sugar Rose. I made that one specifically for her. Felt natural to name it after her too."

"Rose." He looked at her. "She shares your and Penny's middle name?"

"Yeah. So much bad happened with our names." Things she still struggled to process, the outcome of which formed a permanent rift with her parents on one side and Penny and Belle on the other. "What my mom did ... it split Penny and me up for too many years. I wanted to bring healing."

His gaze trailed to Anna, tears moistening his eyes. "And has it?"

"How could anything with this little girl not bring healing?"

As if that answer surged hope in him, his full focus landed on her. "She connects us too, Belle. In so much more than name."

Her heart stuttered. What he offered would be so easy to slip into. And so difficult to let go of a second time. Because she didn't trust herself ... or him. And this time it wouldn't be her heart shattered, it would be Anna's too.

That wasn't an option.

"It's getting late. You should go."

He blinked away his surprise but nodded. "Of course."

They walked to the top of the stairs, and he took the first one before spinning toward her. Down a full step, he still held the height advantage on her. "Thank you for letting me see her."

Too many emotions clogged her throat, so she simply nodded.

"I'm not going to leave, Belle." Straight shoulders, strong jaw, direct look. No doubt he intended to allay her fears with his words.

But she didn't have the luxury of believing him. Maintaining a healthy respect of his ability to hurt her protected not only her heart but Anna's. So she lifted a sad smile and offered an answer that covered both tonight and her fears for their future. "Yes, you are." Then she backed away. "Goodnight, Micah."

Chapter Seven

Indecisiveness had never been a quality Micah possessed. But in the day and a half since Belle's last words to him, he'd picked up his phone and stared at her contact so many times he lost count. His finger would hover over her name until his hand cramped, but he couldn't press dial. He told himself it was because their opposite schedules prevented enough time and privacy for an honest conversation.

That was a lie.

He didn't call because he feared her parting words the other night held truth.

Which was a belief he needed to duck. He might not be the warrior Belle and Anna deserved, but he couldn't give up. The weight of who he'd been wasn't his to shoulder. He'd already settled that with God. Understood he was completely changed and new. Problem was, he'd thought he was prepared to withstand the barbs Belle would throw. To see the hurt and distrust in her eyes. Instead, her words were like a riptide sucking him back to those old fears. To beat that riptide, he couldn't fight it directly. He'd wear himself out trying. Time to stop striving against preconceived notions and allow himself the space to become the man they needed. Someone who loved Belle and Anna. Who'd come home to honor them. Protect them. Selflessly care for them.

Actions louder than words. Turning the volume knob up on his efforts required a move beyond ordering meals, and this warm Saturday morning offered that chance. When he left Belle Thursday night, he ran into Astrid, who casually passed on the information that Belle was scheduled to work AnnaBelle's alone this morning. The older ladies had chartered a bus for some sort of day trip with the single moms, and Belle had agreed way-back-when to cover for the day. Jonah and Penny were watching Anna for her, but there wasn't anyone to watch Belle.

He'd happily step in.

He quickly showered, dressed, and headed for breakfast with Mom. Chloe cast him a glare as he shut the door in her face. No doubt she'd make him pay for leaving again. After an hour with Mom, he hit Starbucks for himself and Belle. Knowing her, she'd already brewed a pot. Plus, he'd had another cup delivered with her breakfast, but showing up with a single coffee would be like attempting to eat candy in front of a child. No doubt he'd end up handing his over to her, so he might as well bring two.

Arriving at AnnaBelle's, he spotted Belle before she saw him. She stood inside near the cracked front window. Her back to him, she worked a shirt around a mannequin's arms. White, bulky, and practically as big as her, the plastic form wasn't cooperating, and Belle fought a losing battle with it. Especially since she'd ditched her crutches and currently listed to the right in an attempt to keep weight off her bad ankle.

The overhead bell dinged as he walked through. She cast a glance over her shoulder, then executed such a speedy double-take that the mannequin gained the upper hand. It toppled against her as she hopped backward, trying her best to right the beast.

Hands full of paper coffee cups, Micah rushed behind her to prevent another fall. She oophed into him, grabbing his bracketed arms to stabilize herself. The mannequin kerplunked to the floor beside them.

He leaned his face down to hers. "That's twice now my mere presence has swept you off your feet."

"More like clotheslined me off of them."

"That's not a saying."

She eyeballed him. "It is now."

Couldn't help it, he laughed. Then, "Seriously, though, you okay? You didn't tweak anything, did you?"

"No." Releasing her hold, she straightened. "And maybe stop showing up in places I don't expect you, so we don't have a repeat performance."

"Maybe start expecting me in places you are." He held her coffee out to her. "I bring treats."

"Along with accidents."

"We'll work on that part." Wiggling her coffee until she took it with a sigh, he then stooped down to nab the mannequin and righted it. "It appears you could use some help dressing this thing."

"I got it."

"Funny. Looked like it had you."

"You of all people should know that looks can be deceiving."

"Ouch." Tapping her coffee with his, he said, "Glad I brought you that because it's obvious you didn't get your fill of liquid happiness this morning."

Her cheeks pinkened, but she said nothing.

A door down the hallway burst open and little feet clamored their way. Belle's eyes widened with fear.

"Aw done, Mama. I go potty aw by myself." Their towheaded little girl barreled toward them with such an accomplished smile one would think she'd won an Olympic gold medal in bathroom skills. "Now I have my donut?"

Words deserted Micah. Belle too, but for very different reasons. Her gaze furtively bounced between Anna and him, but he couldn't tear his from the pint-size version of their two halves now in one whole. Seeing Anna asleep had nearly brought him to his knees, but watching her expressions, hearing her voice, having those blue eyes light on him … Yeah, he was going to need a second.

Backing up, he reached for the clothing rack beside him, grabbing the silver bar and clenching it for balance. The tops of hangers dug into his palm, reminding him this wasn't a dream. His little girl stood a few feet away, chatting with her mama. He hadn't warranted more than a swift glance from her. Not when her focus was on arguing her case for that donut with all the skill of a high-powered lawyer. Which gave him time to drink her in.

She had Belle's blonde hair and his loose curls. Already it was easy to see she'd be tall like him, and—judging by the well-worn pink unicorn she'd smashed under her arm in a tight hold—she held a proclivity toward the sentimental side, one Belle possessed but often hid. Her eyes were the same brilliant blue as his, but as wide and dazzling as Belle's. Wider actually, which seemed unbelievable and completely adorable on her round face framed with full, pink cheeks. And that dimple. He lifted a hand to his own. Same spot, just a few inches to the left of his lips.

Belle glanced his way and a line formed between her brows. No doubt she was trying to read his mind as usual. Good luck with that right now. His thoughts flew in every direction so quickly he couldn't even capture them.

With complete innocence, Anna peered up at him, so very unaware of the weight of her question. "Hi. Whas your name?"

Daddy. You can call me Daddy.

But he hadn't yet earned the right to those words. She didn't recognize him. Didn't even realize she belonged to him. Neither of those realities changed how deeply he loved her or the truth that she was his. So he'd wait until the day when the light in her blue eyes shone with the knowledge that she was his daughter and he adored her.

For now, he'd allow Belle to lead.

His eyes flickered her way, and the myriad of emotions playing across her face revealed she had no clue what to say. His lips remained sealed. Belle mapped the course through this uncharted territory, not him, and he'd follow whatever one she chose.

Turning to Anna, she cleared her throat. "Um, this is Mommy's friend, Mr.

Micah."

"Mista Micah." Anna tried out the words, her little voice dropping consonants, softening the edges of his name, and tugging out a smile.

For years, he'd dreamt of the first time he'd interact with his daughter, but that picture never resembled this. A secondhand shop on an ordinary summer afternoon. Yet somehow, this subtle slipping into her life in the middle of the ordinary felt more real than anything he'd envisioned.

He squatted in front of her. "Hello, Princess."

She giggled. "I'm Anna."

"Oh, Princess Anna then." He cleared his throat, the lump there almost cutting off his words.

"I'm not a princess."

"Are you sure?" he asked. "Because you look like one to me."

Anna turned to Belle. "Mama, am I a princess?"

Belle tugged on Anna's soft curls. "A monkey princess."

Then, as if she caught the scent of her donut again, Anna yanked on Belle's hand. "Come on."

Relief flashed over Belle's face at the easy escape Anna provided. Yeah, they could all use a second to regroup.

"I'll stay down here in case anyone comes in," he offered.

With a nod, Belle handed off her coffee, took the crutches he held out, and followed Anna to their door. They both sat on their behinds and slowly navigated the stairs. He set her coffee on the main counter, then paced the floor, praying no one would walk through the front doors. He owed Belle an explanation, starting with the fact he hadn't planned on Anna being here this morning. But he couldn't conjure up an apology. How could he ever be sorry for meeting his daughter?

Five minutes later, much sooner than he'd expected, the two slid down the stairs. Anna held a donut and sippy cup in her hands and still maintained her grip on her unicorn. Belle positioned her on a stool beside the cash register. Her crutches clunked a rhythmic beat as she slowly made her way toward him.

"I didn't know she'd be here." He dropped his voice to a near whisper. "Astrid told me she was staying with Jonah and Penny today. If I knew she was here, I wouldn't have come."

She peered over at Anna, then to him. "Why did you come, anyway?"

So. They weren't talking about Anna yet.

"Thursday as I was leaving, Astrid mentioned you were working alone today. I came by to help."

"At my secondhand store." She didn't try to hide her skepticism.

"I did work two years at Gap." Because no matter how much money his parents had, his dad was set on him making his own way. Other than necessities, Dad didn't feel the need to provide any extra for Micah. Wouldn't allow him to work at his thriving commercial real estate business, even if Micah did study hard to learn everything he could about that world in hopes of impressing him. The closest he came was the summer between high school and college, when Mom pushed hard enough that Dad pulled strings to put him on one of the construction crews rehabbing his most recent purchase.

Like everything else he encountered in life, Micah was a quick study at construction. But that wasn't Dad's business, more like a way to pacify both Mom and himself after years of attempts to grow closer to him. It became painfully obvious that wasn't going to happen, so Micah ditched that job and threw himself into medicine, something he was not simply good at, but actually enjoyed. And to help offset the costs of college, he worked retail.

Belle was one of the few who knew his full story—or at least the parts he'd allowed her to see. "I appreciate your coming, Micah, but I've got this handled."

"Says the woman who was nearly trampled by a mannequin."

"I'll pull a stool over and sit on it while I change the outfit. Lesson learned."

"Why do I think it'll also be a lesson quickly forgotten?"

She shrugged. "I'll be fine." Another glance in Anna's direction had Belle heading that way.

He followed her stare and broke out laughing. At some point, Anna had finished her donut, then dove into Belle's coffee. She'd managed to yank the top off and was wiggling on the stool, grinning so widely her smile was visible behind the venti cup.

"Anna!" Belle's voice went from the edge of frustration to bubbly laughter as Anna pulled the coffee from her lips, revealing a mocha-colored mustache.

"I yuv this, Mama."

Belle swiped the cup from her and grabbed the paper towel Anna's donut had been on, not hiding her own smile. "Come here, Monkey. Let me wipe your face."

The cheesy grin Anna whipped out was too much. Their daughter carried the potential to knock a person flat with her sheer adorableness. Even better, though? Watching Belle with her. He hadn't forgotten how beautiful she was, but seeing her delight in Anna deepened that beauty. He hid behind his own coffee, allowing himself a minute to live in the what-ifs. To pretend this moment was real—that he had the freedom to walk over and drop a kiss on top of Belle's smile. Steal her breath the way simply looking at her stole his.

She glanced his way, the amusement in her eyes slowly morphing into awareness, her steady gaze saying she read every single one of his thoughts. He read hers too. They'd never had trouble communicating with a look, and the way she slammed her lids closed revealed more to him than if she'd left them open. For a brief second, the two of them had landed in the same exact place, and not only did it freak her out, but she didn't want him to see it.

Too late.

Instead of calling her out and causing a faster retreat, he'd file her response away as progress and keep forging forward. A man could hang on for the long haul when a woman looked at him like that. And he had no doubt he still faced an uphill battle.

Great, just great. Bad enough that her heart actually flip-flopped when Micah caught her in his arms, but did her face have to flash like a neon sign proclaiming she wasn't over him?

Because she so was. Her body simply hadn't caught up with the rest of her yet—and she wasn't about to let her physical side lead again where Micah was concerned. Not that she wasn't thankful every single day for Anna in her life, but she could do without the heartache that preceded her arrival.

Anna pushed Belle's hands away. "I aw done." Then she wiggled off the stool and out of reach faster than Belle could capture her. Darn ankle. Anna raced to Micah and stopped a foot from him, her little neck craning to peer up at him. "Hey-yo, Mista Micah."

"Hello, Monkey Princess."

Did he have to be so adorable with her? This was more than she could take. Her heart burst earlier when he'd met Anna. The look on his face showed how badly he wanted to tell her who he was, but he'd remained silent. The fact that he hadn't taken advantage of the moment didn't change her resolve to protect Anna from a still-unstable situation. But it did put a dent in the ugly part of her that self-righteously wanted him to squirm—and maybe even hurt—a little bit.

She wasn't prepared for this. Especially when not one interaction mirrored any scenario she'd envisioned if Micah returned one day. Like today, meeting Anna. It was all so ... ordinary. But some of life's biggest moments arrived in the most everyday settings.

Grabbing the sleeve of a shirt hanging on the rack beside her, Anna wrapped herself in the fabric as she twirled. "Are you here to pway with Mama?"

His eyes lifted to hers. "I'm here to help her."

"I hep Mama too!"

"That's very nice of you."

Okay. This was too much, too soon.

During her pageant days, she'd attended etiquette lessons and learned her taste buds weren't suited for many dishes she'd be forced to endure. Just like learning to develop an affinity for foods she didn't enjoy, seeing Anna with Micah would have to happen in small doses.

Belle stepped between them. "How about you go play with the toys Mama set out for you in the corner? In a little bit, you can help."

Lured by new shiny objects, Anna released the shirt. "Yes, Mama." Then she skipped to the area beside the counter that held a tiny table, blocks, dolls, crayons, and butcher block paper. She set Uni on the table, gave her a pink crayon, then grabbed a blue one for herself.

"I can leave," Micah whispered, leaning toward her.

Again, the fact that he allowed her the choice stilled her reflex to take him up on his offer. Right now, they sat on a tenuously balanced seesaw, and she didn't want to do anything that might knock them off-kilter. If that steel will of his deployed again, the resulting custody battle could grow ugly. She'd much rather work with him than against him.

"No. You can stay." There'd need to be boundaries, however. "But I'm putting you to work since you offered."

He didn't even bat an eye, just agreed. Hours later, he'd changed out the display in the front windows, cleaned the glass inside and out, and swept the floors while she helped customers. At different times she'd look up to see Anna following him, chatting away, and he'd patiently listen and answer her. When it came time for her nap, Anna raced over and hugged his legs. "Bye, Mista Micah. You come pway again?"

His hand brushed against her curls. "I'd love to play again."

When Belle returned downstairs, monitor in hand, Micah stood in the corner perusing the shelves holding the AnnaBelle skin care line. She clunked over to him.

He turned, moisture in his eyes. "Thank you."

Sometimes simplicity spoke far more than a long string of eloquent words. Most often, it rang truer. Another thing she'd learned through pageants was if unsure what to say, fluff with pretty dialogue. She'd become an expert at spinning answers, which was probably why she appreciated Micah's two straightforward words. They carried much more weight.

"You're welcome."

The front door dinged, and a customer walked in. Short and slightly round, with shoulder-length black hair beginning to gray, she was dressed in a sensible pantsuit. Belle guessed her to be in her early fifties.

The woman walked their way. "I'm looking for Belle Thornton?"

"That's me." Belle held out her hand.

After shaking it, the woman introduced herself with a warm smile. "I'm Natalie Simmons, and I'm with the FDA. I have a few questions for you about a few items you sell."

Her smile was warm, but her words injected cold right under Belle's skin. "The FDA?" she croaked.

Micah placed a steady hand on the small of her back. The gentle touch offered a strength she didn't want to lean into, but at this moment absorbed it nonetheless.

Natalie Simmons must have been used to intimidating people because her smile slipped into compassion. "I promise, I'm not here to shut you down, but there are some changes you'll need to make to the lotions and soaps you manufacture."

More changes could mean more time and money she didn't have. She hadn't even heard them yet, and already her tears threatened. No. She didn't need to leap to worst-case scenario. Maybe they'd actually be easy and free.

Three hours later, she reached the conclusion that *worst-case scenario* had not been an overreaction.

"So here's a list for you to keep track of everything we talked about," Natalie said as she scribbled a few more words on the paperwork. "Plan on me returning in about three months to check on the changes to your production shed. We can email about the other items." Unclipping the loose sheets from her clipboard, she handed them to Belle. "And not to worry, I'll schedule my next visit. It won't be another surprise."

Well, that just made it all hunky-dory, didn't it?

Mustering up a pleasant voice, Belle responded, "I appreciate it, but three months might not be enough time." Not with all the other changes currently on the same deadline. She was out of time and money before she even started.

"I understand, but I will need to see substantial progress, or we may have to pause your production." Again, everything about her remained soft, but her instructions held no bend. "It may not seem like it now, but our goal is to help you, not harm you. All of these changes will make your company stronger and help protect you from potential lawsuits. We want you in compliance for both our sakes and will do what we can to see you succeed." She shook her hand. "I'm serious when I say call or email me with any questions you have as you start to tackle this list."

She could be as sincere as the queen, but that didn't change the fact that this extra work appeared as impossible as obtaining a private audience with Her Majesty.

As the door swished shut behind Natalie, Micah stepped from around the counter and crossed to Belle. Exhaustion settled into her bones. She and Natalie had finished the surprise visit with a trip outdoors to the small shed where they produced AnnaBelle's skin care items. That was after two hours in Belle's tiny office, going over everything from her Etsy site to the need for procedure manuals and something called batch sheets. They hadn't even touched the website Belle hoped to have up in the coming weeks.

Her thoughts twirled so fast she put a steadying hand on the wall.

"Hey," Micah grabbed her other arm. "It's going to be okay."

She believed him about as much as she believed unicorns were real, not that she'd admit that to Anna.

Anna!

Belle started for the stairs, but the sight of her little monkey coloring at the tiny table in the corner stopped her.

"She woke up, and you went and got her?" How on earth had she not even thought about her waking?

The answer was simple, but one she hated to face—somewhere inside, she trusted Micah. No … trust wasn't the right word, at least not for her heart. But she did know in her core that Anna was safe with him. It was the only explanation for why she'd remained hyperfocused on Natalie's visit rather than her daughter's schedule.

Micah took her silence as concern. "I should have gotten you, and I promise if I hadn't met her this afternoon, I would have. But I was trying to help, so when I heard her on the monitor—"

Belle held up her hand. "You're babbling again."

He gripped the back of his neck. "Yeah. I guess I am." His nervousness crackled in the air. "I really was attempting to help."

"I know." And he had. Not that she wanted to grow comfortable relying on it.

She looked at the time. Nearing five. Anna would need dinner soon, and he hadn't mentioned having ordered anything for them. She wasn't about to hint he should. "I'm sorry that I wound up keeping you here all day, but you can head out now. I actually do have one employee to cover close tonight, and she should arrive soon."

"You didn't keep me. I wanted to stay." His lips twisted as if he was unsure of his next words. "Plus, I sort of somehow promised Anna cupcakes. Since I did, I figured maybe I could make dinner for you too, rather than ordering it? Takeout has to be getting old."

Wow. Hadn't taken long for Anna to wrap him around her finger. She had a feeling that string would tighten over time. She, however, could dodge the one he was trying to lasso her with. "I appreciate it, but you've already spent your day with us. You don't need to give up your evening too. I'm sure you have more important things to do."

"I'm not giving anything up, Belle." His gaze, his warm voice; he caressed her without even a touch. "I'm gaining everything important."

And just like that, he roped her in even though she'd tried to evade him.

He took advantage of her silence and slipped out the door while she stood there, emotions swirling. How was she supposed to remain levelheaded in the face of his return? Truth was, she couldn't, because her heart had always been his. Even now, in its bruised state. The moment he'd smacked into her, the sore muscle had begun beating again. Hoping. And every time she was around him, that hope warred with the fear inside. She couldn't seem to let go of either one.

Or guess which would win.

Chapter Eight

She had maybe an hour to prepare herself for round two of Micah. That seemed hardly enough time, but she'd allowed this predicament. Could have turned down his dinner offer. Sent him packing. Instead, she'd let him sweet-talk his way into her evening plans—not that she'd had any. But still. She'd determined to move beyond her boundaries, crumbling in the face of a few sugary words. Yet here she stood.

The day replayed in her mind, right along with how Micah had food delivered all week. Okay. Maybe it wasn't his words that had momentarily toppled her defenses. She hadn't been prepared for him to put actions with them. They'd routed around her like a sneak attack, but now that she spied them, maybe over time she could regroup.

As soon as Kim arrived to cover the store, Belle grabbed her mail from the front counter and called for Anna. "Carry this for Mommy?"

"Yep."

They ascended the stairs, the humidity and heat growing with each step. She should have told Micah to grab something that didn't require the stove because running it on days like this made the small space more unbearable.

Anna set the mail on the table, then hopped all the way to the bathroom. "I go potty, Mama!"

Her words half-hit as Belle flipped through the envelopes, stopping at one holding her summer property tax. Honestly. Could she not catch a break?

The toilet flushed, and Anna's sing-song voice floated toward her bedroom. No doubt she headed to play with her stuffed animals. Popping some aspirin, Belle snagged her ice bag and plopped onto the couch in front of her open window. Not a breath of air moved through the screen. With a groan, she stood and wrestled the box fan into the window opening and turned it on. A hot breeze blew against her clammy skin. Would have to do.

Between the heat, the long day, and her painkiller kicking in, her eyelids must have drifted closed. Next thing she knew, Anna was screaming.

Belle launched from the couch. "Anna!"

Micah stood at the top of the steps. Anna wasn't screaming; she was squealing.

"Co-yee here!"

Chloe attacked her with kisses.

"Yes. I see that." Belle slipped her hand over her chest, attempting to slow her racing heart.

Micah stood with grocery bags in both hands, looking chagrined. "This time I was expected."

"You still could have knocked."

"I did."

"Oh." She focused on Chloe as he moved to the kitchen.

"I hope it's okay I brought her." He dropped the bags on the counter. "She's not used to being alone so much, and she's let me know it too."

His grimace spurred her curiosity. "Oh? How so?"

"Let's see," he began as he unpacked things. "Today it was another of Mom's pillows, the leg of one of the dining room chairs, and my University of Michigan hat."

"She secretly an Ohio State fan?"

"Hush. She's devious but not evil."

Anna raced to the family room with a full-on belly laugh as Chloe chased her. They collapsed on the floor together.

"They've missed each other," Belle said. "We would have taken her to see your mom, but I thought your dad took Chloe with him when he left."

A myriad of emotions flashed across Micah's face. "He didn't." Folding his now empty grocery bag, he leaned against the counter and smoothly changed subjects. "You visit my mom?"

"She and Anna have a special bond." Like somehow they both saw a piece of Micah in each other. A piece they couldn't quite recognize but felt slide into place when they were together. "How are you doing with all this, Micah? Your dad leaving. Your mom in assisted living."

Wasn't sure why she asked, except he'd been such a huge help lately, and something inside said she needed to keep things balanced between them. Plus, a tiny part of her worried if he didn't talk about it, he might be tempted to pick up a drink to cope. She'd much rather offer him her shoulder—for Anna's sake.

He crossed his arms, his biceps pulling against the navy T-shirt he wore. "I've never been close to my dad—you know that—but seeing my mom like this is tough. I didn't realize how bad things had gotten. If I had …"

"You may have come home sooner?" The question cost her, but not as much as his answer could.

His deep blue eyes latched on to hers, holding back nothing. "I never should have left in the first place. And that has nothing to do with my mom."

Wow.

Wow. Wow. Wow.

She was in trouble. Big time. She barely had enough strength to turn away from the unspoken invitation there. The one that said he'd open wide those strong arms and tuck her into his embrace if she just put one foot in front of the other.

Forgiving him couldn't be that simple. Trusting him again certainly wasn't. And she had no business being close to him with neither of those things accomplished. Besides, she was a strong woman, capable of standing on her own two feet.

Metaphorically for now, but still. Micah was here for Anna and only Anna. As if to prove it, her monkey joined them, peering up at him. "Hi."

"Hi." With one last long look at Belle—the determined kind that promised a reprieve but not a retreat—he squatted and shifted the full force of his attention to Anna. "Can I have dinner with you and your mommy?"

Without hesitation, she nodded.

Good grief, but their little girl wasn't immune to his charm either.

"What shall we have?" he asked.

Anna bounced. "Cupcakes!"

Micah's eyes slid to Belle's, wonder swimming under a sheen of tears. Her first few days with Anna had produced the same effect. Even now, there were moments where she welled up in utter amazement that this tiny gift belonged to her. Except Anna wasn't solely hers now—she never had been, even if Micah made it easy to pretend that was the truth.

It hit Belle again how surreal all this was, Micah slipping into their lives as quickly as he disappeared. It was both wrong and right at the same time. They needed to talk. She knew that. He did too. But for now, there was a two-and-a-half-year-old standing between them begging for cake.

"Cupcakes sound delicious, and I did promise to bring them." He hauled out four cupcakes, their whipped frosting twirled to the top of their clear plastic container.

"Cake!" Anna's bouncing went ballistic. She hopped around the tiny kitchen, singing the one word over and over. Chloe joined in with a few yaps of her own.

"You made her night. Good luck convincing her they're for *after* she eats dinner."

Panic overtook his features. "She doesn't know they're dessert?"

"She told you she wanted cake for dinner, and you hauled it out for her."

"Can we have cake for dinner?"

She laughed. "No." Then she took pity on him and knelt by Anna. "Mr.

Micah brought four cupcakes. Which of your friends should help us eat one?"

No hesitation. "Uni."

"Okay. Well, Uni needs to eat a good dinner first, right? Because we don't want her tummy to feel sick."

Anna slowed her hopping and nodded solemnly.

"So how about we all eat our dinner first? Uni can eat with us. We're going to have a picnic downstairs. Does that sound like fun?"

More hopping and more singing. This time her song involved the soft and rounded sounds of her adorable version of the word picnic.

"Can you go get Uni ready for dinner?"

Anna tore off to her room, Chloe hot on her heels. "I get ready too!"

Micah watched the entire exchange with wide eyes. "I have so much to learn."

"You have time."

His focus remained on the hallway for a long moment before switching to Belle. "I know we have a lot to discuss, and you've been very gracious to let me see her. I was honest when I said I want this to move at whatever pace you need. I hope you see that."

"I do, and thank you." She absently rubbed her thumbnail, not wanting to do this now, yet needing to lay the groundwork. "Things are changing fast, but I don't want you to think just because I've opened my door that it will stay open. I'm ... I'm flying blind here, Micah. My emotions are all over the place. I want to be fair to you, but I'm also terrified of letting you into our lives. You can be her friend, but that doesn't automatically mean you'll get to be her father."

His face paled, and he swallowed. "I appreciate your honesty."

"None of this will even have a chance to work unless we can be honest with one another."

"Do you want this to work?"

There was no way she was ready to untangle that answer from the mess of her head and heart. "It's too soon to ask me that. I don't even know what this is."

"Fair enough." Silence reset the space between them before he spoke again. "Hope you don't mind, but I thought we could grill and eat outside? I thought I saw a little area out there?"

"There is. It's not in the best shape, but it works." She watched him unpacking his bags. "That doesn't look like lasagna fixings."

"You hate lasagna." He stuffed a container of fruit in the fridge.

"And you love it."

"I'm not cooking for me; I'm cooking for you." He placed salad fixings on the counter. "Besides, it's about a hundred and fifty up here. No way I'm running your stove." Now he faced her. "Don't you have AC up here too?"

"It's broken."

"And your landlord hasn't fixed it?"

She shifted. Embarrassment at having signed the lease she did nearly tied her tongue, but the last thing she wanted was him believing she couldn't take care of herself and Anna. "It's not his responsibility."

He paused to look at her. "How do you figure?"

"It's just not." The temp seemed to go up another degree under the heat of his stare. "What are you making for dinner then, if not lasagna?"

"Salmon. And don't change the subject. I can't help if I don't know what the problem is."

She loved salmon. He hated it. After three years, why on earth was he showing up here, being the man who should have been here all along? Made her want to hit him and hug him all at once.

"There's no problem. I signed what's called a net lease, and that means I'm responsible for the maintenance of this building."

"You do remember my dad was in commercial real estate, right? I know what a net lease is, Belle. I also know there's several types. So what type did you sign?"

"If you know there are several types, then you should know which one I signed." Hopefully, he'd leave it at that.

He didn't.

"I can narrow it down to two that would require you to shoulder the maintenance. My concern, based on your evasiveness, is you signed an Absolute Triple Net with a few self-serving tweaks inserted by your landlord."

Anna toddled toward them, pink tulle skirt, cherry rain boots, purple T-shirt, and strings of beads dripping around her neck. She'd added one of Belle's past tiaras to top it all off. "I ready for dinner." Uni was tucked under her arm, and the worn unicorn wore her matching tulle skirt. Chloe trotted along beside with her own string of pink plastic pearls dragging against the floor.

"You and Uni look beautiful. Chloe too." Micah knelt before her. "I especially like your tiara. Your mommy used to wear them."

Anna spun on her booted heel. "I be back. I be back." She thunked down the hall, tore into her room, and raced back, another tiara in hand. "I put on Mommy."

Belle shook her head. "No, sweetheart. I'm okay."

"Pweese?"

Anna knew her pleases always worked. With a sigh, Belle leaned down for her to place the tiara on her head.

"Mommy's beautiful now too."

Micah stared at them both. "Stunning, I'd say."

"I can't eat another bite." Belle waved off the spatula of salmon Micah tried to slide onto her plate. "It was delicious, though. Where'd you learn to cook like that?"

Slipping the last fillet onto a clean plate, he settled on the picnic bench across from her. A few feet away, Anna splashed in a kiddy pool while Chloe napped under the tree he'd looped her leash around. Seemed Anna had the magical power of wearing her out.

Across from him, Belle leaned her elbows on the table, finally relaxed again after his honest comment in the apartment had clammed her up. Her reaction reinforced that he should maintain a more subtle approach for now. Like the kiddos he'd worked with on his peds rotation, he needed to find additional ways to heal what was broken without scaring her away. If he could divert her focus elsewhere, maybe she'd let her guard down a little, and he could slip in and start to mend the wound between them.

"Thanks. In California I had a friend, Jonathan. He and his wife, Stacey, had me over for dinner often, and I picked up a few things."

She palmed her stomach. "A few amazing things. I've never had salmon grilled on a plank like that. And the sauce you put on it?"

"Pretty delicious, right? It's what convinced me to finally eat salmon." Belle had always ordered it plain with a twist of lemon. Way too bland for him. Tonight, he'd brought lemons for her and made the sauce for himself, fully expecting to be the sole one to use it. Until Belle surprisingly dipped her finger into the bowl and proclaimed he needed to smear it over all of their portions.

"Uh-maz-ing."

All right, he'd make this dish every night if it delivered that satisfied smile. He pushed the plate her way. "You sure you don't want this last little bit?"

"Not if I want one of those cupcakes."

Now *that* was amazing. "I remember days where you wouldn't even have sauce on your salmon, let alone a cupcake after."

"Yeah, I definitely had some strange ideas." She fiddled with the edge of her plate. "I didn't want to pass them on to Anna. The last thing I want is for her to develop weird habits or freak out over food the way I was taught to."

Her mom trained her to count every calorie that went into her mouth. It was pretty great to see how differently Belle was raising their daughter, let alone allowing herself simple freedoms she never had before. He wasn't the only one who'd changed. "I'd say you're succeeding. She gobbled that salmon right up without even batting an eye. And the asparagus too." He'd actually brought chicken tenders to grill for Anna, but Belle had quickly nixed that option.

"I've always fed her whatever I'm eating—healthy or sweet. I want her to know that everything is good, in moderation."

"Even lasagna?"

She caught the tease to his voice and smiled. "Okay, maybe not everything." Gathering the napkins and plates, she began to clean up.

"Leave it. I'll handle it in a sec." Like after they'd chatted for a while and had those cupcakes. "Tell me more about your lease."

A debate waged in her eyes. She didn't want to divulge the details, but she knew him well enough to understand he wouldn't give up asking. A hefty sigh rounded her lips. "The morning you and I ... bumped into each other again, I had a visit from the fire chief and a code inspector. They left me their own lists. Seems after today I can start an entire collection of them." She fidgeted with the edge of her shorts, her lean, tanned legs smooth and silky-looking beneath her fingers. "You were right earlier. When I found this building, the landlord wrote up a Triple Net with a few extra responsibilities for me as a tenant, but in exchange, he gave me a break on rent."

Earlier he'd taken note on the fixes he *could* see while helping in the shop. Those alone would put a dent in her banking account. Now that he knew the potential of what she faced, he worried her account would be drained. "A break as in free? Because looking around here, it should be."

She bristled. "I didn't realize things were in quite as bad shape as they are. If I had, I most likely wouldn't have signed."

It was the "most likely" that bothered him. Belle was more capable than most people he knew. She was also incredibly determined, a wonderful trait to possess. But he worried that her determination to go things alone, while understandable, had placed her into financial trouble and trapped her there. He shouldered part of the blame for that. Okay, most of it.

While he wanted to pursue more of this conversation, he sensed letting it drop for now was the better course. He reached for her plate.

She swiped him away. "You cooked. I can clean."

"And if you had two working legs, I'd take you up on that."

"My hands still work."

He stopped her as she reached to cap the poppy seed dressing they'd used on their side salad. "They don't have to. Not tonight."

She worked her lower lip.

Relying on him wasn't going to come easy for her, but he wasn't above shifting attention to someone much harder to refuse. A few feet away, Anna jumped up and down in her tiny pool. Seemed she'd been wearing her pink unicorn bathing suit under her clothes the entire time.

"Hey, Anna," he called, "do you want Mama to come play with you?"

"Yes!" Her bouncing intensified.

Belle gasped. "Unfair!"

"Pretty sure it's 'all's fair in love and war.'"

Her head tilted. "Except we only have the war part down."

"And yet that little girl is evidence otherwise." His grin deepened with her blush. "In fact, I remember in clear detail—"

"Stop!" Her hand darted into the air. "You win. I'm going."

She hobbled off, muttering threats of teaching him a thing or two about fair play.

Laughing, he cleared off the picnic table and piled everything that needed to go upstairs into the tote they'd used. Didn't take him but a few minutes to run it all inside.

After washing and putting away her dishes, he found the linen closet, grabbed beach towels, and hustled downstairs. Sweat poured off him from that short time in her apartment. Across the yard, Anna squealed as Belle dribbled water from a watering can over her head. Looked like she'd let Anna take a turn on her too.

"Having fun?" he asked as he approached.

Anna snatched the can from Belle and latched her gaze on him. "I do you!"

Beside her, amusement danced in Belle's eyes. "Oh, that's a great idea, Anna. Mr. Micah looks like he could use some cooling off."

He did, but he'd planned on drinking a cold bottled water from the cooler they'd brought down earlier. But how could he say no to either of them?

Handing the towels to Belle, he climbed into the pool and knelt down. "Would you please water me?"

Nodding, Anna turned the entire can over on his head.

He gasped as water drenched, rather than drizzled, over him. Based on Belle's laughter, she'd known exactly what was coming his way. He opened one eye at her. "Thanks for warning me."

Her shoulders shook from giggles. "All's fair, right?"

He splashed her, and within seconds an all-out water war erupted. Anna's squeals mixed with Chloe's yaps and their laughter. Twenty minutes later, they were all soaked. He'd never known a tiny plastic pool could hold so much fun.

Right smack dab in the middle of splashing him for the hundredth time, his little girl hopped out and raced toward the picnic table. "I have cake now!"

Micah looked at Belle. "Did someone say squirrel?"

"Welcome to life with a toddler. Their attention spans are shorter than they are."

"I'm getting that." He hauled himself out from the toddler pool, his legs protesting after the twisted position they'd been in.

Belle called out to Anna. "If you bring them here, I'll help you open them."

Toddling to them, Anna held the plastic container up. "Pink, pweese."

Belle opened it and handed her the one with pink frosting. "Sit in your chair to eat it, and then you can get back in the pool for a little bit."

"Thank you." Her chubby little hands wrapped around the treat, and she shoved a bite in, humming happily as she settled into her princess camping chair. Chloe trotted over to her, ready to pick up any crumbs. Smart dog.

Waiting until Belle had chosen hers, Micah slipped a chocolate one from the container and perched beside her. "She can't say her Ls."

Belle stiffened, her cupcake halfway to her mouth. She set it on her leg. "I'm aware and have addressed it with her doctor, who says her speech is appropriate for her age. If she reaches school age and it's still an issue, I'll put her in speech therapy."

"Whoa. I wasn't calling your parenting into question." He started to rest his hand on her knee but stopped when she shifted away from the movement. "I think it's adorable, is all."

She regarded him with a wary look. "Sorry. Old habit to think people are picking me apart."

"I'm not, Belle." Made him sad he'd destroyed something that had once been so good. Thing was, it hadn't broken all at once. It splintered in one poor choice after another until he finally made the worst one of all—leaving her. Putting it back together would take longer. Fixing things always did. "I never have, and I never will."

She nodded but didn't pick up her cupcake.

He could pray things didn't remain this awkward.

Giving her a little space, he unwrapped his cupcake and dug into it. After a few moments, she did the same. Anna had already finished hers, but rather than hopping into the pool, she and Chloe raced across the patchy grass to an old swing set. He bit his tongue from asking if it was safe. Belle wouldn't allow her to play on it if it wasn't. Still, the way the rickety thing squeaked as Anna climbed the small slide made his insides twist.

"It's on one of my many lists." Belle crumpled her empty wrapper. "But it'll do until we have the money."

He wasn't so sure.

"Yook at me!" Anna inch-wormed down the slide, both hands up and waving their way.

"Be careful, Monkey."

"I do."

And she was, but still … "Maybe I should go over there."

"She's fine."

They needed wood chips around that contraption. No. They needed an entirely new contraption. But he already knew her answer if he offered to build her one.

In some situations, it was easier to ask for forgiveness than permission.

This qualified as one of those times.

Chapter Nine

Belle might have fought off the beauty queen persona Mom had ingrained in her, but she still believed a woman shouldn't sweat—and she definitely shouldn't wake up sticky and stinky. Sleep wasn't meant to be a workout. Apparently her mind and body didn't agree because she'd spent the entire night fighting her sheets. With it this hot, she wanted a cold shower more than a mug of her morning fuel. Another complete injustice.

And it was Monday, no less.

Shoving up, she limped to her bathroom, checking in on Anna along the way. Looked like she'd tossed and turned all night too. Damp blonde curls clung to her forehead and neck. That was it. She was purchasing a wall unit for Anna's room today. At least one of them would get a good night's sleep. Heck, she may even camp on the floor in there.

An hour later, she rinsed off their breakfast dishes and sent Anna to don her sandals. "You ready to go see Astrid?"

Anna scuffed over, face as grumpy as Belle's mood. Holding her arms out, she lifted those big eyes. "Up."

"Mama can't pick you up, Monkey."

Her little lip pooched out.

Belle pointed to her ankle. "I want to, but remember I hurt my ankle?"

This received a nod.

"Let's sit on the steps together and slide down them."

More furious nodding.

Motherhood challenged her in ways no one could have prepared her for. There was nothing she wouldn't do for her little girl, and the weight of raising Anna right weighed on her constantly. She equally worried that she'd either spoil her rotten or be too harsh. She always worked to stay two steps ahead of a tantrum. Tried hard to provide for her needs while fulfilling some of her wants. And the moment she thought maybe, just maybe, she had things figured out, Anna changed all the rules.

All with no one to shoulder the ups and downs with. Motherhood could be so incredibly isolating even on its best days, and she didn't even want to think about the tough ones. Would some of that lift if she had a partner?

"We go?" Anna's little fist tugged on Belle's pinkie.

Good thing, because her line of thinking was growing dangerously close to Micah territory, and that was the last place she needed to revisit. He wasn't the antidote to her loneliness, he was the root cause of it, and she needed to remember that fact.

But, oh, did he possess the ability to give her heart a bad case of amnesia. Another tug. "Mama?"

"Yes, Monkey, let's go." It was entirely too hot up here.

Fran and Betty staffed the daycare for the morning, both of their faces lighting as Anna joined them. After saying her goodbye, Belle limped to the front of the store to flip the CLOSED sign to OPEN. Her ankle throbbed slightly, but the sharp pains no longer plagued her. If she moved slowly, she could manage without her crutches for longer periods. Good thing too, because she didn't have anyone on schedule until late afternoon, and Monday involved sorting through the donations left over the weekend. Emptying the bin wasn't anyone's favorite job, especially during garage sale season. Not that she wasn't incredibly thankful for each item they received, but sometimes people used them in place of the local garbage dump.

She hobbled to the back room where they sorted contributions and flicked on the light. If any customers arrived, the overhead bell would ring. Until then, she'd make progress in here—a difficult task, given the current condition of their garage door. Last month, someone backed into it, damaging the track so badly that now the door opened only part way. Made retrieving donations tough even on a good day.

After ramming a metal bar under the heavy panels to hold the thing up, she started hauling in everything stacked against the side of the building. Then, she addressed the large green bin overflowing with clothes, toys, and miscellaneous household items. Normally, she'd roll it inside to unload, but its height no longer cleared the narrow opening, so she made several trips with a wagon someone left last week. Already heat and humidity thickened the air. No doubt there'd be another water fight in the works for today. Oooh, maybe once help arrived, she could duck out and buy popsicles too.

An hour into her morning, the bell rang for the first time of the day. Normally she preferred things busy, but with as much as she had to sort here, she wasn't about to complain about the quiet. Slipping from the room, she made her way up front as fast as her ankle would allow. A thin man with dark hair stood with a clipboard.

Curiosity moved her a little faster. "Can I help you?"

He looked from his paperwork to her. "I'm looking for a Belle Thornton?"

"That's me." Caution eclipsed her curiosity. Please, not another list maker. "And you are?"

"Pete from Pete's Heating and Cooling."

And she was back to curious, right along with needing an iced coffee to keep up with things. "What brings you here today, Pete?"

His brow crinkled. "I'm here to drop off three wall units and check on your AC system." He flipped a few pages. "Got an early call that it wasn't working upstairs. Asked me to check on the system and see what it'd take for repairs. Said it may be more than a simple fix, so they asked me to install these wall units in the meantime." He smiled at her. "Can't say I blame you, what with this crazy heat we've been having. Bet it's an oven up there."

And that oven had apparently baked her brain because she didn't remember calling him. She'd only thought about buying the wall unit tonight, right? Definitely not three of them. No way she'd do that. But there stood Pete, giving her the once-over and waiting patiently for her to give him the green light.

"I'm so sorry, Pete, but I didn't call you."

"Your unit isn't broken?"

"No, it's broken, but I didn't put in a service call or order any wall units."

He consulted his paperwork again. "Says here a Micah Shaw called it in."

Clarity parted her confusion like she wished chilled air would cut through this heat, but Micah's solution wasn't quite as simple as he'd no doubt hoped. If it were as easy as one phone call, she and Anna would have been sleeping in comfort for weeks now. Did he think she didn't know how to handle things around here? That he needed to step in and do it for her? For Anna?

Her blood boiled hotter than the air upstairs. "Excuse me one moment."

Pete's brows hit his receding hairline. "Sure thing. I'll be in my truck."

Belle pulled out her cell phone and dialed Micah's number. It rang through until his voicemail picked up. She disconnected and tapped the phone against her leg. She had no clue what his Monday morning entailed. Dialing again might make it seem like an emergency, and while her temper said resolving this constituted one, unfortunately, it didn't. But she was sorely tempted.

Thirty seconds later her phone buzzed in her hand with a text message.

EVERYTHING OKAY? I'M IN A LECTURE BUT CAN STEP OUT IF YOU NEED ME RIGHT NOW.

His text enticed familiar manipulative tendencies she'd worked hard to overcome. Her fingers itched to take advantage of his text so she could unload her frustration all over him and feel so much better … but that was the old Belle. Micah may not deserve the new one, but she'd decided long ago that she did.

Taking a deep breath, she texted him back.

ALL IS FINE. WE CAN TALK LATER.

Probably a good thing as she'd have time to cool down, literally and figuratively. She'd intended to buy a unit later today anyway, so maybe Pete would be willing to let her purchase one of the three he brought.

Her phone buzzed again. BTW, THE AC UNITS ARE PAID FOR.

She blinked at the screen. Held it closer. Read it again. And again. Who did he think he was? Oh! She could throw this phone across the room right now. Instead, her fingers punched the screen.

I DIDN'T ASK YOU TO DO THAT.

I KNOW. I WANTED TO.

So he could use this against her? Try and say he could provide better for Anna? Well, she had three years that said otherwise. Some cool air didn't make up for completely abandoning your child. Did it?

WHAT IF I DON'T WANT YOU TO?

YOU ENJOY SLEEPING IN A SAUNA?

THE HUMIDITY IS GOOD FOR MY SKIN.

AND YOUR SARCASM APPARENTLY. Three blinking dots indicated he continued to type, and then, I ALWAYS DID LOVE YOUR HUMOR, SO MAYBE WE SHOULD LEAVE IT 150 DEGREES UP THERE.

Oh, no. He wasn't misdirecting her suspicions with a cute, well-placed comment.

WHY ARE YOU DOING THIS, MICAH?

She waited for a full minute before he responded.

BECAUSE.

CARE TO EXPOUND?

Those dots appeared again. She tapped her foot, waiting while he typed. Finally, his response appeared, and she could hear his teasing tone right along with it.

YOU KNOW, MOST PEOPLE AREN'T THIS UPSET WHEN SOMEONE HELPS THEM. ESPECIALLY WHEN IT'S TO MAKE THINGS BETTER.

Oh, really.

NOT TRUE. I NEEDED HELP FOR A CAVITY ONCE. THEY HAD TO GIVE ME A SHOT AND DRILL DOWN MY TOOTH. IT WAS ABOUT AS MUCH FUN.

I LIKE THAT ANALOGY. KNOW WHY?

WHY?

B/C YOU TYPICALLY GET CAVITIES FROM SWEET THINGS. SO IN A WAY YOU'RE CALLING ME SWEET.

Agh! Her fingers flew across the tiny keyboard. YOU ARE ABSOLUTELY

INFURIATING!

I'M ALSO BEING CALLED ON. GOTTA GO.

CONVENIENT. WHAT DO I DO ABOUT PETE?

But he was gone.

Belle turned and gazed out the front windows. Astrid stood beside Pete's truck. He now leaned against it, drinking coffee, if she had to guess. She limped outside to them, and he straightened. "You get a hold of Micah?"

"I did."

"He tell ya everything is paid for?"

"He did."

"So I'm good to get to work?"

Astrid, who'd watched the exchange, set her steady gaze on Belle. "Seems like a simple question."

Not anywhere close to it. Still, she'd be an idiot to turn him away. Might not like how this all came about, but she had Anna to think about. If it was only her, she'd let her stubbornness have its way, and darn-it-all, Micah knew that. Didn't even have to ask him if that was true. They'd shared far more years together than they had apart, and during those years they'd given away pieces of themselves to each other. Pieces she desperately wanted back but were his forever. She'd gone about things so backward that moving forward seemed near impossible, and if it weren't for Anna, she wouldn't have made a bit of progress.

But motherhood had a way of shelving stubborn and selfish tendencies.

"Yeah, you're all clear. Let me show you upstairs."

Two hours later, she flopped on her couch, obstinately refusing to let the cool breeze from the family room unit touch her temper. But it sure did feel amazing on her skin. Darn. Him. All. She did not want to need Micah Shaw. Being thankful for some hugely noble action on his part—the man basically slayed the fire-breathing dragon hovering over the apartment—said exactly that. She needed him. Well, she'd already read this story, thank-you-very-much, and at the end discovered that yes, he was a prince. Prince Unreliable, destroyer of happily-ever-afters.

Crossing her arms like the grump she was, she burrowed farther into the couch and her bad mood.

Astrid calmly sat beside her. "For a woman who received a gift she couldn't pay for, you don't seem too thankful."

Belle gave her the stank eye.

She laughed and patted Belle's knee. "What I want to know is, are you mad at Micah for overstepping some boundary you put in place, or at yourself for being glad he did?"

The fact that Astrid made so much sense earned her double stank eyes.

No one made a cup of coffee like Madcap did.

Micah locked his legs around a stool perched in front of the wooden counter lining the massive glass windows along Ottawa Ave. Gazing out, he inhaled the bitter scent of roasted beans. His pour-over had been perfect, and he nearly ordered another but didn't need a caffeine buzz. Overhead, the AC kicked on and he grinned. Hopefully, Belle and Anna had been sleeping better these past three nights. Life had kept him too busy to do more than periodically text with her, but tonight was Lamaze class. Like he'd hoped, it provided the perfect excuse to stop by and see them. Bonus was, he'd be helping Belle in the process.

Sunshine pierced a perfect blue sky outside, and people were out in droves enjoying it. Grand Rapids might not be the largest city he'd ever been in, but it was the best. Small enough to feel like a family place but large enough to offer plenty of entertainment. He had no intention of leaving again.

Eyeing the clock, he realized he had a few minutes until his cousin, Jonah, arrived. Micah had texted him over the weekend to see when he'd be in town. While they'd talked a handful of times over the past three years, there were some things that needed saying face-to-face. Just so happened, Jonah and Penny were coming in a day early this weekend. Had a feeling that decision stemmed from Penny wanting to check on her sister, but whatever the reason, it presented him with a slot of time to offer a long-overdue apology.

Rather than stare at the second hand until his nerves got the best of him, Micah reached in his leather messenger bag and pulled out Mom's journal. Never thought of himself as much of a memoir reader, but as Mom slowly slipped away in front of him, the words on these pages tethered them together. Especially since so much of it showed pieces of her he'd never known. To him, she'd been Mom, but inside this journal, a complex woman unraveled layers of herself, which gave new dimension to the picture he'd always held in his mind.

Love is patient. Another piece of Dad's wisdom that he demonstrated toward me, but I chose to walk away from. Not that I could escape his love, but I sure tried hard. And I definitely didn't live this out in my own life. The brokenness I could have avoided if only I'd tried, but I can't play the "if only" game. I can, however, choose to love patiently from now on. No matter if Todd accepts it or not, I've changed, and there's a peace in patience that I've never known before. Learning to love the right way is healing my own heart in the process.

He stared out the window. What had gone on between his parents? Their marriage definitely hadn't been great, but this pointed to a story he hadn't realized even existed.

His gaze landed on Jonah, who strolled up the street. Micah blinked at the transformation in front of him. Looked like the past three years returned Jonah to the fighting form he had prior to cancer striking his nephew, Gavin. He'd lost the extra weight he'd piled on while walking Gavin through harsh treatments and even regrew his hair. Talk about learning how to love the right way. Back then, Micah hadn't seen it. In fact, he gave his cousin a hard time for the physical changes he underwent to help Gavin feel not so alone during the radiation and chemo that ultimately cured him.

Tugging his hand through his hair, Micah closed his eyes. New man. He was a new man. Not the jerk he'd been. Owning the old didn't mean he had to wear that skin again. He'd accept the guilt of his actions, but he was leaving the shame.

Hopefully, Jonah would extend forgiveness and not his fist, because this was the first time they'd actually see one another since Jonah attempted to stop him from leaving Belle on their wedding day. For his efforts, he received a killer left hook. Micah still cringed at the memory of stepping over Jonah to climb in his car. His parting words rang true, though, because in the end, that punch *had* hurt him far more than his cousin.

The memory of sitting in his car, fingers white as they gripped the wheel, and Jonah lying flat on the ground, revisited him often. In that moment, he'd almost changed his mind and stayed. He wanted to. But he wanted Belle and their baby to have a shot at something normal even more.

He'd gotten that so totally wrong.

Now he was working to make all of it right.

Jonah glanced over the crowd, his eyes landing on Micah. He headed his way.

Quelling the tremble in his hands—the one demanding Scotch but receiving coffee—Micah stood and offered his palm while bracing for a possible blow. "Hey. Thanks for meeting me."

Jonah stared at him for a split-second before tugging him into a hug. "Good to see you, Cuz."

Stunned, Micah didn't move.

Jonah released him and sat on the empty stool beside his as if they remained the best friends they'd been in childhood. "How are you doing?"

Micah slowly pocketed his hands, unable to repress the shock in his voice. "Surprised you hugged me."

"What'd you expect? Me to hit you?"

Uh, yeah. "I deserve it."

"Good thing we don't always get what we deserve." He jostled the leg of Micah's seat, nodding for him to retake it. "Otherwise I'd still be sleeping alone rather than with my beautiful wife beside me."

Spoken like a man still utterly gob-smacked by love, even two years into his marriage. Couldn't say he blamed him. "There's something about those Thornton women, isn't there?"

A grin overtook Jonah's face. "Yes, there is." He clasped his fingers, tapping his thumbs together. "Don't know what I'm going to do if this baby is a girl."

"You'll be toast, trust me. I am, and I haven't even gotten to hold Anna yet."

Jonah grew serious. "How's that going?"

"Not as good as I'd hoped but better than I expected, if that makes any sense."

"Completely." He nodded. "Penelope and I have spent a lot of time with Belle. Saying she was hurt when you left doesn't even touch it. Trust won't grow back easily."

"But you think it can?"

"We're praying for it, at the very least with Anna. She deserves to know her father."

"I want to be a part of both of their lives."

"Unlike leaving, this time it's not your choice alone." Spoken not as a rebuke, just the simple truth. Jonah never was one to mince words.

"She's made that clear." Micah played with the edges of a napkin. "Belle's not why I called you." At least not the main reason, though in the last few days, an idea cropped to mind that he hoped to bring up. First, though, "I owe you an apology, Jonah. What I did the day I left? It wasn't right, and I'm sorry."

Eyes steady on him, Jonah listened without reproach. The barista behind them called out a name. Steam bellowed from the coffee maker, and soft indie music played overhead. All the while, Jonah watched him. The man was going to make an awesome father with that unblinking stare. Almost had *him* squirming.

Then Jonah broke into his wide grin. "Forgiven."

Relief lightened Micah, and he slowly shook his head. "You could teach a course on that subject."

"Nope. There's only one teacher for that subject, and I'm a student in regular need of his lessons. Ask Penelope."

He highly doubted it.

Jonah pointed to Mom's journal. "What's that?"

Micah slid it to him. "Belonged to my mom. I found it while I was cleaning out the house, and I've been reading it." Learning more than he'd anticipated too. "Hey, you don't happen to know anything about any letters Gramps wrote my mom, do you? She's intent on finding them so she can give them to me, but they're nowhere to be found. Maybe Penny ran across them while emptying Gigi's house?"

Jonah flipped through the pages. "Your mom? No. But she did find ones he'd written Gigi when he was in Vietnam."

Micah did the math. "He could have written to my mom then too. She would have been little when he was over there." Made sense she'd treasure letters like that. Especially since as an adult, her relationship with her parents hadn't been close. "You sure there weren't any mixed in with Gigi's?"

"Not that I can remember."

Still, he wasn't ready to relinquish the first real lead he'd had. "Could there have been some in something that got sold?"

Jonah contemplated it before shaking his head. "Doubt it. Penelope's pretty thorough about going through every nook and cranny so something like that doesn't happen. But I can ask her."

"Thanks." Though he doubted anything would come from it.

"The entries look pretty recent."

The journal was dated in the front. "They are. She started it a few months after Gigi's death. Most of them are from that first year, before her own memory began to fail more." Something she'd been aware of, based on her own words. "I didn't realize the rift between her, Gigi, and Gramps was so wide."

"Yeah, my mom talked a little about it. Said yours always was the independent one. Left home right at eighteen, but things didn't start to go really downhill until closer to when you were born."

"Because she got pregnant outside of marriage? So did your sister, but Gigi and Gramps never treated her poorly." So he couldn't see that being the reason here either. Gigi and Gramps never did anything but love on Rachael all throughout her pregnancy. Even more so after Gavin was born. They wouldn't have done any less for their daughter.

"Never said, but I never really asked." Jonah closed the book, then slid it over to Micah. "Sorry that I can't now."

Grief played across Jonah's face, but love overshadowed his heartache as if the memory of his mom now brought more joy than pain. Micah wasn't surprised. His aunt had been an amazing woman.

"You know, if it weren't for your mom, I'd have hardly seen any of you." She'd been the one to pick him up and bring him to Gigi and Gramps for sleepovers with Jonah. His own mom always claimed to be too busy to drive them. It was an excuse, he recognized that now, but he was no closer to understanding why she used it.

"I loved those weekends. Gigi and Gramps would spoil us rotten." Jonah fiddled with the edge of his coffee cup. "That's something I'm really going to miss. Seeing my mother holding my child."

Micah remained silent. The past few years, he'd sat with enough people in tough moments to understand sometimes a quiet presence spoke much louder than filling the space with words.

Finally, Jonah swiveled in his seat. "So, you want to come hang at our beach house one of these weekends? Belle and Anna typically visit for at least a day."

"I would, but I plan on being pretty busy for the next several. I actually hoped you'd help me with a project one weekend."

"For them?"

Micah nodded.

"Then I'm in." Strong and decisive. Typical Jonah. "What are we doing?"

The actual list ran longer than he stood tall, and he'd spent the morning triaging it. Anything to do with the FDA list could be completed without professionals—those items were knowns, and he'd already brought in the retirees next door to assist. Root issues with the building remained largely unknowns, and he'd begin hunting down their sources tonight, starting with the roof. Whatever he could do himself, he would. Anything that needed a permit or specialists in that field, he'd help to hire out.

Then there was one item he'd already diagnosed and crafted a plan to address. He just needed extra muscle. "Knocking down that rickety death trap they call a swing set and building something safe."

Jonah laughed. "Death trap might be overselling it a little."

"Would you let your kid on it?"

"Right." He sobered. "Tell me when, and I'll be there."

"The product will be available in two weeks." One of the slides was on backorder, or he'd start sooner. "I work nights, so it'll be during the day."

"No problem. I'll come up that Friday morning, and we can make a weekend of it."

One of the perks of owning the family business was Jonah maintained full control of his schedule. He never took advantage of it, and he always worked harder than he required his employees. So when he did take time off, they never questioned it.

Micah made a note in his phone. "I'll schedule delivery. Say we start around noon?"

"That give you time to sleep?"

"Enough." Though he didn't see a lot of it in his future. "Did you know Belle signed a Triple Net lease?"

"Yep." Jonah scrubbed a hand through his hair. "She signed it before I could read it. I offered, but she insisted she had it taken care of." His jaw tightened. "I still don't know the details of it, but I have heard of her landlord."

The way his voice dropped low with an edge of disgust put Micah on guard. Jonah wasn't one to throw bad opinions around easily. "Who's the guy?" Maybe he'd recognize the name.

"Rick Mastiff. New in town here, but he's owned some buildings in Chicago. Walter's had some run-ins with him. The guy's not known for having his clients' best interests. Only his own."

"Obvious with what he had her sign." Not that he'd read the contract, but he had seen the repercussions of it. "Did you know she had a fire chief and code inspector on her doorstep? They left her a bunch of repairs she needs completed in ninety days."

Jonah's jaw tightened. "She's already poured too much into that building as it is."

Maybe he'd fill him in where Belle had kept quiet. "Such as?"

"Broken windows she started to replace. Resurfacing the crumbling parking lot. Even replacing a leaky pipe in that small room they consider the community kitchen. And it's about one-twenty in that upstairs of hers, so I'm guessing the AC is shot, but she can't afford to fix it. I told Penelope that I'm calling someone if it's still broken this weekend."

It was worse than he thought. His pulse throbbed behind his left eye. "No wonder she's so strapped for cash."

"Yeah. I don't know what her actual rent is each month, but I do know it's increased at least once since she signed."

"Nice." His hand clenched. He was going to look up this Rick.

"We've tried to help however we can, but she's pretty stubborn."

"Don't I know it." Made him grateful and curious why she let Pete stay and install the units he'd purchased. "I had someone there Monday to handle the AC. He called me later that day. It's completely shot and needs to be replaced. She's lucky it's pumping anything into that lower level at all. He put us on his schedule for next week, and in the meantime, he installed window units upstairs."

Jonah straightened. "She let you hire someone?"

"I didn't exactly give her a choice."

"Huh." He rubbed his chin.

"Huh, what?"

"One, I can't believe you got away with that. Two, I can't believe Penelope hasn't heard about it yet."

"I'm not exactly sure I have gotten away with it. I haven't seen her since

Saturday, but I'm headed that way soon. For all I know, she shoved those window units out the moment the guy's truck left."

Laughter peppered out of Jonah. "Thornton stubbornness."

"It's alive and well, I'm afraid." A trait he hoped to break through. "Here's to hoping it won't interfere with our upcoming plans."

Because he intended to do whatever he could to remove the burdens he'd placed on her shoulders.

Chapter Ten

W hat was that saying? "The days are long, but the years are short"? Belle would happily turn that sucker on its end today if it meant she could crawl back in bed and tug the covers over her head. She hadn't reached the end of her rope, she'd slid right off its tattered edge straight into an emotional free fall, with no bottom in sight.

Two of the kiddos in daycare had pink eye, so they'd had to send them home and disinfect everything—and pray that none of the others came down with it. One of the sick kids belonged to the mom on schedule for AnnaBelle's today, which meant instead of catching up on paperwork, Belle had to man the store alone. All on no sleep because Anna had been up all night with the start of another ear infection, thanks to a recent trip to the community pool. So now Belle sat waiting for a return call from the doctor in hopes that they'd see Anna today or, even better, call in a prescription without an office visit. Not like they hadn't been down this road several times before.

And she still had to survive dinner with a cranky toddler before Lamaze class—with Micah, the cherry on top of her crud-tastic day. The man had barely been home two weeks, and he'd somehow successfully infiltrated her space and her life. The air upstairs might be cooler, but her temper certainly wasn't.

"Betty came over to watch the littles, so I can spell you for a while." Astrid joined her at the sales counter. "Thought you could make an early dinner for you and Little Bit, then maybe rest that ankle of yours before Lamaze class."

"My ankle's fine, but if you're offering to help, I'll let you. I have a boatload of work waiting for me and hopefully a prescription to pick up for Anna soon."

"Your ankle is not fine."

"It's better than it was."

Astrid merely shook her head. "At least prop it up while you're working."

"Will do." Not that she needed the instruction. While it was feeling better, the joint still ached if she'd been on it too long, which she had been today.

With a slight limp, she headed to her tiny office. Her cell rang as she settled into her chair. Dr. Townsend's number flashed across the screen. The call didn't take but a minute. He wanted to see Anna, and no amount of begging persuaded the nurse to ask him to reconsider.

Looked like she'd be doing paperwork after Anna went to bed. Yep. Some days proved to be insufferably long.

Nearly two hours later, Belle returned home armed with Anna's medicine and a referral to an ENT. After checking Anna's ears and confirming her fourth ear infection in under six months, he'd handed out a prescription right along with his professional opinion—Anna most likely needed tubes in her ears.

Belle hopped out of her car, then opened Anna's door. After unclicking her from her car seat, she picked up her baby. "How you doing, Monkey?"

"My ear hurt," she whined.

"I know. Mama's got medicine that'll help." And hopefully, dinner arriving soon. It was going on five, and typically someone knocked on her door right around that time. She'd tried, really hard, not to rely on Micah, but tonight proved she'd failed miserably. She may kiss the delivery man when he showed up because she definitely wasn't kissing the man who sent him. Shivers raked through her as that wild thought conjured up the memory of Micah's kisses. Geesh. What was wrong with her? So the man definitely knew what he was doing in that department. Didn't mean she had to revisit it. Even if she could really use his strong arms to help her and Anna up the steps right now.

Argh! Okay. She was tired and hungry, and that combo was obviously making her a little crazy.

Anna lay her head on Belle's shoulder. "I hungry."

"We'll eat in a little bit." She hobbled to their door, then set Anna on the ground so they could both hop up the stairs. After turning on the TV, she grabbed Uni for Anna, along with her favorite blanky, hoping to distract her until dinner arrived. By five-forty-five, two things were painfully clear. Distraction wasn't going to work anymore, and she should have trusted her gut when it warned her not to rely on Micah Shaw. Why was it that he always chose the worst times to not show up?

Her mind filtered through options, not that she currently had many. Jump in the car and hit a drive-thru or scrounge something up in here. She glanced at Anna, who was on the edge of a meltdown. No way she'd go willingly into her car seat. Guess it would be PB&J, which sounded better than grease, but still not the healthy, Pinterest-worthy meal she'd once thought she'd serve her future children.

If she wasn't so exhausted, she'd laugh at her old self.

Heading for the kitchen, she called over her shoulder. "Mama's gonna make you a sandwich."

"Don't want a sandwich," Anna replied with a stomp.

Belle let it go. Right now silence was the best way to dodge the brewing tantrum rolling inside them both. While *PAW Patrol* babysat, she slapped together a gourmet plate of PB&J, bananas, and chocolate milk. The fruit was to appease her; the chocolate milk hopefully would have the same effect on Anna. As she placed Anna's plate on the kitchen table, her cell rang again. Micah. She didn't have the energy or filter to speak with him right now. But if he was calling to cancel on her tonight ... Okay, she wasn't sure if that'd actually make things better or worse. Either way, she needed to know.

With Anna fixated on her cartoon, Belle turned and slid her finger over the screen. "Yes?"

Pause, then. "Everything okay?"

"Yes. Why?"

"You sound tired."

"I'm a mom. I spend my life in a state of tired, Micah."

"And grumpiness?"

She didn't miss his lighthearted tone, but still, "Not the time for jokes." Or for him to try and make her feel better when he was the one who'd sent her frustration plummeting over the edge.

"Sorry." Immediately contrite rather than prickly. Must every situation be used to frame how he'd changed? Clearing his throat, he continued. "Anyway, I hope I'm not interrupting dinner, but I showed up early to check on that leak in your roof. I didn't want you to freak when you heard someone walking around up there."

Seriously? She couldn't figure him out, and she was too tired to try.

In her peripheral vision, Anna toddled to the table. "Knock yourself out, Micah." Not that he'd follow through if he found the leak.

"You sure you're okay?"

"Yes," she grunted. Anna's little lips pooched out as she glared at the sandwich on her princess plate. Oh boy, things were about to implode.

Belle raced to the table, tweaking her ankle in the process. She gasped both from the streak of pain and from the sandwich now flying toward her as Anna frisbee-tossed her plate. "I no want sandwich!"

"Anna!" Belle tried to snatch the sandwich from the air but missed.

"Belle?" Micah's slightly panicked voice rang in her right ear, while Anna's wail pierced her left one.

"Everything's fine. Just fine." Except it wasn't. Belle squeezed her forehead. That was the last of the jam since she'd procrastinated grocery shopping. Hard enough with a toddler, but a toddler and a sore ankle? That combo landed the task right up there with having to call the local health-care hotline with insurance questions—something now on her list as well, due to Anna's impending need for surgery. "I need to go." Maybe they still had cereal in the cupboard.

"Belle, wait. What can I do?"

Rewind the day? Or the past three years? Never leave her to do this parenting thing alone with a broken heart?

"Nothing." Tears pressed her eyes as Anna stood in the middle of the dining room in a full-on tantrum brought on from her own exhaustion, pain, and toddlerhood itself.

"I'm coming up."

His three words reached out like a lifeline from the enemy's ship, but a drowning woman didn't have much choice other than to grab it and hold on, did she?

"Fine." She hung up, doing her best to ignore the encroaching relief. Right now a convict could be on his way up, and she'd open her door in wide welcome for the extra set of shoulders to lay things on. This had nothing to do with a yearning inside for the specific muscle now pounding up her stairs to be the partner he once promised he'd be.

Anna continued her tirade in the middle of the kitchen floor, and Belle hopped her way. Behind her, Micah knocked but didn't wait for her response. No doubt the screaming in the background propelled him through the door. She ducked her head, not wanting to see his initial impression of this out-of-control scene. This was the non-glamorous side of parenting. They'd both been so much about the picture-perfect lifestyle when they were together. The past three years had chipped it out of her. For some of it, she'd happily submitted to the chisel, adding her own strength to removing old habits she gladly shed. But others were painfully carved out, like during the nearly nine full months of morning sickness where the one thing that sounded good was carbs—and her hips still testified to that fact. Or when, as a newbie mom, she'd packed a change of clothes for Anna but not herself and—thanks to simultaneous spit-up and a diaper blow-out—wound up a hot mess as she gave the keynote to a ballroom full of hopeful girls entering the pageant world. That was a night none of them would forget.

Probably functioned as a service announcement for birth control too.

Anna's wails intensified.

"Anna, you need to go sit on your bed."

"No." She stomped her foot.

Yeah. Well. Back atcha, baby. Least that's what she wanted to say. Instead, she swooped in and picked Anna up, holding tight as her precious princess kicked and swatted at her. Belle caught her tiny wrist. "No hitting."

So she chomped on her hand instead.

"Ow!"

"Enough." Micah's steady voice startled them both into silence. Strong and sure, he stepped over to them. "You do not hit or bite."

Anna, crocodile tears running down her face, gave him a wide-eyed nod.

"Now, tell your mama you're sorry."

She switched her attention to Belle. "I sorry, Mama."

Her soft little voice said she truly was. "Okay, Monkey." Even as an adult, fighting a hard day could turn her own self into a tiny monster. Or maybe not so tiny. Anna's actions weren't excusable, but they were understandable. And she'd apologized. "You're forgiven." She placed a kiss on her cheek. "I love you."

"Yuv you too," Anna replied with a sniff.

Belle hugged her close, then set her down at the table, crisis averted but not prevented because Anna's tummy still sat as empty as their cupboards.

Micah bent to pick up the sandwich and plate from the floor. "Is this what started it all?"

"Is that what …" Belle drove her fingers into her hair, yanking it back. "No, Micah. Me believing you'd follow through on a promise is what started it all."

He'd expected to walk into the middle of a raging battle between mom and daughter but hadn't anticipated taking shrapnel from it. "Come again?"

Was she really rehashing their past right here and now? Because, yeah, he could see how his leaving her to parent Anna alone would feel overwhelming even on a good day, but he highly doubted that was the cause of Anna's current fuss. Not when she didn't even know he was her daddy.

"Just"—she released her hair, the golden strands floating down to frame her face, and limped to the kitchen—"never mind."

Uh, no. She'd accepted him into this combustible moment, then tossed that flare onto it. No way he was never-minding her comment. "Finish your thought. I can't help if you don't talk to me."

She opened a cupboard and rummaged through it, coiled frustration in every movement. Anna lifted to her knees, peering into the kitchen. "I still hungry."

"I know you are, baby. Mama's making you something." She sliced up one more-brown-than-yellow banana and placed it in front of Anna. "Have some of this while I make your dinner."

Anna shoved two pieces into her mouth, and he waited till Belle returned to his side of the kitchen counter before moving in close and lowering his voice. "Didn't she like the tacos?" He was sure if she'd eat salmon, she'd eat tacos.

The way Belle's beautiful face screwed up, he might as well have been speaking Klingon. "What tacos?"

"The ones I sent from Adobe." Except even as he said it, everything from the tantrum to her comment, right down to her frustration with him suddenly made sense. "They never showed up, did they?"

She shook her head.

And she'd automatically thought the worst of him. His own annoyance flared. He was well aware he had a lot of ground to make up for, but he hoped he'd at least gained a few inches.

He sighed and yanked out his phone. Double checked the order, then showed it to her. "Should have been here by five-thirty." He tapped again. "Says it's been delivered."

Belle threw out her hands. "Well, it hasn't."

"Clearly." He typed something, then repocketed his phone. "All right, I'll take you two ladies out."

Maniacal giggles escaped her. Ones that turned to all-out deep laughter. He looked behind him at Anna, still sitting at the table as she watched Belle with a completely lost expression that no doubt mirrored his. Belle lifted her hand to her mouth. "Sorry," she spoke through her chuckles, then took a few deep breaths as she attempted to control her outburst.

"Am I missing something?" he asked.

"Common sense, maybe, but definitely not courage." Another long breath. "Eating out isn't currently an option."

"Let me guess," he quickly deduced, "toddlers and restaurants don't mix."

"Especially not tired and hungry ones."

"Okay." He rolled up his sleeves. "Then let me see what you have on hand that I can make."

"Absolutely nothing. That sandwich was the last of my jam." Her cheeks pinkened. "I don't normally let the cupboards get so empty around here but—"

He held up his hand. "You don't owe me any explanations, Belle. But if you felt like you did, my guess is it has to do with your ankle. And had I really thought things through, I'd have someone delivering groceries too."

"You've done enough."

"Not possible." She deserved more than just *enough* from him. She deserved his all in every area of her life, and he'd happily spend his lifetime figuring out every square inch of those areas if she'd only grant him access again.

Until then, he'd keep showing her she could trust him to be that man. Action and patience. He had this.

Anna banged her plate on the table. "Aw done. Can I have more, pweese?"

Belle looked from him to their girl. "One sec, Monkey." Then back to him. "Suggestions?"

He opened her fridge and leaned down to peer into its near-empty depths. One important ingredient remained on the top shelf. He cast her a grin over his shoulder. "You still have bread and peanut butter?"

"Yeah," she drew out. "Why?"

He reached in and pulled out the jar of pickles. "So I can make the best sandwich known to man."

Pickles and peanut butter. His favorite. Eaten the first time as a teenage dare, now he had at least one a week.

"Anna won't eat that."

"Have you given her one before?"

"No way. I love her too much."

He chuckled and set the pickles on the counter. Then he looked at Anna. "Can Mr. Micah make you a yummy sandwich?"

She crossed her arms. "I no want sandwich."

Belle lifted her palms with an *I told you so* glance.

So he leaned close, his lips near her ear. "Care to place a bet with me?"

"No."

"Chicken."

She slid her gaze to his but didn't turn her chin. No doubt she didn't want her lips that close to his. "I'm not chicken."

"Then take my bet."

Her arms crossed, and she sighed long. "Fine. What is it?"

"If I get her to eat this sandwich, then you'll eat one too."

Now she did look at him, though she took a tiny step away to add space between them. "That's all?"

"Yep."

She eyed him, trying to figure out his angle. Other than having fun with her, there wasn't one.

"All right. But if she doesn't eat it, then you keep delivering dinner through the weekend."

He held out his hand. "You have a deal."

She shook on it. He'd keep making bets if it meant being able to hold her hand even for a moment.

Belle pulled away, then leaned against the kitchen counter. "Better have a backup plan, because she isn't going to last much longer."

"I got this." He nodded to the couch. "Go put your foot up. It has to hurt."

"It doesn't."

"Pageant voice."

"Fine," she huffed, but her lips edged up. "I'm going." Rather than the couch, she hobbled to the table and sat beside Anna. "Mr. Micah is making dinner."

"What he making?"

Micah spoke before Belle could. "Uni's favorite sandwich." He unscrewed the top of the peanut butter. "Did you know unicorns love sandwiches?"

Anna's blue eyes widened as she shook her head.

Belle's look said he wasn't playing fair.

"Love and war," he mouthed, then chuckled as her eyes darted to the side and her cheeks darkened. He turned to Anna. "Well, they do, and it's a very special kind." He came around the counter, plate in hand, and set it in front of her. "And Uni said she can't wait to share it with you."

Anna looked up at him, then at her plate. She picked up one of the four triangles he'd cut her sandwich in and studied it before showing the piece to Uni.

"Want me to make her one too?"

Anna nodded.

"One sandwich for Uni, coming up." He strolled to the kitchen and returned a minute later with another sandwich. Anna still held hers. Micah settled into the chair beside Uni. "Unicorns always take their first bites with their eyes closed. You want to try?"

Another nod, and she closed her eyes to bite into her sandwich. Micah lifted one of Uni's triangles and took a tiny bite as well, quickly setting it down before Anna reopened her eyes. As she did, they widened. "Uni eat hers too!"

All the while Belle watched them both, so many emotions floating over her tired face that he didn't even try and start naming them all. But he understood, because in the last two weeks his own had unloaded on him like a teenage girl, and he was still trying to get them in line. Had a feeling they might never completely be. Loving someone was like having a pacemaker in your heart that they controlled. And loving your child? His heart would never be fully his again.

And he was more than okay with that.

"So what do you think of your sandwich?" he asked Anna.

She smiled and took a huge bite. "Yummy."

"No talking with your mouth full," Belle lightly admonished.

As Anna glanced at the puppy cartoon playing on TV, he picked up another of Uni's triangles and nipped the corner off. When she looked back to sip some of her chocolate milk, her eyes grew large again. "She eat more!"

Right. Okay. He could do this every night.

Ten minutes later, Anna snuggled on the couch again, a soft pink blanket covering her, and her tummy filled with her freshly declared favorite sandwich.

The new air conditioning units definitely were doing their job, evident the moment he'd topped the stairs and discovered the only thing heating the space tonight was his little girl's temper.

He rinsed Anna's cup and plate and placed them in the dishwasher, watching as Belle limped over to give her a dose of medicine. He'd noted Anna's flushed cheeks earlier but wrote them off as a remnant of her tantrum. Then through dinner, she'd been tugging on her right ear.

"Does she have an ear infection?" he asked as Belle placed the bottle on the counter, then sat again at the table.

"Yeah."

A weariness infected her tone, raising all his red flags. "This isn't her first?"

She slumped in her chair. "Try her fourth. In six months."

That punched at him. "She'll need tubes." His little girl. On the operating table. Yes, it was routine, but it was also his heart that someone would be cutting into. She might not know he was her daddy, but that didn't stop him from loving her deeper and wider than her tiny heart and mind could ever comprehend. "When are they scheduling it?"

"How do you know they are?"

"Two little letters after my name that I've worked awfully hard for."

"Thought they went in front."

Dr. in front. MD after. Didn't matter. She was simply having fun needling him, based on the glint in her eye. "Take your pick, but either set tells me Anna will need surgery. And before you ask, I did a rotation with an ENT surgeon. That's how I'm familiar with ears too." Well, that and all his years studying medicine in general.

She fiddled with her fingernails. "I need to check with her insurance to see the next steps before scheduling the surgery. I have her under MiChild."

Michigan's insurance for children whose parents were uninsured. It was good, but not as good as what the hospital provided him. Lord, grant him wisdom on how to approach that subject with Belle.

Maybe he'd start with, "Who did they refer you to?"

"A Dr. Martin Clinard."

"His name is familiar. Pretty sure he has privileges at Spectrum, but I'll check into him."

Her demeanor lightened slightly. "You will?"

"Yes. And if you let me know when her appointment is, I'd like to go with you."

"I ... I'd like that."

Progress, no matter how small, he'd take. While they waited for that appointment, he'd check into what it would take to add Anna to his insurance. For now, he'd at least let Belle know she wasn't in this alone. "I also don't want you worrying about her medical bills. I'm here to help now, and I won't let you tackle those by yourself."

Blinking rapidly, she swallowed. "Thank you." Silence settled between them, not quite awkward but not yet easy. Until she lifted a tiny smile his way. "I suppose you're making me one of those detestable sandwiches too."

Oh, he would, but not tonight. "Nope."

"But I lost the bet."

"I know."

"So I have to eat one."

"Yep."

She looked at him, confused.

And as if they were making up for having created this whole mess in the first place, Grubhub knocked on her door with perfect timing. He held his hand up to stop Belle from rising. "I got this." Answering it, he grabbed the bag, thanked the kid, then delivered it to Belle.

"You reordered the tacos."

"I did." He returned to the kitchen. "You still like them, right?"

"They hold my heart."

Maybe next time he'd show up at her door in a taco costume. Chuckling, he shrugged at her quizzical appraisal of him as he grabbed her some water. "For future reference, how does Anna feel about them?"

"She'll eat hers and then steal yours if you don't eat them fast enough."

"Sounds an awful lot like someone else in this room." Not that Belle had ever stolen more than a bite. She'd wanted to, he'd always seen it in her eyes, but she'd counted calories like a miser counted money, always aware exactly how much she had to spend and never giving one up easily.

Setting her drink in front of her, he nodded to the door. "I can handle tonight alone. You enjoy that taco and stay with Anna. You're both exhausted and can use the quiet night."

She set down her food. "The girls barely know you."

"I bet Astrid will join me if I ask her."

Indecision warred on her face until she spotted Anna reaching for her favorite picture book. "Mama read dis to me?"

Oh, their little girl was a force to be reckoned with, and one that had just toppled Belle.

She turned from Anna to him. "Okay. I'll stay."

Those last two words laid something bare between them, because he should have clung to them three years ago. Now they were hers to wield and his to hope for, and he saw it in her eyes. But he planned on doing everything in his power to pursue her until she relented and used them in regards to a future with him.

Chapter Eleven

Persistent knocking roused Micah from a dead sleep. Chloe's piercing yips punctuated the sound, ensuring he remained in the land of the living. Groaning, he rolled over and landed on the ground with a thud. He cracked open his eyes. That's right. He hadn't made it farther than the couch when he returned home from his shift. In his exhausted state, he'd succumbed to the soft plush cushions after deciding his upstairs bedroom was too far away.

More knocking. More barking. Micah pushed to his feet. Scrubbing his hand through his hair, he called out, "I'm coming," and twisted his wrist to check the time. Noon? That meant he'd clocked almost three hours of sleep. Nowhere near the six he'd hoped for to start catching up and possibly feeling human again.

Reaching the door, he scooped up Chloe in one hand and answered with the other, doing his best to control his surprise at the sight of Belle standing on his front step. In her hands, she held a tinfoil-covered pan.

She greeted him with a smirk. "Thought it was my turn to bring you food."

His foggy brain couldn't form a verbal response, so he stepped aside and allowed her and the amazing smell from that pan to enter. She breezed past and headed for the kitchen. Micah placed Chloe on the ground, and they both followed Belle.

She set the pan on the granite countertop as she moved to the coffee pot. Having spent hours in this home, she didn't need to ask where he kept the grounds. An expert multitasker, she scooped the coffee and addressed him at the same time. "Go ahead and help yourself. It's nothing too fancy, just some cinnamon rolls." She filled the pot with water. "Anna helped me make them."

"How? Your cupboards were bare." He'd planned to send groceries her way sometime today.

"I had flour and sugar on hand. Borrowed a few other things from Astrid." And as if she'd deduced his plans, she added, "I'm going to the store this afternoon. My ankle is feeling a lot better."

"I noticed you're off your crutches." He scanned her. "Also noticed you're still limping."

"I said better. I didn't say it's healed."

He lifted the foil and grabbed one of the gooey rolls. "Speaking of which, if Anna helped you make these delicious-looking treats, I assume she's feeling a little better too?"

"She is. The medicine really took hold overnight, and she slept straight through till eight." Which explained why Belle seemed better rested as well. "Astrid's watching her right now. Even with a full night's sleep, she's gearing up for a long nap today."

He took the plate and paper napkin she handed him. "That's good for her. She was obviously tired last night. Didn't even wake up when I was clomping around on your roof." He set his roll on the plate and pulled off another piece. "I'll call on those estimates today. Sorry, it's more of a repair than I can handle on my own."

"No apology necessary. It's not your responsibility, and I can call on the estimates."

"I don't mind, truly."

"Even so, I'll handle it."

While the coffee brewed, Belle began tidying his cluttered counters. His normal bent was toward messy, but the current state of the house suggested someone should name a hurricane after him. Not that he had time to clean even if that was in his nature. That reality became more evident as he glanced around to see the place as if through her eyes. Every dish he'd used this week covered the counters or filled the sink. Mail stacked on the table and the evidence of Chloe's displeasure at being left alone lay strewn about from the kitchen floor clear to the family room.

He stood to help, but she turned on him. "Sit. Eat your breakfast."

"And let you clean up after me? No way."

She stood there, a plate in each hand and an amused look on her face. "Huh. Not so much fun when the shoe is on the other foot, is it?"

"Least I have two working feet."

"But not two working hands?" She piled the dishes in the sink. "Or are you going for the ransacked look here? If so, you've succeeded."

"It isn't that bad."

Crossing to the table, she attacked one of the piles. "You have junk mail forwarded from California that you ripped in half and left here." She sorted through more, a smile lifting her lips as her eyes landed on an open pet catalog. She waved it at him. "Please tell me it wasn't you who circled this."

"I've never seen that," he lied, but she had him.

Her finger pointed to the Chloe-size Yorkie modeling a U of M doggy sweatshirt. "I don't believe you."

"Fine." The little furball trotted into the kitchen as if she knew they were talking about her. "It was going to be her penance for destroying my favorite ball cap."

"Right." Belle dragged out the word, disbelief in every syllable. Then her eyes caught on another partially covered envelope, and she picked it up. "This is from Walter. From what I heard, you two weren't talking."

Seemed the family grapevine worked just fine in her direction.

"We're not."

"You know, he's come into AnnaBelle's before. He's actually bought some of the lotions for his eczema." She ran her finger along the edge of the envelope. "Even tried to give me some advice on my building, which I thought was funny until I remembered you once told me he dabbles in commercial real estate."

If making millions could be called dabbling, then yeah, Walter dabbled. It wasn't the only fire he had his irons in, though. The man lived and breathed business of any kind, which was how he'd wound up on the board of AllWaste. He'd been a silent partner for the company's first few years and also Gramps's best friend.

"Sounds like Walter."

Behind her, sunshine reflected off the lake, the brightness hiding her features. "Are you still upset about his decision on AllWaste?"

He shifted away from the glare. "No. I understand why he made the choice he did, and I agree with it."

"But?" she prodded.

"But it hurt, and that led to a wedge between us. It's going to take more time and energy to patch up our relationship, and I don't have any extra to spare right now." All true, which lent validity to the excuse.

Belle exchanged the letter for the torn pieces of junk mail and walked them to the trash. "Then it's a good thing I'm about to free some up for you."

"By cleaning my house?"

She leaned against the counter, holding its edge. "By telling you I appreciate everything you've done for me, but it has to stop."

Now they were both using excuses because this had nothing to do with Walter. This was about last night. He'd slipped past her cracked open door, and she was attempting to shove him back out.

After Lamaze, he'd inspected her roof before knocking on her apartment door to fill her in on his findings. She'd actually allowed him to stay and work on her FDA task list with her. He'd grabbed his laptop, scooted up to the table alongside her, and began reworking the lotion descriptions she needed rewritten. Felt like old times, them brainstorming solutions and finishing each other's sentences. Even a few moments of laughter slipped in. They'd spent most of their college nights the same way. By the time he needed to leave for work and she joined him at the door, it seemed like he wasn't alone in the shift toward something familiar. That stirring obviously freaked her out enough to show up on his doorstep this morning.

Too bad for her, he wasn't the kind of man to turn tail and run anymore.

The coffee pot beeped. He crossed to her, stopping with his toes nearly touching hers. She craned her neck to look up at him, hesitation on her face as she tried to figure out what he was doing.

"Why?" he asked.

Now *her* brows dropped. "Why, what?"

"Why does it have to stop?"

Her mouth tightened. That's right. If she wanted him to stop, then she needed to admit why, and it wasn't because she didn't need his help. It was because she didn't want him this close. Because he still affected her, and he could see it in the pulse beating wildly in her neck.

She swallowed. "Because."

"Uh-uh. *Because* is not a valid reason." He tilted his head, studying her as he smiled. "I know you know how to string words together. Unless, of course, I rob you of them with my sheer animal magnetism."

She matched his smile. "Or your morning breath."

Laughter erupted, and he covered his mouth. Right. "Maybe if you hadn't woken me from a dead sleep, I'd have had time to brush."

"It's noon."

"And I worked all night."

"Okay. I'll give you that." She crossed her arms, probably a flimsy attempt at a barrier between them.

Reaching around her, he grabbed two mugs from the cupboard, then waited until he was by the coffee pot to respond. Morning breath might be funny, but it certainly wasn't sexy. "I'm still not giving you your answer, though." He poured them both coffee, then hit up the fridge for creamer. "I will, however, give you space from my pungent mouth." He added Half-and-Half into his mug, then walked the bottle over to her.

She took it and dosed her coffee. "Much appreciated," she teased as he settled on his stool.

He took another bite of his roll and chased it with some caffeine. "Still waiting."

She hadn't moved from her spot, only now she held her mug instead of the counter. If she'd thought coming over here with yoga pants, a faded tank, and her hair in one of those crazy buns would deter him from still finding her captivating, she was wrong. He always loved it when she stepped out of her makeup and evening gowns and was just Belle. The fact that she dropped the perfect persona she'd portrayed around everyone else created an intimacy this moment recalled. Her plan backfired in an epic way.

"What?" One eye narrowed with suspicion.

"Nothing." He shrugged. "Just thinking how cute you look this morning."

Bullseye. She straightened with a huff, but not fast enough to cover the pleasure his comment elicited in her eyes.

She set down her mug and finally answered his prodding. "It has to stop because I am not your responsibility. You have enough legit ones, like school loans."

No doubt she thought she had him. Money had been one of their biggest concerns when they found out they were pregnant. He'd already been in the hole for his undergrad, and medical school wasn't cheap. His parents could have helped out, but Dad told him that when he turned eighteen, he was on his own financially. That sparked another huge argument between his parents. Mom wanted to help, but Dad refused. Said he was a legal adult and needed to start acting like one.

It hadn't deterred him from pursuing medical school. If anything, it energized him. He'd even made a plan for repaying every penny within five years of graduation—turned out, he didn't have to.

"Nope. My school loans were paid off."

Wish he could snap a picture of that priceless look on her face. Had to be what he'd looked like when he opened the letter. He still struggled to believe his debt had been paid.

"What? When?" she asked.

"Out in California. A foundation I hadn't heard of chooses a candidate from the hospital where I interned. They award money to pay off the winner's remaining education and any already accumulated student loans. I was the lucky one picked."

"Just like that."

"Apparently." He was still unsure how it all happened, but thankful it had because it enabled him to help her now. "So, see, I can help you. I mean, my pockets don't run as deep as Jonah's, but everything I'm doing is within my reach." Though it wasn't all about money. "And not only the financial side. We work well together, Belle, and I think last night reminded you of that. I want to keep helping. You don't need to shoulder everything alone anymore."

"I ... I don't know."

She wanted to say yes, he could see it. She wore the same expression she had when a waiter tempted them with the dessert tray. She even licked her lips.

Okay. He'd sweeten the deal to make it irresistible. "What about a trade of sorts?"

She straightened, listening.

"Look around. Chloe is a terror in this house. She's not used to being alone for such long stretches, and every time I come home, something new is destroyed. Maybe I could drop her off at your place before my shift. Kind of like a doggy daycare? You help me and I'll keep helping you." Her eyes flickered over him, wariness there, and suddenly it became clear what else he needed to add. "No strings attached. I promise. Just a mutually beneficial arrangement."

That seemed to seal things because she nodded. "Okay. But you have to let me help you clean up right now too."

He held out his hand. "You have yourself a deal."

After a brief second, she slipped hers into his. He resisted the desire to pump his other fist in the air in victory. Might look like he'd been lying, but he hadn't been. His offer came with no requests for anything more. He wasn't asking, but that didn't stop him from wishing for it.

He'd keep that wish to himself, though. After all, a wish once told, wouldn't come true.

She shouldn't be taking the afternoon off. She really shouldn't. But Anna was finally feeling better, the sun was shining, and her sister was in town for the weekend. That was one relationship she never envisioned reconciling, yet here she was, ignoring her massive to-do list to spend a few hours with Penny and Jonah at their beach house.

Thoughts of a similar reconciliation between her and Micah swept over her like the breeze coming off the water, except they didn't produce the same relaxing feel. Trusting him again was a whole different ball game—and she had never been good at any sports. Wasn't about to start playing them now.

"Yay! You're here!" Penny waddled down the steps to the gravel drive, hands on her round belly.

Belle wrapped her in a side hug. "How're you feeling?"

"Huge." And her smile said that, for once, the word didn't bother her at all. "Jonah's on the deck with Evan, blowing up a new floaty he found for Anna."

Their neighbor, Evan Wayne, a Holland police officer, had been adopted into their little group. More like he finessed his way in one night when the scent of the burgers Jonah was grilling wafted over to his deck. Next thing they knew, Evan was at their door with a bowl of some savory pasta salad he'd created in one hand and the thickest chocolate chip cookies she'd ever seen in the other. He expertly negotiated a deal to help polish off their burgers in exchange for the dishes he brought. His genuine smile got him through the door. His amazing food secured his spot.

Least, that's what they told him.

She released her sister and popped open Anna's door. "Where's Rach and Gavin?"

"There's some concert in Chicago this weekend that Gavin wanted to go to with his friends, so Rach stayed nearby."

"How's she doing with him getting ready to start his senior year?"

"Depends on which college he's applying to."

The idea that Gavin was old enough to think about colleges seemed surreal to her. It had to be nearly impossible for Rachael.

"Mama! Yet me out!" Anna bellowed.

Penny laughed. "Yes. Let her out. She's got a new inflatable to see."

Their back deck already stored four of them in various silly shapes. "Your husband has a serious problem." She unbuckled Anna and set her on the ground, then reached for their beach bag before closing the car door.

Penny shrugged. "He likes spoiling his girls. I don't think that's a problem at all." She took Anna's hand. "Right, Monkey?" Oblivious to what they were talking about, Anna simply nodded. "See, she agrees."

Tears misted Belle's eyes. Jonah hadn't thought twice about spoiling Anna as though she were his own. He plugged a hole in her heart. Might not be the perfect fit, but he filled it all the same. That could change in two months when Penny gave birth, but somehow she knew Jonah wouldn't disappear from their lives altogether. Unlike his cousin, Micah, Jonah stuck around.

Ugh! There she was thinking about him again. For three years she'd shoved him from her mind, and now here he was invading every corner. Fine, but she drew the line at him reoccupying her heart. Mentally, she began ticking off all the hurts he'd inflicted, using them to fortify her defenses. They needed strengthening before she saw him again.

"You okay?" Penny nudged her. She followed her to the porch.

"Yeah. Why?"

"You looked a million miles away." The screen door screeched as Penny opened it. "Jonah doesn't want to fix the squeak. Says it'll help us know if our kiddo ever tries to escape. I had to remind him that it'll be a few years before he or she is even walking."

"Goes faster than you can imagine." Her eyes stayed on Anna, who skipped toward the slider at the rear of the house. "In fact, I think Anna bypassed walking and went straight to running and skipping."

Penny laughed. "She does love to move."

In here she had plenty of room. Nearly the entire first floor of their beach house was open, the far wall created mainly from floor-to-ceiling windows with the slider positioned smack dab in the middle. The entire space was white, from the walls to the kitchen countertops, to the sisal rug anchoring the family room. But the furniture and accents were all shades of blue, mimicking the best decoration—Lake Michigan itself. A large deck ran off the back of the house connecting with the sandy hill that rolled down to the endless waters.

None of that beauty captured Anna's attention like her uncle holding the newest water toy he'd inflated. A unicorn tube, the top half of its donut hole clear with colorful, sparkly glitter inside.

"Mama, yook! Yook!"

Belle crossed to her bouncing daughter. "What did your uncle get you?"

Excited blue eyes met hers. "A unicorn!"

Evan and Jonah stepped to the door and rolled it open. "Hey, Monkey." Jonah lifted her in one hand, the tube in the other. "Whatcha think of this guy?"

"It's not a boy. It's a gir-yah."

"Is it?" Jonah peered at the tube again. "Oh, I guess it is. What should we name her?"

"Spar-cahs."

"Sparkles." He chuckled. "A perfect name." Kissing her cheek, he stepped inside and set them both down. "If you get on your bathing suit, we can take Sparkles for a ride."

Her ear-piercing squeal nearly deafened them. "I go get it on." She raced for the beach bag and dove into it, coming out with her pink ruffly suit. "Mama, hep me."

"Yes. I'll help you." Belle enunciated the "l" sound as she followed her to the bathroom, Anna leaving a trail of her clothes in their wake along with Penny and Jonah's laughter. Two minutes later, she bounced in front of Jonah again.

Evan chuckled at her. "Maybe we should rename you Roo, with all the bouncing you do."

"Whassa roo?"

He tugged on her piggy tail. "A kangaroo."

She laughed and bounced even more, her hips swishing to some song playing in her head.

With a wave, Evan headed for the door. "I'd stay, but I picked up the night shift for a friend. Gonna run home and catch some sleep first."

"Stay safe, Evan," Penny called.

"I'll do my best." He uttered his standard reply as the door squeaked shut behind him.

Jonah took Anna's hand. "And we're going swimming. You ladies enjoy those lounge chairs out front."

"We'll come down too," Penny said.

Except going down involved about one hundred steps, which would then need to be climbed to return. In this heat with that belly? Belle remembered all too well how that would go over. She started to protest, but Jonah beat her to it.

Kissing Penny, he shook his head. "You take care of this one"—he gently placed his hand on her abdomen—"and I'll take care of my beautiful niece."

Penny smiled and returned his kiss. "Okay. We'll get lunch going so it'll be ready when you get back."

Jonah's face glowed with absolute adoration for his wife. "You can't sit still, can you?"

"Nope."

He shook his head with a grin, accepting he'd won his battle but wouldn't win the war, and took Anna's hand to lead her outside.

Belle turned to her sister and pointed toward the kitchen island. "Tell me what's for lunch, and I'll get going on it while you sit on that stool and keep me company."

"If you tell me how things are going with Micah."

"So, you're cooking lunch after all."

Penny laughed but then grew serious. "If you don't want to talk about it, I understand. I'm here if you need me."

She did need to talk. She simply didn't want to.

With a sigh, she walked to the fridge. "Tell me what I'm making."

Ten minutes later, Belle stood chopping veggies for a salad while Penny smashed together ground turkey into patties. "Jonah said Micah took him for coffee and apologized to him."

"Yeah, he's been doing a lot of that."

"Taking people to coffee?"

"Apologizing." She sliced a cucumber. "He seems to mean it too, but he also seemed to mean it when he told me he loved me. And we all know how that turned out."

Penny stayed silent and grabbed more meat, working it into a circle. As she placed another patty on the pan, she looked at Belle. "I don't think he left because he didn't love you. I think he was scared."

"Of me? I know I was awful, but I wasn't scary." She set down the knife and swallowed. "Was I?" She'd done a lot of introspection over the past few years and faced some ugly truths about herself, but this wasn't one she'd even contemplated. As tough as the question was, she wanted to know.

"Absolutely not." Penny's firm tone assuaged her fears. "I don't think for one second he was scared of you. I think he was terrified of failing you and Anna."

"So he left. Makes perfect sense because that didn't fail us at all." Sarcasm was at an all-time high. She even added an eyeroll.

"Look, I've thought a lot about what Jonah said from that day and everything he's told me about Micah's parents."

"You two talk about our relationship?"

Penny's cheeks pinkened. "Not all the time, but yeah. Especially now with Micah coming back."

"Glad to know we keep you entertained."

"Belle." Penny dropped her voice. "You know that's not it."

She did. "Sorry."

"It's okay." Grabbing another handful of turkey, Penny continued working. "All I know is what Micah said that day. He alluded to the fact that you and your baby would be better off without him. Jonah said at one point it looked like he didn't want to leave, but he'd convinced himself it was the best thing to do. And think about it," she said as she stood to wash her hands, "you two were constantly fighting, and he'd grown up with parents always at war. Jonah said it was miserable in that house. Micah wouldn't want to go home at times, so he'd hang out at Jonah's. I think he was scared the same thing would happen to you guys."

Belle sifted through what Penny was saying, solid pieces of possible truth separating from years of misunderstanding. She'd need to bring those pieces to Micah to test their validity, yet the more she played with them, the more they felt real. She had a sneaky suspicion if she kept digging in this area, she'd uncover a trove of explanations she hadn't allowed herself to entertain until now.

Penny settled onto her stool and rested her hands on her middle. As if sensing that she'd given Belle enough to contemplate, she changed the subject. "I finalized the menu for Jonah's birthday and picked out the cake. Wait till you see it."

"He still doesn't suspect anything?"

"If he does, he's not telling me." She smiled. "Convincing him it's a couple's shower was genius."

"I come up with a good idea now and then." Jonah wore the crown as king of surprises in that relationship, but Penny was determined to dethrone him. This was her chance, and Belle was happy to help. "Made the most sense. We'll build the party right around him, and he won't have a clue. People typically miss what's right in front of their faces."

"Yes, they do." Penny's expression turned soft. "I nearly missed Jonah. I'm so glad my eyes finally opened to the obvious because that man was my best surprise ever. Nothing I expected, but everything I need."

They chatted through party details as they finished making lunch, but Penny's words continued to echo through her brain. The only person in front of her right now was Micah, and she thought she had him figured out. But were her eyes stubbornly locked on who she thought he was rather than seeing who he'd become?

Chapter Twelve

"How's the weekend been going? Anna still feeling better?" Micah's voice drifted over the phone late Sunday night. The hospital paging system sounded in the background, but he didn't hang up, so they must not have been calling for him.

"Yeah. Makes me wonder if she needs to see the ENT next week."

"Everything I've heard about Clinard says he's the best, and tubes are a very simple surgery."

"Still surgery."

"Which we aren't sure she needs. It's only a consultation." His calm, steady voice soothed her nerves better than the mug of chamomile tea she'd polished off. "And I'll be there, so you won't be alone." No hesitation. Just words that mirrored his actions over these past few days.

Every evening, when he dropped off Chloe, he'd peek in on Anna to make sure she was improving. Then later at night, when he was sure it was past Anna's bedtime, he'd call to check on the progress Belle had made with her lists. She nearly believed his calm assurance that they would accomplish everything before the FDA's second visit. He'd end the conversation with an update on the roof or thoughts on ways to improve the prenatal program. Sprinkled in between were questions prodding her to share about her day or her worry over Anna's upcoming appointment. He'd offer a listening ear and big shoulder—whichever she most needed. Last night she'd hung up the phone relaxed and ready to sleep, and it hit her. Micah wasn't mindlessly chatting; he'd been helping her decompress.

Sharing her burdens with someone else was a luxury she hadn't indulged in for years. Honestly, it freaked her out how easily Micah slipped into that void. Relying on him felt so natural, but could she resume that habit without her heart becoming attached? The man proved a dangerous enticement to her well-being.

"Belle?" he questioned. "Did you fall asleep?"

"No, but I'm about ready to." She yawned, one hand covering her mouth while the other pet Chloe. The fluff ball had taken to sleeping with her during Micah's overnight shifts.

"I'll let you go then."

A good idea, even if she wasn't quite ready to hang up on the warm timbre of his voice. "You're still planning on the morning?"

"I am. I'll be there as soon as my shift gets out."

"You're sure? You're going to be exhausted."

"It's easier for me to keep moving, then sleep once we're done."

"Good thing the guys across the street are coming."

"Right." His voice held skepticism.

Understandable, but, "They're in great shape and will be a bigger help than you think."

"I think I'll bring my medical bag with me just in case."

"I haven't seen one of those since I watched *Little House on the Prairie*."

"Those men probably grew up on the prairie." Low and bordered with mirth, his comment elicited memories of easier moments. Once upon a time, teasing marked their relationship, not tension. He used to try to take credit for her toned abs by saying his comedic talent created a giggling abdominal workout. She'd definitely give him the laughter part, though the man was no comedian. But love let joy loose inside a person, and where joy was, laughter often followed.

She chuckled with him now. "Ye of little faith. They'll probably run circles around your tired self tomorrow."

"I guess we'll see."

"I guess we will."

A comfortable silence settled between them, and she risked leaning into it. For Anna's sake, maybe allowing Micah to slip into their lives could be this easy. Pursue a love born of friendship, not romance. It definitely wouldn't risk her heart in the same way, and he did seem changed.

"I hope your night goes well," she said.

"Yours too."

Stretching, she flicked off her bedside lamp. The light of a full moon slipped through the cracks in the blinds, creating shadows on her floor. "I'll be sleeping."

"I know. I hope it's a good night's rest."

"I'll see you tomorrow, Micah."

"Goodnight, Belle."

They hung up, and she burrowed under her blanket, tired but still sifting through the past few weeks. She'd been far from perfect in her relationship with Micah, and she could own those things. They'd both changed. At least Micah seemed different. More relaxed and peaceful as if he was finally comfortable in his own skin. Biggest change of all, from what she'd seen, he hadn't touched one drink. On the surface, everything looked great. Thing was, he'd surprised her before, which meant he was perfectly capable of doing it again.

Therein sat her massive problem, because Micah held a portion of her heart that no other man ever came close to grasping. Being around him made that truth more evident. She'd simply need to proceed with the utmost caution.

Rolling onto her back, she stared at the ceiling until sleep finally arrived. Soon sunlight pricked her eyelids, announcing the dawn of a new day. Within an hour, she and Anna were dressed, fed, and clomping downstairs with Chloe on their heels. "You excited to go to the movies with Aunt Penny and Uncle Jonah?"

"Yes!" Anna bounced up and down.

Penny and Jonah would return to Chicago later today, but they'd asked to help out at AnnaBelle's. There wasn't anything Penny could do here, but taking care of Anna proved even better than lending her muscle—or Jonah's. Throughout the morning, he'd help Penny chase Anna, since anything much past waddling went beyond her current abilities.

They slipped outside as Penny and Jonah pulled up. He helped move Anna's car seat, then buckled her in. "You sure you don't need me here?"

"Positive."

"All right. We'll bring her home after lunch."

"Sounds good." Belle leaned near Penny's window. Her sister's stomach jostled. "You weren't kidding. That baby is a mover and shaker."

"I'm ready for my ribs to no longer be a goal post."

"You're almost there."

"Eight more weeks." Penny smiled. "And I thought waiting for our wedding day was tough."

Jonah grabbed her hand. "Completely different kind of anticipation." With a wink that had her sister blushing, he drove off.

Missing her little girl, but relieved she could accomplish more without her underfoot, Belle strolled into the shed beside AnnaBelle's. This small structure inspired her from the moment she'd first stepped foot into it. Possibilities burst alive as she studied the space. Producing the lotions and soaps in here seemed like a perfect fit, and she'd done her best to keep things sanitary. Everything she created out here she'd use on her own daughter. Unfortunately, the FDA didn't use that for their litmus test.

There was so much work to do before Natalie Simmons returned. Fixating on the timeline wasn't going to help anyone.

Footsteps crunched her way. "Ready to get to work?" Marv's old voice, as gravelly as the ground he walked on, reached her.

She smiled her greeting, and his weathered face returned the grin. Lyle and Don stood beside him. In denim and T-shirts with carpenter belts snug around their waists, they were here to help. "I am." She handed Chloe off to Astrid, who'd joined them with Betty and Fran. "Thanks again for taking this fluff ball."

"Are you kidding?" Fran stole her from Astrid. "She'll be the hit of the Community Room today." They left, fighting over who got to hold her.

Laughing, Belle faced the men. "All right, let's get started."

Lyle hitched up his drooping pants. "Where's that boy you said was joining us?"

Flicking a glance at her phone, she shrugged. "Running late, it seems." A twinge of unease settled in her gut, but she did her best to silence it. Micah promised he'd be here, and until he gave her a reason otherwise, she was going to give him the benefit of the doubt. That felt nearly impossible given their history, so she jumped into work.

Twenty minutes later, they arrived at an organized plan for emptying the space and then started hauling everything out. During her third trip between the buildings, it became clear that her plan of distraction failed miserably. Her muscles burned right along with the same question branding itself on her brain: where was Micah?

Setting down another bin filled with essential oils, she wiped the back of her hand over her brow, determined not to let her thoughts run away from her. There was a perfectly good explanation why he wasn't here. Her phone dinged a text, and she snapped it out of her pocket. Except it wasn't him. It was Lettie.

Micah asked me to text you. He's not sure he'll make it and wanted me to let you know.

Because texting her himself would be too much?

Okay. Yes. There could be several logical reasons for the holdup, but the pit in her stomach told her one thing. Their past wasn't nearly as far away as she pretended. Trusting Micah Shaw to be there for her might be a task she didn't have the strength to complete. Especially when he continued to let her down.

Babies never consulted him about his schedule.

Micah snuck a glance at the clock.

"You have someplace to be, Shaw?" Dr. Hyatt's gruff voice prodded him.

"I did. But this takes priority." That truth never used to bug him. He'd always been able to compartmentalize, a characteristic that often made him better at his job. But since arriving home and slowly slipping into Anna and Belle's life again, that ability proved tougher than ever before. Like right now, with his shift nearly over and Belle waiting for his help. But an emergency C-section took precedence. Didn't mean it was easy.

"Then how about you act like it." Hyatt scrubbed his hands, his gruff voice prodding Micah's full attention. "Two people's lives depend on your ability to focus on them, not that clock. Think you can handle it?"

"I can."

Belle was a mother, she'd understand. He'd asked Lettie to shoot her a text, and he'd call when he finished.

Hands washed, gloves on, he followed Dr. Hyatt into the O.R. and left everything but his patient and her baby behind. Two hours later, he still rode the high of a successful delivery. Mom and baby both perfectly healthy, he scooted from the recovery room.

"Hold up." The dad followed him into the hall and shoved out his hand. "I wanted to say thank you again."

Micah shook it for about the twentieth time. "Your wife did all the hard work." She'd been in labor nearly forty-eight hours and had pushed for three of them when the baby's heart rate plummeted. "We only helped at the end."

"You did more than that." Hands on his hips, he shook his head. "And I can't thank you enough."

That much had been obvious over the past two hours. Understandable, when he'd face the real possibility of losing his child before he'd gotten to hold him. "Listen, my part in taking care of your wife and son was for today. You do that for the rest of their lives, and that'll be thank you enough."

"I think I have that covered." With a smile, he returned to his wife.

Micah's thoughts turned to Belle, and he jogged to the locker room. Lettie confirmed she'd texted but said she hadn't received a response. Snagging his own phone, he checked, but nothing waited there either. He shot off another text before a quick rinse-off and change. Grabbing his backpack, he headed for his car. Nearly ten. His stomach growled and his mind begged for sleep. All-nighters were killer, but he promised he'd help Belle. He might be late, but he would still follow through.

Hitting the golden arches, he ordered a breakfast sandwich and large coffee and kept moving. The mix of protein, caffeine, and sheer will would energize him for a few hours before he'd be forced to crash. Pulling into Belle's lot, he noticed a couple of old guys in lawn chairs drinking their own coffees. They guarded the side door like weathered sentries, stopping him as he approached.

"You Micah, young man?" Tall, thin, with downy white hair and square black glasses squatting on a large bulbous nose, he looked like a stretched-out version of the grandpa from *Up*.

"I am." He held out his hand.

The man ignored it. "You're late."

Pocketing his fingers, he nodded. "I'm that also." He sipped his coffee and scanned the two other men. Both bald, one was nearly as tall but much stockier than Grandpa Up, while the other was shorter by several inches and sported a belly that evidenced a love for good cooking. "Did Belle tell you why?"

"She didn't say a thing other than you weren't coming."

Interesting. "Yet here I am."

"Almost three hours late."

"With good reason, which I did communicate to Belle." He eyed them all. Obviously they'd commissioned themselves as her protectors, and the idea made him smile. Winning them over could go a long way toward winning over Belle. "I'm in my fourth-year residency for obstetrics. There was an emergency C-section this morning at the end of my shift. I came as soon as I could."

The short man stepped forward. "You save that baby?"

"I did."

He thrust out his hand. "Name's Marv. My wife Fran and I lost our firstborn because there weren't no good doctors around. You can be late anytime if that's the reason."

As if Marv's stamp of approval released the dam holding the others back, Grandpa Up shook his hand next. "Lyle. Pleased to meet you."

"You too." Micah moved from shaking his hand to the final man's outstretched offering. "And you are?"

"Donald, but you can call me Don."

The side door opened, and Astrid stepped out along with two other cotton-tops who scanned Micah up and down with a scowl.

"Now Betty," Don sidled up beside her, "you don't need to kill him with those eyes. He's okay."

"He's also late," she groused. "It's not the first time he told Belle he'd be somewhere, then didn't show up, now is it?"

Don kissed her cheek. "I don't know anything about the first time, but I do know he had a good reason today."

Marv joined the other woman and snagged a cookie off the plate she held. "He delivered a baby who was in trouble this morning, sweetheart. Saved its life."

That had to be his wife. The warm look that passed between the two of them was something he hoped to have one day.

She walked over and held out the plate. "Our rule is, if you have a coffee in one hand, you need a cookie for the other." Returning her smile, he nabbed one of the windmill shaped cookies as she introduced herself. "I'm Fran, by the way. That's Don's wife, Betty, and you already know Astrid."

Astrid nodded his way as they all settled on chairs under the big oak to the side of the doorway. Micah remained standing. "Is Belle joining us?"

"I don't think she's ready for a break yet." Lyle's voice revealed more than his words.

"Maybe I'll go check on her." He started for the door, then turned around and grabbed another cookie. Hesitated. Then grabbed one more. "Peace offering." Had a feeling he'd need it.

He strolled down the hall and aimed for the open doorway spilling over with mutters and movement. Inside, Belle strained to lift a ten-gallon bucket filled with some sort of liquid. Looked like her intention was to load it beside another one already on a dolly. "Need some help?"

She startled but retained her grip. "I got it."

He set the treats on a table as he crossed the room to relieve her of the weight. "And now I do."

Her white-knuckled grip didn't release until his fingers touched hers. Then she couldn't back away fast enough. "Thanks." The word strangled out as if her good manners had barely beat her anger into submission.

"You're welcome." Retrieving the cookies, he offered her one. "Your protective detail outside said it was snack time."

"Good. They needed a break." She ignored his attempt at humor and his peace offering and reached for another bucket instead. "I don't. There's too much to do."

Oh, she was primed for a fight, but he didn't want to spend their time together arguing. "Okay. Put me to work then."

"I've got this covered. You can head home, Micah. I don't need you here."

She, however, seemed unwilling to let go of whatever bothered her. Like he was careening toward a cement wall and someone had cut his brakes, he had no clue how to avoid this collision. Only thing he could think of was to eject because honestly, he was exhausted and didn't possess the energy to put up with her prickly self this morning. Not when, for the life of him, he couldn't understand what he'd done wrong.

"Fine." He turned to leave and made it to the doorway before words he'd read yesterday in Mom's journal stopped him. *Don't let anger take root. Hashing things out is hard and uncomfortable, but dealing with issues leads to peace. Ignoring them leads to resentment. I'd rather live in peace.*

Yeah, so would he.

He sucked in a fortifying breath and spun the opposite direction. Belle had already refocused her attention to sorting through a shelf of product. He stopped a foot from her. "Except it isn't fine."

Shoulders lifting and falling with a not-so-silent sigh, Belle faced him. "I'm busy, Micah."

"Then you shouldn't be trying to push extra help out your door."

"I don't have time for this." She moved to skirt him.

He blocked her. "We're making time because we need to learn to communicate like two adults." Her eyes narrowed and her mouth opened, but he continued. "You're angry; I get that, so don't pretend you're not. What I'm not quite sure about is *why* you're upset. I had Lettie text you. Didn't you receive it?" Because that's all that made sense.

"I did." Clipped and final, her words didn't add any clarity to his confusion. Didn't mean he was giving up. "Then you know why I'm late."

"Yep."

"Yet you're still angry."

She shrugged as she set a crate of tiny bottles on the dolly. "I'm not angry."

"You're certainly not happy."

Now she looked at him. "Micah, I'm not upset with you. You didn't do anything wrong. What you're sensing is me resurrecting boundaries so I can protect myself."

Not unfounded words, but man, did they sting. "From me."

"Maybe." She rubbed her thumbnail, eyes focused just over his shoulder. Then she lifted her unguarded gaze his way. "It's safer to only have expectations of myself. I know what to anticipate then."

"And never get let down."

That lifted a corner of her mouth. "Well, I did place myself in quite the predicament with this place, but yes, it's easier to rely only on myself."

"Easier?" He tipped his head. "Or safer?"

She puffed out an amused breath. "Both?" Then she dropped any hint of merriment. "I understand why you were late, Micah. You sent the text. There wasn't anything else you could have done differently. But when you didn't walk through that door…" She lifted her shoulders in a shrug.

Right then it smacked him. Reconciliation with Belle might not be possible, but then again, he watched miracles happen on a daily basis. Even breathed life into a few himself when people around him said it was hopeless. The reward of placing those babies into their parents' arms chiseled new resolve in him. He wasn't a man who gave up easily anymore, and he certainly wasn't going to when the future he wanted stood in front of him, needing him to hold strong for them both.

He strolled to her, stopping just shy of encroaching her personal space. But he wanted her to feel his stable presence.

"I don't have a job where I can hang up the CLOSED sign and walk out every night, but I promise two things. Like today, I will always do everything in my ability to communicate with you, and—outside of my job preventing it—I will always follow through on my word. I know it's scary, but can you keep allowing me the chance to put actions with that promise?"

The question seemed to force a debate inside her. Finally, she answered. "My head completely understands what you're saying, but the rest of me ..." She tugged on a loose strand of hair. "Relying on others is already tough enough. But you? Jumping to worst case scenario is like this crazy reflex I can't control, and I'm worried I'll never be able to."

Honest answers weren't always fun, but they were necessary.

"I get that, I do. I left you with no warning. Even before that, things weren't exactly the best, and I know my drinking didn't help anything." They hadn't talked about that aspect, but she needed to know. "I haven't had a drop in two years."

"Not one?"

"Not one."

She took another moment to absorb that information. "I'm glad, Micah, for you and for Anna, because I was way too quiet about how much you drank then, but I wouldn't be now." Determination squared her shoulders. "Anna deserves better."

"So do you."

Her head tilted back as if his words surprised her, but then she relaxed. "Yes. I do."

"Which is why I don't want to fight with you, Belle. I grew up with arguing parents. I don't want that dynamic for either of us, and I definitely don't want it for our daughter." His answer rose from his own fears. "All I'm asking for in our relationship is peace." Might as well lay it all out there, though. "But if at some point something more develops, then I'm all in." They had to trust each other first, and right now, his hope for that lay seriously depleted at his feet.

Her eyes searched his, and he refused to blink. Every part of him was open to her perusal. There was nothing to hide.

And then, as if her head and heart arrived at some sort of neutral ground, she softened. "Okay. To the peace part anyway. The rest"—she said with a shrug—"is going to take time, and even then, I can't promise."

"If you can't promise, can you 'maybe'?" He offered the compromise teasingly but meant it oh-so-seriously.

Again, she made him wait for an answer, but as he was discovering, waiting for her was well worth it.

"I can 'maybe.'"

One word chased with a tiny smile, minuscule really, but in his world, minuscule things held the power to heal a grown man. That barely-perceptible uptick of her lips breathed life into his hope. Not enough to fully reinflate it, but enough to keep him going.

She nodded to the treats in his hands. "By the way, cookies make a great peace offering."

He held one out.

She took it, then wiggled her fingers for the other. "This definitely calls for a two-cookie peace treaty."

Chuckling, he handed his over as well.

Chapter Thirteen

Thursday night, Belle stood in front of their small Lamaze class, catching everyone's attention—especially Micah's—with her lead-in. "And now for a little truth time."

He wasn't sure these girls could handle more truth. He'd already hit on all three stages of labor, complete with a plastic pelvis and baby doll for demonstration. That illustration drained their faces of color, but Belle pulled them from the brink with a few soft words of encouragement. Then she segued into a "truth" section, which preceded a short break before they'd talk about techniques to use in labor.

Belle picked up an eight-by-ten photo that had been face down on the table and held it up. He grimaced right along with the rest of the girls at the wrinkly newborn there.

"Your baby may not be the most beautiful thing you've ever seen." Laughter followed her words, his own included. She addressed the room but looked at him. "This is Anna right after birth. My first words were, she looks like a monkey." She tilted the picture to glance at it. "You have to agree, I'm right."

More laughter from the girls, but he remained on her description of newborn Anna. It explained so much and tipped his lips into a grin.

Belle set the photo down. "I say this to let you know that it's perfectly normal not to experience love at first sight with your baby. You'll be exhausted and possibly in pain. Plus you'll still have hormones raging all over, and it's all because of this little person. So give yourself time to fall in love with him or her. Trust me, it may take a while, but you will." She held up a more recent picture of Anna and everyone aww'd. "And they will end up the cutest thing you've ever seen."

She excused them with instructions to return in ten minutes. After they all exited, Micah joined her. "So that's why you call her Monkey."

"Can you blame me?"

His grin grew. "Not at all. Though with as chubby as her cheeks are now, I can't believe she was ever that wrinkly."

Belle's nose crinkled. "Yeah, I love her cheeks."

"She does have the adorable thing down pat." He followed her as they started to move the chairs into a circle, preparing for the rest of the evening. "Hey, I meant to ask, but when I pulled in tonight I noticed the garage door along the side of your building is all busted up. What happened there?"

"My guess is that someone backed into it when they were leaving a donation."

"No one said anything?"

"Nope."

He settled the final chair in place. "You need cameras there."

Her brow lifted, but she stayed silent. Didn't need words, though; she'd always spoken loudly through looks. No doubt she owed the ability to her years on stage.

"I'm just saying that it would be helpful for you if something like that occurred again. Or if someone tried to steal your donations."

"If someone steals the donations, then they need them worse than we do."

Valid point. "Does the door work?"

"It does."

He settled his hands on his hips. "You do remember that I know your tones, right? So half-truths don't fly with me."

"It's a whole truth. The door does open."

"All the way?"

Her grin caught him straight in the chest. "Your persistence hasn't waned."

"Neither has your evasiveness."

A few strands of hair slipped from her ponytail and caught on her lips, shiny with gloss. She swiped them away. "Why are you so interested in my door, anyway?"

He blinked his focus from her movements to her eyes, which locked on him, a deep line drawn between them. Hopefully, sooner rather than later, confusion wouldn't be her gut reaction to his concern. "Earlier, I saw Nia trying to haul in donations, and I noticed she didn't have it open all the way. Wondered if it was broken or if that was something she'd done to help keep the space cooled. Either way, dragging items in through a half-opened door didn't look easy."

"It's not." Belle shrugged. "But we manage."

"Wait. You haven't been doing that with your ankle, have you?"

She innocently shrugged, then turned and called to the girls in the hall, "We're ready if you are."

They filed into the room as he leaned over Belle's shoulder, his mouth resting beside her ear. "Just because you change the subject doesn't mean I forget what I learned."

Goosebumps lifted on her skin, but she didn't have time to respond, because

Sydney asked, "Does it matter where we sit?"

Clearing her throat, Belle answered. "Not at all."

After everyone found a spot, Micah stood in front of the class. He pointed to the poster he'd brought with cartoon faces of women in varying stages of labor. "Earlier tonight, we talked about these different stages. Now we're going to go over some techniques you and your partner can use during each one to help ease your pain."

Belle watched him from the far wall. He started by pulling out rice bags and heating pads, which were often helpful during early labor. "Mom will typically be pretty talkative early on. Maybe bring some board games or load up your favorite Netflix show to watch. You never know how long this period will last, but you'll definitely know when it's over. As labor progresses, Mom is going to become quieter. It'll be your job to figure out what she needs."

He talked through a few nonverbal clues to watch for, then moved on to some massage techniques. "Belle, why don't you come up so I can demonstrate?"

She waved her hands in front of her. "I think you're doing fine on your own."

"Please, Miss Thornton?" Kim implored. They'd all brought their coaches tonight, but only one of them came with their baby's father. Everyone else had a relative or friend. "I learn better if I can see it." Then she turned and winked at Micah.

Little matchmaker in the making. Might need to slip the girl a twenty at the end of the night.

With a sigh, Belle limped to the front of the class and presented her back to him. "Have at it."

"As you can see, Mom may not be in the best of moods." He smirked as she glared at him over her shoulder. "But that shouldn't prohibit you from helping her however you can." He slipped his fingers over her trapezius muscles, his thumbs massaging the tension at the base of her neck. Beneath his touch, her body softened. "Massage is one of the best ways for Mom to relax. Your touch can be very healing when she's experiencing pain."

Belle straightened and stepped away. "Or it can be the exact opposite." Turning, she addressed the class. "It's very important to ask her what she wants and then listen to it."

"Though sometimes she may be hurting so badly she either isn't sure or she won't be able to say. It's in those times you need to see past her pain to what she really needs."

"Or back off and trust she'll tell you when she figures it out for herself."

The classroom went so silent he could hear a fly buzzing in the window.

Micah settled on the edge of the table. "And that, friends, is your demonstration on how quickly things can deteriorate during labor."

Laughter broke the tension, and Belle shook her head. "I take my role here very seriously."

"Good, then you won't mind if we move on to demonstrating some different positions?"

Her mischievous grin came out to play. "I think that's a great idea." She grabbed one of the exercise balls he brought and handed it to him. "You'll need this."

"Um ..."

"You weren't expecting me to squat with my sore ankle, were you?"

He narrowed one eye but took the ball. "Of course not."

Belle coached him through several less-than-comfortable maneuvers, requesting he hold them while she explained their uses in slow detail to the class.

"I don't remember any of these being moves I learned," he noted.

She paused and looked down at him. "Which one of us has actually *been* through labor before?"

All right. He'd give her that.

By the fourth position, the soft sniggers of the women floated to him.

He unfolded himself from the crazy stance. "These are not Lamaze positions."

She emphatically nodded—"Yes, they are"—then playfully tapped a finger against her chin. "I may have smashed them together with some yoga and Pilates moves, though." The sniggering in the room turned to full belly laughs. Belle covered her mouth with her fingertips to hide her own giggles.

"Nice," he groused but tossed in a grin.

When the room quieted, she addressed the moms-to-be. "As much fun as this evening was, ultimately I hope you understand that—like tonight's class— you can never expect labor to go picture perfectly. You may have one idea in your head, but once things start, there'll be curveballs. Be prepared to bend with them." She tipped her head in Micah's direction as she spoke. "That's the best advice I can give you."

They finished up with a few more true positions and techniques the women could use, then had them practice with their coaches. A half-hour later, the room was empty of everyone except himself and Belle. He rolled the exercise balls to a corner while she realigned chairs.

"Can I ask you a question?" Because one had been on his mind all night.

She hesitated, then, "Sure."

He crossed the room to help with the final few chairs. "What was your labor like?"

Her mouth scrunched up. "Hard. Long." She met his eyes. "Rewarding."

As they finished, he sat and tapped the open seat beside him. She actually took it.

"I'm sorry I wasn't there."

"I know."

He took her hand, flipped it in his, and ran his fingers over her palm. "And I know my being here again has been a curveball in your life. Thanks for bending."

"Pretty sure I've been equally unyielding. Like the other day." She swallowed. "I know we talked, but I never actually apologized for getting upset with you. I overreacted, but like I said, it hit on all these old feelings, and they kind of took over."

"Thanks." He appreciated the apology but also understood. "It makes sense, though. I was gone three years, and I've only been home two weeks."

"Two and a half," she corrected.

"You're counting the days?"

"Like my mom used to count her gray hairs."

"You say the sweetest things," he deadpanned.

She laughed and moved her hand on top of his. "I really do appreciate you allowing me my time with this. With telling Anna."

"I meant it when I said you set the pace, Belle. There's no time limit on telling her who I am." His heart might beg him to gather Anna up in his arms, tell her he was her daddy, and never leave her side, but he would wait until he was invited. Didn't mean he was any less her father just because she wasn't calling him Daddy. And it certainly didn't mean he loved her any less. There wasn't anything he wouldn't do for her—even wait to be in a relationship.

He stood and hauled her to her feet. "Now, let's go see about your door."

"You're determined about that thing, aren't you?"

"I'm determined about a lot of things, Belle, and you're at the top of that list."

Her open mouth was worth his bold comment. He might be patient, but that didn't mean he had to be inactive, because he had every intention of turning her "maybe" from earlier this week into a "yes."

"Sydney, these are gorgeous." Belle peered over her laptop at the anxiously awaiting face of the young woman and found a rare smile lighting Sydney's face. A wobbly one, as if she was out of practice with the expression, but it was there nonetheless. "I'd never have been able to create these in a million years."

Yet in two weeks, Sydney designed new labels for all Belle's products. Ones that somehow straddled the line of pretty enough for girls but simple enough for guys.

Sydney shrugged. "I'm glad you like them."

"Like them?" Was she serious? "I love them. And I love what you did with the new logo. What I had before was too feminine, and I didn't even realize it until I looked at all of this."

Another shrug. "Guys would stop with their wives or girlfriends at the store or farmer's market, but none of them would shop alone. I thought it could help."

So she had an observant eye too. "You might want to think about switching from a straight business degree to marketing. You're really good at this."

"It's one set of labels."

"That show an amazing amount of talent."

Light brightened Sydney's eyes. "You think so?"

"Wouldn't say it if I didn't." She'd experienced enough fake things in her life. She wanted no part in handing them out. "In fact, I'd love to have you help me shape the website. I'm nearly through with the descriptions, but I could use a hand revamping the overall look. Everything from color scheme to grabbing shots of the product with these new labels. Think you could work something up?" She stood and rounded her desk, leaning against it. "I'd pay you and give you full credit as the web designer."

"Me? Seriously?" Sydney pointed to herself. Doubt eclipsed her earlier excitement. "There's got to be better people you can pay for that."

"I'm sure there are people more trained, but I want you." Belle nudged Sydney's foot with her own. "Don't let your insecurities talk you out of a great opportunity. If I'm willing to take a chance on you, you should be too."

Sydney nibbled her bottom lip. "Can I think about it?"

Let her think too long, and she'd talk herself right out of it. "If, while you're thinking, you work up a few ideas to show me at the end of this week, I promise to be honest about whether they fit what I'm looking for." She reached out her hand. "Deal?"

Sydney hesitantly shook it. "Deal." Then she exited the tiny office, her head a little higher than when she'd walked in. Moments like this fueled Belle's energy to keep AnnaBelle's going. Helping someone find her place, watching her unravel more about herself, or catching excitement over endless possibilities never before glimpsed on her horizon? AnnaBelle's provided all of that.

It provided *her* with all of that.

"Knock, knock." Astrid rapped her knuckles on the wood casing around Belle's door. "You look about a million miles away."

"Just thinking about how convincing these girls to believe in themselves reminds me of last summer. Remember when I tried to persuade Anna to play outside again after that wasp stung her? All she could think about was how she'd been hurt. It took me weeks to convince her it was safe to come outside." She met Astrid's eyes. "It's the same with these girls, and just like then, I refuse to give up."

Astrid listened, nodding. "That's a very insightful analogy. Could be applied to most anyone here." She directed a pointed look her way.

"Anyway"—Belle drew out the word—"it's a great reminder of why this place is so important, and why I need to work harder to make sure it stays open." She pointed to the brown-stained ceiling tiles above her. "And that it doesn't fall down around us."

Astrid's bright red lips pulled up. "Seems you've got some help for that one."

Honestly. The woman was on a roll this morning. As if they were playing Red Rover, Micah had called Astrid to his side and captured her—along with most of the Grands. Now they all held hands and tried to entice her to join them. Well, she was perfectly happy and safe, right over here. Even if her team had grown scraggly.

"Because he's trying to work off his guilt."

"I don't think it's guilt that keeps him coming back."

Belle huffed. "Don't know what else it would be." Besides, her lame explanation kept him at arm's length.

"Now, child, we both know you aren't that dumb." Astrid didn't pull any punches. She had no problem calling out her sad excuse. "But if your heart's not quite ready yet, that's okay. Just make sure you don't keep it locked up forever." She nodded down the hall. "Now come on. It's time for lunch."

No use answering or arguing. Astrid said her piece and wouldn't engage in more conversation unless it involved forward momentum. Fact was, she'd nailed Belle's current state. She wasn't ready for her heart to move anywhere near Micah. Not willingly anyway. It seemed to be tiptoeing closer to him all on its own— especially since their conversations two days ago—and that completely freaked her out. On one hand, she wanted nothing more than to step into his arms, tuck her head under his chin, and breathe him in. The scent of cedar and Irish Spring soap still could make her feel safe, because once upon a time in Micah's embrace, the world, her mom's words, and the pressures of being perfect all melted away.

Until he left her.

It became the strangest juxtaposition. In her memories, he was her safe place. In her reality, he was what scared her most. Yet, her heart continued its march toward him as if it didn't question he was the only man for her. That *maybe* she'd offered him was edging toward a *might*. Which was dangerously close to a *yes*.

With both hands, she covered her face and let out a frustrated growl.

"Should I come back later?"

Belle stilled. Had she made his voice up in her head now? Slipping her hands down until her fingertips rested on her cheeks, she peeked out at Micah, standing there looking oh-so-perfect in faded jeans rolled just above his dark leather work boots, a crisp white T-shirt that fit him too well, and a hint of blond scruff that made her fingers itch to touch his cheeks. With sunglasses on his head and sun-kissed skin, the man maintained his style for every occasion. He'd gone full GQ in college and remained there, and she hadn't minded one bit. She'd never been into flannel or cowboy boots. There was something very sexy about a man who understood fashion and wore it well.

"Belle?"

She glanced away from the awareness in his eyes. He was far too observant.

Her hands landed on her hips. "What are you doing here already?" It was Friday, which meant he shouldn't be here until dinnertime. He'd drop off Chloe, eat with them, and then help out for an hour or so to make progress on her slowly-growing-shorter FDA to-do list before heading to work.

One eyebrow arched. "Nice to see you too."

"Sorry." Her emotions might be all over the place, but she didn't need to be a brat. "You surprised me."

He leaned on the door casing. "That's why I stopped by, actually."

"To surprise me?"

He cracked the grin that had captured her from first sight across their college campus and held her even now. "To *not* surprise you." Swinging his keys on his U of M key chain, he tipped his head toward the back of the building. "I'm going to work on that door today, and it may be loud at times. Thought I'd let you know, so you didn't freak out."

Oh, she was freaking out. "You don't have to keep doing this, Micah."

"You watch Chloe; I help out. Remember?"

"With my FDA list, not fixing every corner of this building." Speaking of Chloe, her bark resounded down the hall. Since he'd arrived early today, it made sense she would too. Still, "With all the extra you've been doing, it isn't a fair deal. I feel like I'm taking advantage of you."

He straightened, strolling into the room until he stood right in front of her. Wearing confidence like he'd invented it, the enticing flirt she'd once fallen for came out to play as he dropped his voice all low and rumbly. "I wish you'd take advantage of me."

Heat rushed to her cheeks, and she punched him in the arm. "Micah!"

But unbidden laughter bubbled from her lips and pulled out his.

"Sorry." The apology floated over his laughs. "I couldn't help it. You set me up so well. Plus"—he drew his finger down her forehead and along the bridge of her nose—"you had this deep line here that I thought needed smoothing."

She shivered under his touch, even as it summoned heat in its wake. He continued the movement, trailing along her cheek and neck until his fingers tickled the skin along her collarbone.

"Is that your polite way of saying I'm getting old and wrinkly?" she asked through her suddenly dry throat.

"Not at all." Warmth filled the icy blue of his eyes. "And one day far, far in the future, when you do get a wrinkle or two, you'll still be the most beautiful woman I've ever seen."

"You assume you'll still be around then." She wanted him to be.

The thought crystallized before her defenses could shoot it down.

"The only way I'm leaving is if you ask me to." His thumb made a lazy circle in the well of her neck. "Are you asking me to?"

She couldn't even if she tried. She seemed to have lost her voice. So she gave the tiniest shake of her head, knowing full well his question had leaped from the future to this very present moment. And fully aware of what her head shake invited.

He leaned down, his eyes never leaving hers, an intensity there that went beyond physical desire. He wasn't playing and this wasn't a passing moment— this was for keeps. Her heart hammered as his hands slipped tenderly to hold her face, softly tugging her closer.

She wasn't ready for this. Wasn't ready to give her heart to him for keeps, because she still didn't trust that *his* forever was the real deal. His intentions were, but those weren't enough. Especially not with Anna's heart on the line too. She wanted promises, but even those could be broken.

Oh, she was in a tangle with no idea how to unknot herself.

And Micah saw every bit of those fears in her eyes. Hands cupping her cheeks, he aborted the almost-kiss and gently pressed his forehead to hers. His minty soft breath brushed against her in a sigh.

"Sorry," she whispered.

He leaned back enough to capture her eyes again. "Don't apologize. A kiss shouldn't make you feel regret or fear. It should make you feel protected and loved." His hands drifted down, over her shoulders, and stopped at her upper arms. "I'm going to go fix that door of yours. Straighten out the track, and see if I can get it to fully open. Like I said, if you hear a few bangs, don't freak out, it's just me." With a gentle squeeze to her arms, he left.

Down the hall, the Grands chatted away. Tiny voices lifted from the daycare beyond that as the kids finished their lunches. Life stirred all around, but hers suddenly felt at a standstill. For the first time in years, she hadn't a clue which way to move. Further into her safe solitude or forward toward the promises Micah offered?

Why couldn't it be as simple as creating another list and tallying the pros and cons in each column? But love couldn't be distilled down to something so black and white. Emotions were messier than Anna's finger painting, and they blurred together into a gray area she didn't know how to navigate. Not when either direction felt like she'd lose something.

So the question was, which way did she stand to lose the most?

Chapter Fourteen

"You look like roadkill."

Micah turned at Nash's comment. "Thanks." He tossed his dirty scrubs into a bag in his locker. "Should have seen me about ten minutes ago."

"Messy delivery?"

"The mom's getting a transfusion right now." He sat to lace up a new pair of tennis shoes. He should wear something more practical, but he couldn't force himself into clogs. A man had to draw the line somewhere.

After stowing his backpack, Nash slipped on his badge for morning rounds. "Ready to fill me in on who's here before you fall asleep?"

"Are you as charming with your patients as you are with me?"

Nash revealed his sparkling white teeth and thickened his accent. "No worries, mate. They're a mite easier to charm than you."

"I'll bet." What was it with women and accents?

They pushed through the locker room door into the hallway, dodging a nurse who raced by. Friday night's full moon made this Saturday morning a crazy one. Micah walked Nash through all his patients, stifling a yawn as he finished. Nash looked at him over the chart he held. "You are going home to sleep, right?"

"At some point." First he had breakfast with Mom, Belle, and Anna. They'd bring Chloe to hand off while also allowing Mom the chance to see her.

"How many days until you're on vacation?"

"Eight. And yes, I plan to catch up on my sleep that week." Or at least catch more than a few hours a day.

"If you don't collapse before then."

"I won't." He signed out, grabbed his things, and headed for the staff lot. His limbs might as well weigh a few hundred pounds, and there was a slight buzz ringing through his head. Exhaustion didn't touch his physical state, but he could handle it. He'd made promises—to himself, to Belle, to Mom—and he was done being the guy who broke them.

If you say you're going to do something, follow through. Your yes means something. So does your no. Use them both carefully. Couldn't remember which day he read that—they were all blurring together—but the words had sunk deeply into him, reinforcing the decisions he'd already made to follow through. No excuses. Which was why he pointed his car toward Mom's and not home, even though he was pretty sure sandpaper had replaced his eyelids and a fog thicker than what rolled off Lake Michigan had invaded his brain.

He took the first available spot in Brookhaven's parking lot, turned off his car, and leaned against the headrest for a quick second. Sleep taunted him, but he batted it away with the image of Belle. She'd nearly let him kiss her. The mere fact that she'd wanted to—even for that brief moment—was enough to sustain his patience. Enough to make the lack of sleep worth it.

With a groan, he hauled his weary body from his car and straight inside. Loud voices erupted from Mom's room, followed by a crash. He broke into an all-out run, rounding her doorway to find Mom's nurses, David and Lydia, holding her.

David glanced up at him. "She's having an episode."

No kidding, Sherlock.

Micah hurried to her side and hunched down to her height. "Mom?"

Cloudy blue eyes met his, and she jerked, fear chasing away those clouds. "I'm not your mom. Who are you?" She tugged against the nurses. "Where's my boy? He was supposed to visit me today." Another yank. "I need to find him."

She kicked at Lydia, who evaded the movement. "You need to go," David quietly ordered.

Go? He couldn't leave her in this state.

But then Mom looked at him, her eyes latching on and widening. "You told him, didn't you?" She wrestled. "Now he's gone. You said he wouldn't be mad." Tears spilled down her cheeks. "I know I messed up. Please tell him I'm sorry. Tell him to come back."

The anguish in her voice sliced through him. Whatever mixed-up memory she was lost in, he had no clue how to extradite her. He'd been trained to stay cool under pressure, knew how to quickly assess and address multiple curveballs, but seeing Mom like this completely robbed him of that practiced calm.

"I …" He blinked to David, who nudged his chin toward the door.

Micah backed into the hallway but couldn't leave. He reached the far wall and slid down it. Bending his knees, he rested his elbows on them and hung his head between his hands. Inside her room, Mom's tears turned to wailing. David and Lydia's soft voices tried to soothe her, making promises that made no sense. That her son wasn't angry. He'd come to visit.

He had. He was right here in the hall.

She simply didn't recognize him.

What terrified him was that she never would again. That the last time he'd seen her was the final time she'd know he was the boy she now cried for.

A few tears slipped from his eyes, and he brushed them away with the back of his hand.

"Mista Micah!" Anna's tiny voice jolted him from the descending sadness. She raced toward him full-tilt, launching her tiny arms around his neck as she reached him. Her little face puckered. "Why you crying?"

Belle caught up to Anna. Concern latched onto her features as she looked from Micah to Mom's room, then back again.

Scooping Anna into his arms, he stood. "I'm just a little sad."

"Why?" She squished his face between her hands.

"Because my mommy isn't feeling good." His words sounded funny through pinched cheeks.

Innocent confusion crinkled her tiny brow. "Why not?"

More cries came from Mom's room, and Belle stood between the open door and Micah. He spun Anna so she couldn't see inside, but that gave him a direct view. The nurses struggled to get Mom into bed, but she fought them. Couldn't help it. He lost it.

Belle snatched Anna from him. "Hey, Monkey, can you walk Chloe to see the birds?"

"Uh-huh." Anna took Chloe's leash—he hadn't even seen the dog—and skipped down the hall with her to the tiny cage.

With his thumb and forefinger, he pressed his eyes, trying to stanch the flow of tears. Then Belle's arms circled around him, and it was a losing battle. He could blame his current level of exhaustion for crying like a baby, but that'd be a lie. That was his mom in there, and she was worth every tear falling.

"Come on." Belle tugged him away from Mom's door.

After another minute, he'd managed to pull himself together enough to offer Belle a sad smile. "Thanks."

She nodded, her own eyes damp. "Bad day."

It was a statement, not a question, but still he answered. "She didn't recognize me. She's waiting for me to show up, but when I walked through the door, she thought I was someone else. I don't have a clue who, but she thinks I took her son." Dragging a hand through his hair, he tugged on the ends. "I couldn't help her. I only made it worse. She's slipping away, and I can't do anything about it." A strangled laugh choked out. "I can't even find the stinking letters she keeps asking me about."

Belle's hand rubbed between his shoulder blades, her touch settling him. Down the hall, Anna pointed to the birds as Chloe watched with interest. "What letters?" Belle asked.

"I have absolutely no idea." He peered down at her, helpless. "That's the problem. She keeps talking about letters her dad sent her that she wants to give me, but I never heard one mention of them growing up. I asked Jonah if he or Penny ran across them when they did the estate sale after Gigi died, but he said they hadn't." He sighed. "If Gramps wrote them, I don't know where they are."

The whole time he spoke, Belle nodded her head as if everything he said made complete sense. As he finished, she gave one last nod, then removed her hand from his back. "Okay. Let's find them."

"What?"

But she'd already hauled her cell phone out and dialed someone. She held his gaze but said nothing until whoever it was answered. "Hey, Penn, can you and Jonah take Anna for the day?" A pause and then, "Great. We'll be at Micah's parents' house." Then she hung up and looked at him. "Did you want to talk to her nurses before you leave?"

"Yeah."

"Okay. I can wait with you or take Anna out of here. What's best for you?"

"Would you mind staying?"

He'd never met anyone with a smile like hers. At least a smile that impacted him the way hers could. At times it fired heat through him, other moments it pulled laughter, and right now, it blanketed him with a calm he desperately needed.

With a nod, she stayed until David and Lydia stepped out to speak with him, Belle's hand touching his arm in reassurance. All the while, Anna wandered up and down the short hall with Chloe, both of them near silent. He wasn't completely sure, but that had to be unusual, so he said a silent prayer of thanks for their uncharacteristically quiet demeanor in the past fifteen minutes.

"You gave her Ativan to calm her?" he asked. "How much?"

"Two milligrams," Lydia responded. "I spoke with her doctor while David helped her to bed. He thinks there's a few things going on."

Micah held up his hand, one question taking precedence. "Is she getting worse?"

David shook his head. "We don't think so. Of course, this episode could point to that, but we think it's due to a change in her medicine."

"Right. Dr. Cho switched her from Razadyne to Exelon." They'd known a medication change could produce worse side effects than what she'd been experiencing, but he'd hoped that wouldn't be the case.

"Now he'd like to try Aricept."

Micah tensed. "Isn't that for severe Alzheimers?"

"It can be, but it's mainly used for mild to moderate."

"The side effects aren't any better."

Belle squeezed gently. "None of them are."

He peered down at her, surprised.

She shrugged. "I'm no doctor, but I can google things."

It wasn't that she discovered the info; it was that she'd gone looking for it. For *his* mom.

He repositioned his arm beneath her hold until his fingers found hers. His turn to offer a squeeze. The slightest of hesitations, but then she returned it.

"She's resting comfortably now?" he asked.

Both the nurses nodded. "She is," Lydia said. "Most likely when she wakes up, she won't even remember any of this."

For once, he was grateful for that fact.

"You'll call me if she has another episode?"

"Definitely," Lydia reassured.

There wasn't much more he could do here. He turned to leave, then stopped. One question he hadn't asked. Didn't want to. But couldn't leave here without voicing it. "I ... Seeing me. It seemed to scare her. Should I stay away?"

Empathy lifted Lydia's face. "She loves your visits. Tells everyone all about her boy. It may be best to establish a more regular routine, but don't stop visiting."

He dragged a hand through his hair, his already crazy schedule spinning him in circles. But if Mom needed regularity, he'd provide it. "I'm on nights for another week, so I'll plan on breakfasts until after that."

David had drifted down the hall to squat in front of Anna. Lydia moved in their direction. "We'll see you tomorrow morning, then."

Still holding his hand, Belle looked up at him. "You okay?"

No. "Yeah."

The corner of her mouth pulled up. "Pageant voice."

He chuckled. "I do not use a pageant voice."

"What should we call it then? When you give the answer you think people want to hear, rather than what you honestly feel?"

"Survival mode?" Because that's what it currently felt like.

"Good thing I have plenty of experience with that, then. Come on." She tugged him toward Anna, Chloe, and the exit.

"Oh. My. Word." Micah held up a picture.

Belle snatched it from him. Their first date. Homecoming of their freshman year in college. "Those are some seriously bad hair choices." Micah's covered his ears, and he'd maintained shaggy side-swept bangs in that decade's resurgence of the bowl cut. She'd gone shaggy too with a bob she never should have attempted. Thank goodness her hair grew fast, and he'd chopped his later that year.

"That dress is still my favorite, though."

Navy, floor-length, and formfitting with a high neck, she'd picked it out herself, away from Mom's strong opinions. That night was one of the few times she'd been fully glammed up yet still felt like herself. She credited Micah more than the dress for that memory. He'd looked her in the eyes as if she was the most intriguing woman he'd ever met. They'd talked and danced for hours. He didn't even make a move on her.

But he had kissed her goodnight. A tender kiss. And in that moment, he reached in and grabbed a hold of her heart.

Something similar happened today when she walked into Brookhaven and saw Micah on the floor, crying. Except instead of his kiss, this time his tears seized her heart, and there was no way she'd leave him. All that remained messed up between them didn't seem to matter right then, because in spite of everything— even though she tried hard to pretend otherwise—she still cared about him.

On a completely platonic, friendshippy level.

She handed him the picture. "You cleaned up pretty well yourself." He always knew how to dress, and his body was made for clothes. Tux, jeans, or the athletic wear he now wore, didn't matter what he put on.

"Thanks." He tucked the photo into the box, then returned that to the shelves full of boxes they'd been going through and grabbed another. His arms flexed under its weight. As a friend, she was allowed to appreciate those muscles, and how good he looked in his running shorts, faded U of M T-shirt, and ball cap. It was perfectly acceptable friendship thinking. After all, friends saw the best in one another, and a person would have to be blind to miss Micah's ... best features.

She most definitely had no problem with her eyesight.

He caught her staring and smiled.

Cheeks heating, she dropped her gaze to the paperwork in her hand while her mind blared a warning. Noticing was one thing. Acting on it was another. Friends did not act on attraction.

Plopping the box between them, he slid down the wall and removed the lid. "Lucky number thirteen."

"Let's hope." She feathered her fingers through the remaining items in hers.

Micah worked quietly beside her. "Thanks again for this morning."

"No problem."

"I'd forgotten how much I love those cherry walnut pancakes from Real Food."

Once Jonah and Penny had picked up Anna, she'd called in a pick-up order at the tiny café they used to spend weekend mornings in together. Not that she ever shared a pancake with him. Probably why his mouth dropped open slightly when she pulled one out of the bag for herself. "They are delicious." And as big as a plate. She'd saved a few bites for Anna later.

"It's nice to see you allowing treats into your life. I always wanted that for you."

She peeked up at him, the warmth in his voice settling into her bones. "I had to want it for myself too."

"I can relate." The air conditioner kicked on around them, but it didn't touch the intensity of his stare. "There's a lot of things I want now that I never thought I could have before, and they definitely make my life sweeter."

A puff of laughter escaped through her nose. "You've gotten cornier these past few years."

"I call it more romantic."

"No. Definitely corny." She wagged a finger between them. "And there will be no romance between us."

He dove into his box. "If you say so." Except his tone contradicted his words.

"Micah," she warned.

"Quiet. I need to concentrate so I don't miss anything."

At least he'd stopped flirting. Except she had this sneaky feeling it wasn't a permanent reprieve.

Box thirteen didn't wind up to be so lucky. Neither did boxes fourteen through twenty-two. Belle shoved her last one away, then stretched her neck until it cracked. "How many letters are we looking for anyway?"

"I have no idea." He dropped his head against the wall. "I did find an old journal of hers and brought that in, hoping it would pacify her."

"But it didn't?"

"Nope. She gave it right back to me." Sliding his knees up, he draped his arms over them. "I've been reading it, and it's been simultaneously insightful and confusing."

Interest flared. "Can I see it?"

"Sure." He disappeared for a minute, then returned with a cracked leather book. "Here you go."

Belle took it and skimmed the pages.

Micah settled beside her. "She talks a lot about how she messed up with my dad. I always thought he was the only one who caused problems between them, but that doesn't seem to be the case." He pointed to the page she had opened. "See. She mentions several times about this bad choice she made, how she knows she hurt him, but she never really mentions what it was she did. Only that she was sorry, and she wanted to fight for their marriage." Above them, Chloe yapped at something. Most likely a squirrel outside. "Doesn't seem like Dad was receptive to any of it."

"Does she say that?"

"He's not here, is he?"

Oh. True.

She stopped on an entry, and Sharon's cursive *love doesn't hold your worst against you* caught her eye. It stuck under her skin like a tiny burr that begged for her attention. She closed the book and handed it to Micah. "Have you asked him about any of this? The letters or their marriage?"

"About the letters, yeah, but he doesn't have a clue. As for their marriage, it didn't seem my place to ask him something as personal as that. We aren't exactly close."

"Neither one of us hit the proverbial parenting jackpot, did we."

A tired smile lifted his lips. "No, we did not."

"At least fifty percent of yours gave an effort."

"Your dad tried."

"With Penny." Though even in that, he refused to truly stand up to Mom. Belle shrugged. "He sort of left me alone. But I can't blame him. I sided with Mom on everything, well aware each time I did that it drove the wedge deeper between him and me. My actions pushed him closer to Penn, but she deserved someone in her corner."

"So did you." Nearly a whisper, his words exuded a quiet strength. "You still do."

No. What she deserved was not having her heart broken again. Safest way to ensure that meant not relying on others more than she relied on herself.

"We should get going so you'll have time to eat with us before your shift starts." She scooted away from him as she spoke. "Jonah's probably already fired up his grill."

"I'm sorry, Belle."

His words stopped her. "You've said that. Multiple times."

"Because I keep seeing new facets of how my leaving hurt you."

"What is it you think you see now?" Her trembling voice betrayed the false bravado she tried to pull off.

He caught it too. That slight tip of his head. The narrowing of his blue eyes. The uptick to the right corner of his mouth. All communicated as loudly as if he verbally called her out on the discrepancy.

Instead, he answered, "You're scared to rely on people because you don't want to get hurt again."

She stiffened at his spot-on diagnosis. "Can you blame me?"

"Not at all. I think it's a natural response to all the people who've left you, and I'm sorry my actions helped reinforce the lie you believe that relying solely on yourself is the safest way to live."

"It's not a lie."

"It may not feel like one, but just because you believe something doesn't make it the truth."

"Did you take counseling classes or something?"

He cracked a grin. "No. I went to counseling."

If he told her he'd flown to the moon, she'd be less surprised. "You what?"

"I saw a counselor in California, and I'm working on finding someone here."

"You're being serious here?"

"I am. It's how I learned I was believing a lie when I left you." Rubbing his neck, he sucked in a deep breath. "I haven't said anything because I don't want to excuse my actions. My leaving, that's on me. But you need to know that the night before our wedding, I told my dad we were pregnant."

She absorbed that fact. "We agreed we weren't telling until after the honeymoon."

"I know, and I wish every day I'd kept my mouth shut."

"Okay," she said slowly, trying to keep up with him.

"I was dealing with Walter's decision to prevent me from joining AllWaste. The fallout left me feeling so insignificant. I'd never been enough for my dad, so Walter's decision spilled those same thoughts over into my relationships with him and my family's company. That morphed into me believing the same about you and our baby. It was like this mental landslide I couldn't stop. My internship was pulling you away from a familiar city and your friends right after you found out you were pregnant. Plus, you wanted me in a nine-to-five job, and that wasn't happening. Then I talked to Dad, and he reinforced my feelings. Said you and our child would be better off if I left you."

"He actually told you to leave me?" Unbelievable.

"Strongly suggested it, and all I could think about was that he was right. I would never be enough for you, and in all my trying, it'd only lead to more fighting. And I couldn't raise a child in a home like that. I was drinking so much by then." Moisture gathered in his eyes, and his voice grew raw. "I honestly believed I was making the right choice for you. That you and our baby could find better than me."

Like tumblers in a lock sliding into place, his revelation finally provided a reason to why he left. No, it didn't change the hurt she'd endured or the fact that things remained broken between them, but she could understand. Reaching out, she squeezed his arm. "Micah, that's not an excuse, that's an explanation. All this time, I thought you didn't want us."

She started to pull away, but he captured her hand with his. "I did. I still do."

"I want to believe that. You have no idea how much."

"You can."

He tugged her closer and cupped her cheek. She closed her eyes, giving in to the feel of his touch. She missed it. Missed connecting with him. Wanted to believe they could have everything she'd once believed they could. But even with the answers to questions she'd held too long, there was still no guarantee he wouldn't leave again. Understanding all the reasons in the world why people left didn't change the fact that they did.

A sigh escaped him, and he released her, his hands resting along the tops of his legs. She nearly squirmed under his assessment of her, like he was trying to ascertain how to mend whatever remained broken between them. But he was the cause of her wounds. Could he also be the one to heal them?

She still didn't know.

But with every interaction and every conversation, she hoped more and more for that possibility to be true.

Chapter Fifteen

A nother letter from Walter. Micah ran his finger along the edges of the envelope. After his conversation with Belle over the weekend, he didn't feel right tossing it. But he couldn't open it either. Thing was, now *he* felt the awkwardness for allowing the grudge to go on as long as he had. What would he say to him?

Ultimately, it didn't matter. He couldn't drop truth bombs on Belle and pretend he didn't hear them slipping from his own mouth.

With a deep breath, he tore open the envelope and pulled out a single sheet of paper. On it was a simple sentence. "When you're ready, I'm here to talk." Underneath that was a phone number. It wasn't the one he remembered for Walter. At some point, he must have finally ditched the landline they'd always teased him about. He'd given that number to very few. Wonder if he guarded this one in the same way.

Micah pulled his phone from his pocket, heart thudding. He could do this. Walter had played a huge role in his life growing up. Filled the hole Dad had torn open in him. Which was why it hurt so badly when Walter passed him over for Jonah, even if that choice made logical sense. To his heart, it felt like one more person found him wanting. But there was no way Walter could have known how the impact of that decision would leave Micah susceptible to Dad's words the night before his wedding. Like throwing open the door holding a storm at bay, his insecurities roared, flooding him with lies he'd taken for the truth.

Counseling, prayer, and a few good friends helped him close that door and lock it for good. Yes, at times he could still hear those insecurities banging, but he refused to answer.

Which meant it was time to call Walter. Before any new excuses could arise, Micah punched in the numbers on the paper. The phone rang and his palms grew sweaty with each trill. After twenty seconds, it rolled to voicemail, and he hung up. This was not a conversation to be had via messaging. It had waited three years; it could wait a little while longer.

"Chloe, you want to go see Anna?"

The Havanese fur ball tore around the corner. She and Anna would be joined at the hip if Chloe stayed at Belle's permanently. He was sorely tempted to make that offer, but Belle would probably renege on letting him help her if she thought the scale was unbalanced.

As he loaded Chloe into his car, his cell rang. His pulse thrummed. Had Walter seen the unknown number and returned the call out of curiosity?

Yanking his phone from his pocket, he peered at the screen. His heart settled into a normal beat as he answered. "Hey, Jonathan. What's up?"

"You were on my mind, so I thought I'd call."

"Glad you did."

He wasted no time. "How're things going there?"

Micah filled him in on Mom's recent episode, all that was happening with Belle, and the possibility of Anna needing a small surgery. He ended with his attempt to call Walter.

"And you're trying to maintain your work schedule."

"Yeah. That too."

Olivia's soft baby chatter filled the background as Jonathan answered him. "That's a lot on you. Been tempted to drink?"

Lying transferred power from him to his old vice, and he refused to return to its grip. "A few times, but I haven't touched it."

"Any luck finding a counselor?"

"I met with one last week that felt like a fit. I'm seeing him again tonight."

"Good. Accountability is key."

Jonathan would know. He'd been there. And when someone walked through the fire and came out smelling like smoke and holding on to the ashes? Then not only survived, but thrived? That's who he wanted to listen to.

They chatted until he pulled up at Belle's. Anna played on the rickety playset while Astrid and a few of her group enjoyed cookies and coffee nearby. They were babysitting today while he and Belle worked on a few things in the shed.

He cringed as Anna slid down the wobbly slide. Next weekend, that thing would be gone. Wished it was sooner.

Her feet landed safely on the ground, and she looked up, saw him, saw Chloe, and squealed. He opened his door, expecting a hug, but she only had arms for Chloe. Yeah, so maybe he was a little jealous of a dog, but making Anna happy provided him the greatest joy. He longed to hear her call him Daddy, but even though she hadn't, he still loved to make her smile.

Anna tumbled onto the grass with Chloe. He somehow managed to clip the leash to the spastic fur ball, then Anna helped walk her over to Astrid and the gang. Their greeting was nearly as enthusiastic as the one he'd just witnessed.

With a wave goodbye, he crossed the lot to the small shed. Inside, Belle printed off labels with the printer he'd had installed. She smiled her hello as he strolled over and picked up a sheet. "These turned out really great."

"Sydney created them. I'm having her redesign the website too. She's incredibly talented."

"She is. So are you."

"Says you."

"Because it's true." He settled on a stool by the counter. "How's the sprinkler system coming? I saw the permit in your window, so they've started?"

"Yep. They'll do my apartment first and work their way down."

"Did you ever hear back from the concrete guys on the new steps out back?"

"I did. They're coming Tuesday."

"Remember, they're billing me." Her spine stiffened. There was one more thing he'd been putting off that might tighten it even more, but with Anna's appointment two days from now, he needed to finally toss it out there. "Along those same lines, I looked into adding Anna to my insurance. I have to wait until the start of our new year, which, with the hospital, is in October. Since that's pretty close, I thought we could ask her ENT to wait to schedule tubes—if she winds up needing them."

Belle started relabeling the bottles in front of her. Knowing she needed space to process, he checked emails on his phone. Sure enough, after a few minutes she turned to him.

"Have you also been looking into custody?" There was no malice in her tone, but he heard an underlying fear tremble beneath her steady voice.

"That's a discussion we'll have together. I know I have legal rights, but I will not pursue them on my own." He fixed a firm gaze on her. "No surprises. I promise."

She visibly relaxed. "Okay."

"Okay, as in you believe my promise? Or okay as in we'll add Anna to my insurance?"

"Both."

He didn't take her acceptance lightly. Standing, he joined her by the essential oils, the slightest hint of all their scents swirling in the air. "I know this isn't easy for you."

"No, it's not. All I keep thinking is how I get hurt when I depend on people." Her soft voice spoke of a truth that painted her past but didn't need to color her future. "But I don't want to keep doing things alone."

He wrapped his fingers around hers. A gentle touch meant to let her know she wasn't alone. "It's funny, isn't it? Relationships are a catch-22. We were created for relationship, so we want them, but they inevitably hurt us because we're all messed up in one way or another. When we hurt, we pull away, which makes us lonely. So we try it again, get hurt again, pull away again until finally we stop trying." A pause. "It takes courage to stay in the fight, and yeah, sometimes you need a breather, but you can't quit permanently." He squeezed her fingers. "You just determined you're not quitting."

Sliding her hand from his, she picked up an essential oil from the counter and stowed it with the others. "You've certainly gotten wise in your old age."

"Careful. We're the same age," he stated. "And, like I mentioned last week, counseling." Once upon a time, he'd thought seeing a psychologist signaled weakness. Now, standing on this side of some very productive therapy, he understood the strength of admitting a need for help and getting it. Not that perfection now defined his world, but he possessed a better ability to navigate any tough stuff thrown his way. And his past certainly loved lobbing all his faults straight at him.

"It definitely seems to have helped you find some perspective."

"It's helped me in a lot of ways." He watched her straighten a few bottles that didn't need straightening. An idea hit him. "Want to teach me how to make a jar of lotion?"

She peered at him over her shoulder, her brow crinkled. "Seriously?"

"Yeah. I think we could both use a little fun." He rolled up his sleeves. "Besides, if I see your process, maybe I can help you create that SOP manual."

"The process may take more than an afternoon."

"Have to start somewhere, right?"

"Okay, but I feel the need to warn you. Most of those had some pretty nasty beginnings before I arrived at the finished product."

He wasn't scared of a little stink. "I'm game if you are."

"All right." She nodded toward the shelf with scents. "Grab the sandalwood, clove, and vetiver."

"Veti-what?"

"It's labeled. Just grab it."

With everything alphabetized, he easily found it. Once she'd assembled all the ingredients, she walked him through the process right up to where the scents were added. "We'll start with equal measures, and then I'll bump one up to see which should be dominant." After blending the mixture, she dabbed a wooden stick in and retrieved a sample. She held it to her nose, and then to his. "What do you think?"

"It's not right, but I couldn't tell you why."

"So don't try and figure out what's wrong. Focus on what's right."

He leaned closer and inhaled again, closing his eyes. "The spiciness of the clove is good, but there's this … grass? Am I smelling grass?" He opened his eyes.

"That's the vetiver."

"It's not bad, but …" He rubbed the spot behind his ear as he walked over to the other bottles on the shelf. One jumped out at him. "Are you making this for a guy or a girl?"

"Both. I'd like a scent that anyone can use."

Smart. It definitely filled a hole in her current product line.

He reached for the bottle and brought it to her. She scrunched her lips as she took it. "Lavender? No man is going to buy lavender."

"Says you. Because this man just picked it out."

Shaking her head, she opened the oil and dumped a few drops in. As she stirred, she mumbled, "Pretty sure your man card just got revoked."

Oh, really.

He slid in behind her, both hands palming the counter on either side of her waist as he skimmed his cheek along the soft skin of hers. Forget whatever scent they were concocting, she smelled amazing. Roses. All woman. Traces of that soft aroma could linger on him every day if it meant he'd been close to her.

"What was that about my man card?" He kept his voice low. "I'm not sure I heard you."

She'd stilled when he moved close, but as he spoke, a shiver raked through her. Her face turned ever-so-slightly, her lips traveling dangerously close to his. "I was saying," she haltingly whispered.

"Mmmhmm?" he coaxed.

Now she fully turned and palmed his chest, giving a tiny shove. "Could you back up a bit?'

He straightened his arms, allowing a fraction of an inch more room. "Better?"

Her eyes stayed focused on his chest. He flexed, and she lifted a massive eye roll. "Overcompensate much?"

"Oh, sweetie, I haven't even begun to overcompensate for that comment." His grin chased the warning, and he dropped his lips to the spot where her neck and jaw met. He slid his hands to her waist and tugged her to him, relishing her swift inhale of breath. But what made it all the sweeter was how she tipped her head, as if inviting him closer.

Man, did he want to accept that invite. His body hummed with a building desire that reminded him he played with fire. This was not the way to fix what lie broken between them.

He pulled away before his mouth actually made contact, instead trailing his breath up to her ear. "Let's be clear. I don't wear flannel, and I actually spend a few minutes on my hair. The only sport I tolerate is football, and I've been known to enjoy the theater. But my man card is most definitely intact." Pressing a kiss to her cheek, he took a step back, rubbing the nape of his neck. "Which is why I'm not letting my hormones make the next move."

Her closed eyes popped open, deep blue and hazy with the same heat that had him taking another step away. She blinked, a tiny shiver going through her, but this one helped clear her focus. "Thank you."

"Uh, for what?"

"For stopping." With both hands, she shoved her hair from her face. "I don't know what came over me."

Couldn't help it. He chuckled. "You and I have never had an issue with starting things up, Belle." He hid nothing in his expression as he said the next words. "And we're good together. Very good." There was no use denying it or pretending their attraction wasn't palpable—or that they didn't have very clear memories of being together.

Ones playing through her mind too, judging by that blush. He rammed his fists into his pockets. "But I never should have let things go that far back then. If I couldn't commit to you in marriage, I never should have committed to you in bed." It wouldn't happen again. "This time, I don't want to give you the *good* parts of me. You deserve my best in every area. Especially in my restraint." Which became easier to deploy the more he focused on his reason behind it. "Because I want the best for us."

"Isn't it a little late for that?"

"Nah." He reached out with the softness of his voice rather than a touch. "It's never too late. Not if we both want it. We just have to try." He picked up the bottle of white lotion they'd mixed. "Kind of like what you said about creating this stuff. Some of your scents started off pretty awful, but you didn't give up, and now you have some best sellers."

"That's not there yet."

She wasn't talking about the lotion. "I know."

She hesitated, then pointed to herself. "I'm not sure if I'll ever get there."

"I know that too." But he had enough hope for them both. "How about we focus on making this right, and take the rest as it comes?"

Rebuilding trust took time, and his love would be patient.

She held up the lavender bottle. "You sure about this?"

"It's a place to start."

"All right." She studied the glass container, rolling it between her thumb and forefinger. "Let's give it a try." Then she peeked up at him. "But I make no promises. We could be creating a disaster."

"I choose to believe we'll wind up with something pretty amazing."

No response, but he did catch the tiny uptick of her lips. More progress. As always, he'd take it.

"Read again." Anna bounced on Belle's lap, waving her favorite *Elephant and Piggie* book in Belle's face. They'd already read it four times.

Belle grabbed the book before Anna accidentally smacked her in the face, then checked her watch. She lobbed a tired look at the door. The one Micah should have walked through ten minutes ago, but he was still MIA. Four unanswered phone calls had rolled to voicemail that he'd yet to return.

That wasn't the only thing rolling.

She unclenched her jaw, flipped open the book, and did her best imitation of Piggie's jovial voice. She oughta win an Oscar for this happy performance.

"Anna?" A sweet-smiling nurse with Bugs Bunny scrubs called from the hall.

With one last glance at the vacant doorway, Belle picked up Anna. "It's our turn, Monkey."

She battled her encroaching anger and attempted to fully concentrate on her baby girl. As the nurse charted Anna's vitals, Belle reminded herself that Micah must have a good reason for not being here. While Dr. Clinard looked in Anna's ears, Belle contemplated different emergency scenarios that could have prevented Micah from contacting her. And thirty minutes later, as she and Anna stopped at the surgical scheduling window, Belle did her best to maintain a semblance of peace.

"Do you have insurance?" Hair in a sensible cut to match her sensible suit, the woman peered at her across a tiny desk.

"Um, I'm not sure." She barely stopped the word *no* from escaping. Micah didn't have to be present for Anna to be on his insurance, but he did need to follow through on filling out the paperwork. Right now, Belle wasn't holding her breath.

Anna fidgeted in the chair beside her.

The woman, whose tag read Bonnie, tipped her head. "You're not sure?"

"It's a complicated situation." She motioned with her eyes toward Anna, hoping Bonnie would understand and fought off a wave of embarrassment.

At least she picked up on Belle's nonverbal cues. "Okay. We'll get you on the schedule, and then you can call us once you've had a chance to figure out those details."

Belle chose a date in mid-fall like Micah had suggested, then scooped Anna up. They made it into the parking lot when his car careened around the corner.

He slammed it into park and hopped out, hair sticking in every direction, shirt untucked and wrinkled, and socked feet shoved into sandals. She was trying to give him the benefit of the doubt—really, she was—but the way he looked erased all acceptable excuses she'd contrived for him in the past hour.

"Mista Micah!" Anna wiggled in Belle's arms.

"Hey, Monkey." He caught her as she catapulted herself from Belle's arms to his, but his attention remained on Belle. "I am so sorry."

His apology sounded sweet, but she was through with his sweet words. Especially when his appearance created an awful alibi. It screamed that he'd overslept. Would he admit it? "What held you up?"

Her anger rose right along with that flush creeping up his neck.

To his credit, not only did he own his screw-up, he also didn't sugarcoat it. "I overslept."

Belle held out her hands for Anna.

"Mista Micah come pway with us?" she asked.

"Sounds like Mista Micah has more important things to do today."

"Belle," he said as he followed her to her car, "that's not fair."

"You really want to talk fair right now, Micah?" Because he sure wasn't acting fair. He expected her to trust him, then reneged on the promise he made her. This wasn't work that kept him away. It was his bed. Sleep trumped his daughter's appointment. She seethed but couldn't go full force on him in front of Anna. Even now, their little girl tipped her head, watching.

He must have noticed Anna's awareness too, because he waited until Belle had her buckled in her car seat. She walked around and started the engine, turning the AC on full blast and closing the door. Then she turned and laid into him. Didn't need volume to get this point across. "This right here is why I don't want to try again with you. You make promises you can't keep, and this time it's not only my heart on the line. I refuse to allow you to disappoint Anna the way you disappointed me."

"Are you kidding me right now?"

"Do I look like I am?" What did he have to be upset about?

Looked like he was going to tell her. "I overslept because silly me thought I could clock an hour between work and here." He paced in front of her. "I am running myself into the ground trying to prove to you that I've changed. If I'm not working or with my mom, I'm at your place. I've run your Lamaze classes, fixed your door, set up your shed, and worked through that FDA list with you—"

"So what? You're keeping some scorecard?"

"No! I'm trying to remind you because it seems like you've forgotten." He stopped and tossed his hands in the air. "And if anyone's keeping a scorecard, it's you. It has one huge mark on it—I left you—written in permanent ink, so no matter what I do, I can't win."

"Leaving me was a pretty *huge* thing. I'm sorry I won't lie down and let you roll right over me and back into my life."

"You think I'm asking you to be a doormat?" He yanked on the ends of his hair. "Your perception is so far off you don't need glasses, you need a telescope."

"That doesn't even make sense."

"Good! Now I'm not the only one completely baffled." He looked up, muttered something, then focused on her again. "How do we keep ending up here? It's like a circle I can't escape."

"No one's holding you here."

He gripped his neck as if he was trying to do just that. After a moment, he slipped his hand into his pocket like he'd relinquished the effort. "If you can't see that everything I've done this past month has centered on helping you, then there's nothing else I can say. I'm not going to stand here and argue with you in the middle of a parking lot." He backed away. "I need to see my mom. You're not the only person I let down this morning, but you are the only one who won't forgive me. Guess I should be used to it by now."

Then he spun on his heel, got in his car, and drove away.

Belle stood there, watching him. Anna knocked on her window, and Belle climbed in the car.

"Where Mista Micah go?"

"To see his mommy."

"We go too?"

Belle propped her hands on her steering wheel as her mind raced through the morning. She had forgiven Micah, hadn't she? Except as she filtered through the weeks he'd been home, it hit her. As many times as he'd said he was sorry, and even when he'd told her the reasons behind his leaving, she hadn't uttered those three words. Yet he'd shown up continuously on her doorstep, not once pressuring her for them.

Whether or not they had a future as a couple, she needed to say them, because she did forgive him.

"Yeah, Monkey. We go too."

Firing up her car, she pointed it to Brookhaven. He'd waited long enough, and—even if her response had been in reflex to their past—she'd been pretty awful to him this morning. No, he shouldn't have overslept, but he really had been burning the candle at both ends. At some point, his body was bound to give out, and she was just thankful it hadn't been in the form of relapsing with a drink.

She pulled into the nursing home, unbuckled Anna, and made her way to Sharon's room. Micah looked up as Anna barreled inside. Surprise widened his eyes, but caution quickly narrowed them.

"Can I talk to you?" Belle softly asked.

He pulled Anna's arms from around his neck. "Sure." Then he set her in Sharon's lap and turned cartoons on the small TV. "We'll be right back."

"Okay," the two responded, attention already on the show.

Micah followed Belle into the hall. Two nurses walked their way.

She rubbed her thumbnail, waiting until they passed, before uttering those three words. "I forgive you."

His brows lifted. "You forgive me? Wow. Okay."

Not quite the reaction she expected. In fact, it almost had a sarcastic edge.

He released a wry laugh. "You know, Belle, for someone who always hated the expectation of perfection, you sure do love measuring me by that yardstick. Here's a news flash, though, I will never measure up, because *I'm human*." He moved to return to his mom's room. "So thanks for forgiving me for my fleshly mistake. I appreciate it."

Oh, he'd completely misunderstood her.

"Wait!"

He actually stopped, but he didn't turn around. "What?" Weariness pulled the word into two syllables.

"I meant, I forgive you for leaving me." Now she made circles on both thumbnails as he faced her. "I, well, I realized after you left earlier that I've never actually said that to you, but you've apologized numerous times. I'm pretty obviously still dealing with some trust issues, but I do forgive you."

His shoulders lifted in a long sigh. "Thank you."

She'd come this far; she might as well keep moving because she'd acted ugly in that parking lot and he deserved her apology right along with her forgiveness. "And I'm sorry for arguing before. I understand why you overslept, and I don't think you want me to be a doormat."

The corner of his lip hitched up. "I don't think you're in any danger of that happening." Down the hall, something beeped in one of the rooms. "I really am sorry for oversleeping. I would love to hear how Anna's appointment went."

She opened her mouth to tell him when Sharon's doctor walked up.

"Micah, can I have a minute?"

He looked caught. Belle made the decision for him. "It's okay. Go. I'll fill you in when you get done."

"You sure?"

"Positive."

He nodded and followed the doctor.

Belle slipped into Sharon's room. She and Anna still watched an old *Tom and Jerry* episode. Belle picked up a pair of Sharon's socks and walked them to her laundry basket. A picture on the dresser caught her attention, and she picked it up. Squinted. It was yellowed with age, and the man in it looked like Micah.

"Oh," Sharon spoke as Anna wiggled from her lap to haul out toys from her backpack. "I pulled that out for you. It's such a handsome picture of Micah, isn't it?"

It had to be from about thirty years ago. Must be Todd, but it looked more like … no, she was seeing things. "Yes. It's a great picture." With one last hard look, she placed it on the dresser, then crossed over and settled on the couch. "Speaking of Micah, he's talking with the doctor. He'll be back."

"Wonderful." Sharon peeked toward the door. "I hope he has my letters. My father gave them to me, and I want to give them to Micah. He needs them." She looked her way. "You'd like them too."

Before she could respond, Micah returned. "They're serving lunch. Anyone else hungry?"

Anna hopped up from the floor. "I hungry!"

He looked at Belle.

She looked at Sharon. "Mind if we join you?"

"That sounds wonderful."

They made their way to the dining room. Today was a good day. While Sharon's mind struggled to stay in the present, she was calm and able to keep up with their simple conversation. Laughter made its way around the table as Anna charmed Sharon. Their bond as Nana and granddaughter remained strong even though Sharon didn't remember it this afternoon.

As they returned to her room, Micah leaned down to Belle. "Days like this are becoming fewer and farther between. I'm learning to cherish them."

She couldn't imagine how hard this had to be on him, watching his mother disappear right before his eyes. Still physically here, but mentally so far away. It was tough enough for Belle, and Sharon wasn't even her mother. Of course, her own mothers—birth and adoptive—had both willfully chosen to desert her. No sickness forced them to. So, maybe she could understand in some small way. She squeezed his hand. "I'm sorry you're going through this."

His fingers closed around hers. "Thanks for coming."

She heard the full intention behind his words. The relief that she'd followed him here rather than let their argument fester. She had to admit, even though it'd been hard, it felt a whole lot better than stewing in her anger all day.

"You're welcome." She smiled.

They settled Sharon in her room, then headed out to the parking lot, Anna swinging between their hands. Micah looked over at Belle. "Got plans for the rest of the day?"

"Working some more on figuring out that batch system. Then I'm covering the store." Above them, the sun shone in a bright blue sky. The temperature crested eighty, and a slight breeze buffered them, all the makings of a perfect summer day. "You?"

"There's a project I'm starting on." That was all he said. No further details, and she shouldn't press, even if her curiosity begged her to.

"Okay. Well, good luck with that."

"Thanks." His mischievous smile spiked her curiosity, but he waved and jogged to his car with no further explanation.

Belle started hers and exited the lot, her mind caught on what Micah might be up to.

About three minutes down the road, she noticed he trailed her in traffic. Strange. He should have turned the other way. Another two minutes, and it was obvious he was following her. Had he forgotten to tell her something? But then he'd call, right?

Her focus split between the road and Micah, she nearly missed the load of lumber in her backyard as she pulled around her building to park. She hopped out, taking in a few plastic pieces in bright colors, ones that looked an awful lot like portions of a tunnel slide.

Micah parked beside her, shut off his engine, and got out, that grin still engulfing his face.

"This is your project?" she asked.

"Yep." His hands slid into his pockets.

She faced him, hands on her hips, wonder in her voice. "Micah Shaw, what are you up to now?"

Didn't matter what he responded, because she already knew the answer—he was up to the same thing he'd been working on since he'd burst into her life again: winning back her heart.

Chapter Sixteen

There was something about making Belle smile that made him feel every inch the man he wanted to be. And when Anna added in that full wattage of hers? He was a goner. Anything she wanted, he'd give her.

"You're building a new playset?" Belle held Anna in one hand and Chloe's leash in the other while her blue, widened eyes roamed from the pile of lumber to him.

"Yep." Quite the eloquent response, but more and more, he discovered these two girls possessed the ability to yank the words from his mouth, the breath from his lungs, and his heart from his chest.

Belle swung Anna's hand. "You hear that, Monkey? Mr. Micah's gonna build you a new slide."

Anna's smile grew even larger, and she did her silly little dance he loved to watch. He looked at Belle, and they shared a laugh over their daughter's antics. Felt good. So much better than their earlier parking lot rumble. He longed for the day when these were the moments that characterized their relationship. When Belle's reflex would be to assume the best in him, not the worst. Anna tugged on his jeans. "When my slide here?"

He squatted. "Tomorrow."

A car pulled into the lot behind Belle, but she didn't turn, her full focus remaining on him. "Tomorrow?" She tipped her head, one hand shielding her eyes from the sun. "How big is this thing going to be if it's taking two days to build?"

"A little bigger than the old one."

"A lot bigger judging by that pile." Jonah strolled up, hands on his hips and teasing in his eyes. "What have you gotten me into?"

Penny, Rachael, Gavin, and another man he hadn't met followed Jonah over. Belle turned. "You're all helping?"

"Yep." Penelope hauled her sister into a hug, her belly creating an awkward angle. "Well, most of us. I have strict orders to stay away from sharp tools and heavy lifting."

Jonah sent her a tender look. "You're doing plenty of heavy lifting."

Belle doled out hugs around the circle. Micah didn't think anything of it until she reached the strange guy dressed in flannel who easily towered over her. The man had muscles that said he stayed in shape and a perceptive look that said he missed nothing. Including how Micah eyed him with Belle. The guy broke off the hug and walked his way, hand extended. "I'm Evan Wayne. Neighbor of Jonah and Penny when they're here in town."

"Neighbor? And here I thought you lived with them because you're always there." Rachael joined them, hand to her mouth as if she meant to utter her next words to Micah alone. "And his name's actually Bruce. As in Bruce Wayne."

"It's Bruce *Evan* Wayne," he amended, "because, yes, my parents thought it would be cute to name me after Batman. It's not."

Rachael fixed a look of pure innocence on him. "Oh, you heard that?"

He mimicked her expression. "Of course I did. Maybe if you didn't listen to that racket you call music at decibels far above the local noise ordinance, your ears wouldn't be shot, and you'd recognize the difference between shouting and whispering."

"These two at it again?" Gavin joined him. No longer a gangly thirteen-year-old fresh off chemo, he'd grown at least six inches, sprouted a thick head of dark brown hair, and dropped the pounds that steroids had added. Not to mention the muscular evidence that he worked out regularly. Looking at him now, no one would know he'd nearly lost his life to cancer.

Micah shook Gavin's hand. "They do this often?"

"Careful, son. You may be taller than me"—Rachael warned with a mock glare—"but I can still reach your ear." She grabbed for it.

He swatted her away. Beside them, Anna squealed as Jonah zerberted her. He joined them along with Penny and Belle, who hadn't wiped the look of awe from her face. It was about to grow because across the lot, the doors of the retirement center opened and the gang exited. Micah waved, and they returned the gesture. "I may have enlisted a few more helpers too."

Wetness pooled in her eyes. "You didn't have to do this. You've already done so much, and this is"—she hesitated—"extra. It doesn't have to be done. Especially with how I acted earlier."

Ignoring the audience, Micah stepped into Belle's space. He cupped her shoulders and leaned down until his eyes were level with hers. It hit him then, how lucky he was that she allowed him close enough to capture the minute details in them. Most people would walk past and only notice their brilliant blue. Few were intimately allowed in to see the silver streaking through them. The navy ring encircling a bright ocean blue.

Right then, he vowed to be the last man she gave that privilege to.

"First off, we've moved past earlier, so let it go. Second, stop telling me I've done enough. There isn't a limit when it comes to you and Anna, because love is limitless. That's how it works."

Tears crested over her eyes like a wave rolling into shore. "Love?"

A puff of breath escaped him much like that word had. No use denying it, though. "Yeah, love. I've always loved you, Belle. I just haven't always done it the right way."

She swallowed.

The retirement gang's voices grew closer while everyone else stood a few feet away, pretending not to listen. Micah squeezed Belle's shoulders, then slid his hands down her arms before releasing her. He wasn't looking for a response. Part of loving her the right way involved giving her the space and time to heal. Reality was, they might never be more than co-parents, but he determined that no matter what, love would mark their relationship.

Love is patient.

Yeah. He was learning that one.

"We'd better get started. I told Anna tomorrow, and it'll be ready tomorrow."

Belle grabbed her sister and Rachael. "We'll go upstairs and make some snacks for you guys." She motioned to the crew from next door. "Ladies, want to help me?"

Jonah stepped beside him as the women headed upstairs. Behind them, Evan and the old men checked out the piles of product. Hands in his pockets, standing shoulder to shoulder, his cousin turned to look at him. "So you two are getting along then?"

"For the most part."

"Hmm." Jonah rocked on his heels with a laugh. "For the most part, it seems you may be downplaying things a tad."

"Or it's that I don't want to get my hopes up." Especially after this morning.

Jonah turned until they were face-to-face, and he blocked Belle's retreating form. "Get your hopes up. Dive fully in. Love doesn't fear. It hopes. Even when things look dim."

"Not sure how much dimmer it can get than me walking out on her while she carried our child." He snapped his fingers. "Oh, right. I did that *while* she waited in a wedding gown at a church filled with our family and friends."

Jonah cuffed him upside the head.

"Ow!" Micah rubbed his temple. "What was that for?"

He shrugged. "You were doing such a good job pummeling yourself, I figured you wouldn't mind if I took a swing too. After all, I owed you one."

"Which you said you forgave me for and weren't going to collect."

"So wait, when someone forgives you something, they're not supposed to still hold it over your head?"

"No."

"Good. I'm glad we both agree on that part." He squeezed Micah's shoulder. "You've been asking everyone else to forgive you, Micah, but you forgot one important person on that list." He paused but didn't need to say the word, because his steely gaze—eyes so much like Gramps's—spoke it loudly enough. "You."

Sometimes truth hurt. But sometimes … Sometimes it did the exact opposite. It lifted the pain carried so long a man didn't even realize the weight of it until it released.

Micah blinked and cleared his throat. "I invited you to work on the playset, not me."

"Two for the price of one. You're a lucky guy."

Huffing a short laugh, Micah clapped Jonah on the back—"That I am"—then stepped away. "How about we get moving on this stuff?"

"Hit your emotional quota for the day, and it's time to break things, huh?"

"Well, I plan on building something, not breaking it, but yeah."

Jonah followed him to the pile of lumber. "Sounds like a great analogy in the making there."

Micah grunted. "If I didn't know better, I'd say Penny and your impending fatherhood have softened you up." He peered over at him. "Except you've always been a softy."

They stopped beside the other guys, who looked as entertained as if they were watching an old Andy Griffith rerun.

"I prefer the term 'in touch with my emotions.'" Jonah grinned wide. A new light in his eyes that said he was one lucky guy. "And Penelope loves it, so I'm not changing."

Easy to say, for a man who had it all together. Change was the only hope Micah had to land in that same spot. That place where the woman he loved looked at him in a way that held him there. Made him proud of the man he was and sent roots so deep, not even a hurricane wind could yank them out.

Hands full, Evan joined them. "Lucky you're not around those two all the time. This pregnancy has made them even more sickeningly sweet."

"Sounds like you've known them for a little while."

"Ever since they bought their place in Holland."

"Evan's a cop," Jonah noted. "He keeps an eye on our place in the winter, and we've enticed him to visit Chicago a few times."

Micah tipped his head. "Not a fan of big cities?"

"Not really. But Chicago has grown on me." He looked at the miter saw in his hands. "Where's a good spot for me to set this up?"

Micah pointed him to an area by the building where their power cords would reach. As he walked off, Gavin followed with the rolling saw stand.

Marv and the boys joined Micah. "Where are we starting today?" Marv asked.

Micah laid out the plans he'd settled on. Two double-floored towers connected by a bridge, with monkey bars and swings between them. A short wavy slide extended from the lower half of the left tower, while the right tower held a curvy tunnel slide off the top floor, along with a climbing rope and wall. Both sides had benches inside the first floors, with steering wheels and telescopes along with a few other fun pieces to explore.

After removing the broken structure, the old guys started building one tower while Evan and Gavin tackled the other. While they worked, Micah tapped Jonah to help him dig a few holes.

"This plan doesn't call for holes." Jonah pointed to the papers.

"They're for something else." Micah walked to the corner of the play area.

Jonah followed. "We're building more than the world's biggest swing set?"

He unfolded a piece of paper from his pocket. "We're building this."

Jonah scanned it. "An arbor swing?"

"For Belle." Anna wasn't the only one he wanted to spoil. "She needs someplace to watch Anna while she plays."

"Let's get to it then."

A couple of hours later, the two bases for the swing set rose tall, while footings for Belle's arbor stood in place, the concrete drying around them. They'd managed to create the monkey bars and the beginnings of the bridge, and now they needed to heft it up and screw it in place. Hopefully, Micah wouldn't drop his end. Exhaustion seeped into his bones a little more with each board he hauled, nail he pounded, and screw he drilled into place. He'd caught a few extra Zs when he overslept his alarm earlier, yet sleep still sought him much like first-year interns sought his approval.

"We're ready when you are." Marv's voice penetrated the fog around him.

Lyle and Don chuckled beside him. "I think he fell asleep on his feet," Don said.

"I'm awake." Barely. Even with all the caffeine he'd consumed each time the women brought new drinks and snacks. But as much as he needed sleep, he wasn't about to break his promise to Anna to have this finished by tomorrow.

"Okay, then let's get this in place." Jonah lifted the end of another beam and followed Micah over. He grunted under the strain of the weight, shifting his hold to set it into place. Gavin threw a level on the boards, then nodded to Evan, who started driving the screws.

Jonah's arms shook, but he held strong. "Any luck finding those letters for your mom?"

"Nope." Micah welcomed the distraction from the burn in his arms. "Belle and I went through all Mom's boxes in the basement and didn't find a thing. She wonders if they exist, and I'm starting to think the same thing. Feels like I've checked every nook and cranny in that house."

"Nook and cranny?" Jonah arched his brow.

Don stood near the second tower and checked that things were level there. "I think we're rubbing off on him."

"Glad for it to happen." Micah's muscles ached under the weight of the load he held. "Especially if you transfer some of that wisdom you've gained on women. You guys seem to have them all figured out." If he and Belle could manage to snatch even a small portion of what flowed between these guys and their wives, he'd be one happy man.

Deep belly laughs peppered the air. Marv's morphed into a fit of coughing, and Don smacked him hard on the back.

"We ain't got them figured out," Marv finally said around a breath. Evan drove the final screw in, and Micah and Jonah released the bridge as Marv kept right on talking. "No one figures out women. You'll spend a lifetime trying, and that's not long enough." His old eyes twinkled as he looked at Fran sitting under a shade tree with Astrid and Betty. "But that trying sure is fun."

"Sure is." Lyle joined them, a tender smile that flirted with sadness softening his face. "Wouldn't have traded a moment with my Ruth."

"She was a good woman," Don quietly said. "No one made peanut butter cake like her."

"My mouth waters thinking about it," Marv added.

Lyle's hands rubbed up and down his suspenders. "I even miss her burnt cookies."

More laughter. The kind that filled the space between grief and treasured memories.

Don dragged a handkerchief over his forehead, wiping away sweat. "I'll tell Betty to burn some for you next time she makes them."

"She have trouble with cookies?" Micah asked.

"No, my Ruthie made the best cookies around." Lyle smacked his lips. "But when we were first married, she burned a batch. I came into the kitchen and found her in tears, so I picked one up and bit into it. Made a big fuss about how surprised I was that she knew burnt cookies were my favorite, and I proceeded to eat the entire panful." He sighed. "Never did get anything but burnt cookies from then on. She'd make an entire perfect batch, then burn one just for me."

"And I bet you wouldn't change a thing should you have the chance to do it over," Jonah noted.

"You'd win that bet." Lyle picked up a short board and tapped it against his hand. "Loving someone isn't always about the sweet stuff. You gotta take the tough stuff too. Every time I ate one of those cookies, I'd think about that."

Micah pointed at Lyle. "And that's the wisdom I was talking about."

"I got some wisdom to add too." Marv tugged on the bill of his John Deere trucker hat. "Someone better test them monkey bars before we get to the next step."

Right. They had a playset to build and a ticking clock that closely resembled a towheaded nearly three-year-old.

Walking over, Micah grabbed two bars and dropped his weight, then swayed back and forth. He moved along, testing each bar. The structure didn't budge.

"So?" Jonah stood facing him.

The strong base did its job, holding everything in place. "I think we're ready for the next step."

As they grabbed more wood, it wasn't lost on him the parallel this project had to his relationship with Belle. Getting rid of the old, rickety beginning, because nothing safe had been built on it. Creating a new, solid footing that could hold their full weight. Testing it. Trusting it. Adding onto it.

It was the adding on that gave him pause, because while he was more than ready to take that next step, Belle wasn't. Sure, he could play on her lingering attraction to him, but he wanted more. He wanted all of her.

If someone had told her three years ago that this was how she'd be spending her Sunday night, she'd have laughed in their face. Yet sitting here at King's Club, surrounded by friends her grandparents' age and her ex-fiancé, the only laughter she experienced was spurred on by the amateur comedian on stage.

Hearty applause capped off the elderly gentleman's act as Micah leaned close to Belle. "Astrid's next." His knee bounced while Astrid confidently strolled on stage to join the MC announcing her.

"Relax. She comes here once a month. This is old hat for her."

"But she said she's trying out some new tricks."

Belle still blamed that announcement for her rogue idea that she and Micah attend as moral support. Yesterday, after finishing the play mansion he'd built their daughter, everyone gathered for a picnic. Astrid shared she'd be debuting a few new magic tricks tonight, and that's when Belle's mouth overrode her common sense. Out popped the invite to Micah that they show up to encourage her. He didn't even hesitate, just smiled and said he wouldn't miss it for the world.

The ease with which he'd answered and then turned that dimpled smile her way had Belle worried he'd mistaken this for some sort of disguised date. He couldn't be more wrong. This was all about supporting their friend, not finding ways to spend more time with him. And to ensure they both knew that fact, she invited the rest of the Grands to join them and volunteered to drive everyone in her minivan. Absolutely nothing about that set-up said "date."

The lights dimmed and a spotlight surrounded Astrid. The sparkles on her glittery silver dress lit up like stars, her smile the brightest shine of all. "Good evening. For my first trick, I need a volunteer." Nearly all the little old men's hands shot up, and her gaze landed on someone in the front row. "Max, you haven't had a turn in a while. How about you come on up here and help me out."

"It's like she's got groupies." Micah scanned the crowd.

Belle laughed. "Maybe we should make them T-shirts."

His soft chuckles joined hers.

"Quiet you two," Fran scolded, though the smile on her face said she was more bark than bite.

For the next twenty minutes, Astrid commanded the stage. She made Max's wallet disappear and then reappear—with her number in it. Birds magically materialized in a cage, then turned into a cat surrounded by feathers. She quickly reassured the gasping audience that the birds were unharmed. As she whistled, they flew from the rafters to her shoulder. But the best was her ability to predetermine another random volunteer's favorite number. That reveal involved her correct guess tucked into the MC's tuxedo pocket.

She left the stage to a standing ovation led by Max. As the next act took the floor, Astrid joined their small round booth at the rear of the room.

Micah stood and let her slide in beside her friends. "You were amazing."

"Thanks." She scooted close to Betty. "I owe it all to my Titus. He taught me everything I know."

"Way I recall it, you taught him a thing or two as well," Marv added.

Having waited for Astrid, they all ordered light snacks to share. She'd been one of the first performers of the night, and they didn't seem to be in any hurry to leave. Surprisingly, neither was Micah.

Belle studied him over their plate of chicken wings. As much as she'd tried to deny it, he'd changed. Still wasn't sure if she fully trusted the change, but she couldn't ignore the evidence any longer. He worked himself to near exhaustion as he finished his residency, helped her and Anna, and maintained a constant presence for his mom. Last night she found him asleep on a blanket beside the playset he'd built. Anna had curled up beside him, and the sight cracked Belle's heart open another notch. Tonight, he was here with the oldest crowd they'd ever hung out with, drinking Coke instead of a martini. In fact, she hadn't seen him touch a drink in all these weeks, which supported the promise he'd made that he was through with alcohol. Not that she was with him every second, but his house didn't have any open containers sitting out, and he never smelled or acted like he was consuming again.

He glanced up from his third wing and caught her staring. "What?" He swiped his cheek. "Do I have sauce all over me?"

"No." She quickly snagged her iced tea and sipped. "Sorry. I was just lost in thought."

"Oh?" There went his dimple. "Good ones, I hope."

Big band music bounced from the stage. Marv motioned for Micah to move. "Time to let me out, son. I'm gonna dance with my girl."

"Me too," Lyle nodded to Belle. "If you'd be so kind as to let us out."

Smiling at the group, the two couples exited to the dance floor. Only Astrid remained. Micah wiped his mouth and hands, took a long sip of water, then held his palm out to her with his most charming smile. "May I have this dance?"

And Belle's heart cracked open even wider.

Astrid looked at Belle, who offered a slight nod. Micah wasn't hers to claim, so Astrid wasn't cutting her out of a dance.

Her old friend accepted Micah's hand. "Try and keep up."

His deep laughter echoed as he followed Astrid to the floor. What Astrid didn't know was she and Micah had taken dance lessons prior to their wedding, and he would have no problem keeping up. In fact, he twirled her around the floor until she looked giddy and breathless, a side-effect of being in Micah's arms that Belle should have warned her about. She never thought watching him dance with another woman would produce those same feelings inside her, but his tenderness with Astrid brought them out in full force.

"Pretty gals shouldn't be sitting alone." Max stood beside her booth, his hat in his hands. "Would you care to dance?"

How could she refuse his adorableness? "I'd love to."

As they took the floor, he twirled her once. "Name's Max."

She nodded. "I saw you on stage earlier. I'm Belle." She kept pace with his steps. Surrounded by her friends, good music, and laughter, she hadn't had this much fun in ages. Happiness slipped over her, sealing the memory with a bow of joy. It was an evening she didn't even know she needed but would never forget.

After two fast dances, the band slowed the tempo, and the old crooner spoke into the mic. "This next song isn't an oldie, but it's a goodie. It's a special request for my granddaughter, who's here tonight with her new husband. She had me learn it for their wedding."

As the notes shifted to familiar ones, Belle stilled. Oh, no. It couldn't be.

"You know this song?" Max asked her.

"Um, yes, it's by a guy named Ed Sheeran."

"Ed who?" He leaned in and practically yelled. Apparently his hearing aids suddenly stopped working.

But there stood Micah, out of nowhere, supplying the answer. "Ed Sheeran."

Astrid took Max by the arm. "Care to buy this girl a drink?"

He looked at Belle. Selfishly, she wanted to keep him as her shield, but one look at Micah's determined face said it wouldn't work anyway. "That's fine, Max. Thanks for the dance."

He nodded and walked off with Astrid. Micah's focus never left Belle. She could feel it hot on her as the strands of "Perfect" played around them. The old man singing the lyrics nailed the song too. Bittersweet memories kept her eyes anywhere but on Micah's.

That didn't stop him from speaking. "I believe I owe you this dance."

Owe?

She stepped back. "You don't owe me anything, Micah."

His fingers gripped hers, preventing her escape. "Yes, I do." He squeezed. "I owe you a good memory to replace the bad one I created." He leaned down until she had no choice but to meet his ocean blue eyes. "Would you give me that chance?"

In his broken voice, she heard what he was truly asking. Would she give *them* a chance?

The song was only a quarter in, and the melody kept moving. Just like time had continued ticking these past three years. Driving them away from one another then somehow bringing them back together. Here. In this moment. And it felt like the choice she made now held power over where they'd go from here.

She wasn't ready to trust that everything would work out between them.

But she still wasn't ready to walk away.

"Okay." One word. Barely a whisper.

But he heard it because a relieved breath escaped him, and he tugged her close. His arms encapsulated her into his warm embrace. She rested her cheek against his chest as they swayed. They didn't use one of the fancy steps they'd learned for this dance. Instead, he wrote a new memory over the old one, just like he promised.

His chest rumbled as he hummed along with the band, and he held tight as if trying to ensure her that this time, he wasn't letting go. As the music drifted away, they stood there. And the irony of the song hit her. She wasn't the girl she was back when they were together. Ten extra pounds. Hair that hadn't been highlighted or blown out in months. Drug store make-up rather than name brands. Dancing to this song in faded jeans and an old Michigan T-shirt rather than the ball gown she'd worn on their wedding day.

"I look anything but perfect tonight," she mumbled into his shirt.

He leaned back barely enough to capture her face in his hands. His thumbs brushed her cheeks. "You are more beautiful to me than you've ever been." His eyes searched her face, taking in every single inch. "Yeah, physically, you're still the hottest woman I've ever seen." He chased those words with a wolfish grin that caused her stomach to dip. "But it's more than that. Watching you run a business. Seeing you with the women who come into your shop. Your kindness with the retirees next door." He paused. "Your selfless love for our daughter." His voice broke, and he swallowed. "The fact that you *are* imperfect, and you're finally letting that show. Belle, sweetheart, there is no one more beautiful to me than you."

She blinked away tears that pricked her eyes, unsure if they were happy or sad ones. Maybe a little of both. For the past three years, she'd changed the station whenever this song played, and in one dance, with a handful of words, he'd scrubbed away another hurt she'd clung to.

Her hands reached up to cover his, and he leaned closer. Was she ready for this? One kiss would change everything between them. But then again, it was already changing, wasn't it?

She pushed up on her toes, meeting him halfway.

"Oof," Micah lurched to the left.

"Sorry." A little old man called as he jitterbugged away.

At some point the music had swapped to another upbeat jazz tune. How had they both missed that?

Micah cleared disappointment from his face with a smile. She wasn't sure if her expression showed the same or relief, though her heart said it was on board with the former.

He reached out his hand. "Want to try some of those steps we learned?"

Reaching for all the good memories, she grabbed his hand. They'd been well-partnered in so many ways, and resurrecting this one suddenly sounded fun. "Sure." A full belly laugh ripped from her as he spun her around.

Two hours later, they waved as their friends disappeared through the doors of

Brookhaven, then Belle walked Micah to his car. Upstairs, Sydney babysat Anna. Belle looked beyond the new play mansion to her own surprise of a gorgeous wooden swing covered by an arbor strung with twinkling lights.

"Thank you again for all this. You didn't just spoil Anna, you spoiled me, and you really didn't—"

"If you say one more time that I didn't need to do it, I swear I'll come back in the morning and cover this entire back yard in wood. A deck. Tree house. Another of those swings."

"Okay, stop." She playfully punched his shoulder. "But seriously, thank you."

"Seriously, you're welcome." He stifled a yawn.

She opened his car door. "You need to catch up on your sleep. In fact, it should be top on your list of things to accomplish while you're on vacation." From what he said, his week off officially started tonight.

"There are things far above that on my list."

"Well, change them."

"Even if they involve you and Anna?"

"Even if."

He snorted. She recognized that noise as his "not happening" response.

"Do I need to come over there and force you into bed?" she threatened.

He lowered his voice suggestively. "You're welcome to come try."

"You wouldn't appreciate my methods." She playfully shoved him into the car.

He sat but didn't move his legs inside. "You know I'm only teasing."

"I do." Her foot nudged his. "You get slap-happy when you're tired, and you're close to exhausted right now. Which is why you should head home."

His hand reached for hers. "It wasn't my exhaustion earlier, Belle. When we were dancing." His thumb rubbed over her knuckles, and vulnerability rippled over his face. "Would you have let me kiss you if we hadn't been interrupted?"

That question was about so much more than their almost-kiss. He wanted to know where her heart stood. If he was bold enough to ask, she needed to be bold enough to answer.

"Probably. But that doesn't mean I should have." She ran her fingertips along the short hair just over his ear. "I won't deny I'm feeling things again, Micah. I'm not sure what that entails, and I'm still struggling to trust it." Trust him. "Kissing you is easy, but I don't want to take the easy way this time. I can't."

"Fair enough." He leaned against her touch, his eyes not leaving hers. There was a resolve there that had only grown each day he'd been home. "How about we both agree to keep taking this one day at a time, and be open to what it may grow into? And acknowledge there'll be the inevitable bump, but that we're going to believe the best in each other. Not the worst. Sound doable?"

In theory? "It does."

"You sound a little wobbly."

"I feel a little wobbly."

He chuckled. "Me too." With a squeeze, he released her and swung his legs into his car. "Well, if I don't want you turning all Dwayne "The Rock" Johnson on me and body slamming me into bed, I should probably get going."

"At least you admit I could take you in a wrestling match."

"Only because I can barely see straight."

Concern had her gripping his door so he couldn't shut it. "Do you need me to drive you home?"

"No. I'll be fine. Promise."

"Text me when you get there, then."

"Will do." He closed the door then rolled down his window. "Do you and Anna want to go to TimberRidge Wild Animal Park tomorrow?"

She recognized a bargaining chip when she saw one. Pasting on her pageant smile, she tossed it his way. "We'd be happy to go with you Tuesday *if* you sleep all day tomorrow."

"Wrestling me without even lifting a finger," he muttered, though his lips tipped up. "Fine. I'll sleep tomorrow and pick you girls up Tuesday morning."

"It's a date."

The word rolled off her tongue, but this time, she didn't want to reel it in. Not when she caught his satisfied smile. There was something about being the reason behind that smile of his that made her want to keep causing it.

She only hoped she could.

Chapter Seventeen

"All these animals here, and she wants to see the snake." Micah tried to hide his shudder but failed miserably. Best he could hope for was to not scream like a girl. Oh, wait, his little girl wasn't screaming. She was reaching for the slimy, slithery creatures. Right beside her, Belle covered her mouth. She could try and hide that smile all she wanted, but it still played brightly in her eyes.

This had not been part of the plan when he'd suggested taking them to TimberRidge Wild Animal Park. Adventure. Laughter. Excitement. Something to build on the moment he and Belle shared two nights ago.

Beady-eyed snakes did not fit.

"Mista Micah, come see!" Anna held the tail of a giant anaconda that he was pretty sure God never intended to create. Now, the fuzzy llamas outside, those were worth spending time on. Heck, he could even handle the arachnid exhibit. But no, all Anna talked about since spotting the sign on the building was seeing the snakes.

He inched toward her. "I bet your mama wants to see it too."

Belle didn't even miss a beat, just stepped between Anna and the resident Steve Irwin wannabe and grabbed the slick, black speckled body of the writhing creature. "Oooh,"—she peeked at Micah—"it's actually not slimy at all."

"I'll take your word for it."

Her head tipped, and she laid those teasing eyes on him. "You're talking like a guy who puts lavender in his lotion."

Beside her, Steve-o chuckled, then skimmed a glance over Belle like that snake had done to its mouse earlier. Yeah. No. Not happening.

Micah edged between them. No question, he'd handle this reptile if it prevented the human one from striking. He turned his back to the guy, fully engaging Belle. "Okay, so you're not wrong. It isn't awful."

"But for the record, the lavender still is."

He smiled. "Still haven't found the right amount?"

"Oh, I have." She released the snake and wiped her hands on her jeans. "It's zero."

"So maybe you need to try something else." He let go too, but inches away, Anna still held on, petting the snake and chatting with it as if the thing understood every word she said. Chuckling, he refocused on Belle. An idea hit. He looked between Belle and Anna. "What about rose?"

Her brows scrunched.

"With that veti-whatever you called it," he suggested. "And some of the clove or woodsy stuff. I think it could work."

She tapped a finger against her chin. "I don't know."

But he did. Already he loved to inhale the light rose scent that she wore. If he could carry a note of it every day, it'd be like having her right there with him. "I'm not saying push it to the front, but I do think it could add a dimension that guys might connect with. Maybe without realizing what they were smelling." But it could conjure up an emotional attachment—and that was a strong marketing tool.

"Mama, yook!" Anna held a smaller snake in her hands, Steve-o standing beside her.

The man smiled as if he was her proud father. He turned his full focus on Belle. "She sure loves reptiles. You should enroll her in our Thursday class. Parents are welcome too."

Seriously, dude? So Anna didn't call him dad, and Belle obviously wasn't wearing a ring, but they were here together.

"She's a little young for that," Belle replied.

"We've got lots of kids her age that attend." He maneuvered to her side. "We spend time learning about the animals, and I haul out my guitar for a few songs." The guy's slick smile reappeared. "My usual set around here is more kid speed, but I'd take requests if you had them."

"Sounds like fun," Belle said. "But it's a bit of a drive out here, so I doubt that'll work."

"Oh?" The guy took the snake from Anna. "Where do you live?"

That was it. Micah grabbed Anna's hand. "Really shouldn't say. We don't want her growing up thinking she should give that information to strangers." Then he squatted down in front of her. "You ready to go on a safari ride?"

"Yes!" She hopped. "Carry me?"

He swept her onto his shoulders and turned to Belle, who watched him with an amused expression.

"Ready for some zebras?" he asked.

"Sure." She followed them outside.

As they hit the sunshine, he peered down at her. "What's so funny?"

"You."

"What'd I do now?"

"Acted like a jealous boyfriend."

Up on his shoulders, Anna sang a song as she wiggled her legs in his grip. The girl never stopped moving. "Of that kid in there? I was trying to ensure Anna knows proper boundaries."

"Sure you were." Belle kicked a stone, watching it roll across the path. "That had nothing to do with Anna. You thought he was hitting on me."

"I *knew* he was hitting on you." Couldn't help the growl in his voice.

"I wasn't flirting back."

"You also weren't shutting him down."

"It's called being polite."

He side-eyed her. "Manners to a guy that's coming on to you is an open invitation to keep trying."

"He was harmless. Not to mention younger than me."

"Not by much. And definitely not enough for him to care."

"You cared enough for the both of you."

They stopped at the safari pavilion to wait for the tram. Anna reached above to grab leaves from the tree he'd perched her under. Micah leaned close to Belle. "And I'm not about to apologize for it. I gave us up way too easily before. I won't make that mistake again."

The tram pulled up before she could respond. That was okay. He kinda liked the way her lips slightly parted and eyes widened; it said way more than her verbal response would have.

A redhead hopped down to greet them. "You ready for a safari?"

Anna jiggled on his shoulders. Had to be nodding excitedly. "Yes!"

He bent to let her down as the redhead squatted to her level. "Have you already seen some animals today?"

"Mmhmm. Snakes!"

"Oh, then you must have met my little brother, Mac, too." She straightened. "I hope he showed you our anaconda. Second largest in captivity."

"He did."

"Quite the charmer, that one," Micah spoke at the same time.

She quirked her head. "Was there a problem?"

"Not at all." Belle smacked his shoulder. Then she held out her hand. "I'm Belle, this is my daughter, Anna, and this"—she faltered for a second—"is our friend, Micah."

Friend. Right.

He shook the woman's hand.

"I'm Elise Wilder, and this is my place."

Belle looked around. "Pretty impressive."

"Thanks. I started with a petting zoo, and it kind of grew from there." She motioned to the tram, which was actually a school bus. They'd removed the top and replaced it with a tarp, then painted the body like a cheetah. "If you climb on, I'll show you some of my favorites."

Anna bounced up the steps and slid into the first seat. Micah went to follow, but Belle turned on him. "Be nice."

"I'm always nice."

She grunted and climbed the steps to sit beside Anna. He took the seat across from them.

"Everything okay?" Elise hopped up a few stairs as she waited for other passengers. "I know my brother can be a little awkward. He's a bit of an introvert and sometimes puts his foot in his mouth when he's trying to connect." Her lips twisted as if the mere thought of him was tantamount to sucking a lemon. "But he's really harmless. Promise."

Belle shot Micah a look, then smiled sweetly at the woman. "He was fine, and we had a wonderful time in the reptile house because of him."

He needed to redefine "wonderful time" for her.

That thought produced a rabbit trail he'd happily follow.

She looked at him, a wrinkle appearing between her brows. "What?"

"Nothing."

"Your face is saying something completely different."

"Yeah?" He let his dimple deepen. "What do you think it's saying then?"

Her cheeks darkened with a blush that said her mind followed him down that trail. She wouldn't admit it, though. Instead, she turned to Anna. "What animals do you think we'll see, Monkey?"

Anna started her long list, and he leaned back in his seat, listening to her chatter. He crossed his arms, more content than he'd been in years. Excitement buzzed under his skin. The kind that arrived with anticipation when something good hovered on the horizon. It grew stronger each time he interacted with his girls. Holding on to hope allowed him to keep trying, but watching that hope morph into the future he desperately wanted energized him to stay the course.

Once the seats around them filled, Elise fired the bus up and took off. A pungent breeze of dust, animals, and fresh-mowed grass wafted through the open top as they slowly cruised the aisles. Wild animals played behind fencing created from mesh wire attached to large, rustic wooden poles. Gravel crunched under the tires, and a few of the animals called to them.

"Can we feed them?" Belle asked.

Elise stopped beside the zebras, who stared at them. "Not these, but when you return to the main area, you can feed the camels and giraffes, along with any of the animals in the petting zoo."

"That sounds fun, doesn't it?" Excitement tinged her words as she squeezed Anna's shoulders.

Their little girl didn't break her stare from the zebras, but she did respond with a giant nod.

Two hours later, they'd seen every single animal TimberRidge offered, along with a repeat trip to the reptile exhibit. They stood beside the anaconda's glass window, and Anna peered up at him. "I hungry."

He glanced at his watch. Nearly two o'clock. The snacks Belle doled out earlier lasted longer than he'd figured they would. Probably because Anna had been so distracted by the animals. "Good thing I packed us some food then." Looking over her head to Belle, he motioned to the picnic area. "Want to take her to wash her hands? I'll grab the food and meet you over there."

"You packed us a picnic?"

"I figured we'd need lunch." He nudged aside the grin that wanted to escape. Wait till she saw what he'd packed. "You game?"

"I didn't have to cook it, pack it, or buy it. I'm definitely game."

He'd remind her she said that shortly.

He jogged to the car, grabbed the cooler and a backpack full of food, then made his way to the picnic area. Belle and Anna already waited at a table under the shade of a huge oak tree. She settled on one side. "How can I help?"

"Just sit there." He tossed her a sandwich wrapped in parchment paper, then passed one to Anna before hauling out chips and watermelon. "I kept it simple. Hope you don't mind."

"I'm thoroughly offended," she said with a grin that slipped as she unwrapped her sandwich.

His, however, erupted full force. "What?" He aimed for an innocence he didn't feel.

Her eyes narrowed. "You are a brat."

"Peanut butter pick-ahs!" Anna's exclamation bellowed from beside them. "I yuv peanut butter pick-ahs."

He tipped his head her way. "She yuvs it."

Belle set hers down. "Tell me you packed me something else."

"See, I would have, but then"—he snapped and pointed at her—"I remembered our bet."

Her head dropped back with a groan. "I completely forgot."

"Lucky for you, I didn't."

"Yeah. I got that," she groused. "You aren't seriously going to make me eat that thing, are you?"

He rubbed his chin with his knuckles. "Hmm ... I suppose we could come to a new agreement." He wiggled his eyebrows.

She picked up her sandwich. "I think I'll take my chances with this."

"Too bad." He held his up too. "You'd probably enjoy my other suggestion more."

"In your dreams, buddy."

"I think you mean in *your* dreams. Me being your dream guy and all."

"Those dreams are picturing you in a pit with snakes, Indiana Jones-style."

"Heroic and handsome. I'll take it."

"See, again, I think you're missing my point."

"Or I know you well enough to hear what you aren't saying." He wiggled his eyebrows again.

"I'm going to tape those in place."

He laughed. "Is that any way to thank me for this amazing lunch?"

"Trust me, I've thought of about one hundred more creative ways to thank you for this." She held up her sandwich. "And that's in the last three minutes alone. Wait until we get home."

Her last word sunk in deep. Picturing home with the two of them produced an appetite that food couldn't touch. Walking through the door. Helping put Anna to bed. Following through with this moment of flirting because, yeah, he could be creative too.

Right. He took a long swallow from his water bottle.

Belle's gaze didn't leave his for a very long moment. She stood in that moment with him, seeing every thought he wasn't giving voice to because, like he'd said earlier, they knew each other that well. Didn't surprise him that she could read him. It surprised him that this time she kept right on reading rather than slamming the book shut.

"I have more?" Anna broke the moment like the good little chaperone she'd become.

He reached for another swig of cold water as Belle smiled. Except this one turned cunning. "You want Mama's sandwich?"

"Unfair sportsmanship." He tried to block her play.

"Yes, pweese." Anna reached for it at the same time.

"There you go, Monkey." With a shrug, Belle handed the sandwich to her and aimed pure innocence his way. "All's fair, right?"

He allowed her the moment, doing his best to sell his disappointment. Lowered shoulders, frown, even added a small groan while she beamed across from him. The woman was much too fun to play with. If he held out a few seconds longer, she'd deploy fully into her cocky triumph. And, yep, there it was.

Arms out, she started to sway back and forth, doing a little dance. That's exactly where Anna got her moves from. And like their little girl, she was too cute to stop. Yet, somehow, he'd manage.

Full focus on her, he reached into the bag. Her swagger stuttered as his revved up. His fingers closed around victory, and, oh, did it taste sweet. "Lucky for you, I came prepared." He tossed it her way. "Bon appétit."

Only thing that could make this moment better was if he could kiss the shocked look from her face.

"Everything all set for tomorrow?" Belle turned to Penny, who sat in the cushy leather chair beside her, Rachael on her other side. They'd already had massages and manicures. Getting their toenails done finished up the day of pampering Jonah had arranged for them.

"Yep." Penny ran her hand over her belly. "He still doesn't suspect a thing."

"I cannot believe you're going to pull this off," Rachael said. "He's never surprised."

Penny grinned. "He won't be able to say that after tomorrow." She pointed out the color she wanted for her toes, then turned to Belle. "Micah's coming, right?"

"As far as I know."

"Okay. I wasn't sure of his schedule."

"He's off this week." And they'd spent nearly every day together. She wasn't about to offer that info, though.

"Things going well between you two?" Penny watched her closely as if she'd picked up on what Belle wasn't saying.

"They are."

"Because you seem to be seeing a lot of each other."

"Yep."

Rachael leaned around Penny. "You're going to make us drag it out of you, aren't you?"

She gave her best innocent look. "Drag what?"

But Penny was having none of it. "Don't mess with the pregnant lady. I'm tired, sore, and cranky."

"Please. We grew up with Mom. Your crankiness doesn't scare me."

"Then how about this? If you want to be one of the first to hold your niece or nephew, you'll spill your guts about Micah right now."

Rachael burrowed into her seat and closed her eyes as if she suddenly hadn't a care in the world. "Never mind, Belle. Go on and take your time. I want to cement my place as favorite aunt."

"Honestly, you two are the worst good cop, bad cop I've ever seen."

The two of them actually had the nerve to laugh.

"But is it working?" Penny asked.

She started to answer, then hesitated. But she had to talk to someone because all she'd managed to do on her own was tangle her emotions even tighter.

The woman doing her pedicure handed her the color options. Belle chose a soft pink, and the woman nodded, then left to find it. Belle fiddled with the plastic cards filled with nail polish samples. Picking one had been infinitely easier than uttering the words she was about to say. "It's been nice having Micah around."

This grabbed their attention, but the looks on their faces said they were waiting for her to add more to the comment. When she didn't, Penny prodded, "And?"

"Isn't that enough? Does there have to be more?"

This time it was Rachael who responded. "There doesn't have to be, but it's pretty obvious there is."

She wasn't wrong. But Belle couldn't say it. The words were too big. Too powerful. Left her too vulnerable. Worse, they came with no guarantees.

Penny reached for Belle's fingers, wrapping hers around them in a secure embrace, then broke the silence. "From someone who knows what it's like to try and ignore feelings you don't want to have, I can tell you that never works. You've got to face them head-on and address them."

"That's never been the issue. I want to know that I can rely on him."

"Isn't that what he's been showing you since he came back?" Rachael asked softly.

"He has," she acknowledged. Resting in that knowledge proved harder, and she couldn't fully release her heart to him until she trusted him implicitly.

Penny's pedicurist finished, and Penny lifted her toes. "Oooh, they're so pretty. Thank you." She showed the turquoise polish to Belle and Rachael. "Jonah's painted them for me a few times, but they never look quite this good."

"My brother's been painting your toenails?" Rachael asked. "That is love."

No. Love was showing up for your child without her yet calling you Daddy. Micah hadn't only been there for Belle; he'd been there for Anna.

Within minutes they were all finished, and they donned little Styrofoam flip-flops to waddle from the shop. "Lunch next?" Rachael asked as she climbed into the driver's side.

"Sure. Whatever the pregnant lady wants." Belle hopped in the backseat.

Whatever the pregnant lady wanted turned into several stops, the final being a specialty chocolate shop with the richest chocolate torte Belle had ever indulged in.

They pulled into Jonah and Penny's beach house and practically rolled themselves from the car. "Where did you manage to put all that food?" Rachael asked as they followed Penny inside.

"This baby seems to suck it up as fast as I can eat it." Penny opened the front door to a waiting Jonah, who kissed her cheek. "It's got to be a boy."

Jonah chuckled. "You change your mind every day."

"Today, I'm convinced."

"We could always call the doctor's office and find out. Do a gender reveal at the baby shower tomorrow."

"Not on your life." Penny let him lead her to the couch, then put her feet up on the pillow he had waiting for her. "What do you think of my toes?"

"As colorful as you." Another kiss and then he looked at Belle and Rachael. "You ladies have fun today?"

"Too much," Rachael said.

"Mama!" Anna raced from the kitchen. "Yook! Uncah Jonah painted my nails!" She showed off her own pretty pedicure and manicure.

"Just because she didn't get to go doesn't mean she had to miss out," Jonah said.

Belle swooped Anna up. "You spoil her." Then she looked at every toe and fingernail, each one a different color.

"It's a rainbow," Anna proudly proclaimed.

"Because unicorns love rainbows." Evan followed Gavin into the room.

Rachael shook her head. "Your idea then?"

"Yep."

"Suggested after I'd already painstakingly painted them pink, so trust me, I've already thought of plenty of ways to thank him." Jonah met Rachael's eyes with a conspiratorial grin. "Several of which I'm sure you'll help me with."

"You know me too well."

Evan settled on the arm of the chair Rachael reclined in. "Remember, I know where you live, and I'm trained to be stealthy."

"I'm terrified of your cat-like qualities." She studied her nails, the hint of a smile tugging at her lips. "Or is it bat-like?"

He reached for her neck, squeezing the tender spot where most people were ticklish. "How's that for bat-like?"

She swatted at him as laughter peeled from her.

Across from their antics, Penny stifled a yawn.

"I think my beautiful wife needs a nap." Jonah tugged a throw off the end of their couch and spread it over her. "You're all welcome to stay, but we'll take this party to another room."

They all stood, and Gavin started for the kitchen. "I'm ready for first dinner anyway."

"That boy can eat." Evan followed him but tossed his comment to Rachael, who was on his heels.

"You're not saying anything me and my grocery budget don't already know."

Gavin's deep voice floated to them. "One more year, Mom, then I'll be at college and that grocery bill will be nothing."

"I'm counting down the days," she teased him. Her face, however, said that countdown was anything but a joyous one.

Evan's forehead wrinkled as he stood in the kitchen doorway watching her. His hand touched her back, ushering her past, and he leaned down to whisper something to her as she slipped by. A soft laugh slipped out of her lips, and his own face smoothed.

Belle bounced Anna in her arms. "It's time to get this monkey home and into the bathtub."

Anna giggled. "I no need a bath."

Burying her nose in Anna's neck, Belle took an exaggerated whiff. "Oh, yes, you do. You smell like bananas."

"No I don't." More giggling.

They quickly said their goodbyes, Anna distributing hugs to everyone in the house, before making their way to the car. Within twenty minutes, they climbed the steps to their tiny apartment, Belle's ankle down to a slow ache at the end of a day like today.

By the time Anna was tubbed, slathered with her sugar-rose lotion, and in her snuggly pajamas, her eyelids drooped. Belle read her two stories, then tucked her and Uni in with a kiss to the forehead. Quietly closing the door, she shuffled to the kitchen and poured a glass of water, then settled on the couch with the mail and her laptop.

The woman from the FDA had emailed her notes on the SOP manual Belle put together. Things looked promising and were nearly set for her return visit. It hadn't been easy listening to all the necessary changes, but in the end, they paid off. Production was smoother. Her website and labels had been updated. And business was picking up. Best part was how it provided even more experience to the women here. Sydney alone found a new passion and pursuit that could carry her into the future.

Tossing aside several envelopes of junk mail, Belle paused on the third piece.

Her eyebrows bunched together as she noted the return address of her landlord. Strange. It wasn't time for her monthly rent bill to arrive.

She ripped it open and unfolded the letter, then scanned the words. Disbelief set in. Rick was calling in her back payments. She had until Monday at five to bring a check into his office, or he would lock her out and begin the eviction process per their lease. Additional words and threats blurred together, and she set the letter aside, leaned her head in her hands, and fought off an encroaching panic attack.

For the first time in years, she didn't know how to fix this one on her own.

Chapter Eighteen

B elle might be fooling everyone else, but she wasn't fooling Micah. Something was bothering her, and he was nearing the end of his patience in politely waiting to find out. So when she plucked up whatever fancy container Penny had used at this party to hold the now depleted infused water, he followed her across the deck.

"Let me help you with that." Hands outstretched, he offered to take her burden from her.

She twisted away. "I got it, but if you can open the slider, that'd be great."

Look at that, rather than brushing him off, she enlisted him for teamwork. Now, if he could convince her to do that with whatever had those lines digging into her forehead, he'd count today a complete success.

"Thanks." She brushed past.

He remained on her heels all the way to the kitchen. Rachael stood at the counter, cutting up more fruit. She smiled at them. "Hey, guys. I'd say the party is a success. Did you see the look on Jonah's face when he realized it was for him?"

His cousin still carried a dumbfounded expression—well, except for when his gaze landed on Penny. Those two were crazy in love, and Jonah didn't seem to care who knew it. He couldn't pass by her without a touch or a kiss, and Penny glowed under his tender care. The two were beyond lucky—they were blessed. Coveting might not be a good thing, but Micah wanted what they had, and he wanted it with Belle.

"I'm just glad my sister was able to pull it off. I think she's actually happier than he is."

Rachael nodded. "He's impossible to surprise, and he reminds her of it all too often."

"Can't make that claim anymore," Micah added.

"Trust me. Penny will have no problem reminding him of that fact."

Belle refilled the container and added more lemon slices and raspberries to it. Then she tore off a few sprigs of rosemary and tossed them in too. As she moved to the fridge to put those things away, he took advantage and picked up the container.

"Thanks," she said.

"Want to know an even better way to thank me?"

Okay, based on her blush, that had come out all wrong. Not that he was opposed to what his words conjured up, but, "By talking. I meant by talking."

"Of course you did."

He readjusted his grip. This thing was heavy. "Something is bugging you."

Surprise flared in her eyes before she narrowed them. "Nothing's bugging me. I'm perfectly fine."

"Pageant. Voice."

"Bothersome. Man." She reached for the water, but it was his turn to twist away.

Rachael swiped the strawberries she'd cut into the large fruit bowl, picked it up, and headed for the door. "I think I'll bring this outside."

Belle's focus remained squarely on him. That was fine. He didn't have anywhere else to be except right here helping her.

After a full minute, she sighed. "You are so stubborn."

"I'd say we're evenly matched."

Her fisted hands planted on her hips. "Why do you think something's bugging me?"

"You're honestly asking me that?"

She shrugged.

Setting the container on the counter but maintaining his grip, he leaned close to her. "You've rubbed the fingernail polish from your thumbs. You let Anna take three trips to the dessert table. You were zoned out during the conversation with Jonah's dad, which is why you pulled out one of your safe responses about the weather. And you've worn your stage smile all day." He straightened. "Want me to go on?"

He couldn't quite tell if she looked impressed, caught, or frustrated. Maybe a little of each.

"No. That's enough." Laughter erupted through the windows, momentarily snagging her attention. Then she returned it to him. "I am a little distracted today, but this isn't the time or place to get into it." She paused, then, "Can we talk later? After the party?"

He did his best to stay cool. Last thing he needed was to scare her away when she was finally coming around. "You tell me where, and I'll be there."

"Down at the beach? I'll check with Penny and Jonah and see if they can watch Anna for a little while once everyone leaves."

He'd hire someone if he had to. "I'll plan on it." Lifting the water jug, he motioned for her to go ahead of him. "Mind getting the door?"

She rolled it open and then went to check on the rest of the food. For the next several hours, she kept busy playing hostess so her sister could enjoy the day. By the time the sun started its retreat through the sky, everyone had departed and most of the leftovers were put away. Penny rested on the couch, Jonah beside her, while Gavin entertained Anna with a game. Evan was helping Rachael finish up in the kitchen.

"Want to sneak down with me?" Belle approached him, nerves evident in her voice. Was she nervous about sharing with him or about the news she had to divulge? Either way, he'd be there for her.

They started down the wooden steps that connected the deck to the beach below. Micah snagged a blanket from the large box Jonah and Penny kept at the bottom. "Need a sweatshirt too?" A few lived in the same container.

"Sure."

The breeze picked up as they neared the water. "It's going to be a gorgeous sunset tonight." He spread the blanket out away from the tiny waves sliding into shore. Belle ignored it and walked to the edge of the water, dipping her toes in. He settled on the ground, giving her space and patience.

After about five minutes, she joined him. Sitting crisscross, she faced him. "I'm in trouble, Micah."

He tensed, a thousand scenarios running through his mind. He worked to keep his voice calm. "Trouble, how?"

Tears welled in her eyes. "Rick is threatening to evict me."

"On what terms?" Facts first. Emotion later. Though he had a pretty good idea what the facts were.

Her face crumpled. "You know why. I'm behind on my rent, and he's calling it in." She buried her head in her hands. "I'm such an idiot. It's why I didn't want to say anything. But, Micah, I don't know what to do."

Micah knew what he *wanted* to do. Unfortunately, that wouldn't help Belle, but it would land him in a world of trouble. "He had you fix that entire place up, and now he's going to kick you out. He played you."

"I let him."

"Hey." He softly rubbed her arm. "We'll figure this out."

Lips trembling, eyes watering, the look she centered on him was one of a woman who wanted to believe his promise but wasn't sure she could. "How?"

He didn't know, but when he faced a problem with a patient, he started with the facts presented and worked out from there. "What do you owe?" If it was only a month or two, he could cover it. When she didn't immediately respond, his gut churned. "How much, Belle?" he coaxed gently. Last thing he wanted was for her defenses to come out. He was on her side, and she needed to feel that.

She shook her head.

"Please, tell me."

"I can't." She refused to look at him.

So he took her chin and tenderly brought her eyes to his. "We all have done stuff we aren't proud of, but you can't keep it to yourself. That gives it too much power. You're not alone in this. Share it with me and let me help you."

Her nostrils flared and she swallowed, battling her reflex to stay strong all on her own. He watched the war play out in her eyes and refused to look away. He'd been all-in since the moment he decided to return. He wasn't going anywhere, and at some point in time, she'd believe him. He prayed that moment was now.

"Forty-eight thousand dollars."

The number hit him hard, but it was nothing compared to the immediate knowledge that she'd been carrying this burden alone. All this time he'd been standing beside her, and she hadn't allowed him to shoulder it with her. That she finally had now wasn't lost on him.

Did he pull her into a hug? Or start working through solutions with her?

That decision was made when the dam burst and her tears flowed.

He hauled her to him, lifted her right up, and snuggled her in his lap. "Aw, honey. It's okay." Stroking her hair, he held her close as she fisted his T-shirt and cried. "I'm here, Belle. I'm not going anywhere. We'll figure this out."

He continued to murmur soft words to her until she slowly calmed. With a tentative glance, she looked up at him, then self-consciously laughed. Her fingertips swiped the moisture from under her eyes. "I'm a mess."

"Yeah. You are." He lifted her chin with his thumb. "But I have a thing for messes."

Pink tinged her cheeks. "You must, because I haven't scared you away yet." As if catching her words, she looked away. "At least not permanently."

Would their past always hover between them?

He nudged her chin back toward him. "And you're not going to. I've tried to tell you, to show you, I'm here for as long as you want me."

She stared at him long and hard as if trying to push the past away to see their future. She wanted it; he caught that truth in her eyes. A hint of fear still remained, but so did a new desire, or maybe not new, but one she'd locked away and now released.

"I think I believe you." Barely a whisper, as if she'd meant the words more for herself than him.

Her palm slipped up his chest and along his neck, to rest against his cheek. He watched the debate in her eyes and held steady. He'd let her lead.

With the tiniest of nods, as if she'd answered her own questions, she leaned into him. It was all he needed to meet her halfway. Her fingers trembled against his cheek as his lips touched hers, and he wrapped his arm tighter around her. Cocooning her. Letting his touch pick up where his words left off. He loved her. He'd protect her. And he wouldn't leave her.

She missed his kisses, but even more than that, she missed being in his arms. Slipping her hands down along his biceps, she held on to him holding her and matched him kiss for kiss. He tasted familiar, of some of her favorite memories along with the promise of new ones. His hands still fit the small of her back perfectly, and his touch still brought out goosebumps. Releasing his arms, she traced her fingers along his shoulders and into his hair, remembering how sensitive the skin at the nape of his neck was. She knew him.

And he knew her. Smiling against her lips, he matched her tease with one of his own, lightly squeezing just above her hips where she was most ticklish. Problem was, right now the feel of his skin on hers was eliciting anything but laughter.

He either heard or felt her intake of breath because he moved his hand and slowed his sweet rediscovery of her lips. Dropping his forehead to hers, he cupped her shoulders.

"We've still got it."

A quiet laugh lifted from her. "Yes, I'd say we do."

His thumbs made lazy circles along her collarbone, and he dropped a kiss on her forehead. "You know I love you."

She wanted to return the words, but that remained a step she couldn't take. They lodged in her throat, the vulnerability of them wielding too much power over her. That curl-your-toes kiss probably outed her feelings to him, but voicing those three little words seemed too much.

He sighed but didn't press. Setting her from him, he wove his fingers through hers and squeezed. "Tell me more about whatever your landlord said."

Way to kill the mood. Yet it needed to be done for more than one reason.

"I've been behind on my rent for nearly all two years but still making payments. I haven't been able to keep up while also making the necessary fixes to the building." Frustration welled. "It's my fault that I didn't have someone more knowledgeable read the lease before I signed it. I got myself into this situation." One she'd merely told him the tip of until tonight.

"And you have me here, now, to help you out of it. Beating yourself up doesn't accomplish anything at this point."

He was right, but she still felt like she deserved a few hard knocks. "I promised him that I would catch up by next November, and he seemed okay with that. But last night, I came home to a letter—which he called a courtesy—that said I needed to have the money to his office by close on Monday, or he'd lock me out of the building and begin the eviction process."

Micah's lips moved back and forth as he digested her words. "First off, from the little I can remember, he can't lock you out. And even once he does file a formal eviction notice, you'll still have a little time to make your account current."

Oh, if it were that simple. "As far as normal leases go, sure, but that's not what I signed. I even pulled it out to look again."

His hands fisted, but she understood his anger wasn't aimed at her. "What's your lease say?"

"That he can lock me out. That if I'm in breach of contract, he can evict me without notice, at least downstairs. I'm not sure about upstairs because I live there. But if I am evicted, he's allowed to sell any of my personal property in the building to recoup his lost rent." Saying it out loud made her feel like the idiot she was for signing the stupid thing.

"It won't come to that."

"I don't see how. Do you have nearly fifty thousand dollars laying around, because I sure don't."

"No, but I have a portion of it." He hesitated. "What if we talk to Jonah and Penny?"

Belle vehemently shook her head. "No. They're about to have a baby. Penny's scaling back on her estate sales, and he's expanding his territory again to compensate. The last thing they need is me hitting them up for money."

"You know Jonah would do it in a heartbeat."

"I do." That was the problem. "At the detriment of his own needs, and I cannot ask that of him. Not if there's another way."

Micah didn't look convinced, but he nodded anyway. "All right, we'll see what else we can come up with."

She'd thought of nothing else since opening the letter. "All I know to do is work up new numbers based on allocating a higher percentage of my sales to him so I can pay things back faster." It'd make things even tighter, but she and Anna could survive on ramen noodles and turn the AC wall units off. "If I bring the changed projections in along with a chunk of the payment, maybe he'll see it as a good-faith effort. He's been willing to work with me all this time. I have to believe he'll continue to do the same."

"We need to prepare for the fact that he might not." Now he met her eyes, his voice firmed by an edge of protection. "Either way, I do not want you confronting this man alone."

"I have no plans to confront him at all. The last thing I want is to make him angry."

"Last thing I'm worried about is his feelings." Micah flexed his hands as if trying to work out his obvious irritation. "In fact, I think we need to start looking for a new building for you. I want you away from this guy."

"Sounds great, but I don't have a valid reason to break the lease." She'd scoured the wording to see.

"Then we'll find something."

"You're a doctor, not a lawyer."

He merely shrugged. "I'll hire one."

The man was on the warpath, battling for her. Kind of made her want to kiss him again.

She startled. What was wrong with her?

"Everything okay?" Concern tugged his eyebrows low.

That concern deepened her craving. "All's fine." She swallowed. Kissing him once would never be enough. She'd managed over the past three years to bottle up that knowledge, but one taste of him uncorked it, and there was no way she'd manage to put the lid on again.

His head tipped, and a slow smile slipped across his lips. "Pageant voice." He leaned toward her, hands braced on either side of her legs. "If you want me to kiss you again, all you have to do is say the word."

She simply held his stare. He raised a brow. She matched the look with a silly grin. He'd always taken the tough moments and made them better. It was a fact she'd allowed herself to forget and now reveled in remembering.

"The word," she teased.

With a laugh, he claimed her lips. This kiss was slow, soft, and tender. Filled with the promise of days to come. He'd told her for weeks he was here to stay. Now his kiss sealed that truth and said how much he treasured her. He broke away too soon, setting her away from him. At some point, the sun had dipped beyond the horizon and a slight chill claimed the evening air. Wrapping her in the hoodie he'd snagged earlier, he stood and reached for her hand. "It's getting late, and I'm going to guess Anna's pretty tired."

Goodness. For once she hadn't been thinking about Anna at all. The fact that Micah was? That warmed her more than his kiss.

"Yeah, probably." She took his hand as he hauled her to her feet, and they started for the stairs.

They slipped into Jonah and Penny's to find Anna on the floor watching *Moana*, while Rachael, Evan, and Gavin sat on the couch with bowls of popcorn.

Rachael held up hers. "Want some?"

"We're good." Belle started collecting Anna's things. "Where's Penny and Jonah?"

"Penny wasn't feeling too well, so Jonah helped her upstairs."

Micah immediately stiffened. "Everything okay? Should I go up and check on her?"

"She's actually asleep." Jonah stepped off the bottom stair, joining them. "I think it was too busy of a day." Still, lines creased his forehead, and he rubbed the back of his neck.

"I can take a peek if you want."

He shook his head. "She says I'm being overprotective, and I probably am. I think what she needs most right now is sleep. Hard to get when you're eight-and-a-half months pregnant." He attempted a grin. "At least I'm told."

"She's telling the truth," Belle said.

"Absolutely," Rachael chimed in.

"It is," Micah agreed, "but if you need me for anything—anything at all— call me." He stooped to pick up one of Anna's books from the floor before handing it to Belle. "Whenever you're ready, I'll walk you out."

"You two just coming up from the beach?" Jonah settled onto the chair beside the couch, swiping Rachael's popcorn as he did.

"Hey," she said.

Without a word, Evan handed her his.

Belle zipped up Anna's bag. Her girl was so tired she hadn't moved from the floor or acknowledged their presence with anything other than an exhausted smile. "We are."

This had everyone, even Gavin, smiling.

Micah swiped a look around the room, met her gaze, and shrugged.

At least they'd confined their teasing to those smug looks. No doubt the next time they'd start digging. She hadn't a clue what they'd find because she wasn't even fully sure herself. Kissing Micah felt like the next step on a blind journey. She was doing her best to feel out the path along the way and not trip.

They said their goodbyes, then Micah walked them to the car and helped her buckle Anna into her seat. Before Belle closed the door, he wrapped her in a hug and kissed the top of her head. "Starting tomorrow, I'm on days, plus I have to cover a shift for Nash, so I'm pretty much at the hospital the next thirty-six hours. When I'm not, I'll be working to find a solution."

"And sleeping?"

"You trump sleep here."

"Micah—"

"I'll sleep Monday night after we handle Rick." He nudged her away so he could see her face, but his arms remained around her. "I'll be at that meeting, and we'll get this figured out. I promise."

Tucking back into him, she nodded against his chest, feeling lighter since she shared her burden. Freaked out a little still, but definitely lighter. "Okay."

"You trust me?" His heartbeat thumped in her ear, strong and sure.

She held her breath, stepped off the cliff, and prayed he'd really catch her. "I do."

Chapter Nineteen

Micah never liked working against a clock. Time always moved faster when forced up against it. That was the only explanation for how Monday afternoon arrived, and he still didn't have enough money to cover Belle's deficit. He refused to admit defeat, though. Instead, he'd called the one person with deep enough pockets to help them. It was a long shot. Other than his single failed attempt to contact Walter a few weeks ago, he hadn't made amends in their relationship. But he was willing to try anything, even if it didn't cast him in the best light.

He dialed Walter's number again. Got voicemail. Again. Where was the man? Micah had left him countless messages. The last let him know of the urgency—not that the sheer amount of voicemails hadn't already done that. But for someone who'd been trying to contact him for three years, Walter suddenly seemed in no hurry to reconnect. Not that a "hi," followed by hinting at a need for money, sounded palatable to anyone. But Walter had always said if he needed him, call.

"Room 3212 is ready for you." Lettie hustled down the hall. "She's moving fast."

He hurried after her, wishing at least for today he was still on nights. Luckily, Nash agreed to arrive early so he could make it to Belle's meeting. Sometime during the six-hour baby boom he faced, he needed to figure out how to fix her problem.

Two hours later, he left another set of new parents with their baby boy and consulted his phone in the hall. Still nothing from Walter. There was, however, a return call from Micah's financial advisor confirming he'd moved money from a few investments and borrowed against his 401(k) like he'd asked. Still, it wasn't enough to meet what Belle needed.

He flipped to his contacts and hovered his finger over Dad's number. Closing his eyes, he pressed the screen. After five rings, it went to voicemail. He cleared his throat. "Dad, it's Micah. I … have a favor to ask. Can you call me back?"

Hanging up, he tapped his phone against his forehead. Within seconds, it rang and Dad's name popped up. Micah immediately answered. "Dad."

"Need help getting the house ready after all?"

"No." He wished it were that simple. Best to dive right in. He explained the situation. "So I wondered if you have available cash that I could borrow? I'll pay it back."

Complete silence met him.

"Dad?"

"Sorry." Though his voice said anything but. "I'm trying to figure out what gave you the impression that you could call me for money in this situation. You haven't been my responsibility in years. Even then, I gave you advice about Belle, and you chose to go against it. You want to make autonomous decisions, then you get to handle the outcomes on your own too." He didn't even pause. "Is there anything else?"

Micah white-knuckled the phone. Dad wasn't acting out of character, so his answer shouldn't sting. And even though it did, this wasn't the argument he needed to spend energy on. "Nothing at all."

"Then I need to go." And he hung up.

While that call felt like a colossal waste of time, he'd had to make it. If he was going to make the next one, he needed to be able to tell Belle he'd exhausted all other options. Scrolling through his contacts, he found Jonah's number and dialed it. Belle might not want to ask them for help, but with their backs against a wall, there wasn't much other choice. Hopefully, she'd understand.

Like he'd done with Dad, he quickly filled Jonah in on everything. "I have half the money—"

This outcome was one-hundred-eighty-degrees different.

"You don't even need to ask. I'll cover the balance, but I don't have all the available cash today. I'll have to move a few things around. I can get you a portion now and the remainder by the end of next week. Think that'll work?"

"It'll have to." He didn't have any other choice. Neither did Belle, but, "She's not going to be happy I called you."

"I'll write it up as a loan. She can pay me back."

Except he'd never call it in. Not like Rick had done. "Thanks, Jonah."

"Is there anything else I can do? I'll go to the meeting too, if you guys need extra backup. The man is already on my list."

"I think we're good. You enjoy this week off with your wife."

He'd taken the week after his birthday off to hang out at the beach with Penny. Something about a babymoon. At least that's what he heard other women at the party calling it.

"Okay." Didn't need to tell him twice. "I'll swing by the hospital in a few hours and drop off the paperwork and a check."

"Have them page me. I'll meet you unless I'm in a delivery."

They disconnected. Micah needed to call Belle and let her know what he'd arranged. This solution wouldn't be her favorite, but it was their only current option.

He just prayed she'd understand.

He tapped her name on the screen and waited for her to answer.

"You're not calling to cancel on me, are you?" She aimed for a teasing note, but he still heard her underlying worry.

"Nope." He walked down to the end of the hall for quiet and glanced out over the city. Overcast and hot today. They were in for a good storm. "Calling to tell you everything is all set."

"How?"

"I had some savings that I moved around." He hesitated then plunged in. "And I called Jonah."

Silence greeted him, then a long sigh. "I didn't want to do that."

"Would you hesitate for even a second to help them out?"

"You know I wouldn't." Anna sang in the background, the sound growing quiet as Belle must have stepped away. "It's hard, Micah. I don't like relying on anyone, and in the space of not even a day, I'm having to do that with Jonah and with you. It scares me."

"Because people let you down."

"Always." She sniffed. "And I don't think I can go through that again. I promised myself I wouldn't."

"You aren't going to. I know you've been hurt in the past and that I had a hand in it. But, Belle, that doesn't mean this time will be the same. Trust us." His pager buzzed at his side. "Trust me."

"I'm trying to."

He checked his waist. "I hate to say it, but I need to go. I'll meet you at Rick's office at ten to five."

"I'll be waiting."

They hung up, and Micah raced to another delivery. The next few hours passed as fast as he'd expected. About an hour before Nash was scheduled, he received a page to the ER. He wasn't on call down there, so he headed to the nurse's station. "Lettie, the ER paged me. Know anything about it?"

"Nope."

He rounded to the phone and called down. "This is Micah Shaw. I received a call."

"Yes, Dr. Shaw, we had a Jonah and Penny Black come in via ambulance. He's asking for you."

Micah's heart rate tripled. "I'm on my way."

He took the stairs rather than wait for the elevator. Hit the door at a full-out run to the ER. "Black?" he called as he raced by the desk there.

"Bay two."

He didn't even look at Jonah as he rounded the corner. His eyes went to Penny's red, puffy face and the monitor behind her. Her blood pressure was off the charts. Preeclampsia.

"What have you given her?"

The doctor who'd had him paged ran through the details, ending on, "She seized en route, and the EMTs administered a bolus of magnesium sulfate."

Not preeclampsia, but eclampsia.

"She's going to be okay, right?" Worry replaced Jonah's typical calm demeanor.

Micah staved off his growing unease. He needed a clear head because that report moved this situation from bad to worse. "Tell me what happened."

"She hasn't been feeling good since the party. Started complaining of a headache this morning, then her vision doubled and she nearly passed out. I called 911."

Micah looked at her ankles. Swollen. He'd noticed them at the party but hadn't thought too much about it. She'd complained of a headache too, but it had been a hot day, and she'd had a lot of excitement.

No excuse. He should have put it together.

Penny's vitals blipped across the screens behind her. He needed the baby's. "Get me a Doppler," he directed the nurse, then squeezed Penny's foot. "How're you feeling?"

She had an oxygen mask over her face and uttered a slow and labored response from behind it. "Not too great."

"Could have fooled me. How'd my cousin ever get such a beautiful woman to marry him anyway?" His eyes remained on her monitor as the cuff on her arm inflated.

"Charmed." She pulled in a breath. "Me."

"Pretty sure it was the other way around." Jonah stood at her other side, his voice shaky.

She smiled from behind the mask. "You never gave up."

He tenderly brushed her sweaty bangs from her forehead. "So you don't either. Deal?"

She nodded.

The cuff released, and the monitor alarm shrilled. "Her BP is still too high." Micah took the wand from the nurse. "Let's hear that baby of yours. No doubt he or she is a strong one with you two as parents."

He moved the probe over Penny's belly. "Stop holding your breath, Penny." She needed all the oxygen she could take in. Jonah's gaze drilled into him as he continued to position the probe, waiting. Finally the heartbeat sounded through the instrument. "There. See? Fast and strong."

Which allowed him to momentarily shift the full weight of his concern to Penny. With her numbers still climbing despite the magnesium sulfate and the fact she'd already seized, there was only one sure solution to guarantee the baby's and her safety. "Looks like today's the day you meet this little boy or girl."

"What?" Penny struggled to sit up.

Jonah clenched her hand with his. "Now?"

Micah nodded to the nurse, who started unhooking Penny so they could move her. She pushed against the nurse, her movements sluggish but determined. "No. It's too early," she slurred.

"Micah?" Jonah's worry dug into his voice, and he held Penny's bed in place even as Micah attempted to move it.

"Jonah, I need you to let go."

"Not happening."

They didn't have time to argue. They had an IV in her with fluids and a magnesium drip to stop the seizure. Her body settled, though Jonah still held his frantic look. It wasn't going to get any better.

"Her BP is still climbing." The nurse read off her number, then removed the cuff and looked to Micah for the order to transport.

He looked at them both. "We need to deliver your baby." Then he directed Jonah to the woman standing near the curtain. "You need to go with her and sign the paperwork. I'll be with Penny. I promise I won't leave her side."

"She's only thirty-five weeks."

He wished he could soften the situation. Simultaneously wished he wasn't the one to be here, while knowing there was no other place he'd rather be. "I can stand here and explain it all to you, or I can go save Penny and the baby."

"Go." Jonah's voice broke over the one word.

Penny nodded her consent.

It was all Micah needed. He signaled the nurse, who had the bed moving before Jonah stepped from the room.

"Wait!" The fear in Jonah's voice froze him.

His cousin jogged to Penny's side, bent over, and kissed her on the forehead. "I love you." Straightening, he speared Micah with his teary eyes. "Bring them both back to me."

Hands on the rails of her bed, Micah pushed it into motion and left without answering. He refused to make a promise he might not be able to keep.

Belle cast another look at the clock. She couldn't wait any longer. She had to go inside and hope that Micah was nearly here.

Legs shaking, she strode to Rick Mastiff's door and pulled it open. The receptionist, Krista, greeted her with a smile. "I'll let him know you're here."

Dark gray carpet met lighter gray walls with cushy navy chairs lined up against them. A few glass tables held magazines. Overhead, light jazz played. The area provided an open invitation to sit and wait in relaxation. No way that she would or could.

Returning, Krista waved Belle through the door to the offices. "He's ready for you."

Belle turned down her offer of coffee. She was already shaky enough. At Rick's office, Krista knocked, led Belle in, then closed the door as she left. Why did she feel like a lamb led to slaughter?

Probably because of Rick's predatory smile. "Belle. It's good to see you." He rounded his desk and offered his hand.

She refused to let hers tremble. Calmly returning the handshake, she settled into one of the chairs beside his desk. Rather than returning to his seat, he took the chair across from her.

"I was surprised to receive the letter you sent me." Jumping right into why she was there allowed for a sense of control. One she desperately needed.

"I figured you might be, but the more I thought about our discussion, the more I came to the same conclusion. As much as I agree with what you're doing, I can't continue to waive the rent. It sends the wrong message to my other tenants and potential business partners."

"I don't know any of those people, so I'm not quite sure how they'd know about our arrangement."

"The commercial real estate world is a small one. Word travels, whether you mean for it to or not."

Again she had the feeling he wasn't being sincere with her, but there was nothing she could say. If Micah were here, he at least had connections to that world. He'd be able to step in.

But he'd ditched her.

She tightened her grip on her purse. "You agreed to give me until next November because of all the fixes I'm paying for on your building."

"Hmm …" He grabbed papers from his desk and slipped on glasses before flipping through them. "I don't see that here. What I do see is your signature on the lease that requires you to make any necessary fixes to the building *and* keep up with your rent in a timely manner. A rent that is already below market value for the area."

"Because you knew the building needed work."

"No, as I recall, it was because I believed in the nonprofit you were starting there. So I provided a break on rent, which you haven't kept up with." He handed her the papers. "It's all right there in the lease."

"I know." She didn't touch it. "I've read it, and *I* recall our conversations that you're reneging on."

He placed the papers on his desk again and removed his glasses, sliding them into his shirt pocket. "Conversations don't hold up in court. Signed contracts do."

"I have all the receipts showing the money I poured into the building."

"Good. It was your responsibility." He pointed to the paperwork. "Written out in black and white." She opened her mouth, but he held up his hand. "Now, I wouldn't want you to think I'd kick you out without another option. I do want to help."

She suddenly understood how Micah felt about that snake the other day. She was staring one down right now that elicited the heebie-jeebies. Difference was, she'd been there when he faced his reptile, and he'd left her all alone with hers.

"How exactly do you want to help?" Talk about tough words to utter.

"By offering a way for you to settle up, so I don't have to follow through on the eviction." His eyes grew dark and calculating as he verbally shoved her into a corner. "Unless you have the money with you."

"I do not." He knew it too, but he was having fun toying with her. He was every bit the jerk she'd suspected.

"As I figured, which is why I came up with this proposal." He reached for the second stack of paperwork on his desk and handed it to her.

She read through it, then looked up at him incredulously. "You want me to sign over fifty-one percent of AnnaBelle's?"

"Only the lotion line."

"Yes. I see that." Or at least that's how she interpreted the words. She didn't have the best track record when it came to contracts, though. "It's not going to happen."

As he spoke, he rounded his desk, opened a drawer, and rummaged through it. "That's fine, but then I'll file a formal eviction notice, and you'll have approximately thirty-five days—give or take when the court date is—to pay me in full."

"I won't have the money by then."

Shutting the drawer, he held out what he'd been looking for, a pen. "Then sign that and we'll wipe the slate clean."

Her heart hammered. "Why do you even want part of a lotion business? It makes no sense."

Talk about a calculating stare. Rick nailed it. "Because I'm a businessman, and as I revisited your numbers, I saw clear potential in the line you created. You owe me money, and this is a way for me to collect while also making what appears to be a profitable investment."

At least he was finally being straight with her.

"It's not an awful proposal. Your debt will be gone, and you'll have a backer for your business." He wiggled the pen. "I think in the end, you'll see we make a great team."

Except she didn't want to be on his team.

She wanted to be on Micah's, but once again he'd deserted her.

Idiot didn't even begin to describe her on, oh, so many levels.

"How do I know you're not going to take my company and still come after me for rent?"

Using the pen, he pointed. "Page two, third paragraph."

She read it. Sure enough, signing here would erase the debt she owed, though it would start accumulating again October first.

"I need to think about this. Have a lawyer look over it before I sign."

He leaned on the edge of his desk. "Please, go ahead and read over it again. Ask me any questions you may have. But this is a one-time deal. You leave my office without signing it, and I'm afraid I'll be signing the Demand for Possession, Nonpayment of Rent on your building."

Putting herself and all the moms out on the street because she had nothing saved to help them move to another building. She had her lotions, though.

"Oh, and also, I'd be forced to come after your entire business to collect what I'm owed."

"You can't do that."

He arched one brow. "Can't I?"

It was a chance she had to take because she couldn't sign that paper. Even if she lost everything—which it looked like she would—she refused to let him shove her any farther into a corner. She could start over. She'd done it before.

Standing, she stared him dead in the eye. "You can try. But what you can't do is blackmail me into business with you."

Head held high, jaw as firm as her decision, she exited his office. At this moment, she wasn't sure who she was angrier with, herself for putting this ball in motion, Rick for taking advantage of her, or Micah for deserting her once again when she needed him most.

Her heart cast its vote for the man who seemed an expert at tearing it in two.

She drove home on autopilot. Her phone rang, but she turned it off. No doubt Micah would call with excuses she didn't want to hear. Dragging herself upstairs, she found Astrid and Anna at the table. Anna giggled as Astrid made a peanut disappear. If only her troubles were as easy to get rid of.

Astrid's grin smoothed as she took Belle in. "How'd it go?" She craned her neck. "Is Micah with you?"

Unable to speak, Belle shook her head. Last thing she needed was to dissolve into tears in front of Anna. Picking up on Belle's crumbling emotions, Astrid stood. "How about this little girl comes and has dinner with us old folks tonight?"

"Yes!" Anna hopped up and down.

Giving her daughter a hug, Belle mouthed "thank you" to Astrid, who nodded and reached out for Anna. They disappeared downstairs, and Belle let the tears fall. She was wiping up her snotty mess of a face when her doorbell rang. Peeking out her window to the lot below, her spine stiffened.

Now he showed up?

Honestly, she couldn't be responsible for what she might do if she answered, so she stayed right where she was. After a few more buzzes, he walked away. She slid down onto her couch. At some point, she'd have to face him, but that wasn't going to be—

The door at the bottom of her steps opened. That sneak went through the storefront.

"I know you're up there. I'm coming up," he warned.

She met him at the top of the stairs. "Of course you are, because that's what you do. Come and go when it's convenient for you. To heck with what I want."

He'd stopped two steps down, keeping them eye level, and remained calm in the face of her fury. "I'm sorry I wasn't there, but—"

"You. Are. Kidding. Me." Until now, she hadn't a clue her voice could reach such decibels. "You're sorry? Oh, that makes it all better."

"Belle—"

"No." She studied him. His hair was a mess. His eyes held exhaustion. His voice sounded wary. But in the face of all she'd just lost, not a bit of it mattered to her. "It's too late. I cannot believe I let you in again. Allowed myself to believe your promises even when I saw the cracks in them. I accepted your excuses because I wanted to believe ..." All the words she wanted to throw at him evaporated. They didn't matter. Wouldn't change anything. She was tired of everything to do with Micah. "This is over, Micah. Don't come around. Don't call. Don't send food, or help, or whatever it is you think you're going to try to do to fix this." She sniffed. "I needed you today, you promised you'd be there, and you weren't."

He absorbed her words. "I know, and I'm sorry. I was—"

"Sorry doesn't cut it." Her voice shook. "You haven't changed, and you're not going to. My mistake for thinking otherwise. But believe me, I won't let Anna make the same one."

That ignited a fire in his eyes. "Are you serious here? What happened to believing the best in each other instead of the worst?"

"Hard to do when you don't have a best side, Micah."

He lowered his voice to a steely calm. "Didn't seem to think that when you kissed me."

She saw red. "Momentary lapse in judgment. Won't happen again."

"No. This"—he waved a finger between them—"is your momentary lapse. You're letting our past color how you see things, and I thought we'd finally moved beyond that."

"So did I." She crossed her arms. "But apparently you're hardwired to leave me when I need you most."

"Oh my gosh, woman, you can be so impossible!" He dragged a hand through his hair and breathed out frustration. "I am standing right here. I. Haven't. Left."

"Here isn't where you promised you'd be, Micah. That was three hours ago, when I stood in a room with my own snake, defenseless." Bitterness soaked into her words.

He moved up a step, his own anger rising, judging by those fisted hands and tight jaw. "What did he do?"

With a light snort, she shook her head. "Offered to forgive my debt."

That answer darkened his eyes. "In exchange for what?" The words a low growl, he seemed to vibrate with his own tightly coiled anger.

But he didn't get to come in late to the fight and pretend to be a protector after she'd taken a knockout.

"Doesn't matter. I handled it." Shaking her head, she leveled her final hit, wanting this all to be over. "I am so thankful I didn't tell Anna who you are because she deserves a father who'll always be there for her. You've proven yet again you're not that man."

The blow landed because he jerked back. "After everything, that's really what you think?"

"No, Micah." The hurt on his face fueled her fire. Good. Let him hurt like she had. Like she was all over again. "It's what I know."

His lips thinned, and he nodded. "All right, then." He turned. "Not that you've asked or care, but your sister had her baby, and *that's* where I was. Saving their lives." Then he descended the steps and walked out her door.

Chapter Twenty

Belle had never seen Jonah look so ... shaken.

"How are they?" She'd tracked down Penny's room to find her sister sleeping. So she'd come up to the NICU and waited in the hall until Jonah appeared.

Not having seen her, he looked up. Exhaustion lines creased his face, and his hair stood on end. He looked at her through bloodshot eyes. "Holding their own. I don't even know where I'm supposed to be. Which one I should stay near."

"Penny would want you here. I'll stay with her."

He absently nodded. "Six hours ago, they were both okay."

"And they're going to be okay," Belle promised as if she had any say in the matter.

Peering past her, he asked, "Have you seen Micah?"

Oh, yes, she had. Her heart still hurt over the words she'd speared him with. "Yeah."

Jonah blinked away tears. "Is he still here? I need to thank him."

"I-I don't know." If he'd returned to the hospital, she hadn't bumped into him. But she desperately needed to speak with him too.

"If it weren't for him ..." He stopped. Shook his head. "He saved both their lives."

She couldn't begin to imagine all the emotions Micah must have faced. Operating on Penny and the baby. Knowing at any moment he could lose them both. Worrying it would be his fault. And forced to break his promise to her.

Then what had she done? Shredded him with her own hurt and pain.

"I'm glad he was here." She meant it now. If only she'd known hours ago. "Have you called Rachael?"

"Yeah. She and Gavin are on their way."

"All right. I'll go sit with Penny for a while. I have your number if anything changes with her."

"What about Anna?"

"She's with Astrid."

"Okay." He scrubbed a hand down his face. "I'm going to go back in."

"Jonah?"

"Yeah?"

"Do I have a niece or a nephew?"

His face softened. "A niece. But I won't share the name without Penelope."

Understandable. They needed a little bit of normalcy returned to the moment. "I can't wait to hear it."

He slipped into the NICU, and she traveled downstairs to find Penny. The doors dinged open on the maternity floor, and she stepped out, turning left. Her eyes lifted, and there stood Micah, staring at her.

"Hey," she softly said.

He simply nodded.

"Can we talk?" She hooked a gaze up and down the hall. "Maybe someplace private?" No doubt he knew of a spot that fit the bill. Would he offer it, though, or walk away?

Looked like he was weighing those options.

"Please?" she added, hoping to tip the scales.

He sighed. "All right." Then he started down the hall, opened the door to a room, and waved her through. He closed the door behind him and stood in front of it, arms crossed, saying nothing.

"I'm sorry, Micah."

He stood there, then finally uttered one tired word. "Okay."

"Okay?"

"Yes. Okay. I accept your apology."

"That's it?"

"Unless you have more to say?" No anger lined his face or words. Rather a resignation that chilled her more than the cold air blowing from the vents.

"I didn't know you were here helping Jonah and Penny."

He sniffed. "You thought I was, what? Napping? Out with the guys? Or maybe drinking again?"

Her tongue glued to the roof of her mouth. Yes, she'd thought most of those things, but admitting them now sounded so petty. As petty as they'd been to think. Still, he'd owned so much of his junk that she owed him nothing less. "I did, but it was wrong of me."

His eyes closed, and he inhaled as if he was trying to suck in an extra measure of patience. After a moment, he opened them. "I can't keep doing this, Belle."

Her heart hammered. "Being around Anna and me?" Something like an "I told you so" rose from deep inside, the words coated in her own voice. "Because you said you were sticking around this time."

"I said I'd be around as long as you wanted me." He corrected her words.

"But you don't want me. You made that very clear earlier today."

"I was tired, hurt, and angry."

"And you'll be all three of those things again at some point in life." His volume raised, and his hands waved out to his sides. He stopped. Took another breath. Calmed his voice. "Our past has to stay in our past if we're going to have a future. But you can't seem to let it go."

"I have."

"No, you haven't. Every time something goes sideways, you assume the worst of me, no matter how many times I've shown you differently. I never expected this to be easy, but it's like I've racked up a debt that I cannot pay off, and I'm so tired of trying."

Okay, so he wasn't wrong. Except, "It isn't just you. I've been hurt over and over, and it's like I expect people are going to leave me."

"I know. You've made that perfectly clear. Repeatedly." Complete acceptance surrounded not merely his words, but his stance, as if he realized the battle he'd been fighting could not be won, and he was in full retreat.

It scared her more than she thought it could.

"Micah—"

"It's okay, Belle. Sometimes things don't work out the way we want, but I meant what I said. I'll be here for anything Anna needs." Anna, not her. Tears welled in her eyes even as he continued. "I want the best for you both, and right now, that means you and I not being together."

"We can still try."

He hesitated, his heart in his eyes. "Do you trust me?"

"I want to."

His probing gaze delved deep. He knew her well enough to see the fear behind her answer. She couldn't hide from him.

A sad smile split his lips. "And yet you haven't even told Anna who I am. You're still convinced I'm going to let you down." His voice cracked. "You can forgive, but you can't forget, and we can't move forward if you're always looking backward." Then he stepped from the room, the door swishing shut behind him.

A dark lonely house, smarting heart, and wrecked future didn't mix well for a guy whose mouth still watered for a drink every now and then. The memories of Penny's delivery kept circling on repeat too, stoking his thirst. Saying this was a bad day was like saying the sun was a little hot. To cap it off, at some point while he'd been saving Penny and her baby, Walter had finally returned his call.

He'd been out of the country, had just landed in Chicago, and was on his way to Michigan. He'd help with whatever Micah needed and asked him to call back.

He would, even though it was too late to make a difference for Belle. Except not tonight. His quota for dealing with messed up relationships had been met. Right now, he didn't have it in him to deal with another one, even if Walter's response hinted at a positive outcome. He'd misinterpreted Belle, so he wasn't exactly confident in his people-reading skills at this moment.

As Micah flicked on the lights, Chloe's yapping headed his way. He scooped her up, thankful for the distraction. "You hungry?"

She barked her answer, and he carried her into the kitchen. "That makes one of us." He set her down, then filled her food bowl. He wasn't sure if his appetite would ever return.

Grabbing a water bottle from the fridge, he settled on one of the stools while Chloe ate. Across from him was Mom's journal. He pulled it over and paged through it, feeling like a failure. Of course, why did he think any of these words would work in his life? Hadn't changed Dad's mind. Dad and Mom were farther apart than ever before.

Slamming the leather book closed, he paced the kitchen. Was that all he had to look forward to? A growing distance between him and Belle? Anna too?

Like someone reached in and cranked up the volume in his brain, his thoughts pulsed louder and louder. If Belle was so determined to see him as the old man, why was he fighting so hard to remain the new one? He was just ... so ... tired.

Tired of trying. Of pushing. Of hoping. He knew their past hurt her, and he willingly bore the responsibility for her pain. But he'd thought she would let him rebuild their broken trust. Instead, she held her hurts over his head, returning to them with any mistake he made. It was like trying to claw his way out of a sandpit. He'd only make it so far before the walls would crumble again, and he no longer possessed the energy to continue climbing. In fact, the entire exercise had left him thirsty.

Changing directions, Micah walked down the hall and stopped outside Dad's office. Hand on the knob, he hesitated a second before turning it. The door creaked as he slipped inside, his eyes on the bar. Dad's Scotch beckoned him. Its burn would eradicate the chaos in his head. Blur it until the sharp edges didn't cut anymore.

He crossed the checkered rug, the pattern more in line than his emotions, and stopped in front of the thick crystal tumblers. No one here to stop him. No one here at all. So why did it matter what he did if his future consisted only of himself?

Uncapping the decanter, he poured himself two fingers. Then he took the glass and settled in the same exact seat he'd been in three years ago. Swirled the amber liquid. Sniffed in its familiar, medicinal-laced oaky scent. Placed his lips on the cool glass rim.

"What are you doing, Micah?" The deep voice, soft and without reproach, reached into the room.

Micah turned, and there stood Walter. Still clenching the glass, he lowered it. "Walter? What are you doing here?"

"You called me." Hands in his pockets, answer given matter-of-factly, Walter strolled into the room. "I told you I was coming."

"To Michigan. You didn't say here."

"Well, I did try you back, but you didn't answer." He shrugged. "But the urgency of your messages told me I should head on over."

Still not letting go of his drink, Micah lowered his head. "I appreciate that, but it's too late for why I called."

Walter took the seat across from him. "Why don't you fill me in and let me be the judge?"

He swirled his Scotch, enjoying the rhythmic circle it turned in. Consistent and smooth, a stark contrast to his internals. To his life, really. "Go ahead. You'll eventually come to the same conclusion as everyone else."

"Which is?"

"That I am lacking. As a potential husband. A father. A son." Another swirl. "Take your pick."

"Okay." Walter's voice held a strange note. He leaned forward, elbows on his knees and hands clasped. "I pick son."

Micah laughed. "Good one. I'm failing my mom. All she wants are some letters her dad wrote her, and I can't find them." He lifted his empty hand, then quieted. Took a breath. Spoke the next painful truth. The one that started it all. "And I have never been enough for my father."

"Yes, you have."

Micah wished he possessed the confidence of Walter's answer. He knew better. "Maybe you should check with him before you answer because he'd say differently."

"No, he wouldn't." Tender, strong, and still so confident. "He doesn't."

The hairs on Micah's neck rose as Walter's final words broke from his throat. Micah lifted his eyes to meet blue ones that reflected a familiarity he'd always seen but never noticed. Words from Mom's journal began to mix with Dad's actions toward him throughout the years, drawing a picture with such clarity it stole his breath.

Still, he denied it.

Until Walter nodded. "You're my son." He blinked rapidly. Sniffed. "I've wanted to tell you for so long."

Micah pushed to his feet and bolted from the room. He made it out the slider, the tumbler heavy in his hand. He hurled it into the night as footsteps sounded behind him. He whirled, but words completely deserted him. Wow, did he just gain a whole new perspective on Belle's response to his unexpected reappearance in her life six weeks ago? Feeling ambushed and betrayed, no wonder she'd run.

Watching him tentatively, Walter maintained distance. "I'll answer any questions you have, Micah, but first you need to know that I have always and will always love you."

"I …" He dragged his hand through his hair. "What do I say to that, Walter?" He turned away from him. "I can't do this right now."

His world already pressed in on him so tightly that he'd nearly succumbed to old tendencies. If he tried taking on any more emotion, he'd break.

"I understand." Walter's tone reinforced his words. "And I'll leave, but not until I know you're going to be okay."

Right. He'd seen him holding that drink.

He might not want to talk to Walter, but he couldn't deny he'd shown up at exactly the right moment. Spoken a truth he couldn't quite accept, yet one that began to pry the past's fingers from its stronghold on his heart. He might not be able to understand the love of Walter as his father, but he did know he wanted to look nothing like the father who raised him.

With new resolve, Micah turned and headed for the study. Starting with the Scotch, he opened the decanter and poured it down the drain. He didn't stop until every bottle stood empty. Both hands on the counter, head dipped, he peeked up at his reflection in the mirror behind the bar. Movement caught his attention. Walter stood in the doorway once again. Their eyes met in the mirror.

Walter nodded. "When you're ready, I'll be here."

Then he turned and left.

After a few minutes, Micah straightened. He needed fresh air. Returning to the deck, he snapped his fingers and Chloe came running. They stepped outside, and Micah settled in one of the chairs beside the concrete gas firepit. He started it up, then pressed into his chair, head tilted to stare at the stars overhead. His thoughts were as scattered as those million pinpricks in the midnight sky, and he wasn't moving until he found some order to them.

Which meant he might as well get comfortable. He'd be out here a long time.

The twinkling stars overhead reminded Belle of how small she felt in such an overwhelming world. She stared up at them, as likely to touch them as she was to ever move from this spot where her past and present converged, trapping her.

She toed the ground, gently swaying the bench swing Micah had built her. Anna's soft snores filtered through the baby monitor, and it struck her that she'd not only have to explain why Mr. Micah wasn't around, but why Chloe had disappeared too.

Didn't seem fair. Not to any of them. But continuing down this road led to greater heartbreak. She honestly didn't see any other outcome.

Footsteps crunched across the gravel. "I thought that was you out here." Astrid stepped into the soft glow of light from the Edison bulbs. "Looks like you have the world on your shoulders."

"A dangerous place for it to be, based on recent outcomes."

Astrid settled beside her, adding her power into keeping the tempo of their motion. "Oh? How about you give me the details, and then I'll see if I agree with you."

"You will."

"Possibly, but it sure would be nice to arrive at a conclusion on my own rather than have you driving me there."

"As if that would even be possible."

"Then why are you trying?"

She wasn't. The facts would speak for themselves, and they pointed to how she'd failed the people around here. She'd done the very thing she feared others would do to her, and she wasn't quite sure how to own it yet. She never set out to let them all down, but that didn't change the fact that she had.

One lone frog croaked from someplace over by the playset, and every few seconds crickets added their chirps. There was the slightest chill to the air, a promise of fall arriving in the next few weeks. Belle kept her eyes on the stars. "I met with Rick. If I sign over half of AnnaBelle's, he'd forgive my debt. But I couldn't do it."

Astrid stayed silent.

Belle continued to rock the swing. "Even after he threatened to evict us and go after everything if I didn't."

"And you thought he was being honest?"

"I didn't know, and I was there alone." For reasons she now understood, but that knowledge didn't change any of the facts. "But I couldn't sign those papers."

"That was a wise decision. Rick can't be trusted. He's not like Micah."

Belle swiveled in her seat. "What's that mean?"

"It was a pretty clear statement."

Right. She had a gut feeling Micah was why Astrid had come out here. Wouldn't she be surprised to know what had transpired? "I told him I wanted to try, and he said it wouldn't be a good idea."

"Because you haven't forgiven him."

"Yes, I have." Belle straightened. "I told him that too."

Astrid studied her. "Was it Micah's words or actions that made you believe you could trust him again?"

"I …" She stopped and thought it through. "Both."

"Right. Because we need both. Talk alone without follow-through is empty."

"But I did follow through. I let him back into my life. Let him into Anna's."

"And kept him on the hook for his past sins the entire time." Astrid wasn't letting her off easily. "You forgave, but you didn't forget."

"Of course not. How on earth can I forget him leaving me? Leaving Anna?"

A smile slipped across Astrid's ruby red lips, and she took Belle's hand. "Harry Houdini is one of my favorite magicians to study."

"I know."

"Did you also know that he bragged he could break out of anyplace someone locked him into?"

"No. But it sounds like him." Where was this going?

"Well, he did, and people took him up on it. There's a story about one of those times. Somewhere in England, they put him in a jail cell and left him there. He worked two hours trying to escape, but he never was able. Finally, it hit him why."

Belle raised her shoulders. "The lock was too complicated?"

"It was never locked to begin with. Every time he thought he was unlocking it, he was actually locking himself in, when all he needed to do was push the door open and walk out." Astrid patted her hand. "The only person keeping him locked up was him."

She allowed the words to simmer.

Still, "My hurts are real, Astrid. My whole life, people have left me, and I'm so tired of that pain."

"Then let it go."

"I thought I had. I forgave my parents. My birth mom. Even Micah." She honestly had, but Micah's words kept picking at her. The truth hurt, especially when she didn't like it, yet felt powerless to change it. "But I can't forget what they did."

"Oh, child, forgetting something isn't amnesia, it's amnesty. It's letting a person off the hook. Knowing what they did, but choosing not to bring it up again. Deciding to move forward with a clean slate." She slipped her hands into her lap. "Remembering protects us from people whose behaviors haven't changed while allowing us to see the ones who have. Your memories aren't meant to be used as a weapon. That will only backfire and hurt you in the process." Apparently emptied of all she'd come to say, Astrid stood. "Good night, sweet girl." She strolled away.

Belle looked up again at the night sky, not ready to go inside until she finally figured this all out. Which meant she might as well get comfy. She'd be out here for a while.

Chapter Twenty-One

It paid to have contacts in the hospital.

The elevator door dinged, and Belle stepped onto the third floor. One phone call to Lettie let her know Micah had several back-to-back Caesarean sections over the next few hours, so it was safe to visit Penny and Jonah. She needed to talk to Micah, to make things right, but she still wasn't sure what that entailed— even after pulling an all-nighter with her thoughts. As this morning dawned with no solution to her problems with Rick or her heartache with Micah, at least her sister had reasons to celebrate, and Belle planned to join her.

Turning left, she walked to their room at the end of the hall and rapped her knuckles on the door. "Can I come in?"

"Absolutely," Penny answered.

Once inside and past the curtain, Belle smiled at her sister. Color had returned to her cheeks since last night, and the medically induced cloudiness had parted from her green eyes.

"Are you feeling as improved as you look?" She set the pink balloons and gift bag she'd brought on the window ledge.

"Yes." Relief filtered over her features and voice. "I'd feel even better if they would stop poking, squeezing, and prodding me every hour."

"Your blood pressure is still high," Jonah cautioned.

Penny peered up at him. "It's coming down. They're not concerned."

"I am." The intensity of his stare showed not only his love but the remnants of his fear.

Penny placed her hand on his where it rested on her bed. "I'm okay, Jonah. So is Abrielle."

"Abrielle?" She hadn't heard the baby's name yet. The soft "A" added a more feminine feel.

Now Jonah smiled. "Yeah. It means protected, which felt right after how she came into this world."

And how her daddy planned on marking all of her days, no doubt. Little Abrielle was loved and protected, and she'd grow up knowing it much like Anna knew Micah's love. Except she didn't understand who he was to her. That hadn't stopped him from unlocking his heart and letting her completely invade its space. Without a second thought, Anna flung herself into his open arms, never once doubting that he'd catch her.

He had. Then he'd stood there and beckoned Belle to make the same leap. She thought she had. Instead, fear acted like a bungee cord, yanking her back to the cliff's edge before Micah's arms could close around her. Heart pounding, she'd clung to that familiar place, because keeping her feet on the ground, supporting her own weight, felt safe.

It was also lonely.

"Where's my niece?" Penny broke through her thoughts.

Belle refocused on the moment and pulled a piece of paper from the gift bag. "I couldn't guarantee she'd stay off you, and your stomach and its stitches wouldn't have enjoyed that. But she colored this for you."

Penny took the picture of a very pink unicorn. "It's adorable."

"She cannot wait to meet her cousin. Do they have any idea when you may be going home?"

Jonah and Penny shared a glance, and he cleared his throat. "Micah was in this morning during rounds. If Penny's blood pressure decides to return to normal and stay there, she could go home tomorrow. Abrielle's doing really well, but we'll most likely go home without her."

"I'm sorry, you guys."

"It's okay," Penny said with a trembling smile. "May not be what we planned, but then again"—she held up her and Jonah's joined hands—"this guy wasn't either, and look how great that turned out."

He leaned in and kissed her. Penny's shoulders lifted as if his very presence steadied her. As he settled in his seat, he met Belle's eyes. "We're sorry too. I know you needed Micah yesterday along with a check from me—"

"Stop right there," Belle interrupted. "I needed my sister and niece safe more than anything else. I'll figure the rest out somehow."

"With Micah's help?" Penny asked.

"I don't know, but right now, you have other things to think about, so don't worry about me."

"That's like asking her to wear all black. It's not going to happen." Jonah chuckled. He loved how colorfully Penny dressed.

"Especially with how off Micah acted this morning. I know something happened between you two."

"And they'll tell us when they're ready." Jonah peeked at Belle. "Right?"

She nodded.

He grew serious. "Will you also let me know if there's anything I can do to help?"

"I will." Reaching behind her, she grabbed the gift she'd brought. "Now open your present."

Penny dove into the tissue paper, smiling at the tiny pink outfits. As she folded them, a nurse arrived with a wheelchair. "Ready to go see that precious baby of yours?"

"Definitely."

Jonah pushed the button to lift the head of her bed, then helped her out of it. "You coming with us?" he asked Belle.

"Can I?" She wasn't sure on NICU rules.

Jonah looked at the nurse, who nodded.

Didn't have to ask her twice.

They went up to the fourth floor, and a nurse met them as they put on gowns to enter the NICU. "You must be mama." The blonde held out her hand, a welcoming smile on her face. "I'm Janette, and I'm Abrielle's daytime nurse." She led them through the door. "Beautiful name, by the way. I love what it means."

"Thanks."

Belle stood back as Penny and Jonah received all the recent details about their little girl. Janette scooped her up from under the warmer and placed her in Penny's hands. Jonah squatted beside them, his hand cupping Abrielle's tiny head. Belle snapped several pictures with her phone, then saw the nameplate on the warmer.

"Her middle name is Rose?" she asked, surprised.

Penny smiled at her. "Yeah. I wanted to carry on what you started with Anna." She looked at her daughter and then to Belle. "You know, Jonah and I were talking about how roses are full of thorns, but then at the top of it all is something so soft and beautiful. They're resilient, yet tender to the touch." She stopped, her emotions no doubt soft from the past twenty-four hours. What Penny couldn't yet know was that they'd stay that way over her little girl for the rest of her life. "It's what I want for our girls. For us." She paused. "For you. There's been a lot of thorny moments that caused pain, but I still believe you can have something beautiful."

Resilient, yet tender. The path there involved being vulnerable, and suddenly, she wanted to pass on so much more than her name to her daughter. She didn't possess the tools to do it on her own, but she had an idea of how to obtain them. It required asking for help, and she finally felt ready to do that, because standing on her own hadn't stopped hurt from entering her life. It left her alone to face it, and she was doing a miserable job.

She wanted better. Deserved better. So did Anna.

It was time to stop fiddling with the lock on her heart and throw open the door. Truly leave the past behind.

Micah pulled into the driveway, exhausted from a sleepless night and intense day. No deliveries like Penny's, but the sheer multitude of them drained the little reserves he had. Then he'd stopped by to see Mom and hopefully find some answers to Walter's bombshell, but his questions began to agitate her. She seemed to want to respond, but she couldn't discover where she'd locked away the facts to their story. All she could say, repeatedly, was that he looked so much like his father.

He never could see the resemblance when she used to say that, but he'd been comparing himself to the wrong man for his entire life.

Inside, Chloe barked. Micah trudged up the front steps and opened the door. He had enough time to shower and change before Walter arrived. He'd called him on the way home, convinced that he was the sole person with the answers Micah sought.

Thirty minutes later, a knock sounded from his front door. Taking a deep breath, he opened it. "Come on in." He stepped aside for Walter to enter.

"I'm glad you called." Walter followed him into the living room. They settled on chairs opposite one another. "I meant it when I said you could ask me anything."

Right now, he needed to stick with facts.

Walter supplied every single one. How, despite their age difference, he and Mom had fallen in love, but they didn't know how to tell Gramps and Gigi. How she was going to break things off with Dad, but then she found out she was pregnant.

"She was scared." Walter filled in the blanks. "Gigi had asked her once if there was something going on between her and me, and she lied. Said there was nothing between us, though I don't think Gigi ever really believed that. Then, when your mom found out she was pregnant, telling them was hard enough. She wasn't prepared to confess that she'd lied about us too. That the baby was mine. So she told everyone you were Todd's, and he married her."

"She lied to you too?"

"Yes." Walter massaged his thumb into his palm. He hadn't stopped fidgeting since he walked in. "Watching you grow up, I always suspected you were mine, but she didn't tell me until after Gigi's death. That's when she shared everything

I'm passing on to you."

It was also when she started writing her journal.

Walter continued. "Your grandparents always suspected, but she refused to confess to them. It's what drove a wedge between them." More pieces of his childhood strung together. "Your dad discovered it when they tried to have more children and couldn't conceive. He was sterile, so he knew you weren't his. Apparently, that's when things changed between all three of you, and over the years his resentment grew."

Yeah. Those were the memories he shared with his parents. They'd colored over any good ones, or maybe he'd been too small to remember them.

"Why didn't he leave?"

"I suspect you'll need to ask him that, but from what your mom said, it was his pride. He'd married her, and all that time, you were someone else's son. Plus, your gramps had helped him financially to start his business. He worried he'd lose it in a divorce, and he felt it was his entitlement for the lie your mother perpetrated."

Micah absorbed it all. Still, "Why didn't you tell me three years ago when you found out?" He couldn't reconcile it. "If you love me like you claimed the other night, you would have told me. Or"—he didn't want to ask, but he had to know—"am I not the son you wanted?"

Walter didn't speak immediately. How could he? What answer would be adequate?

But he didn't offer an answer. Rather, he lifted a question. "Do you love Anna?" Soft, with no reproach, he laid the simple truth out there. He wasn't using it to hurt, but rather to heal, the fact clear with the tender tone he used.

"You know I do," his words scraped out. Every part of him raw.

"But you haven't told her you're her father. Why?"

Fresh wounds that wanted to gape open fought to mend. "Because the time hasn't been right."

Walter nodded. "When I found all this out, you weren't speaking to me. Your life was in a downward spiral. I worried that telling you would add to it, so I kept contacting you, and I waited until you were ready to let me in." He stood and came over by Micah. "But there hasn't been one second that I have not wanted you, Micah. You're my son. That's the only qualification you need to be enough, and the only reason *I* need to love you as much as I do."

And because he loved Anna the same way, he could believe Walter's words. Oh, they had a long road in front of them, but he was taking the first step on it. Tears in his eyes, he looked at this man he'd known for years but now held a new role in his life. It felt strange and yet right. "Thank you."

Walter gripped his shoulder. "You're mine, and nothing will ever change that. The difference is now you know it. Soon others will too, starting with Rick Mastiff."

Confused, he straightened. "What?"

"You mentioned his name on one of your messages. I think it's time you filled me in on the rest."

Chapter Twenty-Two

"Hard to believe she's three weeks old." Micah handed off the tiny nugget to her daddy. A twinge of jealousy nipped at him as he watched Jonah have the freedom to hold his daughter and kiss her cheeks.

Jonah side-eyed him. "Not until tomorrow. Don't rush it."

He wasn't. In all honesty, the days had dragged by, each one longer than the last. He needed to speak to Belle. They might not be able to make things work, but this not seeing Anna wasn't going to continue. He was her daddy, whether Belle liked it or not. At some point, she needed to let Anna know.

Penny entered the room, looking tired but stronger. She crossed the fluffy white rug to their couch and smiled down at Jonah. She pointed to the cushion beside him, and a tender look passed between them. "This seat taken?"

"That's my line," he said, giving her a kiss as she settled beside him.

"You stole my heart; I stole your line." She snuggled into him, reaching to gently stroke little Abrielle's cheek. "Seems fair to me."

"Not even close. I came out way ahead." Another soft kiss.

"Ellie can't say it, so I'll say it for her. You two get a room." Abrielle's nickname—one Anna had given her, especially adorable knowing the way she said her Ls—rolled off his tongue.

Jonah broke away, laughing. "Can't help it. I love my wife."

"And that little girl is all the evidence we need to that fact." Micah stood by the whitewashed fireplace. Any minute, the rest of the crew would pour inside, but he'd make a hasty exit first. He had shown up at the back of the church to watch Ellie's baby dedication, then bust out of there to meet Penny and Jonah at home, knowing they weren't staying for the entire service. However, they'd invited everyone over for brunch, and that everyone included Belle.

Cooing at her daughter, Penny spared him a fast glance. "You sure you won't stay for brunch?"

"Yep." Tires crunched on the gravel outside. "In fact, that's my cue."

Jonah handed Ellie to Penny, then followed him out the slider. "You know you're welcome to stay."

"I do, but the last thing I want is to make Belle feel awkward or pressured to speak with me."

"You two still haven't spoken?"

"Nope." And it was the biggest lesson in patience he'd ever undertaken. "I'm waiting on her." He hustled down the stairs and over to Evan's, where he'd parked so Belle wouldn't know he was here.

Thirty minutes later, he sat on the deck of his parents' house overlooking Reed's Lake. Chloe lay at his feet, gnawing on a bone. These first few weeks of September resembled summer more than fall, and he loved this time of year. Maybe later, he'd take a kayak out and paddle around the lake before going to work tonight. Definitely would help relieve some of his stress.

The slider behind him opened, and Chloe started barking. Micah swung around and nearly dropped his water bottle. Belle stood in the open space.

"Did you honestly think I wouldn't recognize your car just because you parked it at Evan's?" she asked.

"Obviously I did."

"And obviously it didn't work." She fidgeted nervously. "Why did you leave?"

"Because I wanted to give you space."

As if his answer provided the antidote to her brewing worry, the lines that furrowed across her brow and bracketed her mouth smoothed. It seemed to inject her with courage too because she stepped outside, closing the door behind her. "I kind of like you in my space, though." Then she stepped into his. "How are you doing, Micah?"

Seriously? She dropped that line, then asked him that question? He swallowed. "Okay."

She smiled. "Pageant voice."

"All right. I'm miserable. Is that better?"

That wiped away her smile. Those lines reappeared across her forehead, and sadness flickered in her eyes. "No." She motioned to the seat he'd been in and the one beside it. "Can we sit?"

"Sure." He waited until she settled before taking his own. "Why are you here, Belle?"

His heart wanted to offer its own suspicion, but he couldn't afford to buy into the hope until Belle confirmed her reason.

She hauled out a piece of paper. "I received something in the mail on Friday." She held it out to him.

Micah took the letter and smoothed it open, already aware what it said. "Walter bought your building."

"After he paid off my debt."

Much like he'd paid off Micah's student loans. Yeah, that had come out too during one of their many recent talks. Walter was all about canceling debt for his children, and the moment Belle fell in love with Micah, she'd come under that heading as well.

She tipped her head. "You don't seem surprised. In fact, you seem like you already knew." Her eyes narrowed. "You called him, didn't you?"

"I did."

"When?"

"Does it matter?"

"No, I guess it doesn't." She rubbed her thumbnail. "Thank you, Micah. I know that wasn't easy."

"It wasn't." He refused to lie to her. He'd also refused to allow her to think she owed him anything in return. Loving someone right meant you did it selflessly, and he planned on loving her right whether or not he could ever call her his again. "Not because of what he did for you, but because of what I found out when I talked to him."

Her hand stilled. "He's your father, isn't he?"

How had she …

Before he could ask, she started listing the clues that led to her correct conclusion. "The journal entries, his eczema like Anna's, the picture—"

"What picture?"

"The one your mom has. She said it was you, but it was a really old photo. I thought it was your dad at your age, but it looked so much like Walter."

"Because it *was* him."

They sat in silence for a minute before Micah filled her in on everything Walter told him. "He knows Rick Mastiff too. They've had run-ins before. And it was Rick who called the fire chief."

"What? How'd you find out?"

"Walter knew who to ask." Micah rubbed his palms together. "Rick pushed your back up against the wall, thinking he could corner you."

"And then Walter stepped in." She sniffed. "Why though? I'm the one who got myself in the mess. I didn't deserve a bailout."

Now Micah gave a sad smile. "Because, while it might not still be true, you loved me once. That was all Walter needed to consider you a part of his family. To him, you're his daughter, and there's nothing he wouldn't do for you."

Nodding slowly, she seemed to absorb that truth. "He loved me, even though I didn't know our connection." Her eyes found his. "Sounds a lot like his son with his daughter."

"Anna is mine. Doesn't matter if she knows it or not."

"I think it's time she did." Sliding off her chair, Belle knelt in front of him.

"You were supposed to be at Penny and Jonah's, but we found you anyway." Then she nodded toward the slider. It opened and Anna raced out.

His heart started a funny beat.

"Mista Micah!"

With a tiny wave, Rachael slid it closed and disappeared into the house.

"Hey, Monkey." Micah nearly collapsed under the weight of her hug. "I've missed you."

"I miss you too!" Always bouncing, she bopped up and down in his arms.

Beside them, Belle sniffed. "Hey, Monkey, remember we talked about calling Mr. Micah by a new name?"

Anna's beautiful blue eyes—Belle's shape, his color—widened. "Yes!" Oh, he saw the direction this was headed and already was a blubbering mess.

With Belle's encouraging nod, Anna clapped her hands together. "Daddy." Her bouncing turned into one of her one-word song and dances as she wiggled in front of him. "Daddy. Daddy. Daddy. Daddy."

And, yeah, he was a grown man sobbing on the back deck of his parents' house.

Anna stopped. "Why you crying, Daddy?"

That did him in. He slipped off the chair and hauled her to him, burying his face in her neck, inhaling sugar and roses. "Because I'm very, very happy." Lifting his gaze, he met Belle's eyes and found them as watery as his own. He yanked her into the hug too.

His little family, and they fit in his arms perfectly.

Anna started squirming. "Aw done." She ducked from under his arms and raced for Chloe.

Belle dug a tissue from her pocket and swiped at her nose. She handed another to him. "I came prepared."

"Thanks."

They shared a tiny laugh, both still on their knees. The slider opened again, and Rachael stuck her head out. "Who wants a cookie?"

"I do!" Anna raced to Rachael. "Chyoe too!"

With a wink, Rachael closed the door behind them.

"You aren't kidding when you say you came prepared." He pocketed his tissue, but before he could settle into his seat again, Belle took both of his hands.

"I am so sorry for the things I said. You are exactly the kind of man Anna needs for her daddy. Patient. Kind. Self-sacrificing." Another rogue tear escaped her eyes. "And I forgive you, Micah. Like really, truly forgive you. As in, I'm choosing to forget too. Not that our past didn't happen, but I'm working on not holding it anymore." She paused and nibbled her lip, the action working hard to distract him from what she was saying, but then her still-tumbling words clicked and brought him back around full focus. "I'm seeing a counselor. I have been for a couple of weeks because I needed to start really working through some things, and I didn't want to come see you until I had a better grip on them." He was nodding, falling in love with her a little more with every rambling word as she kept talking. "I'm still trying, and she suggested—and I wondered—if maybe you'd want to go with me? Because I want a fresh start. I want to release our past for good so that I can hold on to you." She brought their shared hands to her heart and finally took a breath. "If you'll have me?"

If? "You really need to ask?"

"I do because I'm a mess. Full of thorns. I can be prickly and difficult, and I'm asking you to—"

Before she could rev up again, his lips landed on hers with a confidence that answered for him. In case she had any lingering doubt, he unclasped their hands and wrapped his arms around her, cocooning her in his embrace. Deepening the kiss, he ensured she knew that yes, he'd have her. Today. Tomorrow. For the rest of their lives.

He slowly leaned away, just enough to tease her. "You can never give me a hard time about babbling again."

"I wasn't babbling." She grinned.

"No?"

"I was sharing my feelings."

"I think you used up all your words."

"That's okay. I don't need them."

Then she dove all in, proving that actions spoke way louder than words, and he pulled her close, so he didn't miss a syllable.

Pounding slowly broke through the haze of his response, and he broke the kiss. They turned toward the source of the noise. Anna stood at the glass door, smiling at them. Rachael raced into the room and grabbed her. "Sorry!" her muffled voice called.

Belle dropped her forehead to Micah's, laughing. "Just a warning. Alone time with her isn't very easy to come by."

"Then we better make the most of it." Lips covering her laughter, he went to work happily completing that task.

Epilogue

"I cannot believe she requested peanut butter and pickle sandwiches for her birthday party." Belle placed the platter on the pink and purple plastic table cloth covered in unicorns. "I also cannot believe the sheer volume of unicorn paraphernalia you found."

He'd purchased his parents' house, and every surface of the kitchen and family room had the magical animal on it, and if they weren't sitting on something, they were hanging from the walls or floating in the air. He'd even found a unicorn costume for Chloe, who trotted after Anna as she bestowed a name on every one of the single-horned creatures.

"What? It's the first time I've gotten to celebrate her birthday with her." Based on the goofy grin he'd worn all day, that simple fact made him deliriously happy.

She wasn't buying it was a one-time deal, though. "I have this sneaky suspicion you'll spoil her every year."

Snagging her around the waist, he tugged her close and nuzzled her neck. "I thought you liked how I spoil you two."

She shivered in his arms. "There's a lot I like about you. Spoiling is just one."

He skimmed the tip of his nose along her neck and cheeks, stopping when it touched hers, and his lips hovered over her mouth. "Care to tell me something else you like?"

Oh, this man had her heart. "How 'bout I show you?"

"I was hoping you'd say that."

She laughed against his lips, diving into the kiss with a familiarity she'd never find old.

Something tugged them apart. She looked down to find Anna squeezing between their legs. "No kissing."

Micah dropped his forehead to Belle's shoulder. "You weren't kidding about that whole *alone-time* thing."

Cupping his face between her hands, she lifted his lips to hers and planted a quick kiss there. "You're just now realizing that?"

"No." He scooped Anna up, holding her between them. "Which is why I stocked this party with carbs, candy, and lots of games so this one"—he bounced her till she giggled—"will fall asleep early and stay asleep."

"I no suh-yeep," Anna protested.

"Not now, Monkey. First we're going to have your party."

"Yay!"

He set her on the ground, and she tore off with Chloe, her excitement already at crazy level.

Belle shook her head. "You do realize your plan means she's going to be a handful until she passes out."

He whipped out that wolfish grin. "Well worth it."

She groaned and returned to the kitchen. Together they finished up the rest of the prep, putting the last of the food on the table as the doorbell rang. They'd decided to have the party here so there'd be more room. Plus, Anna loved this place—a large driving factor in his decision to buy the house. They'd swam along the shore until the cool nights turned the water too cold. When fall hit hard, they'd raked leaves and jumped in the piles. And after the first snow, they'd made their very own Frosty. She'd even helped Micah decorate a tiny Christmas tree here, and just last week, as her January birthday drew near, he'd bought her a pair of ice skates to try on the now-frozen lake.

Four months had passed in a blur, and she'd loved every moment—even the ones filled with hard work. They saw a counselor weekly, alternating between their private appointments and ones together. That work was paying off in huge dividends; she loved Micah more every day. Fear no longer marked that love. Rather, a hopeful anticipation settled into her heart every time she looked at him.

Voices drifted from the hall as their friends and family descended. Belle reached for Ellie. Holding her niece awakened new longings in her. She looked across the room and found Micah watching her. His smile said he knew exactly what she was thinking, and he'd be more than happy to help her fulfill that desire.

"Nice blush, sis." Penny looked from Micah to her. "He better put a ring on that finger and soon."

"Hey!"

"I didn't know a person could grow so red." Rachael added her two cents, then opened her arms for Ellie. "It's time for her favorite aunt to hold her."

"She already is." This had become a running gag whenever they were all together. Ellie giggled in her arms as Belle bounced her. "See?"

Rachael made a silly face, and Ellie laughed even harder. "I do see—quite clearly—that she prefers me."

Evan snagged Rachael's arm. "She's not going to if you get hangry. Come eat first, and then you can keep pulling those crazy faces."

"I do not get hangry." Rachael tugged from him and looked at Gavin. "Do I?"

His eyes widened, and he stuffed a chip into his mouth.

"Smart boy." Jonah strolled up and handed Penny a plate. "You should eat your dinner too before Ellie demands hers."

"Don't have to ask me twice." She took the plate and followed him into the kitchen.

Evan motioned that direction. "You coming?" he asked Rachael. "Because that's me asking you twice, but I'm happy to go for a third. It's a charm, I'm told."

She rolled her eyes. "Don't believe everything you're told."

He followed her into the kitchen. "And yet, it worked."

Everyone made their way through the buffet, humoring Anna with the peanut butter and pickle sandwiches while grabbing the "real food" Belle had insisted on. That was one bandwagon she wasn't going to jump on with those two.

As they finished eating, Anna entertained her guests with a dance, while Belle handed off Ellie to Rachael, then scooted up beside Micah, who stood in the corner with a pensive expression on his face.

"Miss your mom?" she asked.

In the last few months, she'd declined even further, to the point where she remained most calm in the familiarity of her room. Micah visited her daily. This morning, he'd told her about Anna's unicorn-themed party. Tomorrow they'd bring her one of the matching cupcakes, and she'd most likely ask what it was from.

"Yeah." He wrapped his arm around her shoulders and pressed a kiss to the side of her head. "I love you."

"I know." She leaned into him. "I love you too."

"Yuv me too?" Anna tugged on his pant legs.

Micah scooped her up. "Yes, Monkey, I love you too."

"Yuv you three," Anna replied.

He tapped her nose. "Love you four."

"Yuv you more!"

"Love you more!" Micah's words blended with Anna's.

He'd caught on to their saying, but Belle still grew a little misty-eyed listening to them use it. Those two adored each other.

Walter joined them. "The new scent is selling well."

AnnaBelle's Lotions was really taking off with him as a backer, and their sandalwood rose scent was quickly becoming a top seller. Belle smiled at Micah. "It was a collaborative effort." A little of him and a little of her, and she'd finally struck the right balance.

"You should make them more often."

"Yeah, we should," Micah agreed. Then he stepped away from her. Turned. Smiled.

"Micah?" Her heart beat funny as if it knew something she didn't.

Holding up one finger, he handed Anna to Jonah, disappeared down the hall, and returned a few seconds later with his mother's Bible. Turned out, those were the letters she kept asking for. Walter put the pieces together for them. Seemed Gramps had often referred to his Bible as letters from his Father, and then he'd passed that Bible on to Sharon, who'd finally passed it on to Micah when he brought it to her. Now he stopped in front of Belle with it in his hands. "When I visited Mom today, I talked a lot about you."

"You did?"

He grinned. "I tend to do that quite a bit."

"He does," Jonah called from the edge of the kitchen, holding Anna.

Everyone laughed, then grew quiet as they watched what had been such a long journey unfolding into its next chapter.

Micah flipped through the worn pages of the black leather book. So many sections were underlined or highlighted. "You know Gramps gave this to her, and all she wanted was to give it to me. It's like getting a little piece of her back because all throughout the pages are her little notes on life lessons she learned. They're intertwined with ones Gramps made too. Some pertain to their personal lives. Some to their family. And some to marriage." Closing it, he held her gaze. "I couldn't ask for a better handbook to start our own marriage with, and if we're lucky, we'll have years to add our own markings before we pass it on to our children one day."

Belle cocked her head. "Our marriage?"

"Yeah." He bent to one knee and took her hand. "And this second time around, I promise to love and cherish you the way I should have the first time." He pulled out a ring. Two stones wrapped in more diamonds creating an infinity symbol in an endless band. "The first time I gave you a solitaire. This time I want you to know you aren't alone, and I'll love you forever."

She knelt too, her free hand resting against his cheek. "I wouldn't trade our story for anyone else's. You are worth every heartache and every tear shed because it's taught me to cherish every moment. And, Micah Shaw, I don't just cherish you, I adore you." She kissed his cheek. "More than that, I love you with all my heart, and I'd be forever blessed to call you my husband."

He kissed her then. A kiss filled with the sweetness of second chances and surrounded by the love and support of their family, because life wasn't meant to be lived alone. It was meant to be shared.

And she planned on sharing every second with this man who held her heart in his tender, safe hands.

THE END

Author's Note

As I was writing Belle and Micah's story, the theme of forgiveness continued to return to the page. It pushed hard on memories and moments in my own life. Much like in the book, I want to ensure that you know there's a difference between reconciliation and forgiveness. Reconciliation requires two people. They not only must forgive one another, but there must be a change of heart and habit on both parts so that the relationship can be reestablished. Forgiveness, however, is all about our hearts. Forgiveness can—and sometimes should—happen without reconciliation. Forgiveness brings freedom to our lives as we release the pain and anger from what another did to us. It is integral to our own heart's well-being. The only way we can have the power to forgive another, especially if they haven't changed or aren't seeking forgiveness themselves, is through Jesus Christ. I know this because in my own life, leaning into His strength is the only way I truly released old hurts so that I could move forward. And just know, Jesus not only wants to help you, but He is waiting for you with open arms. Even if you've never called Him Father, you are His child, and He loves you with an unconditional love. If you'd like to know more about Him, please reach out to me at susanltuttleauthor@gmail.com. He's one story I'll never grow tired of sharing.

Discussion Questions

1. Belle has made an effort to change how she views and speaks to other people. She notes early on that, "Now she understood how razor sharp her words could be, wounding without even a direct hit. But she also knew how one well-placed word of kindness could burrow into a person and unfurl courage, confidence, and beauty they didn't even realize existed inside of them. She could destroy or build others up." What are some memorable words or actions of kindness you remember giving or receiving in your life?

2. Belle and the other single moms work to make skin care products. Are you someone who creates or crafts? If not, what hobbies do you enjoy?

3. If you could create your own lotion, what scents would you combine?

4. What part of Micah and Belle's first scene together did you most identify with? Would you have handled any of it differently? If so, how?

5. Do you believe people can change? What must they demonstrate for you to trust they're a different person? In what ways did Micah and/or Belle display they've changed?

6. Who was your favorite character and why?

7. What part of the story struck you as most romantic?

8. Toward the end of the story, Astrid tells Belle that, "forgetting something isn't amnesia, it's amnesty." How does this apply to the saying, "forgive and forget," and do you believe this is possible?

9. What was your favorite instance of Micah putting "actions with words" in this story?

10. One of the themes of this story is trust. Name a few ways this theme played out over the course of the story.

11. What scene was your favorite and why?

12. Would you ever eat a peanut butter and pickle sandwich? If not, what's the strangest thing you've ever eaten?